Pirates
and
Prejudice

by

KARA LOUISE

Cover Image by Dreamstime.com
Cover Design by Kara Louise

ISBN 978-0615815428

Published by Heartworks Publication
Printed in the United States of America

Library of Congress Cataloging-in-Publication Data

Kara Louise
Pirates and Prejudice

A note from the author to my readers -

You may be reading this book because you love Jane Austen's *Pride and Prejudice*. If that is the case, you love the characters as much as I do, and I hope you will enjoy this variation that takes Elizabeth and Mr. Darcy on quite an adventure.

If you are reading this book because you enjoy pirate stories, my hope is that you will be intrigued enough with the reference to *Pride and Prejudice* that if you haven't read it, you will want to.

This story begins after some important events have taken place in Miss Austen's novel, and refers to them in backstory. While you can read this book without reading her novel, I think your enjoyment will increase having done so.

I have several people I wish to thank who were a great help in getting this book written and into your hands. Thanks to Mary Anne Hinz and Gayle Mills for their copy edits, Jakki Leatherberry for her story edits, and to my sisters, Donna Natale and Cheryl Wallace, for their suggestions, support, and encouragement.

I also wish to thank Jane Austen for her original inspiration of the characters and storyline. Little did she know how deeply all her novels would touch people two centuries later.

I hope you enjoy *Pirates and Prejudice.*

Chapter 1

London

A harsh, accusing voice inside Fitzwilliam Darcy's head uttered the words he had heard repeatedly the past few months, words that tormented and haunted him.

"You are the last man in the world whom I could ever be prevailed upon to marry!"

The words came unexpectedly and seemingly without reason. Each time he heard them, he futilely tried to ignore them or push them away. Unfortunately, they sounded as loud and clear as the first time Elizabeth Bennet indignantly expressed her decided estimation of his person.

Darcy shook his head, wishing to free it of the assaulting voice. In a gruff whisper he said, as much to himself as to the voice, "I have had enough of this!"

He drew in a deep breath as he attempted to clear his mind, but he was in too great a stupor for it to make a difference. He covered his ears with his hands as if that would prevent him from hearing those hurtful words. He desperately wanted the voice to go away, and he wished for some inner strength – inner resolve – to shake off this feeling of utter despondency. He could not believe the extent to which he had allowed himself to be tormented and to fall into such a reprehensible state.

Each time he recollected the words Miss Bennet had lashed out at him, he felt a dagger pierce his heart. "Pull yourself together, man!" he muttered to himself. He felt trapped in a quagmire of self-pity and regret, from which it seemed impossible to extricate himself. His heart ached at both the memory of her and the despondency she had brought upon him.

Darcy walked along a bumpy cobblestone road in London, not far from the docks on the River Thames. He hoped no one would recognize him in this less than desirable part of town. The possibility always existed, however, of encountering someone who might begin spreading rumours about his appalling state.

A couple of street urchins skipped past him, not bothering to inquire after money. They barely glanced at him, as if they thought he was as destitute as they were. He *was* destitute in the depths of him. He had never, in the course of his eight and twenty years, allowed himself to become so negligent in his person, unbridled in discipline, nor tormented in his heart and mind.

He inclined his head at the sound of footsteps behind him, but could only discern two men who had stopped to talk beneath the low-hanging branches of a nearby tree. He narrowed his eyes at them, thinking for some reason they seemed out of place, but he found it difficult to see them clearly enough to determine why he felt that way.

He looked down and absently kicked a loose stone that lay in his path, sending it spiralling into the shrubbery.

Darcy had come to London hoping to hide in the dark, crowded streets. He allowed his valet to take time off to visit his family and told him that he would notify him when he was again needed.

When he first arrived in London, the persistent cold and rain seemed to echo his disposition. When the sun finally began shining a week ago, however, it did nothing to brighten his mood.

Darcy let a small room near the docks owned by an elderly gentleman. The innkeeper was grateful that his new renter, although keeping much to himself, did not seem like one to cause problems and was always prompt with his payment.

Initially Darcy had reasoned that the noise and constant activity in London would obscure his tormented thoughts. But it had done little to alleviate the real pain he felt in his heart.

Normally when in London, he attended lavish parties and balls, went to the theatre or a concert, and met with family and friends.

As he walked the darkened street, he realized how much he had wished – had even anticipated – doing all those things accompanied by Elizabeth Bennet.

His hand went up and rubbed his stubbly chin. He had not shaved nor trimmed his hair in close to two months. He could now walk the streets of London in an unrecognizable state. No one would suspect that he was the ever-fastidious Fitzwilliam Darcy. He seemed very much unlike the man on the inside, as well.

He dropped his head, and the layers of his greatcoat flapped in the breeze as he walked nearer to the docks. The odour of fish and garbage pervaded the air, and his stomach writhed as the pungent smell assaulted his senses. He grasped a nearby railing that looked over the murky waters to steady himself.

Footsteps behind him quickened. He twisted his head and noticed a somewhat fashionable couple walk towards him. He ducked his head so there would be no chance that they would recognize him, but not before seeing a look of disgust and revulsion etched on their faces at his despicable state. The gentleman ushered the woman away, muttering something indiscernible as he did.

Relief washed over Darcy that they did not seem to recognize him, but any gratefulness he felt was soon overpowered by the feeling of shame that infused him. He swayed, and his knees threatened to buckle. He felt as though he had little or no strength left.

He grasped the railing more forcibly as he felt himself begin to collapse onto the ground. He had a fleeting thought that it would be best for him to jump into the river and end it all. He was calculating just how many steps he would have to take to reach the edge of the dock, when he heard another voice inside of him. This time, however, it was louder than normal.

Get a grip, man! You know who you are!

Darcy raked his fingers through his long, unkempt hair, letting out a groan. Looking up to the heavens, as if the voice came from the Almighty Himself, Darcy uttered a soft, "Help me."

He began to feel dizzy, and his body trembled.

He heard approaching footsteps again, more strident than the others. He lowered his head down onto his hands, waiting for them to pass. Before he could formulate another thought, he felt himself being grabbed forcefully about his arms. His jerked his head from side to side, glancing up for a moment as he yelled in protest. It was the two men he had seen earlier lurking nearby.

As he was pulled to his feet, he struggled to free himself saying, "I have little money, but take want you want and leave me be!"

Their grip tightened, and they shoved him up against the railing. Darcy's heart thundered in his chest as the wooden beam jabbed into his stomach. Fear rose in him that the men were going to throw him into the water. He thought it odd that just moments before he was pondering jumping in himself, and now everything inside fought against it.

Darcy's hands were suddenly pulled back behind him, and he felt something cold encircle his wrists. Handcuffs! "What are you doing?" he mumbled. "I demand to know what is going on!"

"Yer time is up, Lockerly! Ye won't be makin' an escape this time!" one of the men said.

"Ye will likely be hangin' before the week is out!" the other said with a sneer.

Darcy shook his head and tried to make sense of their words. He struggled one more time to free himself from their grasp and the cruel bite of the handcuffs, but was unable. Although nothing had sobered him up in the past month, this had quickly done it. But he was still at a loss to understand what was happening.

He skewed his head to look up at the man on his left. "What do you mean? Who are you talking about? Who is this Lockerly?"

The man let out a gruff laugh. "He is someone who don't have much time left in this world. Now start walkin' and don't you be trying to git away again, or we'll shoot you, we will! The reward for ye is dead *or* alive!"

"But *more* if ye is alive!" The other man laughed viciously.

As Darcy staggered slowly, he felt a harsh push from behind. It was all he could do to keep from stumbling. As his feet reluctantly obeyed, his mind struggled to comprehend. The name Lockerly sounded familiar, but he could not recollect why.

The two men shoved him along impatiently, talking between themselves about the reward they would receive and how fortunate they were to have caught him. They occasionally gave him a sharp jab or roughly tugged his arm, ignoring any protest Darcy was able to mutter. He could not believe anyone would be treated in such a manner and began to wonder what they intended to do with him.

He wriggled his hands, trying to free himself from the cuffs, but that only served to bring about more pain, as the metal rings gripped his wrists without mercy.

"Where are you taking me?" Darcy asked, his voice and head a little clearer. "I demand to know who you are and why you are treating me in such a contemptible manner!"

The two men laughed. One said, "I think Lockerly has been trying to pass himself off as a gentleman, with that smooth, polished voice." He laughed again. "Too bad he don't *look* the part of a gentleman!"

Darcy winced. In refusing his offer of marriage, Miss Bennet had accused him of acting in a most ungentleman-like manner. He had always thought he displayed nothing but the opposite.

At another harsh push, Darcy steeled himself. "I am Fitzwilliam Darcy! You have no right to treat me thusly. I demand to know where you are taking me and why!"

Both men laughed again as if it were a joke. "You are Fitzwilliam Darcy?" asked one. "Well, beggin' your pardon, but *I* am the Prince Regent!"

They turned down a dark alley, and Darcy could not be sure that his feet would cooperate much longer. He was being dragged along and had no means by which to steady himself since his hands were bound behind him. At one point, he faltered, and then stumbled to the ground. Turning his face just in time, the side of his head crashed into the dirt.

Instead of asking whether he was hurt, the two men laughed again and jerked him up. Darcy felt warm liquid streaming down his neck. He knew he was bleeding from somewhere near his ear.

"You have no right to be doing this!" he cried out to them. "I demand some respect and to be taken immediately to the authorities!"

"Take you to the authorities?" the taller of the two men asked. "Now *that* we can do! As a matter of fact, we is takin' ye to the Thames Police Headquarters!"

They began to walk faster, and Darcy realized that they were indeed headed there. His body noticeably relaxed, and he found it much easier to walk when he was not fighting the two men. He took in a deep breath and hoped this misunderstanding might be cleared up shortly.

They came to the large brick building, the men holding onto him in a firm grip.

"We got 'em!" one of the men hollered. "We got Lockerly!"

"I am not this Lockerly!" Darcy repeated as he attempted to recollect who Lockerly was and why they thought it was him.

Several men rushed out. Darcy found himself in the grip of two more men. "Bring him in at once!" one of the men demanded.

Darcy was forcibly brought inside, and another man rushed past them. He heard the sound of keys and a metal door being opened. He was then thrown inside, and he crumpled to the ground. One of the men came in and removed the handcuffs from his wrists. He slowly lifted his head as the door was closed and locked.

He realized immediately that he had been put inside a cell. *Perhaps it is merely my drunken state that has me here,* he thought. *I shall sleep it off and be released in the morning.*

The men remained outside the door speaking in low voices to each other. Darcy heard a little.

"It is him; I am sure! Look at this drawing!"

"He had much longer hair and beard," said another.

"Probably had it cut and shaved to disguise himself," another suggested.

"Just think!" one man shouted. "We have recaptured Lockerly, the pirate! He won't escape this time, and he'll soon suffer the same fate as all his shipmates!"

Suddenly all the men laughed. "Looks like we'll be having another hanging soon!"

Darcy suddenly realized why he had recognized the name. Lockerly had been captured a while back, along with his band of pirates, but somehow he alone had escaped. All the men had been found guilty of piracy and hung. He shuddered as he thought that they had mistaken him for this evil man.

He determined that he was not in a state to argue with these men and decided he would wait until morning when he had a clear head. He glanced about at his primitive surroundings and saw a block slab upon which a blanket and pillow rested. He pulled himself up onto it and lay down, finding it cold and hard. He closed his eyes, not bothering to unfold the blanket.

Chapter 2

The sound of men's voices slowly roused Darcy. It was damp and cold; his muscles ached. The light of dawn barely lit his quarters, and he squinted, trying to adjust to the dim surroundings.

As he looked about him, it took several moments to ascertain his whereabouts. When he saw the bars across from him, he was jolted awake at the recollection of the events of the previous night.

He ran his fingers through the tangled curls in his hair and warily sat up. He could not decide whether he dreaded more being assaulted this morning by the consequences of his hard drinking last night or by the mercenary men who believed him to be this infamous escaped pirate named Lockerly.

He shook his head in anger and despondency. He was furious with himself and despaired of his current situation. He had allowed himself to wallow in the depths of his misery to such an extent that he was no longer recognizable as Fitzwilliam Darcy – neither inwardly nor outwardly.

"God, help me!" he uttered in a hushed pleading, his eyes closed and his hands clasped together tightly. "Is anyone to believe who I am, or shall I go to the gallows and die?"

He leaned against the wall, and his head fell back. He tried to swallow, but his mouth was dry, his lips cracked, and his throat parched. Looking to his right, he noticed a basin of water and a cup. He dipped the cup in the water and took a sip.

He spit it out immediately as the bitter taste assaulted his tongue. But even the small amount of moisture felt good in his mouth, so he took another sip and swallowed, grimacing as he did. Despite the foul taste, it did help ease his thirst.

I must convince them that I am Fitzwilliam Darcy and be set free from this detestable place!

"Hello, there!" He stood up and walked to the door of his cell, grabbing the bars tightly. He could hear the men off in another room.

He called out again as he rubbed the tight muscles in his arm. "I demand to talk to someone!" His head began to swim again with dizziness and pound with pain, and he was only able to mutter weakly, "I am not this Lockerly! You have the wrong man!"

When no one took heed of his cries, Darcy returned to the hard slab that had been his bed. Sitting back down, he put his head in his hands and massaged his forehead with his fingers. He took in a deep breath to help calm his stomach.

The image of his sister, Georgiana, came to mind, and he wondered what she would think if she came to learn of the disgraceful condition – and place – in which he now found himself!

He had not seen her since he first returned from Kent. It had been futile to try to keep his melancholy from her. She knew him so well. He could not tell her – he could not tell a single soul – that the one woman he had allowed himself to love had refused his offer of marriage. It was far too great a mortification; not only because she had turned him down, but also because he had been so completely wrong in his estimation of her regard towards him. *And in the man he thought he was.*

Georgiana had readily seen in his face and demeanour the anguish he felt. She repeatedly asked him what was wrong, and he continually assured her – with little success – that nothing was amiss. He could see the look of worry deepen on her features.

He finally deemed it prudent to distance himself from her before she became more concerned about him than she already was. He decided he must leave before she discovered the truth.

He sent her to Pemberley to spend the summer there, which she did each year. As he bade her farewell, Darcy had forced a loving smile on his face, which was not too difficult where his sister was concerned. He told her that he would not be staying in London for long, but would be visiting friends and would try to write to her as often as possible.

He closed his eyes as remorse flooded him that he had only written her once. He shuddered at the thought that she might come to learn he had been thrown in prison. It was imperative that they release him!

Darcy heard the sound of footsteps, which came to a stop in front of him. He slowly lifted his head and found himself looking into the face of a tall, well-dressed man.

"Finally!" Darcy exclaimed, steeling himself against the painful throbbing of his muscles and head. "Please, you must tell them I am not Lockerly."

"They say you claim to be Fitzwilliam Darcy." The man looked at him through narrow eyes. "I am slightly familiar with *who* that gentleman is, but I must confess I was not aware that Mr. Darcy of Pemberley was such a slovenly character as is before me."

"You must believe that I am he!" Darcy implored him.

"Hmm…" The man continued to scrutinize Darcy, rubbing his chin as his eyes swept over him. "In order to do that, you must open your shirt and show me your right shoulder."

Darcy shook his head in disbelief. "You want me to what?"

"Lockerly has a very prominent scar that goes from his shoulder to the centre of his chest. If you have no scar, you cannot be him."

Darcy fumbled with the buttons on his shirt and opened it.

The man gave a wave of his hand. "You may close it now."

Darcy looked at him with pleading eyes. "And?"

"I would have to agree with you. You are *not* Archibald Lockerly."

"Heavens, I am grateful to hear that." Darcy felt a surge of hope flood him. "You believe me."

"Yes, but I must confess that in your current condition," he waved his hand through the air, "you look a great deal like Lockerly and I would surmise not at all like Fitzwilliam Darcy."

"But at least you believe me."

The man unlocked the cell door and walked in, extending his hand. "I am Edward Foster of the Thames River Police."

Darcy reached out and took his hand. "It is good to make your acquaintance, sir. I am, truly, Fitzwilliam Darcy."

Foster sat beside him. "I am of the opinion that if Lockerly was truly trying to pass himself off as Fitzwilliam Darcy, he would have done it a little differently." His gaze swept over Darcy and his attire. "I hope you will accept my apologies for the unpleasant manner in which you have been treated and realize it was a simple mistake."

"How is it that you could see that I am not Lockerly, but no one else here could?"

"He was being held down in Brighton, so no one here has actually seen him. I, however, have been in the man's putrid presence a great deal. These men were basing their conviction that they had the correct man strictly from a drawing."

"So I may go?" Darcy asked and started to stand up.

Foster reached out and stopped him. "Not quite yet." Foster raised his shoulders as he took in a sharp breath. "Look, Mr. Darcy, I will not bother you with questions about why you look like this, but I believe your showing up here – looking as you do – was very providential."

Darcy cocked his head at him. "How is that?"

Foster took in a deep breath. "This Lockerly is a slippery one. We had him and his ruffian band in custody, locked up, and when he was being transported to London, he was snatched out of our hands." Foster paused and looked intently at the man next to him. "Mr. Darcy, we may need you to do something for us."

Darcy let out a breath he had been holding. The relief of Foster's words coupled with his curiosity had helped clear his mind immensely. He leaned towards Foster. "Exactly what do you want me to do?"

The man stood up and faced Darcy. "We would like you to impersonate Lockerly for a short while. We will spread word that he is recruiting men to make up a new crew."

Darcy bolted to his feet and then sank down quickly as his head began to spin. "You want me to what?"

"The news of your capture... that is, Lockerly's capture, has spread like a wildfire. At the moment, I am the only one who knows a mistake has been made." Foster spoke, his voice barely a whisper now.

Darcy shook his head in disbelief. "This is absurd! I cannot be someone I am not!"

"Even for the good of the country? For the lives of innocents that may be lost?" Foster sat down again. "Unfortunately... or fortunately, I suppose it depends on how you look at it... in the state you are in now, you do look a good deal like Lockerly. If we could use you as bait to lure him into our net, we would be forever grateful."

"But I am no sailor. I have some basic knowledge of sailing, but not a large vessel and definitely not out in the high seas."

Foster let out a laugh. "You are getting ahead of yourself, my good man. We expect that Lockerly will hear that someone is claiming to be him and will make himself known. I will have two men with you at all times for your protection. They will be passing themselves off as two of your sailors."

"You actually want me to recruit pirates?" Darcy asked incredulously.

Foster nodded.

"Definitely not! No, it is too risky," Darcy replied, shaking his head. He looked into Foster's eyes. "What if one of these men realizes I am not Lockerly?"

Foster let out a puff of air. "You look just like him. But in addition to that, all of his men were hung. Not one is left. He is probably hiding out somewhere, but I doubt he is anywhere near London."

Darcy forced his mind to think. "Then how will he come to hear about me... him... another Lockerly?"

"Word travels fast around the docks and up and down the Thames and the English Channel. We will spread word around, and I can guarantee he will hear about it. If you can give me a week... no more than ten days... hopefully he will show up to confront this imposter. We will be waiting for him when he comes."

Darcy was not convinced. "Confronting that imposter is what has me concerned, as well as rounding up a crew of disreputable men to be pirates!" Darcy let out a huff. "Both are ludicrous and could put me in a very precarious situation!"

"Calm down, Mr. Darcy. When Lockerly comes, we will be ready for him. And chances are the men who want to join you will be young lads who are only looking for adventure. You will have nothing to worry about with them."

Darcy sat still and groaned, the shaking of his head the only movement.

"I do not know how much you have heard about Lockerly, but the man has rarely taken a life on his own. Granted, he will seize a ship and leave it burning while the crew of that ship is stranded in lifeboats, but his main goal has been to *liberate* its treasure and be on his way. It is true that at his hands many lives have been lost at sea when they were not rescued, but he is not a man prone to fighting or taking a life intentionally when he does not have to." Foster paused and cradled his chin in his hand. "Yet, I have heard amazing stories about his fencing ability. More often than not, his captives surrender before any harm is inflicted."

"I am still not convinced of this. Certainly someone else can do it."

Foster regarded Darcy for a moment. "By the looks of you, I would guess that you have gone through some sort of adversity. Consider this a way to work your way through it while helping us out." Foster shook his head. "There is no one else who can do this. Pictures of Lockerly are everywhere." He pulled out a drawing and showed it to Darcy. "You have to admit there is a resemblance."

Darcy scowled at the likeness. "Anyone with a week's worth of beard and unkempt attire would suffice."

"No, only you will do."

Darcy stood up and walked over to the door again and grasped the bars. "Let me go home and think about this."

Foster cleared his throat. "Unfortunately, Darcy, you will need to remain here another day. We have to keep up the illusion of Lockerly being in custody." Foster slapped Darcy on the back. "Besides, I would surmise that you would not return home unless you had cleaned yourself up. Can I assume that you have not been staying at Pemberley or your home here in this condition?" He said this as more of a statement than a question.

Darcy groaned.

"In addition, I do not think you would wish for news of your imprisonment and your destitute state to reach your family. I fear if I release you as Fitzwilliam Darcy, there would be no way to prevent that."

Darcy abruptly turned around. "How dare you!"

Foster shook his head. "It would not be by my doing, Mr. Darcy. That would be what would happen if you left this place as

Mr. Darcy. But…" Foster stood up and stepped to Darcy's side. "If you leave this place with me as Lockerly, no one would need to know."

Darcy looked down and covered his head with his hands. "If that is how it is to be, then so be it."

"Excellent! I need to work on the details of how we are going to play this out, but I will get back to you on the morrow. In the meantime, do not mention to anyone here about being Fitzwilliam Darcy. I do not want word of this to get around."

Darcy let out a sigh. "Just make sure no one hangs me while you are gone."

"You have my word!" Foster said with a laugh.

"Good! And Foster?"

"Yes?"

"May I please have something to eat?"

~~*

Throughout the day, men came by the cell and peered in, making spiteful and disparaging remarks. With each accusation, Darcy felt awash with contempt – at them and himself. He was only able to remain silent against his tormentors because he knew who he was. He was at least thankful that after a good night's sleep and meal, his head was much clearer than it had been in quite some time.

As he considered Foster's proposition, he thought how this would truly be the only way to prevent news of his being thrown in gaol from being bandied about London and amongst his friends and family.

He raked his fingers through his hair and shuddered as he wondered what had become of him! He was Fitzwilliam Darcy, after all – meticulous, proper, esteemed… He had always considered himself fully capable of handling any situation. Yet he had been completely powerless in securing the hand of the one woman he truly loved and then in conquering the hopelessness and despair that had been wrought in him because of that.

He sat up erect and considered how this obligation might help take his mind off Elizabeth Bennet. That day she had refused his offer of marriage, he stormed out greatly incensed at her. But throughout the night, as he had recollected the words she had lashed out at him and then penned the letter to her, he had realized she had not spoken flippantly or even without basis.

Her misunderstanding of George Wickham's character was not her fault, and he could readily see how that scoundrel had deceived her about *both* their characters. He had grown up with George Wickham, but that young man had become a thorn in his flesh. And yet it was her accusation that he had unduly interfered with his friend Charles Bingley and her sister Jane that made him realize how wrong he had been.

He thought back to the words he had spoken that night and put his hand over his mouth, closing his eyes. How could he have been so presumptuous in stating to her – in an offer of marriage – that her family was unsuitable and so far beneath him? He let out a groan as he realized he was now more upset with himself for his behaviour than he was with Elizabeth for refusing him.

Yes, he would agree to impersonate this infamous pirate Lockerly despite abhorring all manner of disguise. But once all was behind him, or perhaps as he was in the midst of it, he would make every effort to address those traits she had claimed were so offensive to her. He vowed to improve his person, even though he would likely never see her again.

Chapter 3

Longbourn

Elizabeth Bennet linked an arm through Jane's, and the two sisters walked down the stairs. The sun greeted them warmly, a welcome reprieve from the dreary cold and rain that had plagued them over the past month. Elizabeth reached up on the tip of her toes to touch a dust-filled ray of sunlight with her free hand. She wiggled her fingers, sending the tiny motes whirling, and causing both sisters to laugh.

As they took the remaining steps downward, Elizabeth looked at Jane and smiled. It was good to see her laugh again.

The improvement of the weather this morning seemed to have improved both girls' dispositions. Several months ago, Jane's joy had been shattered after a futile attempt to see Mr. Bingley during her stay in London. She had visited with his sisters, and they had returned the courtesy with a call to her at her aunt's home near Cheapside, but their brother had never made an effort to see her.

Elizabeth was concerned. She and she alone knew the truth about why Mr. Bingley had not visited Jane. It had been Mr. Darcy's influence that had tempered Mr. Bingley's affections for her, and the conspiracy – of sorts – between him and Miss Bingley not to divulge Jane's presence in town to him.

Since then she had made every effort to help keep Jane's mind off Mr. Bingley, encouraging her in any way she could. But

Elizabeth was facing an inner battle of her own. She found herself repeatedly going over Mr. Darcy's words in his unexpected offer of marriage and futilely tried to recall the words she had angrily lashed back at him in her refusal.

The letter Mr. Darcy had written to her addressed several of the accusations she had made against him. Sometimes in the quiet of the night, alone in her room, she would pull out the letter to read it again. It did not give her much comfort; in fact, it often produced a myriad of conflicting feelings: anger, regret, despair, and even an unwelcomed sense of honour at the thought of being singled out by such a man. If only she could put Mr. Darcy's proposal out of her mind as easily as she had the one made by Mr. Collins.

At the mere thought of their cousin, she shuddered.

"Are you unwell, Lizzy?" Jane asked with a quick glance.

They reached the bottom of the stairs, and Elizabeth stopped. She bit her lip and wondered whether she should tell Jane the truth. Jane knew about Mr. Darcy's proposal and how her sister had refused him, while no one else in her family had that knowledge. Her mother would be displeased beyond measure if she knew Elizabeth had turned down a man of such great fortune. But Elizabeth had never told Jane that Mr. Darcy had been partly responsible for keeping Mr. Bingley from seeing her by not divulging to him her presence in town.

"I am well, Jane," she answered reassuringly. She let out a more light-hearted sigh. "I am merely contemplating my trip with the Gardiners to the Lake District."

"And you shall have a wonderful time! I enjoyed it immensely when they took me!"

Jane and Elizabeth came into the dining room, finding both their parents there. The sunny morning had not had a positive effect on their mother, however, as she greeted them with, "Oh, my head is pounding so!"

"Good morning, Mama. Good morning, Papa!" Elizabeth walked around and gave her mother and father kisses, followed by Jane doing the same. The two eldest Bennet daughters sat down at the table.

"It is a beautiful day," Elizabeth said. "I hope it is not too terribly muddy out. I long for a good walk!"

Her father smiled; however, he did not seem as cheerful as he normally did in the morning. "I daresay, Elizabeth, that you will take a walk today whether it is muddy outside or not! You are the adventurous one, are you not?" He did not wait for an answer, but picked up some letters that were folded up next to his plate.

Elizabeth recollected the day she had walked through the mud to visit a sick Jane at Netherfield and made no response. She glanced at Jane, who was looking down into her cup as she poured herself some tea. She knew Jane was thinking about it, as well.

Wishing to change the subject, Elizabeth motioned to the letters. "And what news have you, Papa? Anything important?"

"Yes, but prepare yourself for some bad news."

"Bad news?" both sisters asked.

Mrs. Bennet was quite agitated. "Why must letters always contain such vexing news? I despise getting a letter! People have no compassion for my nerves!"

"What is it, Papa?" Elizabeth asked, her brows narrowing in concern.

"One is a letter from my sister. Viola, as you know, lives with her family on St. Mary's in the Isles of Scilly. It has been many years since we have seen them. And the other is a letter from the Gardiners."

"Our Aunt Gardiner has written?" Elizabeth's face lit up. "What has she to say? Does she mention our trip to the Lake District?"

"I cannot wait to see her children again!" Jane interjected. "I so enjoyed them when I was in London."

"But you said there was bad news! Tell us, Father!" Elizabeth exclaimed.

"Well, Lizzy," her father said. "I shall leave it to you to read."

He handed the letter to Elizabeth, and she began to read it aloud.

Fondest greetings to all my family,

I hope you are all well. I know that we have been planning with much anticipation a trip to the Lake District with Elizabeth, but something has arisen, and we are now not able to go. We had hoped that perhaps a shorter trip to Derbyshire would be possible, but now, that is also out of the question. We are so disappointed, but know that the greatest disappointment must be felt by Elizabeth (and our children, as well, who were so looking forward to seeing

Jane again). We promise to make an effort to go next summer. We shall count down the days! I hope you can find it in your heart to forgive us.

M. Gardiner

Elizabeth took in a deep breath and let it out slowly. "I *am* disappointed, but I know if it were at all possible, they would have made the effort."

"Oh, Elizabeth," Jane said as she reached out and touched her sister's hand. "I know you were so looking forward to it! I feel terrible that I have talked so much lately about my trip with them two years ago. Pray, forgive me."

Elizabeth put her other hand on top of Jane's. "Dearest Jane, please do not fret. There will be another opportunity for me to go with them."

Mrs. Bennet waved a handkerchief through the air. "Upon my word! Something else will come up if you make other plans, and they shall likely all come to nothing!"

Elizabeth let out a long sigh and looked at her father. "And the other letter? Does it contain bad news as well?"

"Yes, but I have something to ask of you two after you have read it, especially in light of the Gardiners' letter." He handed it to Elizabeth with a sombre look.

Elizabeth began reading the letter.

My dearest brother,

I do hope this finds you and your family well. I am not quite sure how to tell you this other than to just come out and say it. I am very ill and become weaker by the day. The doctor is not certain how much longer I have and has given no hope for a cure. I long to see you again and would make the journey to Hertfordshire in a heartbeat, if I could, but that is not possible.

Elizabeth looked up at her father. "I am so sorry to hear this, Father."

"I cannot bear to even think about this!" Mrs. Bennet uttered. "Poor Viola, and then it will be your father's time to go, and then those Collinses will have us out of our home!"

Elizabeth turned to her mother. "Please, Mama, have some

consideration for Father."

"This whole dreadful affair has me…"

"I see no occasion for this type of prattle, Mrs. Bennet!" her husband declared impatiently.

Jane paled and her eyes glistened with tears. "Oh, Papa, how sad it would be to never see her again. I remember when they last visited us. Their daughter Melanie was about eleven. She was the same age as Elizabeth."

Her father nodded. "She mentions the two of you. Read on, Lizzy."

I know the family was never pleased when I took that sea bathing excursion to the Isles and ended up meeting and marrying Henry, but trust me, I have truly been happy here. Brother, I do not know if this is asking too much, but would there be a possibility for you to make a journey to see us before I am too feeble to enjoy the visit? You are certainly welcome to come alone or with any or all of your family. Our daughter, Melanie, has the fondest memories of both Elizabeth and Jane, and she has asked particularly if they might be able to come, as well. While she is bearing up tolerably, it would do her good to have her cousins here to cheer her up. Please consider this, my dear brother, for otherwise, I know I shall never see you again.

I promise you that I will not allow this to be a sombre visit. St. Mary's, our island, is a beautiful place with rocky outcroppings, sandy beaches, and rolling hills that are laden with heather. I trust that you will find pleasant weather (apart from an occasional storm) and a nice secluded place to sit and read. The ladies in your family would all find it much to their liking.

If you choose to come, we have found the most economical way to travel is to book passage on any of the merchant ships that carry passengers, either out of London or more southern ports. Please respond with your answer as soon as possible.

All my love, Viola

Elizabeth lowered her hand slowly. "What are you thinking of doing, Papa"

"He is going to get himself killed; that is what he is going to do!" cried Mrs. Bennet.

Mr. Bennet slowly shook his head. "Now, now, Mrs. Bennet, I am going to do no such thing! Lizzy, Jane, I am very much inclined to visit her. She is my only sister, and I now regret never having taken the time to travel to the Isles. Your mother and I were just discussing the possibility of the two of you joining me. With the Phillipses living nearby and the younger girls to help your mother, I think a few weeks without us would not be too burdensome."

"Not too burdensome!" Mrs. Bennet cried. "I can well imagine what calamities might befall us while you are all away!" She waved a handkerchief nervously. "And I dare not think what might happen to Mr. Bennet and you two girls on a voyage across the sea!"

Elizabeth gently placed her hand over her mother's and turned to her father. "Oh, Father! How I would love to make the journey with you." She looked at Jane, hoping she would eagerly accept, as well, despite her proclivity for becoming sick on a boat. She was certain doing something like this would be a diverting way to help Jane take her mind off Mr. Bingley.

Jane began shaking her head. "Oh, I cannot fathom it. When the Gardiners took me sailing on Windermere Lake for merely an hour, I was dreadfully ill. And it was calm waters!"

"But, Jane, perhaps you would not get sick this time."

"I would not wish to take such a chance. But certainly you two must go, especially since the Gardiners had to cancel their trip with you."

"Yes, but… oh Papa, can we afford something like this?"

"We had bountiful crops this year, and I think it is very feasible. I intend to inquire about the merchant ships to find out what the fares would be. I cannot bear to think I may not see my sister again."

Elizabeth brought the letter to her heart and let out a sigh. "As difficult as it will be to see Aunt Viola so ill, I think I would enjoy it very much. Earlier you said I was adventurous. You knew I would agree to go, did you not?"

Mr. Bennet nodded. "I did indeed!"

Elizabeth turned to her mother and squeezed her hand. "And do you truly mind if we go, Mama?"

Mrs. Bennet shook her head. "I suppose there is nothing to say to convince him to do otherwise. If he wants to risk his life and that of his daughter at the hands of marauding pirates or becoming shipwrecked during a storm, what am I to say about it?"

Elizabeth smiled and patted her mother's hand. "I am so pleased you understand!"

Later that very day, an invitation arrived that created a stir amongst the ladies, specifically Lydia, Kitty, and Mrs. Bennet. Lydia was ecstatic that she was invited to join Mrs. Forster and her husband's regiment when they departed for Brighton. Mrs. Forster had singled Lydia out as her particular friend, and Lydia would not rest until her parents agreed to let her go. Kitty felt it extremely unfair that she was not invited, while Mrs. Bennet envied her youngest daughter for the honour of such an invitation.

Elizabeth was not happy with the idea and decidedly expressed her opinion to her father.

It was finally agreed upon, however, that she should be allowed to go under certain conditions. She would travel to Brighton with the Forsters, but Mr. Bennet and Elizabeth would send for her when they stopped in London on their return trip. It shortened Lydia's anticipated stay, which vexed her exceedingly, but at least she was able to go.

The house was much calmer when Lydia departed with the Forsters two days later.

~~*

Mr. Bennet quickly made the arrangements for them to sail out of London. Elizabeth would share a cabin with a single woman who was travelling to the Isles of Scilly with her brother and his wife. They would be in the cabin next to theirs, while Mr. Bennet would be travelling in a cabin down the hall with two other men.

Two days before they were to leave, Mr. Bennet and Elizabeth bade farewell to their family and took a carriage to London. They spent the night at the home of the Gardiners, enjoying the company of Mrs. Bennet's brother, his wife, and their four children.

Early the next morning, the household awakened to a rather bleak day. Clouds hung low in the sky, and a light mist chilled the air. They ate a quick breakfast and then gathered their belongings before leaving with Mr. and Mrs. Gardiner, who decided to accompany Mr. Bennet and his daughter, to the wharf.

When Elizabeth stepped out of the Gardiners' home, she hugged her pelisse tightly about her, bringing the hood up over her head. She and Mrs. Gardiner stepped carefully, but quickly, over the muddied cobblestone path that took them to the waiting carriage.

Once everyone was seated and the carriage was making its way down the narrow road, Elizabeth suddenly felt her heart begin to pound.

"Oh!" she said as she put her hand over her heart. "As much as it grieves me that Aunt Viola is not well, and that is the main reason we are making this journey, I cannot help but feel a good deal of excitement!" She reached out to grasp her aunt's hand. "Are we really doing this?"

Her father looked over at her. "There is still time for you to change your mind, Elizabeth. You may remain with the Gardiners if you prefer. But once you are on that ship, they will not turn around if you suddenly decide you do not want to go!"

Elizabeth let out a laugh. "Father, you know me too well to suggest that I would ever consider that."

"I do not doubt that at all!" he said with a laugh.

As they drew near the river, the cry of seagulls rang in their ears and the smell of salty seawater filled their nostrils with every breath. When their eyes first beheld the tall masts of the sailing ships, Elizabeth reached out and again took her aunt's hand. "I hope you know how much I truly wanted to go with you to the Lake District, dearest Aunt, but I think I shall enjoy this immensely."

Aunt Gardiner covered Elizabeth's hand with hers. "Trust me, Elizabeth. I know you shall. I can readily see you skipping across the sandy beaches in your bare feet, letting the waves lap up above your ankles, and exploring every inch of that island. An opportunity like this does not come along often. I know that you will have a life-changing adventure!"

Chapter 4

Darcy awoke the next morning feeling, for the first time in a long time, a semblance of being his old self again and was eager to depart this appalling place! He felt grimy both inside and out, and wanted nothing more than to have his valet give him a shave and a good scrubbing from head to toe in a nice, hot bath. But he knew that was not possible.

He ate a barely tolerable meal and then sat down to wait, wondering what the day would bring.

Shortly thereafter, Edward Foster walked in and began talking with the warden. He then followed him to Darcy's cell. The warden opened the door and told his prisoner he was to go with Foster.

Darcy shot a look of surprise to Foster, who gave him a slight nod.

"Come," Foster said with a wave of his hand. "I have a carriage waiting for us outside."

Foster led Darcy out to the carriage parked directly in front. The door was open, and two men were sitting inside. Darcy stepped in and sat across from the men. Foster spoke to the driver and then joined them, taking the seat next to Darcy.

Darcy gave Foster a questioning glance. "Did you tell the warden I am not Lockerly? Does this mean I am no longer expected to portray him? Is the scheme at an end?"

"Far from it. I shall explain, but first, Darcy, may I introduce you to the first two recruits who shall crew your ship? This is

Evans and Lindel."

Darcy looked at the two men and nodded, wondering where Foster had found them. Their clothes were tattered, torn, and embedded with stains. Both the men and their clothes most likely had not been washed in at least a month. They were unshaven, and each sported hair that was long and curled at the napes of their necks. The putrid smell that emanated from the two of them assaulted Darcy's nostrils.

"You certainly look a lot like Lockerly," the one named Evans said in a fairly respectable manner, which actually surprised Darcy.

"I suppose if you look closely, you can see the difference," Lindel replied.

"I can assure you that I am not he," Darcy replied. "I am Fitzwilliam Darcy."

When he noticed the men scrutinize him from head to toe, he realized he should be grateful Foster believed him.

"Well now, let us get down to the particulars of what is going to happen," Foster said, as if they were going to discuss a business transaction. "As I began to plot out our little scheme, I realized I had best inform at least some of the authorities what we were going to do, so no one would come and arrest you again. I told the warden you were not Archibald Lockerly, but advised him not to speak of it to anyone. As far as everyone else knows, Lockerly was arrested last night and is in my custody."

"That still leaves me with a great deal of concern that my sister and other family will find out it was me."

"No need to worry," Foster said, casually leaning back in the seat. "I told them you were Benjamin Smith."

Darcy started. "Who is Benjamin Smith?"

Foster smiled. "I have no idea, but I thought the name suited you."

Darcy folded his arms about his chest and let out a huff. "So I am now Fitzwilliam Darcy portraying an unknown Benjamin Smith, who in turn is portraying the pirate Archibald Lockerly?"

Foster paused for a moment and then smiled. "I believe that is correct!"

"If you only knew how much I abhor disguise of any sort!"

"Now," Foster continued as if he had not heard Darcy's last words, "since there is always the possibility that someone still might come to arrest you, thinking you are Lockerly, I am advising the authorities that in order to prevent another case of mistaken identity, they must make sure it is Lockerly by checking for his scar. If anyone seeks to arrest you again, you will have to bare your chest."

Darcy sat back in the seat, his arms rigidly crossed in front of him. "I would hazard a guess there are worse things one might be required to do, but I hope I shall not have to!" He absently ran his fingers up towards his shoulder.

"It is only to ensure the mistake is not made again."

Darcy shook his head. "I thank you for that. I wonder what he may have done to receive such a scar!"

Foster nodded. "We can only imagine, can we not? A sword fight, perhaps?"

Darcy laughed, but there was no humour in it. "I suppose it is fortunate that I enjoy fencing and even excel at it, but mainly in the defensive manoeuvres. Offensively, I might not be such a proficient opponent if I was called upon to take up the sword!"

"Remember, Darcy, you will have my two men with you at all times! I will be in the vicinity, keeping my eyes and ears open for any sign of Lockerly or trouble with the men who come to you. You will be safe."

Darcy let out a huff and combed his fingers through his hair. "I am glad you feel so confident. I only wish I could be as certain as you seem to be!"

Evans spoke. "Whilst we cannot completely guarantee anyone's safety, we can certainly do everything in our power to protect you. We will be watching out for anything out of the ordinary – anything that may indicate that some sort of trouble might be brewing."

Darcy let out a sigh. "I shall portray this Lockerly for just a week, correct?"

Foster nodded. "We first must work with you for several days, however, to prepare you for your role."

"But then, if after seven days Lockerly does not show up, I am free to go?"

Again Foster nodded. "Of course. Are you willing to do this?"

This time it was Darcy who gave a single, reluctant nod of his head. He folded his hands and placed them firmly in his lap.

Foster slapped Darcy's shoulder. "Good! I am glad you agree. From now on, you are no longer Darcy. This is the last time any of us will refer to you as such. From now on, we shall call you Lockerly."

"I only hope I remember to respond to that name."

"Oh, that will be the easy part. The next order of business, and likely to be more difficult, is to teach you to lose your gentleman-like behaviour – your manners and speech, for instance."

Darcy turned abruptly at the words. "You expect me to begin exhibiting those mannerisms that I find so repulsive? I fear I… I cannot do that!" Darcy exclaimed, shaking his head. He wondered how years of formal training could suddenly be erased, but his heart began to beat fiercely as he recollected Miss Bennet's accusation that he was severely wanting in that area.

"Lockerly claims to have some education, so he does have a little polish, but not to the extent you do. When you speak, you must slur some of your words, shorten them, and use some common slang."

"I fear I am ill-qualified for this," he said, turning his head to glance out the window. "I have not the talent to change a lifetime of formal training."

"But ye ken do it," Evans said with a smile. "'Tis not too hard."

"Jest thinks of people whose tongue 'as offended yer ears an' talk like 'em." Lindel said. "You'll be talkin' like a commoner in no time."

Darcy shook his head, recollecting many people in London who would come up to him begging… beggin' for money.

"I do not… I don't know…" Darcy said with a slight grimace.

"There you go! I dunno is better," Foster laughed.

They continued to work with Darcy as they drove through London. After they had been on the road for close to an hour, Darcy asked, "Where are we going?" Darcy cleared his throat and tried again. "Where're we goin'?"

Foster smiled. "We're almost there. We'll be at a secluded place where we ken git ye out an' spend some time wi' ye workin' more on yer speech an' on a few other things. Yer posture, for one. Although from what I 'eard, ye were stumbling about fairly well the night they picked ye up."

Darcy groaned. "That is all behind me!" He bit his lip as he wondered whether in truth it really was!

"Mebbe." Foster said softly. "But it'd do ye well to put yerself back into the frame of mind in which ye was found that night."

"Trust me. That would not do me well at all," Darcy said with a quick shake of his head.

"Well," Foster said, as he slapped Darcy on the shoulder, "whatever it takes to walk an' talk a little more like that ne'er-do-well, I would suggest ye do it! I'll remain wi' ye fer jest tonight an' then leave to find a ship, get it ready, an' start spreading the word 'bout Lockerly. I'll interview any men that show up before you do to git rid of any troublemakers. Evans an' Lindel will stay an' work wi' ye fer the next three days to rid ye of yer refined manners, an' they'll also instruct ye in the basics of sailin'. Then in four days we'll meet at the ship."

Darcy was amazed at how quickly and thoroughly Foster could change from talking properly to speaking like the most uneducated ruffian. He also thought Foster looked a little too eager, as though he thought that this was an excellent plan. Darcy, however, had his doubts.

They rode the remainder of the way in silence. The silence was deafening to Darcy, for in all the talk of ridding himself of gentleman-like behaviour, Miss Bennet's accusations resounded loudly.

~~*

At length, they pulled off the main road and came to a small house situated behind some trees. It looked like a cottage, smaller even than the main dining room at Pemberley.

"Here we are! Yer trainin' – *Lockerly* – will continue 'ere."

The carriage door was opened and Darcy began to step out, but Foster stayed him with his hand. "One more thing. I'll no longer be Foster. Me new name is Forrest, an' Evans an' Lindel are now Ellis an' Lansing."

Foster did not wait for Darcy's response, but extended his hand for Darcy to step out and directed him towards the house.

As Darcy walked towards the small structure, Foster called out, "A lit'l more swagger an' a limp might be nice!"

Darcy tightened his jaw and then did what Foster said. He heard the men snicker softly.

They entered the small home, and the aroma of bread baking and some sort of meat dish greeted them. Darcy wondered how long it had been since he had eaten a decent meal.

He was shown to his room, and Foster turned to leave, saying, "We'll be eatin' in half an hour. Clean yerself up... but only jest a little."

The room was small, but Darcy was grateful it was clean. The last place he had stayed – before being thrown into a gaol cell – most likely had not been cleaned in months. An opened satchel was on the bed, and when Darcy peered in, he saw clothing.

He was anxious to get out of the clothes he was wearing, but when he pulled out a white shirt with ruffles down the front and billowing sleeves, much like the sails on a ship, he threw it back down into the satchel.

He shook his head. "I refuse to wear this nonsense!"

He walked to the basin and picked up the pitcher. He poured water into the basin and dipped his hands into the cool water, bringing them up and splashing it onto his face. His fingers ran over his stubbly beard, and again he wished for his valet's attention. How much he would love a bath. How much he would love – and desperately needed – a shave.

He picked up a towel and patted his face dry. At least that part of him felt clean. He walked over to a mirror and braced himself for what he would see when he looked into it.

The person who stared back at him seemed a stranger to him. His hair was longer than was deemed decent, just brushing his shoulders. The natural curl was flattened with oil and grime. His beard had filled in a good deal since the last time he had seen his reflection. His eyes were red, and dark shadows lay beneath them. His lips were dry and cracked, and he wore a scowl. Perhaps he actually *was* turning into a pirate!

Darcy let out a huff and sat down on the small, narrow bed. He was tempted to lie down and fall asleep, hoping he would wake up from this nightmare. But the nightmare was not only having to pass himself off as a pirate, but having to face the accusations about his character that Elizabeth Bennet had attributed to him.

The dinner bell rang. *Good!* He would push that thought aside for now and enjoy a decent – he hoped – meal.

He walked down the hall to the small dining room and found

the three men already there. He greeted them with a nod of his head.

"No need fer all that formality, Lockerly," Foster said with a smile. "Jest come in an' sit down wi' the rest of us."

"Thank you," Darcy replied.

"Now where'd ye learn all yer manners, Lockerly? No need to say please an' thank ye to us."

Darcy sat down, deciding he would not speak unless spoken to. He placed the cloth napkin on his lap.

"No, no, no!" Lindel cried out. "Ye 'ave no need fer a napkin! Yer shirt sleeve'll serve the purpose better."

"You mean the shirt in my room with sleeves big enough to sail a ship and ruffles that should only be worn by a woman?" Darcy shook his head. "Indeed, I shall not wear that!"

"Ye must look the part, Lockerly, in addition to speaking an' acting the part." Foster took some potatoes from a bowl and set it back down in front of him. "But there are other shirts in there without the ruffles. Ye ken wear those."

"Good! Please pass me the potatoes, Foster."

Foster was looking down at his plate and turned his head slowly, lifting only his eyes to Darcy. "Who is ye talkin' to? Me name is Forrest an' I'll do no such thing. Ye'll reach across the table for 'em, as ye'll do fer anything else ye want!"

Darcy sat there for a moment stunned, and then suddenly he began to chuckle. Then he began to laugh out loud.

"What's so funny?" Evans asked.

Darcy shook his head and extended both hands. "This! All this! I would have loved to have gotten away with this behaviour as a child, but having proper manners was instilled in me with severe repercussions if I exhibited otherwise. It has been so long that I have lived that way, that it has become a part of me. I am really not sure I can do this."

"Trust me," Foster said. "By the end of our stay 'ere, ye'll not think twice 'bout 'aving to speak or act a certain way."

By the time Darcy retired for the evening that first day, his mind reeled with everything the men had tried to teach him. The inarticulate din that had been coming out of his mouth caused him to shudder. But if he had hoped that having a diversion such as this would rid his mind – and his heart – of Elizabeth Bennet, he was mistaken. Every mention of ridding him of his gentleman-like behaviour made her accusation as fresh as if it had happened yesterday, not just over two months ago.

Chapter 5

Elizabeth stood at the rail of the ship, a hand tucked through her father's arm. The fog had begun to lift, and rays of sunlight could be seen dancing across the water. A mild breeze moved the ship steadily along the Thames towards the English Channel.

"My dearest Lizzy, I am glad you agreed to accompany me to see my sister. I would not have wished to travel alone, and you are sensible enough to know that you are the one person whose company I find most pleasing and suited to my temperament."

"I am delighted you wished for me to come along."

He reached over and patted her hand. "Truth be told, I am concerned about Viola. I have no idea how she will be when we get there. She most likely will be in a sickly state, possibly worse. I needed to have someone strong by my side if we find her at death's door. I know you will prove to be invaluable to me." He shook his head sombrely and took in a deep breath. "I only wish I had made more of an effort to see her these past few years."

Elizabeth placed her hand over his. She felt his long, bony fingers and the rough calluses on his knuckles and gave his hand a light squeeze. "I shall be there for you, Papa. If you need a shoulder to cry on, use mine."

Mr. Bennet waved his other hand through the air. "Upon my word, you know I never cry…"

Elizabeth stole a glance at her father and thought she saw his eyes glisten.

He was silent for a moment, and Elizabeth finally said, "We

shall make this a very special visit, Papa. We shall enjoy every moment with her and take good memories home with us."

"Yes, yes, my dear, we shall."

The two stayed up on deck until the boat reached the English Channel. They passed the White Cliffs at Dover and ventured further out into the sea. The waves became a little choppy, and the wind picked up, moving the ship briskly along. Salt water sprayed into their faces, and they both decided it would be best to return below deck.

~~*

The ship made good progress to the Isles of Scilly with a steady wind, relatively calm seas, and a very knowledgeable and courteous crew.

Elizabeth's cabin was small, but clean. It had two beds, a chest of drawers, and a single mirror on the wall.

Elizabeth got along splendidly with her travelling companion, Miss Alice Whiting. She was thirty-seven, never married, but seemingly content in her circumstances, living with her brother and his wife. Mr. and Mrs. Whiting loved to travel, and his sister almost always accompanied them. This was their third journey to the Isles of Scilly to visit friends. They loved the beautiful beaches, mild weather, and lack of crowds.

Despite a rather large age difference, Elizabeth and Miss Whiting discovered they had much in common. They both delighted in observing people, and more than once they shared a laugh over something someone said or did that they found diverting.

They were both early risers, and the first morning out at sea they enjoyed a leisurely walk on the deck of the ship before most people were up. They found that the morning waters were calmer than later in the day.

The two ladies also discovered that they had read many of the same books and enjoyed the same favourite poets, which prompted lively discussions between them.

There was one other thing they had in common. They had both turned down a proposal of marriage.

Miss Whiting confessed to Elizabeth that she now regretted turning down the proposal from a man for whom she had felt only a friendship. She was under the impression that she would have had more strength of feeling if she truly loved him.

Elizabeth admitted to Miss Whiting that she had also turned down a proposal, but one that she did not regret at all. She could readily laugh as she told Miss Whiting about Mr. Collins and his oddities. Then she told her about how her friend Charlotte readily stepped in to mend any sort of broken heart Mr. Collins may have suffered at Elizabeth's refusal, and promptly secured his offer of marriage for herself.

"I honestly believe," Elizabeth told her, "that his pride was wounded more than his heart by my refusal." She smiled and shook her head. "He would have had a difficult time going back to his patroness Lady Catherine de Bourgh without having secured some sort of understanding with a lady."

As much as Elizabeth could laugh about refusing her cousin's offer and readily talk about his unpleasant ways, she could not bring herself to mention refusing Mr. Darcy's offer of marriage. It was something that still aroused a great many mixed feelings within her.

As they walked together the second day out, Miss Whiting brought up the subject again.

"Do you think it wrong, Elizabeth, for me to wonder how different my life would be now if I had only said yes to him? I am not unhappy living with my brother and his wife, but I wonder if I truly made a mistake."

Elizabeth took her arm and patted it. "We all wonder about things like that, Alice. I often wonder how different my life might be if I had had a governess growing up, or maybe even a brother. From time to time we all ask how things might be different."

"Yes, we do, but there is a difference in wondering about being in different circumstances that you cannot control and wondering about having made a decision that affects you the rest of your life."

Elizabeth looked straight ahead. Accepting Mr. Darcy's proposal would certainly have changed her life, but she could not say that she actually regretted her answer to him.

"Do you know what happened to the young man?" Elizabeth asked after a few moments of silence. "Did he ever marry?"

Alice nodded. "Yes, within a half year. I think it was then that all my regrets surfaced."

"I can understand that," Elizabeth replied. Then with a laugh, she added, "I was more shocked than anything else when I heard of my friend's engagement to Mr. Collins. I could not understand how she could do such a foolish thing."

"Well, it is good that you know you did not make a mistake. I, on the other hand, do not have such assurance."

Elizabeth tried to smile, but could not. Mr. Darcy had not turned out to be the villain she had first thought him to be, yet she still felt he had acted injudiciously in discouraging Mr. Bingley in his affections for her dearest sister, Jane.

Elizabeth let out a mournful sigh. She had the assurance that she did the right thing in the one proposal, but did she have it in the other?

~~*

The journey to the Isles of Scilly took them just within sight of the English shoreline as they made their way south and west. Occasionally the coast would be out of sight, and then different points of land would jut out enough to give all the travellers a feeling of reassurance that they were not drifting aimlessly out in the middle of the vast sea.

On the morning of the third day out, the two ladies were up on deck, knowing they would be arriving soon at their destination. Miss Whiting told Elizabeth to watch on the right side of the ship for the small rocky outcroppings that were off St. Martin's island.

"They will keep a good distance away from those dangerous rocks," she said. "Apparently the rocks all around the Isles of Scilly have taken many a good ship down, including a fleet of four naval ships in the 1700s."

"Heavens!" Elizabeth replied. "That would certainly make for an undesirable adventure!" She let out a laugh keeping a lookout on the starboard side. "Let us hope that our captain keeps well away from those rocks!"

The boat finally docked at the port on St. Mary's without any such adventure. Elizabeth and Miss Whiting wished each other God's blessings and went on their separate ways.

Elizabeth joined her father, and they disembarked the ship. She held on to his arm as people rushed past, eager to reach their loved ones or set off to their final destination. The merchant ship had been transporting a variety of produce and textiles, and large crates were offloaded onto carts, which were now making their way out of the harbour.

A young boy walked towards them, asking people he passed if they needed assistance. Mr. Bennet reached into his pocket and pulled out some coins and a slip of paper. He stopped him with a wave of his hand.

"Young lad, we need a carriage to convey us to this address. Would you be so kind as to find a driver to take us there?"

The boy bobbed his head, taking the coins and the piece of paper. "Yessir, I'll fetch one fer ye at once!"

They waited just a bit longer before seeing a carriage round the corner, the young boy running alongside as he directed it to Elizabeth and her father. The carriage driver stepped down, and Mr. Bennet pointed out their luggage. He gave the boy another coin for his promptness.

With a quick nod of his head and a "Thank ye, sir," he skipped away.

Elizabeth and her father stepped into the carriage and sat across from one another. As the carriage moved along, Elizabeth turned her head from one side to the other, enjoying the view out of each window. They climbed a small hill and Elizabeth looked back at the harbour. Although smaller than the one in London, there were a good many ships of all different sizes. They rose and dipped in harmony at the command of the waves. And out beyond, in the other direction from which they had come, she could just barely see the perilous rocks, some large and some small, that stood ready to battle any ship that dared come near.

"So, Elizabeth," Mr. Bennet said after a while. "From all that I could collect by your manner of speaking, you and Miss Whiting seemed to enjoy each other's company. Of what interesting topics did you speak to find you so engaged?"

"We talked about things women like to talk about. I am quite certain you would find it all tedious!"

"I suspect you are right, Lizzy, but I have no objection to hearing about your new friend."

Elizabeth laughed. "We spent many late nights talking about how she has had to live with her brother and his wife as she never married and how I live in a household with four sisters, three of whom are quite silly, but one who is my dearest friend."

"Miss Whiting seemed pretty enough. She has had no suitors, eh?"

Elizabeth bit her lip. "She did tell me about a proposal she once turned down and now regrets – just a little."

Mr. Bennet laughed. "Splendid! I suppose you were able to lament about the proposal *you* turned down and now regret, eh?"

"You know I most certainly have no reason to lament turning down Mr. Collins's proposal, for I do not regret it in the least! What I did lament was how Charlotte took it upon herself to secure his engagement herself."

"Imprudent affair on her part, indeed. But I fear, my dearest daughter, that your mother still begrudges you for refusing him."

"Still? But she does not say anything to me about it anymore."

"That is because I admonished her not to say another word to you about it," Mr. Bennet said as he reached out and patted Elizabeth's hand.

"I thank you for that, Father."

"Oh, she had a difficult enough time of it when you visited Charlotte in Kent. I do not think a day passed when she did not wonder aloud how you felt now that you had seen how content Charlotte was being married to Mr. Collins. For you must know how often Mrs. Lucas talks about it."

"I imagine so," Elizabeth said softly.

"No need to fret about it. I believe your mother was more upset about not being able to boast to Mrs. Lucas about your marriage to my esteemed cousin and instead has had to put up with Mrs. Lucas boasting to *her*."

"If only your cousin had been a more sensible man."

Mr. Bennet laughed. "Yes, if only. I cannot think of one sensible man in my family. Not that I know them all, mind you."

They rode a bit longer in silence. Elizabeth had never once thought about what might have been different had Mr. Collins been handsome and sensible. She may have been more than pleased to accept his offer of marriage.

She glanced at her father and wondered of his thoughts. Did he regret not having a son or not putting away a good sum of money as a handsome dowry for his five daughters? She never really saw him worry. She imagined her mother did enough worrying for the two of them.

"Well, Lizzy, there were no stormy seas or pirates," he said after a while, conveniently changing the subject. "Will not your mother be most disappointed?"

Elizabeth laughed. "I believe, Father, that the journey was so calm, that even Jane would have managed nicely."

"Ah, yes! She just may have," he answered. "But then, there is always the journey home."

~~*

They reached the top of the hill and looked out over the vast ocean and rocky beaches on one side, and heather-filled fields on the other. Wisps of clouds were strung across a deep blue sky, seemingly content to remain where they were and enjoy the view below. Elizabeth did not think she had ever seen anything so beautiful.

The carriage slowed down, and both Mr. Bennet and Elizabeth looked out the window. "Ah! I believe we have arrived." Mr. Bennet took in a deep breath. "Are you ready, my child?"

"I believe I am; but are *you*, Papa?"

Mr. Bennet tightened his fists and rubbed his thumbs and fingers together. "Yes, Lizzy. The only other alternative is to turn around and return home, and I will not do that."

The carriage door opened, and the two stepped out. Someone must have been watching for them, for as soon as they had taken a few steps towards the house, two young men hurried out, followed by a tall gentleman.

Elizabeth smiled as she realized it was her uncle and his twin sons. As her father extended his hand to his sister's husband, Elizabeth watched, eager for a sign in his features of the condition of his wife. As she watched them converse, she felt someone take her hand. She turned to see a young lady smiling at her.

"Melanie!" Elizabeth said, grasping her hands. "I would recognize you anywhere, even though it has been almost ten years!"

"And I you!" Melanie replied. "I am so glad you have come."

"I am, as well, but pray tell me, how is your mother?"

"Only fair. She is inside. She does not get around easily, never goes outside, and stays either in her room or in the western sitting room." Melanie bit her lip and squeezed Elizabeth's hands. "We do as much as we can to make things easy for her." A tear slid down her face.

"I am so sorry, Melanie. I know my father cares deeply for her."

"And she feels the same towards him. Her spirits have been so improved since hearing that he was coming!"

Elizabeth greeted her uncle, Henry Clower, and noticed the fatigue in his eyes. She felt the grief that was reflected on his face. She then greeted Melanie's brothers, Martin and Adam, who were four years younger than she was. Elizabeth remembered them as being quite young when she saw them last, and now they were turning into very nice looking young men.

They walked into the house, Elizabeth keeping an eye on her father in case he needed her at his side.

They were immediately ushered into the sitting room, where they saw a small, frail woman sitting in a chair. She had been watching for them and came to her feet when they walked in.

Mr. Bennet walked towards his sister with his arms outstretched.

"Viola!"

She embraced him as tears trailed down her face. Elizabeth marvelled at how much the two resembled each other. She had not recollected that when they visited all those years ago.

"Now, you must sit down!" Mr. Bennet admonished her.

"I am not that much of an invalid, Brother!" She looked up into his face as if to etch his features in her mind for all eternity. "You look exactly as I remembered!"

"Ha!" laughed Mr. Bennet. "And you were always the tease!"

She turned to Elizabeth. "And my lovely niece! Elizabeth, how good of you to come. I know you and Melanie will enjoy each other's company."

Viola coughed into a handkerchief and waved at the chair. "I think I will sit down now." She lowered herself into the chair and took a few sips of water from a glass on the table next to her.

She looked at her husband with an almost apologetic smile. "Henry, will you please make the introductions?"

There were several other people in the room. Elizabeth looked around, not recognizing anyone, but noticing a young man standing across the room whose eyes rested on her.

"I believe, Edmund, that you remember your cousin, Jenny Adams?"

Mr. Bennet nodded. "Certainly! It is because of her that the two of you met!"

"Hello, Edmund. And do you remember my husband, Calvin? I believe you met several years ago."

"Calvin and Jenny have been so kind as to come," Viola said. "Our two families have spent a good deal of time together over the years."

Mr. Bennet extended his hand. "It is good to see you again, Adams. It has been many years, but I do recollect when you and Jenny passed through Hertfordshire. That was over twenty years ago, before any of our girls were born."

"Indeed, it was!" Mr. Adams exclaimed. "And our David was barely walking around!"

Mr. Adams waved his son over. "David, this is your mother's cousin, Edmund Bennet, and his daughter, Miss Elizabeth Bennet."

The young man, whom Elizabeth had noticed earlier, smiled, stepped forward, and extended his hand to Mr. Bennet. "It is a pleasure, sir." He turned to Elizabeth. "Miss Bennet, if I had known I had such a lovely cousin in Hertfordshire, I would certainly have gone out of my way to pay a call."

Elizabeth was flattered. "You are very kind, Mr. Adams. I would have liked that very much, and I have four sisters who certainly would have enjoyed it, as well."

"Please, Miss Bennet. We are cousins. You must call me David."

Elizabeth nodded. "And you must call me Elizabeth." Elizabeth felt a blush warm her cheeks, and she turned away. His manners were certainly amiable; he had an intelligent look, a ready smile, and was tall and rather handsome. His family seemed warm and open. Elizabeth bit her lip as she considered that her father may have a sensible – and rather suitable – relative after all.

Chapter 6

After four days of loathsome preparation for his role as a pirate, Darcy grudgingly donned the wardrobe that he had earlier refused to wear. He walked to the mirror and looked in dismay at his reflection. The clothes he saw on his person were suited for the most flamboyant pirate, definitely not for him. He grumbled as he beheld the loose white shirt with billowing sleeves, the bright red sash about his waist, a double breasted jacket with large gold buttons, and boots with garish bronze buckles. His hair now hung in loose coils that peered from beneath the tri-corn hat and almost touched his shoulders. His beard and moustache were nearly as thick as his hair, but fortunately, not as curly. Despite the warmth of the day, he was tempted to don his oilskin coat just to conceal his ridiculous appearance.

Before venturing out to be seen by anyone in this outlandish garb, he sat down at the desk. It had been far too long since he last penned a letter to his sister. He was uncertain what he should say to her, but he knew it must be written before they set out for the ship.

He dipped the quill in the inkwell and put it to the paper. Usually the words flowed as easily as the ink flowed from the pen, but this day they did not. He knew any hint as to what he was about to do would worry Georgiana.

He perused the letter once he had finished it.

My Dearest Georgiana,

I hope you are finding great enjoyment in your summer stay at Pemberley thus far. I trust you have been able to pull yourself away from practising on the pianoforte to enjoy some walks about the grounds with Mrs. Annesley and have had the opportunity to visit with some of your friends.

Regretfully, it shall likely be another few weeks before I return. I have been visiting with acquaintances just outside of London and shall return to my town home in a little over a week to meet with my steward to discuss some matters. I shall then return to Pemberley as quickly as possible once my business is complete.

I hope, dear sister, that you will forgive me for such neglect. I shall be home shortly and will explain fully what has been taking up so much of my time. I greatly look forward to our reunion.

Until then,

Your loving brother

He read it several times, hoping he had not written anything that would alarm his sister. She knew him so well, and he hoped any indication of his former state of mind or his present circumstances would not find its way to her. Once satisfied, he folded the missive, sealed it with wax, and addressed it to Pemberley, Derbyshire.

Darcy picked up the one last piece of his pirate's wardrobe: a thick gold chain from which hung a large ruby surrounded by gold nuggets. He twirled the chain around his fingers a few times, and then clasped it tightly. He refused to slip this around his neck.

When he stepped out of his room, carrying both the letter and the ruby, he came upon Evans.

"Whoa! I ken't believe me eyes! It's Lockerly fer sure!"

Darcy held out his letter. "Ev... Ellis, would you be so kind as to have this letter mailed?"

Evans leaned in towards Darcy. "Would I what?"

Darcy closed his eyes and slowly shook his head. "Would ye see that this 'ere letter be mailed?"

Evans took it from Darcy. "O' course."

"One more thing, Ellis." He held out the ruby, dangling from the heavy gold chain. "You really expect me to wear this? I could never wear something this pretentious!"

"I'm sorry?" Evans replied. "What was that ye said? I cuddunt quite unnerstand ye with those big words ye use."

Darcy let out a huff. "I can't wear this! I could never wear somethin' as appallin' as this!"

"That is much better, Lockerly. Yer speech 'as so much improved. But, aye, ye must, for you, Lockerly, are known for wearin' precious jewels that you have seized!"

Their eyes locked in a gaze, and Darcy tugged at his beard. "I fear Lockerly is bein' a bit more cautious about the jewels he used to flaunt until he knows he ken trust 'is crew. He will *not* be wearin' it." He held out his hand, and Evans took the jewelled chain from him.

Evans chuckled and shook his head. "If ye insist."

~~*

Darcy, Evans, and Lindel set out soon after to meet up with Foster. Evans and Lindel had also dressed in their pirating attire. Unlike Darcy, however, they wore the same tattered clothes they had worn the first day he met them, but added loose caps that drooped over their forehead. Darcy wished that Lockerly did not dress so outrageously. While he might wear something like this to a masquerade ball, he felt completely ridiculous walking about in such attire! He had earlier hoped no one would recognize him when he walked the streets of London in such an appalling state; now he desired that to an even greater degree.

In addition to the way he was now dressed, Darcy was expected to continually display the most shocking manners, talk like the lowliest of miscreants, and master a walk that included a lowering of his right shoulder, a long stride, and resting his hand lightly on his sword, sheathed in a leather baldric which hung from his shoulder. He absolutely refused, however, to limp!

Evans leaned towards him. "Lockerly, ye 'ave proven yerself quite well in acquirin' da style an' manners of a pirate, but ye 'ave one fault!"

Darcy looked up. "An' what is that?"

The two men looked at each other, and Evans continued. "When ye find yerself in a situation in which ye feel uncomfortable or surprised, ye forget everythin' we have worked so hard to teach ye! Ye say everythin' the wrong way."

Darcy kept his eyes on Evans, but all he could see was the anger in Elizabeth's face as he stumbled over his words in his disastrous proposal. He had taken the time beforehand to think about what he wanted to convey to her and how to express his love. When he actually had begun talking, however, it had proven to be more difficult than he had imagined, and nothing seemed to come out right! When she had refused him, his shock at her response made his ability to speak even more of a challenge.

As he focused back on Evans, he nodded. "We can only hope, then, that nothin' will 'appen that will throw me back to me ol' ways!"

"Aye," Lindel agreed with a laugh. "We ken only hope."

Evans and Lindel had received word from Foster that the ship was ready for them. He hoped *they* were ready, as well. The ship was docked in a rather remote bay along the English Channel. It was nearer to Brighton than London, as Foster hoped Lockerly was still in the vicinity.

It took about four hours to make the journey. As the carriage turned off onto a secluded road, Darcy saw the masts of a sailing ship moored at a small inland dock. They could not see the English Channel at all, as it was hidden by large trees.

When Evans and Lindel saw the ship, they each let out a surprised gasp.

"He got it!" Lindel said.

"Got what?" Darcy said. "What is it?"

"He actually got Lockerly's ship. 'Tis the *Devil's Seamaiden*, it is."

Darcy looked back at the ship, a feeling of dread rising within him.

Evans slowly shook his head. "Lockerly ain't gonna be happy if he hears 'bout this!"

"But it might be the thing to bring him right to us!" Lindel added.

When the carriage came to a halt, the men stepped out. Lindel took in a deep breath and said, "An' so it begins!

~~*

Foster rushed over to greet the two men. Darcy barely recognized him. He had a good four-day growth of beard and was dressed much like Evans and Lindel, but in place of the loose cap, a bandana was tied about his head.

"Well, if it ain't Lockerly!" Foster smiled at Darcy, giving a nod to his clothes, and then turned to a small group of men, calling out, "'Tis Lockerly! Our Cap'n be finally here!"

Darcy grimaced, took in a deep breath, and then stepped over to Foster, mimicking the walk he had perfected over the last few days. He patted the hilt of his sword with his right hand and asked, "Is this motley group of boys me crew?" A scowl seemed permanently etched on his face.

Foster smiled and nodded. "A shoddier group of miscreants you'll not see."

"Why does that not relieve my apprehensions?" Darcy asked softly.

Foster waved his arm through the air. "No need to worry, though we do need a few more men. But tell me, before I introduce them to ye, 'ave my two men wiped clean every evidence of polite society from ye? I dun't have to fear something proper inadvertently tumblin' out, do I?"

"'Tis my hope not to 'ave that 'appen!"

"Good! Come then, Lockerly. I'll take ye to yer new crew. They hold ye in the highest esteem. Yer reputation is known far an' wide."

Darcy shot a menacing glare at Foster.

As the group of four men walked towards the young men who had gathered in front of the ship, Foster whispered under his breath. "Remember, my name is Forrest, and these two are Ellis and Lansing."

"Yes, I'll remember," Darcy said.

The four men walked up to the ship, gathering the men around them as they did.

"Men!" Foster said, extending his arm towards Darcy. "Meet the illustr'ous Cap'n of the *Devil's Seamaiden*! Lockerly 'as come!"

Darcy stepped forward and eyed the men who eagerly formed a line and eyed him back. He stood taller than all of them. One hand patted his sword while the other rubbed his bearded jaw.

"I hope ye turn out to be better at sailin' than ye are at dressin'!" Darcy bellowed as he glanced out over the men. He then waved a hand down his own clothing and said, "But ye have my respect, as ye must know that I am Lockerly an' must appear to advantage over the lot of ye!"

Foster, Evans, and Lindel chuckled softly, feeling quite proud of Darcy's transformation.

"I'll have ye come up one at a time so as I ken meet ye!"

He nodded his head towards Foster, Evans, and Lindel to join him, for his two companions needed introductions, as well.

Darcy decided to take a somewhat aloof demeanour as Foster introduced him to each man. He wanted to personally scrutinize each one under the guise of feigned disinterest. It was not that he did not trust Foster, but he felt he might notice something that Foster perhaps had missed. If he suspected any of these men had violent tendencies or might know he was *not* Lockerly, he would dismiss the man.

The men were all young. Foster had been right in his assessment about who would show up to join Lockerly's crew. As he heard each man's story, many were the same, coming from poor families and having no trade and no source of income.

A scrawny young man, who looked not a day over eighteen, came and stood before the men.

"Me name's Michael Jenkins. I'm eighteen, the youngest of seven children. Me two older brothers work for me father in his milliner shop, but he can't afford to hire me. He tol' me to find meself work. So when I hears about this, I said to meself, I could do that!"

He paused, as if unsure whether to say any more. Darcy casually nodded for him to continue.

"I ken sew. If sails tear or if clothin' needs fixin', I ken do it." The young man smiled weakly.

"Good!" Darcy replied. "Yer prob'ly someone we ken use."

Edward Webber stepped forward and introduced himself. "I growed up in London. Me father passed on a cupla months ago. I need to help me ma out. I dun't have no sailin' experience, but I learn quickly and I ain't afeard of nobody."

Webber shuffled from one foot to the other and seemed unable to meet Darcy's eyes.

"Will ye hire me, please? I'll do anythin' ye ask!"

"Anythin'?" Darcy asked and walked over to him. He stood

several inches taller than the young man. "Will ye climb the ratlines an' swab the deck?"

The young man looked up quickly with hopeful eyes. "I will, Cap'n. I will. I will even kill someone if ye tell me to!"

Darcy's heart stopped, but he controlled his response, placing his hand on his sword, patting it a few times. Meeting the young man's eyes, he said, "But will ye *not* kill someone if I tell ye not to?"

Webber's eyes grew wide. "Like I said, Cap'n, I will do anythin' ye ask."

"You'll do," Darcy replied. Before he waved him on, he asked, "How old are ye, lad?"

Webber paused and bit his lip. "I'm almost sixteen."

Darcy nodded, concerned about his age, but appreciating his avowal of loyalty.

Most of the young men had no source of income or any ability to secure it. They were putting their trust in Lockerly, and while they most likely had great hopes of securing a vast fortune while pirating, he hoped that they would each find a good future someday. Foster would pay them for the few days they were unwitting participants in this scheme, but once the real Lockerly showed up – or the week was up – they would all go their separate ways.

After Darcy had met – and approved – all the men, Foster told the men to remain where they were while Lockerly had a chance to inspect the ship. The men had been working hard to get it in shipshape condition.

The four men boarded alone so Foster could actually acquaint Darcy with the ship without arousing suspicion. As they walked around, he showed Darcy where things were stored, the galley, dining hall, hatches, and the cabins on each level.

He then came to a door and stood there. "Now this, Lockerly, is your cabin, and I must say, it is quite nice."

When Darcy walked in, he was amazed. Lockerly certainly had fine and expensive tastes. He would not be uncomfortable here. He noticed first the small paned windows that looked out the back of the ship. Polished wood shelves, a wall mirror, and mounted desk looked as though they came out of the finest home. Shiny brass fixtures, from wall sconces to rivets in the chair and bed to hooks on the wall, reflected the early afternoon light. Plush deep red cushions rested upon a single chair and the bed. An intricate Asian rug lay across the floor.

Darcy shook his head and let out a long puff of air. "It appears Lockerly 'as an appetite fer expensive things!'"

"That he does! Now, there are a few more cabins on this level, but the crew will sleep down in the berth." He paused. "There is one more cabin, Dar... Lockerly." They stepped out and walked down the narrow passageway. Foster slowly opened the door, and the men stepped in. Each gasped.

"Who in heaven's name is *this* cabin for?" Darcy asked, his refined language sneaking back in. "No sailor in his right mind would claim this as his own."

The room had the same polished wood and shiny brass, but the cushions were a deep pink. Lace curtains hung across the windows, and a thick rug lay in the centre of the cabin. A small table, secured to one wall, was covered in a pink tablecloth with a lace border. A plush cushioned chair sat in the corner, as well as a wooden chair at the table. A rose-coloured silk counterpane lay over the bed.

"No," Foster said. "As you can imagine, this is a cabin for ladies. Lockerly wanted any woman he brought on board to be comfortable, so he fixed this up according to a woman's taste. The door there connects to your cabin."

"I will have no use for this!" Darcy exclaimed. He looked at Evans and Lindel. "And I will not allow any man to bring a woman on board this ship!"

"We shall make sure the men abide by your wishes," Foster reassured Darcy.

Foster left later that evening once he was satisfied everything was under control. He told Darcy, Evans, and Lindel that he was going to see what more, if anything, he could find out about Lockerly. He would return as soon as he had additional information. Or, he would return at the end of seven days when this scheme – and Darcy's charade – would come to an end.

Chapter 7

Melanie took Elizabeth up to her room, which the two ladies were to share, so they could dress for dinner. The room was decorated in soft blues, with lacy pillows piled high on the bed. A few paintings of the ocean lined the walls, and a small bookcase held some novels.

"You have a very nice room, Melanie," Elizabeth said as she glanced about. She walked to the bookcase and ran her fingers over the spines of the books. "And I see you are a reader."

"Yes," Melanie replied. "I adore love stories and gothic novels. What about yourself? Do you enjoy reading?"

Elizabeth nodded. "Indeed, I do, very much. I love historical and adventure novels, and, of course, sweet romantic stories." She turned to Melanie with a twinkle in her eyes. "You may correct me if I am wrong, but do I see a little romance story being acted out here on the island of St. Mary's?"

Melanie lowered her brows and tilted her head. "I fear I know not what you mean."

Elizabeth leaned towards her with a sly grin. "Between you and Mr. Adams, of course! I could not help but notice how well you two get along, and he appears to be a fine, young man. Quite handsome, too, which is an uncommon advantage in completing a man's character!"

Melanie shook her head, and a blush coloured her cheeks. "Oh, indeed, there is no one finer than David, but there is nothing of that sort between us. We are merely good friends, having known each other all our lives."

Elizabeth drew back a little as she murmured, "Hmm. I confess I am surprised. I thought I had seen admiration as he looked at you."

Melanie looked down at her hands as she knitted her fingers together. "I think, perhaps, that he has felt more for me than I have for him."

Elizabeth pursed her lips as she thought about Alice Whiting and how she regretted turning down an offer of marriage because she only thought of the gentleman as a friend.

Melanie walked to the window, pulling back the curtain. "To own the truth, Elizabeth, my heart belongs to Robert Mintner, who is currently serving in the Navy. I often come and gaze out at the ocean from my window, longing to see his ship come in."

"I hope it is soon." Elizabeth said as she joined her cousin to look out. "Melanie! You have the most beautiful view from here!"

"Yes, I do love it. But I would love it more if I knew Robert was home and safe." She let out a long breathy sigh. "The sea can be so deadly, especially when we are at war with France."

"Are the two of you engaged?"

Melanie slowly shook her head. "Not yet. But I hope to be once he returns."

Elizabeth walked to a chair and sat down. She ran her hands along the arm rests. "Do you know if your cousin… *our* cousin… David, has an affection towards any lady?"

Melanie reached out for Elizabeth's hand. "I think not, and you just say the word and I will do everything in my power to help the two of you get to know one another while you are here!"

Elizabeth smiled. "I think I should like that very much!"

That night at dinner, Elizabeth was delighted to discover that she had been placed next to David. He seemed as interested in finding out about her as she was about him. True to her promise, Melanie was willing to assist in furthering their acquaintance.

"Tell me, Elizabeth, what is it like to grow up with four sisters?" Melanie asked. "Having only two brothers, I cannot imagine it."

Elizabeth laughed. "Oh, we are all quite different, both in looks and personality. My eldest sister, Jane, however, is five times prettier than any of us and at least three times more agreeable."

David smiled. "You make her sound like perfection itself, which I find difficult to believe. Despite having known you for only a few hours, I cannot comprehend that she could be prettier or more agreeable than you."

"Well, we shall not argue on that, but my position would be easily proven true if you ever have the opportunity to meet her. I must insist, however, that Jane is the most agreeable in my family and of my whole acquaintance, as she has the ability to see only the good in a person while I tend to be a little more severe in my estimation of one's character."

"Heavens!" David declared with a look of mock distress. "I wish I had known that from the start. I would have taken better care to leave you with only a good impression of me!"

Elizabeth smiled. "You have nothing to worry about, my good cousin. I have seen nothing in your character that has given rise to any objectionable notions!"

"I am most relieved!" David picked up his glass of wine and looked at Elizabeth over the top of it. "Most relieved, indeed!"

~~*

Elizabeth woke the next day to the sun shining through the window. The window faced east, and she quietly slipped out of bed to see something she had never beheld before – the sun was rising up out of the sea on the horizon.

Wispy clouds were splashed with colours of red, orange, pink, and yellow. The blues of the sky ranged from the softest blue, to a deep azure, to an almost navy darkness as it stretched overhead.

She sat down and propped her arms on the window sill, lowering her head and resting her chin on them. She watched in amazement as, before her eyes, the colours in the sky and water changed from moment to moment.

Elizabeth felt that if she lived in such a place, she would sit at the window every morning just to welcome this amazing display of creation. She unwittingly let out a sigh at the awe-inspiring sight before her, which caused Melanie to stir.

"Elizabeth?" she said yawning, as she stretched her hands up to the ceiling. "Are you awake already? Did you not sleep well?" She slowly sat up in the bed.

Elizabeth turned to face her. "On the contrary, I slept wonderfully. I normally rise early, and when I looked out the window and saw the sun rising out of the water, I could not take my eyes from it. It is beautiful."

Melanie fell back down onto her pillow. "I always wished I could get up early to see the sunrise, but I just find it too... early."

Elizabeth laughed and peered out the window again, noticing someone walking. After a moment, she said, "Oh! It appears that David is out for a morning walk."

Melanie groaned. "He always does that. You should go join him."

"I might just do that, but not today. He will be long gone before I am ready, and chances are good I would not find him, or heaven forbid, get lost!" She turned back to Melanie and smiled when she saw that her cousin had quickly fallen back asleep.

Elizabeth went downstairs a little later and found her aunt and father visiting in the sitting room.

"Ah, come in, Elizabeth," Viola said. "I see that you take after the Bennet side of the family and know the pleasure of rising early."

"Of my five daughters, she is the only one that does," affirmed Mr. Bennet.

"Good morning, Papa. Good morning, Aunt Viola. How are you feeling this morning?"

"Tired, as usual. But I am very happy. I have some of my favourite people here, and that gladdens my heart." She took Mr. Bennet's hand and gave it a quick, frail squeeze. "If I had more strength, I would take you out on a walk about the grounds and up to the top of the hill. There is a view from there of the ocean on almost all four sides of our little island." She coughed into her handkerchief, and it took a while to catch her breath.

An expression of concern flooded Mr. Bennet's face.

She waved her other hand through the air. "I am... all right. Just need... a moment." After a few minutes she said, "I shall ask Melanie to show you both around. She and David know almost every inch of this island."

"I should like that very much," Elizabeth said.

Mr. Bennet winked at Elizabeth and then turned back to his sister. "I should not wish to intrude on the young people, nor would I be able to keep up with them. I should very much like to just stay here and visit with you."

Viola shook her head. "Nonsense! I know you, Brother, and very soon all the people in this household shall compel you to flee from its midst."

Elizabeth laughed, knowing her aunt was probably correct.

"Well, if that proves to be true, I shall be content to take my book and find a spot nearby to read in solitude."

Viola nodded her head. "Yes, you always were the reader. There is a bench about half-way up the hill that has a view of the ocean to the east. You shall find it an easy walk and a splendid place to get away from all the folly that goes on here."

As they continued to chat, more of the family came downstairs and joined them. The aroma from breakfast being prepared grew stronger, and Elizabeth found herself greatly looking forward to eating.

David came in after a while, looking refreshed from his walk. "Good morning, everybody! Did anyone see the sunrise this morning?"

"Yes!" Elizabeth said. "I saw it from Melanie's window. It was a beautiful sight."

"It is one thing I have always enjoyed seeing when we come here. But there is nothing finer than to view it from the top of the hill on a clear, sunny morning with only a slight breeze."

Viola waved her handkerchief in the air. "Yes! You and Melanie must take Elizabeth to see the view at the top of the hill."

He turned to Elizabeth and grinned. "That is a splendid idea. We can have a picnic up there today, and perhaps we can walk up to see the sunrise tomorrow morning?" He gave his head a toss. "I am not certain Melanie will want to go. She enjoys her morning sleep too much."

"I enjoy what?" Melanie said as she came in. "What are you saying about me?" She walked up to David and poked him in the ribs. "I hope it is nothing unkind, for if it is, I shall be forced to tell Elizabeth about all the pranks you used to play on me when we were younger!"

He abruptly turned to Melanie, bracing his hands on his hips. With a smile he said, "You would not dare!"

"Tell me what you were saying about me!"

David gave her a deep bow. "As you wish! I merely said that you enjoy your morning sleep. Do you think you might join Elizabeth and me on a walk tomorrow morning to view the sunrise?"

"Only if Elizabeth is able to wake me up." Melanie walked over to her mother and gave her a kiss. "Good morning, Mother." She then proceeded to greet everyone else in the room. When she came to Elizabeth, she leaned over to whisper in her ear, but spoke loud enough for everyone to hear, "Do not let me forget to tell you about the time David scared me silly when he pretended to have fallen down a short embankment."

"He did not!" Elizabeth exclaimed with a look of feigned shock.

"Yes, well, I was a silly lad of fifteen who was only hoping for a little *comfort* from Melanie."

"Shocking!" said Elizabeth with a laugh. "Did it work?"

"I suppose it worked if you consider *comfort* to be Melanie shaking me violently, all the while screaming for help. I only wanted her to think I was hurt, not dead!"

"Well, you deserved it for scaring me like you did!"

"All right, you two," Viola warned. She turned to her brother. "These two behave more like brother and sister than Melanie and either of her two brothers ever have."

Elizabeth watched the two of them and felt a slight stab of jealousy, as she had never had a close relationship with a young man close to her own age. Despite Melanie's insistence that he was only a friend, she saw something between them that she truly wished she had.

After breakfast, the three young people chatted with the family while food was prepared and packed for their picnic. While Melanie and David had a lifetime of acquaintance that led to a friendly camaraderie, Elizabeth felt a kinship with the two of them. They were both fun, teasing, lively, and intelligent, and she knew that in a week's time when they returned home, she would miss both of them.

Once they had the food and supplies for the picnic, they set out for the top of the hill. It was a mildly warm day, the breeze had picked up, and the salty scent in the air tickled Elizabeth's nose. She had never experienced anything like it.

The trio stopped for a while at a lookout that gave them a view of the eastern sea down to the south. "This is beautiful!" Elizabeth said.

"Are you getting tired?" David asked.

"Not at all! I frequently walk up Oakham Mount, which is not much higher than this."

"Good! Shall we continue to the top?" David extended both his arms. Melanie took one as if she did it all the time, and Elizabeth took the other. He looked down at her and smiled.

When they reached the summit, it was true that they could see at least parts of the sea surrounding the island. Elizabeth wrapped her arms about her and slowly turned, taking in the different views. Looking to the east gave her a full view of the sea, while she could see other islands and rocky outcroppings dotting the horizon in the other directions. Looking down, she could see the waves lapping up onto the shore.

"Do you think that we can go down to the shore? I would love to walk along the beach."

"Most definitely!" Melanie said. "We shall do that tomorrow!"

David spread out the blanket and set out the food that had been packed for them. He invited the ladies to sit down first, and then he sat down at Elizabeth's left.

After they had finished eating, Melanie looked at Elizabeth. "Do you see why I love it here so much?" she asked. "And wait until we go up to Star Castle! The view from there is even more spectacular! I do not think I could ever live anywhere else!"

Elizabeth let out an appreciative sigh. "Oh, it is wonderful."

"The weather is milder in the winter, although we do get some pretty strong gales. The summers are warm, but the air is so clear! Whenever we go across the Channel to London, it always seems so stifling!"

David looked down and began picking at the grass. "That is so true! Melanie even gets restless when her family visits our estate. Even the country with its clean air and open spaces do not suit her."

He shot Melanie a look that did not escape Elizabeth's notice. She wondered if this was the reason Melanie would not return his affections. She did not want to live anywhere but here.

When they were walking down the hill, they encountered Mr. Bennet about halfway down. He was sitting on a bench reading.

"Papa! You have found a most pleasing spot to read!" Elizabeth turned to look out at the sea. "Lovely view, is it not?"

Mr. Bennet closed his book and looked out. "Yes, it is, and now I wish even more that we had come here before. I think your mother would have enjoyed it when she was younger."

Elizabeth looked at him in surprise. "Truly?"

"Well, she would probably not have ventured out on a walk up here, but I daresay she would have enjoyed the weather and a little sea bathing. You know how she always talks about that!"

Elizabeth laughed and kissed him on the cheek. "I believe you are correct, Papa."

~~*

The following morning, when Elizabeth woke up, she gave Melanie a gentle shake to awaken her, and the two met David just before sunrise. They ascended the hill in silence. Melanie walked slower than her cousins and bade them go on ahead, assuring them she would catch up with them at the lookout. Elizabeth knew she was probably tired, but wondered if part of it was to allow Elizabeth some time alone with David. As they walked ahead, he did not offer his arm to Elizabeth, but he did take hers a few times to help her up small inclines.

When they reached the lookout, the first fragments of light and colour were beginning to fill the skies. Elizabeth sat down on the bench, and David sat beside her. They both looked down the trail and could see Melanie slowly making her way up.

"I was actually surprised you were able to wake Melanie this morning. She and I came up here once to see the sunrise." He let out a laugh. "It was in the autumn so it was not nearly as early as it is now!"

Elizabeth laughed softly. "It took me several attempts to waken her. I fear she does not like the mornings."

"No. That is the only thing about us that is different. Except, of course, where we live."

"You care for her deeply; I can tell."

David nodded. "Since I was very young." He glanced towards Melanie as she drew a little closer. "But she has made up her mind." He clasped his hands together and turned back at Elizabeth with a pointed look. "I think I have finally realized we shall always be just friends."

He called out to Melanie, "You have almost made it! Come! The show is about to begin!"

~~*

Elizabeth and her father enjoyed touring the island the next few days. They began by going down to the beach, where Elizabeth bravely removed her shoes and stockings and ran along the shore in her bare feet.

The following day Mr. Bennet wished to visit some of the historical sites. They walked across the ruins of Star Castle, which was built in 1593 during the reign of Queen Elizabeth. They also went to Harry's Walls, the remains of an unfinished artillery castle begun in 1551. It was left unfinished because the site was eventually found to be unsuitable.

Two days before Elizabeth and her father were to leave, Melanie, David, and his mother, Jenny, joined Elizabeth as they visited Hugh Town. This was the main town and port on St. Mary's which all ships sail in and out of. Now that she was at her leisure, she was able to take pleasure in the amenities of the small town. They walked along the winding streets lined with stone houses, pausing to shop at beckoning stores, and then stopping at an inn near the dock for tea and cake.

At one point in the outing, Elizabeth found herself alone with David's mother. She came alongside Elizabeth and took her arm.

"I hope you know how much David is enjoying getting to know another cousin," she said. "He and Melanie have always had a special bond, but she has made it clear to him that she only views him as a friend."

"Yes," Elizabeth said. "She informed me of that."

Jenny patted Elizabeth's hand. "I can see that you are a lot like Melanie, and David is enjoying your company. I hope that our paths will cross again soon. Perhaps you would consider visiting our estate in Staffordshire? We have wonderful forests and lakes around us. Melanie was never able to truly appreciate it, and I think that has affected how she feels about David." Jenny let out a sigh. "I know that he cares for her deeply, but she claims her heart belongs to another. I think he is finally ready for another lady to take hold of his heart, but I would not wish for him to be hurt again."

At those words, Elizabeth's heart began to pound. Her mouth suddenly felt dry, and no words would come. After a few moments she was finally able to mutter, "I would... I would welcome his attentions if he so desired it."

Jenny smiled. "That would make me so happy!"

They walked a little farther and found David eyeing a sign that had been posted in the window of one of the small shops.

"Now, you ladies have no need to fear, for I shall protect you with my life!"

Elizabeth laughed and asked, "From what?"

He pointed to the sign. "From pirates!"

Elizabeth leaned in to read the sign. *Ships have been sighted in the vicinity of the Isles of Scilly engaging in the illegal act of piracy. Whoever can provide information leading to the capture of these ships or the crew will receive a reward of £500.*

She shuddered. "The reward would certainly be most welcome, but I think I shall pass on the opportunity of encountering – let alone capturing – a pirate!"

"You must leave this sort of gallantry to me, then!" David pushed his chest out proudly in a display of bravado.

Melanie gave David a friendly push. "I have lived here all my life and have yet to see even *one* pirate!" Laughingly, she turned to Elizabeth. "We see these signs all the time. While we hear occasionally that there *are* pirates, they do not come to the big islands, but hide out in the rocks and caves of the smaller uninhabited ones." She directed a wink at Elizabeth. "But if David wishes to be gallant, we shall not dissuade him."

Later that day, Elizabeth and David were enjoying a stroll in the garden. He extended his arm, and Elizabeth slipped her fingers around it.

"Elizabeth, I cannot tell you how much I have enjoyed getting to know you, and it grieves me to think that you and your father will be leaving in just two days." He looked up to the sky and let out a puff of air. "Would you mind terribly if I were to go to London with you on the ship? I need to return to the estate shortly." He turned and took Elizabeth's hands in his. "If I may be so bold to say, I should very much like to further our acquaintance."

"Oh!" Elizabeth said, biting her lip. "I am flattered." Her heart began to pound, and her cheeks flooded with warmth. Looking straight ahead, she said, "If it is acceptable to my father, I should enjoy it very much!"

"I will speak with him immediately upon our return, and if he is agreeable to it, we shall see if arrangements can be made to accommodate me on the ship."

Later that evening, David approached Elizabeth with a broad smile on his face. "Your father has agreed! As long as passage can be obtained, I will be sailing back to London with the two of you!"

Chapter 8

Darcy was a natural leader, having the ability to inspire loyalty among his crew which readily earned him their good opinion. He gave orders to the men in a quiet, yet commanding voice that brooked no opposition, but still treated them with the utmost respect, prompting them to obey willingly. Darcy was surprised to discover that he enjoyed this role and almost wished they could take the ship out to sea. He realized, however, that it might prove too risky.

As first mate, Lindel knew precisely what needed to be done in regards to the ship, but he tended to be harsher with the crew when Darcy relinquished control of the men to him. Not surprisingly, the men did not hold him in as high esteem as they did their captain.

Darcy watched him closely not only to learn the ship's routines, but also to patch up the many grievances his first mate instigated from within the ranks of the men.

By the end of the fifth day, six more men came by, bringing the total to twenty crewmen. But still there was no sign of Lockerly.

Early in the morning of the sixth day, Foster returned. He gathered Darcy, Evans, and Lindel in the captain's quarters and gave them some discouraging news. In the privacy of the room, the men dropped their accents. "I have come upon information that Lockerly is not anywhere near here but is across the Channel on the Isles of Scilly."

"The Isles of Scilly?" Darcy asked.

"Do you know of it?" Foster asked.

"Yes, but only slightly. I have read a little about it and have seen it on the maps of England."

"It is known to be a haven for pirates and smugglers who often hide out in its rocks and caves, is it not?" Lindel asked.

Foster nodded his head slowly. "A perfect place to hide out." He turned to Darcy. With a slight laugh he asked, "You would not want to go on a real adventure and set sail, would you?"

"To Scilly? Certainly not. If you wish to proceed there on your own, you have my utmost wish for success, but *I* shall not accompany you!"

Foster let out a long sigh. "I cannot change your mind?"

Darcy shook his head.

"I did not think so." Foster put out his hand to Darcy. "I appreciate all you have done, Darcy. Enjoy your last night as Pirate Lockerly. I know the men have a great deal of respect for you."

"I am sorry it did not turn out as you wished."

Foster nodded. "As am I." He clasped his hands together and returned to his common way of speaking. "Well, I came only to briefly check on things an' see if ye might reconsider stayin' with us a wee bit longer. I need to see if I ken pinpoint exactly where Lockerly is holdin' up. I'll come back 'ere in a day or two. Darcy, I imagine you'll be gone when I return, so let me say again, I thank ye for bein' willin' to humour me an' me scheme."

"And I am grateful to you, Foster, for believing in me when I was in that cell."

"Aye. Once ye are gone, we'll tell the men what we 'ad 'oped to accomplish. There's no need for ye to do that, and I'll pay the men their wages."

"I hope the men prove useful to you. They are all fine men and lack only some good direction."

"Which you have provided well, Darcy." Foster smiled. "But take care to watch yer tongue fer the rest o' the day. Ye still 'ave a bit more time left."

Darcy chuckled. "Aye! I will!"

The men talked a bit more, and then Foster left.

Later that day, Darcy, Evans, and Lindel watched as a man slowly approached them. His sandy blond hair brushed his shoulders, and he had a beard just as long. He was taller and broader than Darcy, and his steely blue eyes peered out from a grimy, weather-beaten face. He appeared to be in his forties.

Darcy kept a cautious eye on him as he drew closer.

"Needin' some help?" Darcy asked.

The man dropped the knapsack that he had been carrying. "You Lockerly?"

Darcy tilted his head as he addressed the man. "Who's askin'?"

"Name is George Bellows. Heard Lockerly is hirin' a new crew for 'is ship. I should like to be considered."

Darcy did not like the looks of the man. He had a bad feeling about him. "Won't be needin' ya. We 'ave all we need," he replied.

Bellows looked out over the crew and let out a laugh. "From the looks of things, ye only 'ave a bunch of scrawny kids. None of 'em would fare well if they was in a skirmish. A trio of old ladies would 'ave no problem bringin' 'em to their knees." His eyes shifted to look at Darcy. "Ye need someone like me."

"Do ye 'ave any sailin' experience?" Lindel asked.

Bellows nodded. "I 'ave worked on a merchant ship fer a few years."

"Why are ye no longer wi' them?" Darcy asked.

Bellows laughed and slowly turned his face to Darcy. "Me an' the cap'n didn't quite see things eye to eye. Me thinks this arrangement would suit me much better."

Darcy shook his head. "No, we..."

Evans put up his hand, halting Darcy's speech.

"Me name is Ellis, an' this here is Lansing. As Lockerly says, we do 'ave a full crew, but if he does not mind, ken I ask ye a question?"

"Go ahead."

"Ever sail to the Isles of Scilly?"

"One of our regular shipments was to St. Mary's. Did it 'bout every other month fer a few years."

Evans and Lindel looked at each other and then to Darcy, who just realized what they were thinking. If Foster wanted to take the ship to the Isles of Scilly to search for the real Lockerly, it would help to have someone on board who had sailed there before.

Darcy sat with his hand rubbing his chin and then suddenly said, "Ye'll do, Bellows. Lansing will show ye to yer quarters."

As Lansing took the man to the ship, Darcy turned to Evans. "I don't like 'em, but I knew what ye were thinkin'. I'll be leavin' tomorrow, and you, Lindel, and Foster can deal with 'im if he causes trouble. I shall be long gone."

~~*

That evening Darcy allowed the men time off from their duties. The young Michael Jenkins pulled out his flute and entertained the men with lively songs. Occasionally, they would dance a reel with each other or sing out a favourite song by the light of a fire. Darcy merely sat and watched. He had grown to care for these men and hoped that each of them would benefit – even if in only some small way – from this week spent with him. He hoped that if they did set sail to go after Lockerly, they all would be kept safe. But most of all, he hoped that their thirst for a pirate's adventure would not lead them down a criminal or violent path.

The men did not seem to grow tired of their festivities, but soon Darcy excused himself for the night. He debated whether he should just quietly disappear in the morning or announce to the men that he was leaving when they gathered for their morning duties. He determined he would decide in the morning.

He read a little before going to bed. The music, muted though it was, and the soft rolling of the ship in the water, wrought an ethereal peace that pervaded Darcy's soul. He had done a good thing, even though it had been to no avail. But he felt he had had an even greater triumph in ridding his thoughts – and hopefully his heart – of Miss Elizabeth Bennet, at least for a greater part of the past week.

Darcy drifted into a sound sleep as the music played. It was only in the early hours of the morning that he awakened with a start. The boat was swaying rather forcefully. Powerful waves were splashing against the hull. As he scrambled out of bed, the ship rose suddenly and then crashed back down, flinging him to the floor. The ship seemed to shake down to its keel. He knew immediately they were no longer docked, but were out at sea!

Darcy grabbed his oilskin coat. He struggled to put it on as the ship leaned from one side to the other. He grasped the bedpost to keep from being hurled down again. When the ship settled, he cautiously reached for the door and opened it, not bothering to light a lantern. He felt his way in the dark up the hold to the deck.

Darcy felt the sting of rain and sea water against his face. Between booms of thunder, he could hear Bellows barking orders to the crew. He tightly gripped the top of the stairway as another wave rocked the ship. When it settled, he made his way up the quarterdeck.

"Bellows! Why are we no longer docked? Where are Ellis and Lansing? What is going on?" Despite shouting at the top of his lungs, the wind practically swallowed up his words.

Bellows did not answer, but called out to the crew. "Be quick! Furl the main sails or they'll be ripped to shreds! Batten down those hatches!" He finally turned to Darcy. "Got rid of 'em!"

"You did what?" Darcy asked, his face contorting in a mixture of rage against Bellows and fear for his friends. His hand gripped the hilt of his sword. "I demand to know what has become of them and order you to turn this ship around!"

Bellows wiped the spray of saltwater that splashed over his face. "Ye'll thank me when I tell ye what 'as 'appened!" He glared at Darcy defiantly. "Ellis and Lansing – they wasn't who they said they was. They was workin' with Edward Foster – the man ye know as Forrest – who works wi' the Thames River Police. I dun't know what they was doin' or plannin' ta do, but I done took care of 'em an' figured we best escape while we could."

"What did you do with them?" Darcy demanded, enunciating his words very pointedly. He gripped the railing of the quarterdeck when the ship rose and then made a sharp drop.

"Oh, no need to worry. They'll be found soon enough. Just wanted to get 'em outta the way until we were out at sea. I didn't want ta waken ye, Cap'n. I told the men ye had given me the order to set sail. They was more than happy to finally put her to the water!"

Darcy felt a sense of relief that the two men were not harmed, but his anger burned towards Bellows. He had known from the start the man could not be trusted.

"You should have consulted with me before doing anything of the kind!" Darcy said. He inhaled sharply and fisted his hands in frustration. He knew that due to the critical turn of their situation, he had neglected to speak as the lowly pirate Bellows believed him to be. "You... ye was completely out of line!" The ship leaned deeply to one side and then the other, throwing both men off balance for a moment. When they were steady on their feet again, Darcy asked, "Where are we?"

Bellows looked up to the sky. "Can't say fer sure!" he shouted over the noise of the wind. "Didn't quite expect the storm. We is pretty much at its mercy." His hands held tightly onto the helm, attempting to keep the ship moving straight ahead. "Judgin' by the winds, we may just end up close to the Isles of Scilly."

Darcy lowered his brows and whispered softly, "The Isles of Scilly…"

Bellows extended his hand. "Do ye want to take the helm?"

Darcy shook his head. "No! Continue on, but we'll talk 'bout this once we are out of harm's way!"

As the sea continued to churn, and the storm prevented them from any sort of effective navigation, Darcy did his best to ensure that his crew and vessel were kept safe. Throughout the night, Bellows proved his proficiency acting as first mate, save, of course, for following through on his duty to consult first with the captain!

Darcy remained on deck, knowing he would not rest easy until the first light of dawn made an appearance… and he knew it could not come too soon for his peace of mind.

~~*

It was early in the morning when Elizabeth, Mr. Bennet, and David Adams said their goodbyes to family and set out to board the ship for their return voyage to London.

Mr. Bennet's sister had repeatedly expressed her gratefulness to him and Elizabeth for making the journey to see her. While each day she had grown weary early in the afternoon, there had been no noticeable decline in the week they had been there, for which *they* had been grateful. They left her with the hope and prayer that she would find strength to face each day for many years to come.

Mr. Clower and Melanie joined them for the carriage ride down to the harbour. Melanie and Elizabeth talked as they held each other's hands tightly. They recounted the events of the past week, how much they had enjoyed each other's company, and occasionally laughed at something David had done. He watched in silence, a twinkle in his eyes and a slight tug at his lips being the only indications that he was listening.

The two older gentlemen spoke very little. Elizabeth could see that her father struggled to keep his composure, knowing this was likely the last time he would see his sister.

When they arrived at the harbour, they said their goodbyes, giving hugs all around. Elizabeth watched David as he took Melanie's hand, bringing it up and giving it a slight kiss. He leaned in and whispered something softly to her. Elizabeth could not hear what he said, but watched as Melanie smiled sweetly.

He turned away quickly, extending his arm to Elizabeth. "Shall we go?"

The three boarded the ship, along with the other passengers, crew, and dock workers loading materials being shipped to London. Elizabeth was anxious to meet the three women with whom she would be sharing a cabin. Elizabeth, Mrs. Joyner, Mrs. Keller, and Mrs. Dillard were the only women on board the ship. There were five men travelling as passengers, and to accommodate them, the husbands of the three ladies were put in one cabin, while Mr. Bennet and David were put in the cabin across the hall.

This merchant ship was larger than the one on which Elizabeth and her father had previously sailed. Again, their accommodations were simple, yet comfortable.

It was smooth sailing that first day as they made their way towards London. Towards evening, however, it was obvious to Elizabeth that the crew was keeping an eye on a storm out on the horizon. Dark, threatening clouds, pierced occasionally by jagged streaks of lightning, seemed to be bearing down upon them.

As the last traces of light disappeared on the horizon, and all the passengers settled into their cabins for the night, the sea began to toss the ship ruthlessly. Elizabeth, along with Mrs. Keller, who had sailed frequently, did their best to calm the other two women in the cabin, but as the storm worsened and the sea raged in fury, they felt a good deal of concern, as well. Mrs. Keller suggested the ladies pull the blankets and pillows off the bed and lie on the floor to prevent them from being tossed out of their beds when the ship rose and fell and feverishly swayed from side to side.

A light tap of the door startled the ladies, and Elizabeth warily stood up and wrapped a blanket about her.

"Yes?" she called out.

"Elizabeth, it is David. Your father and I were worried about you. How are you ladies faring in this storm?"

She opened the door slightly. Although she could not see him, she sensed his caring presence.

"We are huddled together on the floor. Tell me, David, have you ever sailed in anything like this?"

"I have been in some strong storms, but this does appear to be severe. I went up on the deck, and they have furled the sails to prevent them from being ripped apart or blown away."

"What does that mean?" Elizabeth asked, a small tremor noticeable in her voice.

David reached out to find her hand, which rested on the edge of the door. He placed his over hers reassuringly. "We are likely going to be blown slightly off course, but the crew know what they are doing. We shall be safe!"

"Thank you, David. How is my father faring?"

David laughed. "He is doing well. In fact, he is regaling me with stories about your family."

Elizabeth was glad David could not see her as she rolled her eyes at his words. She could only imagine what her father might be saying about them.

"Remind me to ask you later about one Mr. Collins and his offer of marriage!"

"Oh, that man!" Elizabeth exclaimed.

"Is that sentiment referring to your father or Mr. Collins?"

"Both!" Elizabeth said with a laugh, gripping the door as the ship heaved suddenly. "You had best get back to your room and hunker down!"

"I shall, and you do the same!"

As she closed the door, Mrs. Dillard laughed. "Will you enlighten us about this Mr. Collins?"

"Oh, I beg of you not to ask me to speak of that laughable man now! Perhaps when we are out of danger, I shall be more in the mood to tell you about him."

When Elizabeth and the other ladies found themselves feeling ill, Mrs. Keller advised them to take in slow, deep breaths. While it did not remove the offensive feeling, it did help.

The storm did not let up at all during the night, but at some point the ladies fell asleep from exhaustion. It was early in the morning when the ladies were awakened by a thunderous jolt that seemed to shake the ship from bow to stern and all the way down to its keel. All of the women screamed, and Mrs. Joyner cried out, "God, help us! We are going to die!"

"What do you suppose happened?" Elizabeth asked. "That sounded ominous!"

"I have never heard anything like it," Mrs. Keller said. "It sounded – and felt – as though we hit something!"

Elizabeth was of the opinion that Mrs. Keller was correct but did not think it could have been another ship, for despite the pounding of the waves, the ship seemed anchored in one spot, as if something had it in its grip.

The sounds of shouts and pounding footsteps could be heard, and at length, a sharp rap at their door.

Again Elizabeth grabbed the nearest blanket and put it around her. When she opened the door, the captain stood before her, holding a candle. Anxious blue eyes looked out from his weathered, bearded face.

"We have hit some sort of rocky outcroppin', an' my men are surveyin' the damage. But we must ask that ye ladies get dressed an' come up on deck as quickly as possible." He handed Elizabeth the candle he was holding. "Take this an' light one of the candles in your cabin."

"Thank you, Captain." Elizabeth took the candle, lit one of the wall candles in the cabin, and then returned it to the captain.

As the ladies scrambled to get dressed, Mrs. Joyner sat down on the bed and seemed unable to do anything. She began to pant heavily and put her hand over her heart. "I know we are going to die! I know we will sink, and no one will ever find us or know what happened to us!"

Elizabeth walked over and sat down beside her. "We shall be fine. The captain knows what he is doing." She gently helped the woman dress and then got dressed herself. The ladies put on their warmest outerwear over their dresses, anticipating inclement weather on deck.

As the ladies walked out, several of the men, led by David, were coming to their room to check on them.

"Good! You are ready!" David said. "Shall we go up and see what the captain has to say?"

David took Elizabeth's arm as they quickly took the stairs up to the deck. They gathered together and watched as the captain spoke solemnly to a few of his crew members. It was no longer raining, but the wind sliced across the ship fiercely. The spray from the still turbulent waves stung their faces.

The captain walked slowly over to the small group of passengers that huddled together. "Durin' the storm the winds an' waves pushed us far off course. In fact, as far as we can determine, we were carried back towards the Isles of Scilly. The sound you heard earlier was the ship hittin' a rocky outcroppin', most likely north an' east of the islands."

"Are we going to sink?" Mrs. Joyner asked, her voice shaking.

"While the ship is takin' on some water in its hull, we are not in deep enough water to be swallowed up. My men are down in the bowels of the ship attemptin' to make some repairs an' to keep the flooding at bay. At daylight, when I can survey our position, I shall determine whether we can attempt to get you off the ship an' onto nearby land. Then we shall hope that we ken make repairs to the ship or that another ship might come by and assist."

"Oh!" cried Mrs. Joyner. "How are we to get off the ship and onto land when we are nowhere near the docks? I cannot swim!"

The captain scratched his bristly beard. "We have a small boat that'll carry you. Have no fear; we shall ensure your safety getting to land." He paused and took in a deep breath. "That is, *if* there is land reasonably close."

The captain ushered the passengers into the dining room where they would wait for dawn to reveal their location and fate.

Chapter 9

When the first rays of sun lit the skies, the passengers aboard the merchant ship came up on deck and positioned themselves at the rail, anxious about what they might see. The storm had passed, and the sea had calmed, but a fog engulfing the ship kept their surroundings hidden.

As the day grew lighter, they gradually were able to see the large mass of rock that held the ship tight in its grip. The fog, however, kept what was beyond secret, allowing only for an occasional brief glimpse of more rock. They muttered their concerns amongst themselves, but felt it was not the time to bother the captain or crew with their questions and worries. Each time the ship shifted, fearful glances passed amongst them.

The captain stood on the foredeck with a spyglass pressed to his eye. He looked about him, speaking with fervour to his first mate and several other crewmen. Occasionally they would glance down at a map, pointing at it and either nodding or shaking their heads. At length, he approached the passengers.

"My men are workin' feverishly below deck to patch the gash in the ship, but it is still takin' on water. While there is little danger of the ship sinkin' because of the rock beneath us, there's still the possibility of it capsizin' if the hull fills with water."

Mrs. Joyner put her hand over her heart and began to sway. Her husband was ready and caught her when she collapsed.

"Take her to the dinin' room an' give her some tea. Please try to reassure her that there is no imminent danger. We have formulated a plan to assure your safety."

When the couple left, the captain continued, "We were just barely able to see a small uninhabited island to our port side through the fog. When the fog recedes a bit more, I think it would be prudent to remove the passengers to the island until the ship is repaired or another ship comes by. The dinghy we keep stowed on the ship should be able to get you there without any mishap. We will keep watch for other ships while we make our attempts at repairin' this one."

Mrs. Dillard slowly lifted her hand. "But how are we to get down into the dinghy from up here?"

"We'll board you while it is still on deck. One of my men will be with you while we lower it into the water with winches. We shall take the women and Mr. Joyner over first. I am quite sure Mrs. Joyner will appreciate her husband's reassurin' presence. Once you are in the water, two more of my men will climb down the ropes from the ship to join you an' help row. When you are safely on the island, they shall return to get the remaining men passengers."

The ladies were excused to gather some items to take with them. Mrs. Joyner joined them, and Elizabeth assisted in helping her decide what few things she would need, as fear seemed to take away any ability to make a decision.

When they returned to the deck, they saw that the fog had lifted towards shore, and the small island could be seen. Looking out towards the sea, however, they could see nothing.

Once it was determined to be safe to make the short journey, Mr. Joyner and one of the crewmen, who introduced himself as Timmons, climbed into the boat. They assisted each of the ladies as they stepped in. Once settled, the boat was slowly swung over the side of the ship and lowered into the water as the women held each other's hands tightly. Two more crewmen climbed down ropes that were hung over the side of the ship. The men then proceeded to row to the island.

Mr. Joyner was grateful that Elizabeth held his wife's hand as the men manoeuvred carefully around the protruding rocks, occasionally using their oars to push away. When they crashed against one from the force of a strong wave, Elizabeth did her best to reassure Mrs. Joyner that they all would be safe. She was grateful for Mrs. Keller, who diverted them with stories of more perilous trips she had experienced at sea and assured them this was nothing to be overly concerned about.

It took almost an hour for the small boat to reach the island. Two of the crewmen jumped out when they came near the beach and pulled the boat up to shore. Once up on the beach, the men assisted the ladies as they stepped out. Despite the fatigue of the rowers, the two crewmen immediately began rowing back to the ship.

The group watched as the small boat grew smaller and smaller until it finally disappeared behind a rather large protruding rock. The fog had grown more dense and it now completely hid the merchant ship from their sight. A light mist began to fall, and Timmons gathered the group together.

"From what the cap'n could see from the ship, an' what 'e knows of the area, there should be a good sized cave over 'ere." Timmons pointed to the east. "If ye'd follow me, we'll be waitin' in there fer them to return wi' the others so we ken keep dry."

The ladies gathered their few belongings and carefully picked their way across an uneven beach that was strewn with rocks of all sizes and a variety of vegetation washed up from the sea. Elizabeth bit her lip to keep from chuckling as the women struggled to maintain their footing. They were doing everything they could to walk like the graceful and fashionable ladies they were, but with little success.

As they drew near the cave, the rain began to fall more heavily. The ladies pulled their pelisses tightly about them and walked hurriedly. When they reached the shelter of the cave, they let out a sigh of relief. Several large rocks quickly took on the role of hard chairs as Mrs. Joyner, Mrs. Dillard, and Mrs. Keller sat down, huddling close together. Elizabeth sat down on a smooth sandy spot on the ground, tucking her legs beneath her.

Timmons opened a knapsack and pulled out some items.

"Mr. Joyner, if ye please, stay wi' the ladies an' give 'em a biscuit an' a piece of fruit. I'll be searchin' fer some wood to build a fire to dry us off an' keep us warm."

"Oh, thank you, so much!" Mrs. Dillard exclaimed. "I do not know whether I am more uncomfortable from being so hungry or soaked from the rain!"

The ladies laughed as Timmons turned to leave, but he abruptly stopped. Elizabeth looked up when she heard a gasp and saw four men standing menacingly at the entrance to the cave. She felt a great sense of foreboding as the men suddenly drew swords, muskets, and pistols from their belts. She shuddered as she noticed their glaring looks and threatening posture.

"Pirates!" Mrs. Joyner screamed and crumpled into a heap on the ground.

~~*

The winds and rain finally subsided, and Darcy rested his elbows on the port side of the ship waiting eagerly for the first hint of dawn to give them some indication of their location. The clouds prevented them from seeing the skies, and the only light seen for the past few hours was the lightning displaying its fury off in the distance. Darcy felt that same fury deep inside as he considered what Bellows had done, the situation in which they now found themselves, and what he should to do about it.

The sea was calmer now, and the ship rose and dropped steadily, propelled slowly to the west by the movement of the waves. Darcy watched with a keen eye for any sign of land in the distance each time lightning bolted across the skies, but he could see nothing. The sails would remain furled until they had a better idea of where they might be. There was no sense setting out in a particular direction when they did not have their bearings. The last thing they needed was to crash into an unexpected outcropping or even worse, another ship. And despite Darcy's anger at Bellows for acting so recklessly, he refrained from admonishing him further, as he was the only man on the ship fully capable of being at the helm.

As the first hint of light touched the skies, Darcy felt a great sense of disquiet. There was a dense morning fog that prevented him from seeing anything farther than a stone's throw from the ship, and he could see nothing of the skies above.

Darcy marched up to the foredeck and picked up the spyglass, pressing it to his eye. He searched futilely through the fog for anything that might indicate where they were. As he did, he spoke with Bellows.

"As soon as we see land, I insist that we find a place to dock. I have not... I 'aven't..." Darcy paused. "Wait! I see something!"

Bellows looked at him and then out to sea. "What is it, Cap'n?"

Darcy gathered his composure, knowing he must remember to speak as Evans and Lindel had instructed him. They were correct; he did revert to his refined manner of speech when startled or surprised... or angered!

"I'm not sure; I don't see it now. It may 'ave been a ship. It keeps disappearin' in the fog." Darcy's heart thundered as he considered what they might encounter. If it was a ship, the men might want to act out their pirating aspirations, despite any protests he might have. Or worse, they may be encountering real pirates!

"I see it!" Bellows said. "'Tis a large ship; may'ap a merchant ship. Don't seem to be movin'. I wonder if the vessel hit some rocks."

"We need to take care, then, so we don't do the same." Darcy was silent for a moment, but his mind assaulted him with questions. What should he tell his men? And an even greater concern was Bellows! What did Bellows expect Darcy to do as Lockerly, and if he did not do what Bellows expected, would he turn the men against him and lead the crew in a mutiny? He shuddered when he thought of what they might want to do upon reaching that ship.

"I ken see it better now. Me thinks they be in distress," Bellows said softly. "The ship is listin' on its port side."

Darcy blew out a puff of air, and his hand patted his sheathed sword as his mind whirled with thoughts.

"Are ye thinkin' of assistin' 'em... Darcy?"

Darcy turned sharply to Bellows, his jaw dropping. "You know who I am?"

Bellows slowly nodded. "I 'ave known all along. Foster hired me to be part of this whole scheme to get you an' the ship out to sea an' to the Isles of Scilly."

Darcy closed his eyes as his anger now burned for another reason. "That man and his schemes! I have been so angry at you, and now I find out *he* is behind this! And Evans and Lindel?"

"Yep! They was, too."

Darcy balled his hands into tight fists, and his jaw tightened so fiercely he felt his face shake.

"You have me apologies, Darcy."

"But why did they have to resort to such a thing? They had Lockerly's ship; *I* did not need to continue on with this charade!"

"Aye, but therein lies the problem. Ye 'ad such a good rapport wi' the crew; they seemed to respect ye. Neither Evans nor Lindel felt they could secure the trust of the men like ye 'ave." He waved his hand over the ship. "The men'll do whatever ye say, even if it's *not* piratin'."

Darcy turned back to the ship. "We cannot be certain of that, but we shall have to see. Can we get very close to the ship? They hit rocks; might we not also?"

Bellows shrugged. "'Tis always possible, but that ship is larger and her keel extends deeper. We should 'ave no problem as long as we ken see where we're going. If only the fog…"

Bellows stopped and his eyes widened as the fog lifted briefly. "I don't believe it! 'Tis the merchant ship I used to sail on!"

"The ship whose captain you disliked?"

Bellows winced. "Not exactly. That were jest me enhancin' the story. We actually got along decent."

Darcy closed his eyes and shook his head. "Did you men ever consider that what you were doing could put us in grave danger?"

"I regret we didn't."

"I thought not."

"Me thinks ye need to decide what we're goin' to do an' what ye is goin' to tell *them*." Bellows nodded his head towards the crew.

"I know exactly what we are going to do, and what I am going to tell them!" He turned to walk away, but stopped. "I am going to tell them I am *not* Lockerly, I am *not* a pirate, and that we are going to see how we can be of assistance to this ship!" Darcy let out a huff and yanked off his tri-corn hat. He raked his fingers through his hair. "An' I am goin' to tell 'em that my name is… *Smith*!"

"Smith?"

Darcy turned to look at Bellows. "Yes… *Smith*! I do not want anyone to know my real identity, so pray, do not call me Darcy."

"An' does Cap'n Smith speak the way of a gentleman or a commoner?"

Darcy groaned as he considered this. "No, I'll still be speakin' the way of the common man. As much as disguise of any sort is my abhorrence, I ken think of no good purpose lettin' them know I am of the finest circles of society!"

Bellows grinned. "Go to it, Cap'n Smith! After ye 'ave talked to the men, we'll unfurl some of the sails so we ken catch the wind an' sail towards 'em."

Darcy gathered his crew together. Those who had been up on the masts climbed down, and those who were below deck were brought up. The men gathered, their faces filled with a mixture of excitement and fear, having seen the ship wafting in and out of the fog.

Darcy eyed them carefully so he could watch for any sign of mutiny as he told them what they were about to do. At least he knew he had Bellows on his side.

The men listened in surprise and just a little confusion as they were told their captain was not Lockerly, he was not a pirate and neither were they, and they were actually going to be of assistance rather than plunder and pillage the ship that was in distress.

When Darcy finished, he said to them, "I know ye joined me under the misapprehension that I would be leadin' ye all on a variety of piratin' adventures. I am sorry, truly, but this was never my intent. The goal was to lure the real Lockerly to us so he could be captured. But if ye trust me an' do as I ask, ye shall all be receivin' the highest commendations to be hired on other sailin' vessels when we return to London. All of ye 'ave proven yourselves excellent workers."

The men received the news reasonably well. While there was some disappointment, two of the younger men, Michael Jenkins and Edward Webber, confessed that they had secretly hoped they wouldn't have to kill anyone, although obtaining some treasure might have been appealing.

When Darcy returned to the foredeck, Bellows said to him, "Foster knew t'would be this way. The men trust ye completely an' will follow yer orders to the letter."

"'Tis one thing to say you'll do somethin' an' another to do it." Darcy said, folding his arms across his chest. "We shall 'ave to wait an' see."

Bellows pointed to the ship in distress. "As we draw close, I will need to signal 'em so they know we ain't pirates in case they recognize the *Devil's Seamaiden*. Once they know I'm on board, they'll know all is safe."

"How will you signal them?"

"Signal flags that ye arrange in ways that form messages. Cap'n Meeker will know their meaning."

Darcy leaned against the quarterdeck railing and looked up. With a sly smile he said, "I am very grateful you did not hoist the Jolly Roger that Lockerly had stowed away. I truly thought you might do that."

"Ye thought that 'bout me? Sorry. I suppose I did pass meself off as a real scallywag!"

"Ye certainly did!"

"Cap'n, if you'll excuse me, I'll see to raisin' the signal flags before they begin firin' warnin' shots at us."

"Thank you, Bellows."

Bellows left, and Darcy stood at the helm gripping the wheel. He kept an eye on the listing ship, still drifting in and out of the fog. He could see cannons positioned on the side of the deck and would have been concerned, but for the fact that due to the tilt of the ship, the cannons most likely would not be able to hit them.

Bellows worked with a few of the crew to hoist the signal flags, being very particular in the order they went up. When he finished, he instructed the same men to unfurl the topsail, top gallant, and outer jib sails. He watched as the men climbed out on the rigging and released the sails. They dropped with a thud and immediately caught the wind and billowed out. The ship began moving slowly.

Bellows returned to the helm, but allowed Darcy to continue steering. He picked up the spyglass and looked out. "I think we ken get fairly close to the ship. It'll take some careful manoeuvrin' aroun' some of these rocks, but I think we ken do it. We need to approach close enough to throw the grapplin' hook over to pull us in close."

"Would ye mind takin' the helm, Bellows?" Darcy asked, and then suddenly tilted his head and raised a brow. "Is that *your* real name?"

Bellows laughed. "Aye, Cap'n. I 'ad no reason to change it as I was not wi' the River Thames Police, or any police, for that matter."

Darcy watched as Bellows steered the ship and gave orders to the men. The ship drew slowly and cautiously towards the disabled ship, now in full view. As they drew closer, Darcy noticed men coming to the rail armed with muskets and drawn swords.

"Ahoy!" Darcy yelled. "Are ye in need of assistance?"

"We are armed!" yelled one of the men. "We have no valuables on board this ship, if you be pirates!"

"We are not pirates!" Darcy answered back. "I'm Cap'n Smith, an' at the helm is George Bellows, a former crewman on yer ship." Darcy waved for Bellows to come over.

"Lower the anchor an' furl the sails!" Bellows hollered as he took the steps down and walked to the rail. "Good mornin', Cap'n Meeker! I thought ye knew better than to get yerself into this kind of predicament!"

"Couldn't do much in the storm! What're ye doin' on that ship? If I didn't know any better, I'd swear that is a pirate ship an' ye had become a pirate! I wasn't trustin' those signal flags you hoisted. Anyone can claim to be anyone these days!"

"'Tis a long story, but tell us, what ken we do?"

"I ken barely hear ye. Can ye get closer?"

Bellows looked down into the sea, noticing the shadow of rock just beneath the surface.

"I don't think so. But gimme a few minutes!"

Bellows gathered about five men who effortlessly climbed the rigging and stepped out onto one of the masts. He pulled down a rope, releasing the winch that held it taut. Before Darcy could even blink, Bellows jumped. He swung down on the rope, out across the water, and landed on the deck of the other ship. The others followed.

Bellows and the captain spoke fervently while the others went below deck to help with the damage. Bellows then climbed the rigging of the other ship and returned in the same manner. He rushed over to Darcy as the remaining crew huddled close.

"They 'ave a gash in their hull, but that is not the worst of their worries. Apparently they rowed four ladies to a small island just to the north in case the ship capsized. They're there wi' the husband of one of them an' a crewman. They tried to send the rest of the passengers across, but the dinghy just returned to the ship with all of 'em still aboard. There were pirates who fired on the boat as it tried to approach! They 'ave taken the ladies prisoner, an' they are now in greater danger than if they 'ad remained on the ship!"

Darcy removed his tri-corn hat and raked his fingers through his long hair. This was grave, indeed, but he could not turn his back on those in danger. He looked back to the ship and noticed an older man at the rail. He was not dressed as a crewman, and Darcy thought he looked somewhat familiar. He brought the spyglass to his eye and focused on the man.

"You must rescue my daughter!" the man called out. "I cannot bear to think of anything happening to her!"

Darcy's heart stopped. It had been well over six months since he had last seen him, but the gentleman on that ship was most certainly Mr. Bennet! He froze, fear coursing through him. Which of his daughters was in the hands of pirates? Whoever it was, he would do everything in his power to rescue her. As he determined what he could do, Mr. Bennet called out again.

"Please! You must rescue my Lizzy!"

Darcy almost dropped the spyglass and gripped the rail tightly with his other hand. His knuckles turned white, and he felt his chest constrict, finding it difficult to even take a breath. Forcing himself to think, he rubbed his temple. He looked around him at the sea, the rocks, and out towards the lonely island.

He turned to Bellows. "We must make every attempt to rescue these ladies. Can we manoeuvre the ship directly away from the merchant ship so the pirates do not see us and then move stealthily through the fog around the island? Perhaps we can come in and have surprise in our favour... if they have not already seen us."

"I doubt they 'ave. The merchant ship is bigger an' we 'ave been on the other side of it from the island the whole time. With the fog, I doubt they could make us out."

"Well, let us away, quickly!"

Bellows turned to go and then stopped, looking back at Darcy. "It looks like we'll be 'aving a pirate's adventure after all, Cap'n!" He returned to the helm and gave the order to unfurl more sails.

Darcy stood at the rail, staring out into the fog. He could not formulate one thought except that he must save Elizabeth and would make every attempt to do so. Looking up into the heavens, he softly muttered, "Lord, keep her safe! I will do anything, even give her up in my heart, if that is what is needed to ensure no harm comes to her!"

Chapter 10

It had been two hours since the pirates had appeared and taken the party captive. The ladies huddled together in the back of the cave, shivering more from fear than cold. They were sheltered from the mist enshrouding the island but were too far from the small fire at the end of the cave to benefit from its heat. Timmons and Mr. Joyner had been ordered to sit back to back, and their hands were bound together.

About an hour earlier they had heard shots fired. The prisoners had silently looked at each other with anxious glances. They had hoped that the men who were coming over to join them had been the ones doing the shooting, while at the same time feared that they were the ones being shot at. They had waited with great dread while one of the pirates, who was called Torch, was sent out to discover what had happened. When he had returned, the news he brought was disheartening to the captives. Apparently there were two pirates on the beach, Bloody Clem and Scarface Jack, who had indeed shot at a dinghy bringing men over. Torch had assured the other pirates that the dinghy returned to the merchant ship. Fear had consumed the ladies that now no one would come to rescue them.

In the hour since they had heard the gunshots, the pirates had become a little less attentive, save for the one who stood at the entrance to the cave.

Two pirates were lazily sprawled with their backs against the wall of the cave, their muskets and swords at their side. They would occasionally take a drink from a flask or take a bite of some food they had stowed. The one named Torch stood near the ladies, pacing back and forth. Elizabeth could not determine whether he was nervous or trying to act as though he was guarding them against an escape.

The fourth man had remained just inside the cave, looking out. His gaze swept back and forth as if waiting and watching for something. Every once in a while he would look at the ladies, glaring at them with a wicked smile. Elizabeth felt a sick tightening in her stomach at his bold perusal, which more often than not landed on her.

Elizabeth had determined he must be the leader. He was tall, with long, dark curly hair that brushed his shoulders. His beard was full, dark, and wiry. To Elizabeth's discerning eye, he also seemed to be the most capable of inflicting injury. The other men were rather thin and almost appeared unsure of themselves and what was expected of them. They seemed to obey more out of fear than out of bravery.

"Oh, I know we are all to die!" Mrs. Joyner cried out in a hushed tone.

Elizabeth patted her hand. "These men have been drinking too heavily to do us much harm. They can barely walk upright."

"Yes!" agreed Mrs. Dillard. "We must have faith that we shall all come through this unharmed!"

Elizabeth hoped these words would alleviate Mrs. Joyner's fears. For herself, she remembered Reverend Hoover saying that the good Lord was as close as a prayer and to call out to Him when in need. She closed her eyes and without thinking squeezed Mrs. Joyner's hand. All she could murmur was, "Lord, keep us all safe from these pirates!"

She opened her eyes and looked at Mrs. Dillard, who seemed to be praying, as well.

Elizabeth was uncertain how many pirates might be on the island, but from the conversation between the four men in the cave, she knew there were at least two more out on the beach, and possibly more. She felt her heart beat wildly as she considered the safety of her father, cousin, and the rest of the men as they had attempted to come ashore. She hoped they had been able to return to the merchant ship unharmed.

The rain had stopped, and the sun was trying to peek through the clouds. As irrational as it seemed, Elizabeth thought to herself that if the sun succeeded in shining down on them, they would be safe. Or at least they would be warm. She dreaded what might happen once the sun set.

Elizabeth watched as Torch sat down by the other two men, picked up the flask, and began to drink.

"Put that down, Torch! You 'ave 'ad enough to drink and we need to stay alert!" He looked at the other two men in the cave. "That goes fer you, too!"

Torch meekly put down the flask. "Yes, Cap'n Lockerly."

Elizabeth's eyes narrowed. *Lockerly! I have heard that name before!*

As she tried to recollect why the name sounded familiar, Mrs. Keller suddenly whispered, "Lockerly is a pirate who recently was captured by the authorities but somehow escaped!"

"You are right!" Elizabeth replied softly. "I remember reading about it." Elizabeth blew out a long puff of air and looked over at him. "His entire crew was hung. These men must be ones he has recently engaged to join him."

"Oh!" Mrs. Joyner trembled. "This is grave, indeed!"

"Perhaps not," Elizabeth reassured her. "If these men are not experienced pirates, we can hope that we might somehow free ourselves. They do not appear to me to be very clever men or competent combatants. And they are all quite jug-bitten."

"Shall we pray that they continue drinking?" Mrs. Dillard asked, attempting to inject some levity into the situation.

Elizabeth suddenly stood up, and Mrs. Joyner gasped, trying to pull her back down. "If you please, sir, the ladies need a little privacy... to take care of some personal business. If you would be so kind as to allow us a few moments to ourselves outside the cave."

Lockerly grunted. "And 'ave you run off? Me thinks not."

Elizabeth put her hands on her hips. "And where do you think we are going to run off to?"

"She 'as a point," Torch said with a laugh.

Lockerly glared at Torch and then turned back to the ladies. "Aye, then, but only two at a time." He raised his sword and pointed it at Timmons and Mr. Joyner. "An' if ye don't return quickly, ye'll regret it. We'll come afta ya *an'* kill one of the men!"

Mrs. Joyner began to sway, and Elizabeth turned to grab her. She told Mrs. Keller and Mrs. Dillard to go first, while she attempted to calm Mrs. Joyner. This might give her time to compose a plan.

When the two ladies returned, Elizabeth pulled Mrs. Joyner to her feet. "Come with me," she whispered. "The air will help you."

The ladies walked away from the cave. Mrs. Joyner held tightly to Elizabeth's hand and leaned as close to her as she could as they walked past Lockerly. They set out for some dense shrubbery where they could discreetly take care of their needs. As they walked back, Elizabeth began to pick up large rocks and then slipped them into the pockets of her gown.

"What are you doing?" asked Mrs. Joyner in an alarmed whisper. Fear was etched in her features, and her voice shook.

"I am merely arming myself. Here, you take some."

"Oh, I could do no such thing!' exclaimed Mrs. Joyner.

A noise brought the conversation and walk to a halt. Elizabeth brought a finger to her lips in the hopes that Mrs. Joyner would remain calm and silent. She could hear the distinctive sound of someone walking hurriedly through the brush. Her heart thundered at the prospect that whoever was coming might be here to either rescue them or ravage them.

Elizabeth forcefully brought Mrs. Joyner down behind some rocks and bushes as the person drew near. If she could only see who it was! It might not help, but it could not hurt. She knew it could not be anyone from the cave, and she did not think it could be the men who were on the shore. The person was walking from the other direction.

Elizabeth peered through the dense foliage and watched with eyes like a hawk, waiting for the person to appear. She gripped one of the larger rocks in her pocket, fingering it tightly. Suddenly a man came out from around a bend. He was alone! But to her dismay, he looked much like Lockerly, with his long, unkempt hair and beard. He was wearing a tri-corn hat, billowy white shirt, and red sash. He walked stealthily, patting his sword, which was sheathed in a leather baldric. She quickly deduced that he, too, must be a pirate!

Just as he passed, Elizabeth took aim, bit her lip, and struck him in the head with all her strength!

~~*

The *Devil's Seamaiden* had been able to pull fairly close to the small island around to the south. The fog shrouded them as they drew near. As the sea on that side was relatively free of rocky outcroppings, there was no fear of striking one. Darcy and Bellows hand-picked four men from the crew – those they deemed most reliable and loyal – to accompany them onto the small island. The remaining crew were left to man the ship.

The six men rowed across in the small dinghy, making it quickly it to shore. Darcy's plan was to have two men search along the beach in the direction of the pirates who staved off the merchant's ship boat with gunfire and have the other two walk along the shore in the opposite direction to see what they would find. He asked Bellows to give the men a course of action should they encounter any pirates and then to follow him.

As Bellows spoke with the men, Darcy quickly looked about him, alert to any sign that the pirates might be close by. When he was convinced they had not been seen, he hurriedly began walking inland in hopes of finding the prisoners, particularly, Elizabeth.

The rapid beating of his heart propelled his pace and lengthened his stride. A great fear gripped him that any delay could mean disaster for Elizabeth.

He lowered his head to pass through some shrubs. As he brushed aside some branches and came through, he saw a flash of movement to the side and instinctively raised his hand as something came towards him. He felt a searing pain above his right eye, which stunned him momentarily, taking him to the ground.

Darcy lay dazed for a moment, hearing voices.

Another voice – Bellows – sounded from a distance. "Cap'n Smith, are you hurt?"

"Oh, Lord!" a woman cried. "Here comes another pirate! We shall all die now, I am sure of it!"

"Ladies, fear not, we are here to rescue you!"

Suddenly Bellows was beside him, gently shaking him. "Captain Smith, do you hear me?"

Darcy groaned and brought his hand up to his forehead. "What happened?" He could feel the warm trickle of blood and tried to open his eyes as he heard Bellows again.

"Ladies, my name is Bellows. This is Cap'n Smith. I used to serve with Cap'n Meeker, of the merchant ship ye were sailing on. He told us about ye being held by pirates. Ye 'ave Timmons with ye, correct?"

He spoke so rapidly that Darcy could barely make sense of his words.

Suddenly another woman spoke. "You know Timmons? You are not pirates?"

That voice! It was Elizabeth!

"No, we aren't, despite 'ow we may look," Bellows reassured her.

"Oh, I am so sorry! Shall he be all right, do you think?"

"I doubt it is a mortal wound. He'll recover."

Darcy felt Elizabeth kneel down next to him. She dabbed his forehead with a soft cloth, perhaps a handkerchief. He revelled in her gentle touch. But he had to see her! Despite the pain, he slowly opened his eyes.

He was not quite ready for the shock of actually seeing Elizabeth Bennet so close after so long. Soft, caring eyes looked down upon him instead of the sharp, accusing ones he had last seen at Rosings. Something inside of him reacted with great force, and he found himself unwittingly reaching out and grasping her hand.

"Oh!" Elizabeth exclaimed, trying to pull her hand free. "I am so sorry, sir... Captain... I thought you were a pirate! If I had but known! Pray, forgive me! Truly, you must believe me. I did not mean to harm you!"

Darcy loosened his grip slightly, but he did not release her hand.

"No, no," he said. "I am... I'm sorry. I... I didn't mean to frighten ye." He tried to sit up, but a wave of dizziness forced him back down. "I... am a trifle dizzy."

"We must get back," the other woman said, tugging at Elizabeth's free hand. "They threatened to come after us and kill one of the men if we did not return directly!"

Elizabeth looked with an expression of worry at Darcy. He could not take his eyes off of her and was still in possession of her hand. He did not wish to release it, as he felt that as long as he held it, she would be safe.

Elizabeth touched the handkerchief to his forehead again. "I fear it is still bleeding, Captain. I am so sorry!"

"You had every reason in the world to think ill of me. You... ye thought I was another pirate. How many pirates are there?" he asked, gently giving her hand a squeeze.

Elizabeth furrowed her brow and bit her lip, a look of confusion passing over her features. "There are four in the cave, and I believe two are on the beach. They shot at the men who tried to come over after us! My father and cousin were on the boat!"

"They are all safe," Darcy said. "We stopped to give assistance to the ship when we saw it had struck rock. The men had just returned. No one was hit."

"Oh, I am so relieved! The women will be, as well. But please, you must be careful. One of the pirates is named Lockerly, and he seems..."

"Lockerly!" both men said at once, looking at each other.

"This Lockerly, has he harmed you... any of the ladies?" Darcy asked, his hand squeezing hers again in dread.

Elizabeth shook her head. "No, fortunately he has not."

"We 'ave to send the ladies back to the cave," Bellows said. He turned to Elizabeth. "If Lockerly 'as threatened the lives of the others, ye probably should go. We shall gather the rest of our men an' devise a plan to git ye all away from 'em."

"There are more of you? Oh, thank heavens! You may have a fighting chance against them as they are a little unsteady from too much drink."

"'Tis good to know," Bellows replied. "Ken you point out exactly where the cave is?"

Elizabeth pointed in the direction of the cave and then said, "We truly must go. Thank you, and again, I am truly sorry." She looked at the captain, and with a gentle smile said, "Excuse me, Captain Smith, but may I please have my hand back?"

Darcy released it immediately. "Sorry, so sorry! Please be careful!"

"We will. You, as well. And pray, keep my handkerchief. It is the least I can do after what I have done." Elizabeth looked back to Bellows. "Lockerly stands guard at the entrance."

Bellows fingered his jaw. "If ye ken think of any way to distract 'im, that might help."

Elizabeth nodded. "I shall certainly try!"

Darcy watched the two ladies walk away. He felt a mixture of relief that she was safe but still had a great deal of concern for her welfare.

Bellows stooped down. "Are ye quite well, Cap'n? Ye seemed a bit odd jest now."

Darcy looked up at him. "I did? In what way?"

"Well, in the first place, graspin' the lady's 'and like ye did an' 'oldin' it fer so long. I thought ye'd never let go!"

"Oh, that. I suppose it was a little reckless of me."

"Ahh, but a perfect display of unrefined behaviour! Good move on yer part. But I regret to tell ye that yer speech were not always that of a commoner. No matter 'ow perty they may be, ye ken't be speakin' to the ladies one way an' yer crew another."

Darcy rubbed his head. "I was a bit taken aback." He looked up at Bellows. "My head... me head, ye know. I need a moment."

That was the truth. He needed to clear his thoughts and determine what they should do.

Darcy took in a deep breath. "Ken ye go find the others? See what they've found? Bring 'em back 'ere. We ken't wait too long, though, to go in and take care o' the pirates."

"I'll go see if I ken find them. Ye wait here an' gather your wits. I'll be right back!"

Darcy was left to his thoughts... and to gather his wits. He still felt dizzy, but he did not know if it was due to his head injury or to being in such close proximity to Elizabeth. He had not been able to formulate one thought with her so near, let alone speak to her in the unrefined manner he had practiced so extensively. He sat up slowly, leaned against a nearby rock, and examined the situation.

If the men were indeed as drunk as Elizabeth thought they were, the advantage would be in his and his crew's favour. He and his men also had the benefit of surprise, but he and Lockerly were equally matched in the number of men each had. Unfortunately, Lockerly and his men might have their greatest advantage in possessing better fighting skills.

As he waited for Bellows to return, he thought about Elizabeth. Looking down at her blood-soaked handkerchief, he let out a sigh. He had to admit he enjoyed her close presence, the lavender scent that permeated the lace and linen fabric, the few loose strands of her hair that framed her face, and the look of care and concern with which she looked at him. If he told her who he really was, would she pull away, allowing all her resentment and anger towards him to resurface?

He looked down at his clothes and fingered his full beard. No, he would not tell her who he was. He would not want her to see him in such a state. Perhaps someday, but not now. He only hoped she would not recognize him… or had not already. And he would have to make every effort to speak as the common sea captain she thought he most likely was.

"No, Miss Elizabeth," he said softly, wiping some sand and dirt off his sleeves. "I won't be puttin' ye in an awkward situation by announcin' to ye that I'm the man ye despise most in all the world. But…" he added with a sigh, "I'll do everythin' I ken to keep ye safe. That, I will do!"

"Talkin' to yerself?" Bellows said with a soft chuckle, suddenly appearing with Webber and Jenkins.

"No…no. Did ye find out anythin'?"

"We saw a small ship to the east," offered Jenkins." Prob'ly holds a crew of only 'bout eight to twelve men."

"The ladies believed there were only six men on the island. There might be more still on the ship. And 'ave you seen any of our other men?" Darcy asked.

"No, they hadn't returned," Bellows said. "We thought we should git back an' do what we ken to git the ladies away from these marauders first."

"I agree." Darcy looked from one man to another, noticing their willing, but somewhat troubled, faces.

As Darcy cautiously stood up, he said, "Jest keep yer 'ead, grip yer cutlass tightly, be aware of what's goin' on around ye, an' watch out fer one another." Darcy touched his brow with the handkerchief. The soft, silky fabric reminded him of the feel of Elizabeth's skin and seemed to give him strength. The only pain he felt now was the one in his stomach that had been there ever since hearing Miss Elizabeth Bennet had been captured by pirates.

"Are ye ready, men? Let's go an' capture those ruthless pirates!"

Chapter 11

As the two ladies hurried back to the cave, Elizabeth cautioned Mrs. Joyner not to mention a word about the two men they had seen. The poor woman was so distraught Elizabeth was not certain what she might do.

"How do we know we can trust them?" Mrs. Joyner asked. Her eyes were wide, and her face had drained of all colour. "For all we know, those two men could be the two pirates at the beach, Bloody Clem and Scarface Jack!"

Elizabeth leaned towards Mrs. Joyner and spoke in a fervent whisper, hoping to reassure her. "I do not believe they were." She took Mrs. Joyner's hand and said with a light-hearted chuckle, "I am certain someone called Scarface Jack would have a scar on his face. I did not see a noticeable scar on either of their faces, although poor Captain Smith will likely have one after what I did to him!"

"But they may have been pirates who are just as ruthless and looking to fight Lockerly." Mrs. Joyner patted her heart. "You saw how they looked at each other when you told them Lockerly was here."

Elizabeth bit her lip and took in a deep breath. "I did notice it, but for some reason… I am not certain why… I believe we *can* trust these men."

"Ye took a long time!" barked Lockerly as they approached. "We was about ready to go after ya!"

"We apologize. We took a wrong turn and had to find our way back." Elizabeth was grateful when they seemed to accept her story.

Lockerly stood fixed at the opening to the cave, looking out. If he remained there, the men would not be able to take him by surprise. Elizabeth had to do something to distract him. But how would she know when the men were close by?

Torch was adding wood to the fire with a wide grin. He seemed to be rather enjoying his employment.

A few minutes later, Elizabeth heard the whistling of a bird. Lockerly seemed to notice it as well, turning his head curiously in its direction. It did not sound like any bird Elizabeth had ever heard before, although she knew a myriad of different birds inhabited these islands.

She heard it again, and her heart began to beat thunderously as she realized it was probably the men. Lockerly began to walk towards the sound, seemingly intent to find out what it was. She had to do something directly!

Elizabeth stood up and began to walk over towards the edge of the cave. "May I stand by the fire? I am quite chilled."

Lockerly spun around. "What are you doin'? Where do ye think ye are goin'?"

"I merely wanted to warm myself by the fire."

"Git back where ye were!" Lockerly ordered.

Elizabeth turned around to walk back to the ladies, but as she did, she fell to the ground. "Oh! My ankle! I think I may have twisted it!"

Lockerly stormed towards her, anger etched in his features. "Ye should've stayed where ye was!"

As he looked down at her in disgust, a commotion drew every eye to the cave entrance, where four men stood with their swords drawn.

Lockerly deftly spun around, lifting his sword to the ready. His three fellow pirates, however, struggled to get up and arm themselves.

Captain Smith and his men stepped into the shelter of the cave, their eyes all fixed on Lockerly.

Lockerly appeared more amused by their appearance than troubled. He unexpectedly laughed. "Ha!" he said with an evil grin, pointing his sword at the captain. "I take it *ye* are the one who 'as been impersonatin' me! What a poor excuse fer a pirate!"

"I order ye to give yerself up an' release yer prisoners," the captain said. "If ye do as we say, we may jest spare yer lives!"

"I 'ave never been known to give up, even when faced with a *formidable* foe!" he replied with a sneer. "By the looks of yer feeble crew, it won't be much of an effort to 'ang ye all up by yer thumbs!" He sent a leering glance at the ladies, his eyes as black as his hair. "An' then we'll enjoy the ladies right 'ere in front of the lot of ya!"

Elizabeth noticed the captain glance in her direction, his face filled with rage. Their eyes met for a brief second before his turned back to Lockerly. "You had... ye 'ad best not lay a single 'and on any of these ladies!" he demanded.

Bellows intervened. "By the look of *yer* crew, I doubt they will be of much use to you! They're all swimmin' in the drink!"

"Bellows!" Timmons suddenly cried out when he recognized his friend's voice. "Thank heavens you're here!"

This drew Lockerly's attention, and Elizabeth watched as Captain Smith took advantage of the opportunity to come at him with his sword drawn. Mrs. Joyner screamed as the clang of metal resounded in the cave. The two men danced around each other, the tips of their swords slicing through the air with precision.

Elizabeth shuddered as Lockerly threatened his opponent. "I so look forward to piercin' you through wi' my sword. No one...*no one*... impersonates me an' gits away with it!" She wondered why the captain had been impersonating the pirate, but had to admit they had great similarities in their appearance.

Lockerly's men fumbled about as they attempted to pull their pistols and swords out of their belts. When they found themselves surrounded by Bellows and the other two men, one of Lockerly's men grabbed his pistol. The air suddenly exploded with a loud crack as it was fired. Whether he was aiming at someone, Elizabeth could not determine, for his aim was neither accurate nor did his countenance reflect someone who truly wished to kill another person. He almost appeared more frightened than threatening.

Shooting his pistol did give him a little advantage, as Bellows and his men drew back. He shot it once more, a little more confidently, and he and the other man who had been sitting next to him were able to manoeuvre past the group of men and escape out of the cave. Bellows sent Jenkins and Webber after them and then turned to Torch, raising his cutlass as Torch raised his.

Captain Smith sidestepped Lockerly's swinging blade, spinning around and thrusting his sword towards him. Lockerly quickly brought his sword up, meeting the captain's with a loud clank, preventing it from piercing him through. The pirate's face reddened with even more anger as he deftly swung back and forth.

Reacting with lightning speed, the captain met each thrust with one of his own. Elizabeth could see that the two men were fairly equal in their parries, but realized that Bellows was concerned for the captain by the way he frequently glanced over at him as he duelled with Torch. They fought with shorter cutlasses, and Torch, while not as proficient at wielding it, seemed better skilled at the footwork required to avoid being hit.

When their two blades clashed in the air between them, Bellows gave a twisting swing and brought his opponent down next to the fire. He stood over Torch, pointing his cutlass at him. "I'd surrender now, if I was ye!"

Torch looked at him as if he were weighing his options. But with a cunning laugh, he suddenly grabbed a burning log from the fire and hurled it at his unsuspecting adversary. As flames began licking Bellows' shirt, Torch scrambled to his feet and ran out of the cave. Bellows brushed down the small area where his shirt had begun burning and took off after the man.

The ladies looked at each other with wide eyes, knowing that the captain had to be victorious, as he was the only one left in the cave to protect them. Elizabeth wished she could just get over to Timmons and Mr. Joyner and untie them, but in all truth, she was not certain either one could stand up against the likes of Lockerly.

Elizabeth reached into her pockets and felt for the rocks. She found a rather large one and gripped it tightly in her hand. She dared not throw it; she would likely miss. She watched as the captain and Lockerly seemed intent on battling to the death! Mrs. Joyner was crying with heaving sobs, Mrs. Keller was standing as rigid as stone, save for the shaking of her hands, and Mrs. Dillard seemed to be praying, again.

Lockerly unexpectedly swung wide, and the captain's sword

flew out of his hand. Elizabeth gasped as she watched the pirate inch his way towards him, extending the blade of his sword towards the captain's heart.

"So now ye leave me with no choice but to display to these ladies my superior strength an' ability. Me thinks no one will challenge me now!"

Elizabeth gripped the rock tightly. Very quietly, she came up behind Lockerly and swung with all her strength, hitting him on the back of his head.

Lockerly's hand went to the back of his head, and he spun around, his face twisted with fury. He came at Elizabeth, clear in his intention to make her pay dearly for her action. The captain took full advantage of Lockerly's distraction and reclaimed his sword, swinging it through the air. The blade sliced across Lockerly's right arm, sending a gush of blood that spread across his shirt, then dripped to the ground.

Lockerly seemed almost undaunted by his injury, and with rough, coarse hands grabbed Elizabeth, positioning her between him and the captain. Backing up out of the cave with Elizabeth in a tight grip, he threatened anyone who might come after him.

"If you harm her, I shall find you," the captain declared in clear, precise speech. "I shall hunt you down for all eternity! You shall pay for it!"

Lockerly pulled Elizabeth outside the cave, and she winced at the foul odour of his breath and his abrasive hands. Rather than fear, however, she had a rather odd thought. Despite their similar appearance, the captain's hands, unlike Lockerly's, had been soft and smooth.

Lockerly turned, as if to run off with Elizabeth in his grasp, but instead, he pushed her down to the ground and dashed away. Elizabeth braced herself as she went down by putting out her hands, scraping them on some rocks.

The captain rushed over to her. "Are you all right? Are you hurt?"

"Only some minor scratches, thank you."

"I am… I'm goin' after him. Will ye see if ye ken release the men?" He pulled out a dagger and handed it to her. "Do ye think ye ken cut through the rope that binds them?"

Elizabeth nodded. "I can certainly try. Now go! But please, be careful!"

The captain nodded, but did not immediately leave. He stood staring at her. "I... I..." Rather than finish his sentence, his shook his head. "Use the dagger on any of those vile men if they return!"

Elizabeth tilted her head slightly. "Do you not think my supply of rocks sufficient?"

She pulled out a few rocks to show him, prompting a smile.

"Ye do quite well with those."

"Too well, perchance. Your wound is bleeding again."

"I'll worry 'bout that when I return."

"Please do," Elizabeth looked at him pleadingly.

"Do what?" the captain asked.

"Return," she said softly.

He nodded, turned, and was gone.

Mrs. Joyner joined Elizabeth at her husband's side as she worked to cut through their restraints. The two other ladies hurried to stand by the fire, eager to warm themselves.

Once the two men were free, they jumped up, zealous to join the men as they pursued those wicked pirates.

Mrs. Joyner held tightly on to her husband. "Pray, do not go! You will be killed!"

Timmons put up a hand. "You stay here, Mr. Joyner. The ladies will need ye if one of 'em comes back!"

Elizabeth was not certain that Mr. Joyner would be of any assistance, but at least that seemed to appease Mrs. Joyner.

It seemed an eternity before any of the men returned. The women sat quietly huddled together around the fire as Mr. Joyner stood alert at the cave's entrance. With each passing minute, Elizabeth could see the concern deepen on everyone's faces as they could only imagine what may have happened to the men.

At length, they heard the sound of men's voices approaching. They sat frozen; all eyes set to see who it was. Mr. Joyner raised the dagger, ready for whatever might be expected of him.

A collective sigh of relief could be heard as the captain and Bellows appeared. The captain, however, was leaning on Bellows' arm.

"What happened?" Elizabeth asked. "Has he been hurt?"

The captain gave her a weak smile. At least Elizabeth thought he smiled. She did not have a clear view of his expression with the fullness of his beard and the mud smeared across his features.

"Tis muddy out there. I merely fell."

"Come, sit by the fire," Elizabeth suggested. "I cannot help but think this is partly my fault. I know you were dizzy after I hit you with the rock, and you likely overexerted yourself fighting Lockerly and going after him."

Bellows helped him over to the fire where he sat down with the others.

Elizabeth sat down alongside the captain. He removed his hat, and his hair, dark and wavy, had stains of blood along the length of it. She looked closely at the wound, which in addition to bleeding was now a bluish colour. She lightly touched it with her fingers and could feel a prominent lump. She looked over to where Lockerly's two pirates had been sitting. "Mr. Bellows, would you be so kind as to hand me that flask?"

Bellows picked up the flask and brought it to Elizabeth. She opened it and sniffed, making a face as she did. She shook her head but said with a smile, "This will do splendidly!"

The captain gazed up into her face. "I didn't think ye'd be the drinkin' sort, Miss..."

"I am Elizabeth Bennet, and you have no need to worry, Captain. This is for *you!*" Looking about her, she asked, "Has anyone a clean handkerchief that I may borrow?" Elizabeth suddenly laughed. "Well, perhaps borrow is not the most fitting word. I doubt that after I am through with it, anyone will want it back!"

Mrs. Dillard pulled one out of her pocket. "It is clean, Miss Bennet."

"Not for long," Elizabeth said as she poured some of the vile smelling liquid onto it and gently dabbed the alcohol into the wound.

The captain winced, but kept his eyes on Elizabeth.

"I am terribly sorry, Captain, to pain you again, but this will help clean it out. Now," she said looking up to Bellows, "please tell us what happened out there."

Bellows relayed the story to them. They believed the pirates had been on the island quite a long time as they seemed to know it well. The two men that had been sent to the beach confronted the pirates there and then were led on a wild chase through the brush.

They ended up back on the beach where they had started, but the pirates had disappeared.

The same thing happened to Jenkins and Webber, who had chased their pirates around in circles and then down to the beach on the other side of the island. When they got there, they saw them getting into their small boat, quite a distance away. Torch and Lockerly did the same, leading the men away from their ship, and then losing them, at which point they made their way to join the others.

By the time Captain Smith and his crew got there, the ship had already set out from shore. Fortunately they were headed north, away from the *Devil's Seamaiden.*

"I am glad none of you were hurt," Elizabeth said. "We were so worried!"

"Where are the other men?" asked Mr. Joyner.

Bellows answered. "Well, two of 'em are keeping a lookout to make sure those jackanapes don't return. They'll stay there 'til dusk. Lockerly don't dare return to the island at night with all the rocks surroundin' it, but they'll make sure he don't. The other two went back to the beach ye all arrived at to light a fire as a signal to the merchant ship. Their crew will be watchin' fer some sort o' sign that yer safe, and I know there'll be some celebratin' when they see it. Then they'll return to our small boat to git a trunk that we brought over containin' food an' supplies. The sea is getting rough again an' another storm might be 'eadin' our way." Bellows shook his head. "Looks as if we won't be gettin' back to our ship anytime soon."

Elizabeth turned her attention back to her patient. "How does your head feel, Captain Smith?"

He looked intently at her and said, "'Tis still a bit painful. Perhaps it needs more of the alcohol. I ken bear it."

"If you insist, Captain Smith." She poured more alcohol onto the handkerchief and dabbed it again to the wound. He winced, but there was a trace of a smile in his eyes. "There! Now, we must keep it clean. I fear I must ask you to remove the sash that is around your waist."

"Me sash?"

"Yes, the red sash. It is long enough to tie around your head and cover your eye to offer it more protection." Elizabeth smiled. "If you do not mind."

"I'm sure he don't," laughed Bellows.

Elizabeth saw the captain shoot his first mate a warning glance as he untied the sash and then handed it to her.

She took the sash and positioned it over the wound, which ended up covering that whole eye. She reached behind him to tie it. "I hope you do not mind, Captain."

"Oh, again, he don't!" Bellows answered for him.

"Bellows! Would ye please show some manners around this lady?"

Elizabeth tied it tight enough to be snug and leaned back to look at him. "*Now* you look more the part of a pirate!" she said with a glimmer in her eyes.

Jenkins and Webber walked in after a while carrying the trunk. They opened it and pulled out blankets, food, and water, distributing it to everyone. As they did, they explained how they had been successful in getting a rather large fire going on the beach to signal the merchant ship that all were safe. They had been rewarded with a cannon being shot off from the ship when those on board spotted it.

Elizabeth took a blanket, but instead of using it herself, she placed it over the captain.

"I don't need this, Miss Bennet; tis fer ye."

"Oh, but you must rest and keep warm. Please."

"Trust me, Miss Bennet, I'm feelin' quite warm enough without a blanket." His uncovered eye locked onto hers.

Elizabeth felt a warmth course through her from her toes to her cheeks. She met the captain's penetrating gaze and then turned away. A fleeting memory teased her thoughts.

Bellows stood by them with his arms folded across his chest, and he let out a hearty laugh. "Now it's yer turn to mind yer manners, Cap'n. Ye aren't above the rest of us an' need to act like a gentleman, yourself!"

Elizabeth was stirred from her thoughts and noticed that the captain's eyes had softened and almost looked sad.

"Forgive me, Miss Bennet, if I behaved in an ungentleman-like manner."

Elizabeth laughed nervously. Her mouth suddenly felt dry, and she licked her lips. "I assure, you, Captain, I took you to mean you were perfectly comfortable and required no blanket."

The captain smiled up at her. "I believe, Miss Bennet, that yer me guardian angel!"

She smiled softly and shook her head. "I am no such thing! I am the very one who caused this dreadful thing!"

"You are perfectly right, but I hold no grudge."

There was something in his words that left her feeling somewhat disconcerted, but she stood up, swiped her hands together, and said, "Now, Captain Smith, I beseech you to rest. I am going to go sit with the ladies and see how they are all faring."

The captain lifted his hand to stay her. "Thank ye, Miss Bennet, for all ye 'ave done."

"I have done nothing but cause you distress from our very first encounter, Captain Smith. You are too gracious."

He shook his head. "No, no, ye 'ave done so much more."

Chapter 12

As Elizabeth joined the other ladies, Darcy closed his eyes. He had never, in the whole of their acquaintance, had the fortune to gaze upon her at such close proximity and for such a long time. Twice in one day! He could barely contain himself.

Even with his eyes closed, he could readily see the dark curls framing her lovely face and her smooth bisque skin, a hint of rose tinting her cheeks, deepening when she blushed. Her lips were full and flawless. When she licked them, they glistened, and it took every bit of self-control not to lift his head to meet her lips with his. He could see her fine eyes looking down at him. *Fine* was how he had described them to Miss Bingley, but they were much more than that. They danced and sparkled and laughed and mocked beneath long, dark lashes. Yet her eyes exuded intelligence and compassion and strength.

Her laughter rang out, and he longed to observe her, so he sat up slowly and leaned against the wall of the cave. He felt helpless, not so much because of his injury, but because all he wanted to do was watch and listen to her.

He had forgotten how enchanting she was when she laughed. Their last two encounters had been under inimical circumstances, which had later driven him to despair. Whereas her anger towards him had propelled him to try to forget her, her laughter now seemed to erase any memory of what had transpired, and all he wished to do was remain in her presence. How much easier and enjoyable it was, however, being someone *other* than the man she so despised.

~~*

Later that evening, the remaining two crewmen returned to the cave. They had climbed to the top of a rocky hill, and with hawk-like eyes had watched the ship until it disappeared as the sun set on the horizon.

They eagerly ate some of the food that had been brought ashore. There was just enough remaining for morning. If they were not able get back to the ship, however, the men could do some hunting and fishing.

After hearing the men's story, the four ladies decided they would take advantage of the last remaining light of day to take care of their personal matters outside the cave.

"If you will be so kind as to allow us some privacy," Elizabeth said, looking at the captain. "We shall return directly."

The captain, with an air of authority, ordered all the men to remain in the cave until the ladies returned. Elizabeth thanked him, saying she was certain they would all comply.

When they returned, Elizabeth expressed surprised to see the captain up and walking around. The ladies returned to the place in the cave they had come to call their own, but Elizabeth walked over to him.

"Are you feeling well enough to be up and about?" she asked.

He nodded. "I am much improved… thanks to your… yer care. Is there anythin' I ken do to make you an' the ladies more comfortable?"

"You have already done so much. But do you think you can you provide us with nice, plump pillows on which to rest our heads?" She tilted her head with a smile.

The captain met her teasing gaze. He was tempted to offer the use of his arm to serve as her pillow, but he refrained. "I'm sorry, but we brought no pillows. I wish we 'ad thought of it."

Elizabeth laughed. "We shall manage. We can roll up some of our belongings. But thank you for providing us with blankets." She put her arms about her and shivered. "It is getting cooler."

"Aye, it is." The captain chewed on his bottom lip and then looked out into the darkness. He wanted to pull her into his arms and take away any chill she might feel with the warmth he now felt.

When he turned back, the flames from the fire flickered in her eyes. "Miss Bennet..." He took a deep breath. "I..."

Elizabeth waited for him to continue, but Mrs. Keller came up and interrupted any further discourse. "Come, Elizabeth, we need something to cheer us up and want to hear more of your amusing stories."

"I assure you I have no more amusing stories!"

"Yes! You remember! You were going to tell us about that foolish man whose offer of marriage you simply had to refuse."

"Now?" Elizabeth asked.

"Yes! We are all waiting expectantly."

Mrs. Keller grabbed Elizabeth's arm and began pulling her towards the ladies. She turned back to excuse herself from the captain but saw that he was no longer standing there.

~~*

Darcy walked quickly away from the cave... away from Elizabeth... pounding his chin with his fist. He could only thank the good Lord for not allowing him to say whatever it was he was about to say to her. He had no idea what that was going to be, but his feelings at that moment were so strong that he had felt compelled to say something.

Was he going to profess his love? Reveal his true identity? He had no idea. He could not formulate one thought now, save for the fact that the laughter he heard from the ladies inside the cave was directed at him, even though they were unaware of that fact. One thing he did know was that the contented glow he had experienced earlier now felt like a lead weight deep inside, and he could barely breathe.

Darcy's stomach churned as he considered what Elizabeth might be saying about him. He desperately wanted to flee as far away from her as he could get... or else to go in and apologize for being the fool he was when he so recklessly declared his love *and* his misgivings in his offer of marriage.

He slapped his hand against a rock and cast his gaze to the ground. If only this had happened *before* he had allowed his senses to come fully alive in her presence. He had fooled himself into thinking she could care for him. He fisted his hand and slammed it against the rock, this time more forcefully. A small trail of blood trickled out between his fingers. A small trail of blood trickled down his hand. As he wiped the blood away, he resolved that he would no longer allow his senses to be saturated while in her presence.

"Captain!" Bellows' voice called out.

"Here!" Darcy answered.

"The ladies are gettin' tired an' would like to know what should be done 'bout sleepin' arrangements."

"Tired?" Darcy asked, unable to disguise the disgust in his voice. "It sounded like they were... was havin' a good laugh in there over somethin'.

Bellows narrowed his brows at him. "So it would seem. I were not privy to it, other than that it concerned a rather foolish gentleman an' a rejected proposal."

Darcy fisted his hands again. At least he knew she had not recognized him. She would not dare talk about him like that to the other ladies if she knew his true identity.

Darcy ran his hand across his forehead and through his long hair. "I know not what we ken do 'bout the sleepin' arrangements, but I suppose we ought to station two men to guard the cave throughout the night. We ken take shifts, like we do on the ship."

"Aye. But the ladies wondered if there was some way to give them a little privacy."

"I wish we could jest git them back to their ship! That would take care of everything!"

"Cap'n? Are you all right?"

Darcy took in a deep breath. "It has jest been a rather stressful day an' I'm ready fer it to be over with."

"I would've thought you 'ad been rather enjoyin' the day."

Darcy turned sharply towards him. "Why do ye say that?"

"Why, tis perty obvious you think fondly of Miss Bennet an' 'ave been quite enjoyin' her company."

"Well, yer mistaken! Ken't imagine why you'd think that!" Darcy turned and began walking back to the cave. "Come! I supposed we must see what we ken do."

When the two men returned to the cave, the ladies had gathered their belongings and blankets in the far back corner of the cave.

The trunk had been conveniently moved in front of them to afford a little privacy.

Mr. Joyner had positioned himself on the opposite side of the trunk, away from the ladies, but between them and the men. As the women made the final preparations for their sleeping arrangements, Darcy walked over.

"It appears ye ladies have yer sleeping arrangements set. Is there anythin' else I ken do?"

He would not allow himself to look at Elizabeth. She walked over and stood in front of him, however, making it difficult.

"Yes, Miss Bennet? Is there somethin' ye need?" He folded his arms across his chest and looked beyond her. Her scent, however, was not that easy to ignore.

"Captain, the ladies were wondering whether you think their husbands... and my father and cousin... might try to come over again tomorrow."

Darcy shrugged and looked down at his feet as he kicked around some of the dirt. "If the seas are still rough in the mornin', they likely won't risk it."

"They are wondering... if we have to row out to *your* ship... how we might board it. Do you have winches that can raise the dinghy up to your ship?"

Darcy furrowed his brows and ran his hand down his bristly beard. He had not even considered how the ladies would get onto the ship if they needed to.

"We don't. We only 'ave a rope ladder that is thrown over the side. Do ye think the women would be able to climb it?"

"Oh, dear!" Elizabeth whispered as she turned to look back at the ladies. "Mrs. Joyner believes she is going to die at every turn. I doubt she would have the presence of mind to even take the first step out of the dinghy. I doubt Mrs. Dillard could manage it either, but perhaps Mrs. Keller could."

"And you?" he asked as he unwittingly turned his eyes to her.

Elizabeth smiled and her eyes sparkled as she looked back at him. "I believe so. I climbed up and down a rope ladder a great many times when I was younger."

"Did you? An' what was this rope ladder used for?" Darcy regretted the moment he asked. His resolve to distance himself from Elizabeth seemed to have completely evaporated.

"A magical fort our father built in a tree for my sisters and me. Although I fear it has been several years since I last attempted to climb it."

Darcy lifted a single brow. "A magical fort? An' what was magical about it?"

"Oh, you know how children are. To my elder sister, Jane, it was a castle. To my sister, Mary, it was a cathedral, and to my two younger sisters, it was a ballroom."

"And what was it to you?"

"Whenever I had the opportunity, I would escape up there by myself to get away from all the clamour and commotion that has always been a part of life at Longbourn."

"So it became an escape for you?"

She leaned in to him with a smile. "Well, to own the truth, I called it my library."

"Library? Why a library?" he laughed.

"I often noticed how my father would sequester himself away in his library with all his books and read. I soon realized he did it to get away from the noisy din of a household of ladies. So I learnt from him and would take a book with me and spend hours up there reading."

Darcy could well imagine having to resort to something of the sort if he was confined with all the Bennets on a continual basis. Excepting Elizabeth, that is.

He suddenly thought of Georgiana and chuckled. Without thinking he said, "When my sister was younger, she loved to entertain herself in the play castle that my father had built for her."

Elizabeth looked at him with a surprised look. "You have a sister, do you? And she has a play castle?"

Darcy shook his head. He had to be more careful – both in what he said to Elizabeth and how he said it!

"It was... 'twas not a castle, really, that was jest what she called it. And it wasn't in a tree." He drew in a sharp breath. "Miss Bennet, I need to discuss wi' Bellows the issue of gettin' you ladies out to the ship. We'll come up wi' somethin'. If you'll excuse me." He gave a short bow and began to walk away.

"Thank you, Captain."

Darcy stopped. "Oh, an' Miss Bennet," he said as he looked back at her, "ye may reassure the ladies that fer their safety we'll 'ave two men guardin' the cave throughout the night in case the pirates return. I doubt they shall, but just as a precaution."

"I shall inform them. Thank you."

Darcy walked briskly away. His emotions were as turbulent as the seas had been the night before. Trying to navigate through them was positively futile, and if he was not careful, he would end up being battered upon the rocks much like the merchant ship had been!

~~*

Elizabeth returned to the ladies. It was dark in the back corner of the cave, and they felt some sense of privacy as they settled quietly into their makeshift beds behind the trunk. There was little conversation save for what the captain had told her about the guards. She did not want to worry them tonight by mentioning the problematic boarding of his ship and what that likely would entail for the ladies.

Elizabeth bundled up a cloak she had brought along, using it as her pillow. She took the blanket and lay down on half of it, bringing the other half over her.

It was not long before the other ladies fell asleep. It had been a long, rather harrowing day. She was grateful for Captain Smith and how he had done everything in his power not only to keep them safe, but to make them feel safe, as well.

She lifted herself up onto her elbow, resting her head on her hand. She could see the captain speaking in fervent whispers with Bellows and Timmons. Both the captain and Bellows were tall, with broad shoulders and confident stances, and they dwarfed Timmons, who was not much taller than Elizabeth. The captain's back was to her, and his arm rested casually on a small rocky ledge.

She was struck by a thought that for some reason he looked familiar. The way he stood, his posture. Even sometimes his voice.

Elizabeth shook her head. She would have had no occasion to meet him. He spoke as a commoner and most likely grew up near the sea. And yet... There were times when he actually sounded like a refined gentleman. Occasionally he would enunciate a word precisely, without any accent or dropping letters, almost as if he had once learnt to speak properly. And just now when he gave the short bow, it was if he did it without thinking, as if it had been ingrained in him.

She pinched her brows. But there was something else that troubled her. Something had changed in him. He had seemed more abrupt just now, almost as if he was agitated that the lot of protecting this group of stranded passengers was more than he would have wished for. She had noticed a slight scowl that had not been there previously.

She let out a sigh and lay back down. She was too tired to think any more on it tonight. She pulled the blanket up and tucked it around her shoulders, closing her eyes and anticipating a good night's sleep. She hoped to be reunited with her father and cousin on the morrow.

Her cousin – David! She pursed her lips as she considered that she had barely thought of him since the captain had arrived!

Chapter 13

In the middle of the night, the sudden flash of lightning lit the cave, followed at once by a resounding boom of thunder and the sound of pouring rain. Everyone stirred, awakened by the storm announcing its arrival.

Elizabeth sat up, hugging the blanket tightly about her. The mild temperatures that had given everyone relative comfort earlier that day had long been chased away by the brisk wind that drove cold air directly into the cave.

As raindrops hit the red hot wood from the fire, it sputtered noisily, as if angry for being unexpectedly disturbed. The captain rose and threw two pieces of wood onto the fire, stirring it with a third piece before tossing that one in. He stood between the fire and the opening to the cave, allowing the new pieces of wood to begin burning without hindrance from the rain.

"Looks perty nasty out there!" Timmons said. "Anyone know what time it be?"

The captain pulled out a pocket watch, holding it near the flame to read it. "It is close to three o'clock."

He walked over to the two men who had been standing guard at the cave's entrance. "Ye ken get some sleep, now. I'll keep watch til' morn."

"Thank ye, Cap'n." They quickly came in and stretched out on the ground.

Elizabeth watched as the captain donned his oilskin coat and walked close to the entrance. He stood staring out with his hands braced against his hips and his legs in an alert stance. His curly dark brown hair peeked out from under his tri-corn hat, which shielded his face from the rain.

Elizabeth narrowed her brows and tilted her head as she studied him. She thought back to last night, wondering what had prompted the change in him. She knew he was likely concerned about getting the women *off* the small island and getting them *onto* a ship, whether his or the merchant ship. And now he was likely even more concerned that they may be stuck on this island even longer due to the storm.

Elizabeth lay back and closed her eyes. The pounding rain, flashes of lightning, and ominous cracks of thunder prompted disquiet within those in the cave, but for some unaccountable reason, she felt safe and secure with Captain Smith on watch.

~~*

Elizabeth opened her eyes and was greeted with muted rays of sunlight peering into the cave, now serenely silent. The others about her all appeared to be sleeping soundly.

She lifted her head and saw that the captain still stood where he had been last night. He was leaning against the inside wall of the cave, near the outside edge. He had removed his oilskin coat; his loose white shirt stirred in the breeze. The red sash had fallen about his neck.

As Elizabeth contemplated the dark curls caressing Captain Smith's neck, a sudden recollection of a dream teased her thoughts. There was a ship and a storm. Captain Smith stood gallantly at the helm with much longer hair blowing in the wind. His white shirt billowed out like the sails of the ship, and his hand rested on the hilt of his sword. Instead of the sash covering his eye, a true eye patch served its purpose.

Parts of the dream were hazy, but she recalled how rough arms suddenly went about her. Although she could not see who had so forcefully grabbed her, she knew it was Lockerly. He pulled a sword and approached the captain, who had drawn his.

They stood for some time staring at each other, neither one moving. The captain finally said, "I am not afraid of you!"

There was a fight, and she could not remember much more. She could not even remember who won the fight. She bit her bottom lip as she tried to recall more. Then she slowly smiled as the end of the dream came to her.

She remembered standing next to the captain at the helm. Lockerly had been tied up and taken down and locked in the hold. Captain Smith turned to her and wrapped his gentle arms about her, pulling her close. She readily welcomed his affection and looked up at him. Ever so slowly he lowered his head and met her lips with his.

Elizabeth's mouth went dry as she felt every fibre in her body come alive at the remembrance of the dream. Her face warmed, and she placed her cool hands over her cheeks. At that moment, the captain turned and looked at her.

Her heart raced, almost as if he had truly just kissed her. She took a few deep breaths to calm herself, got to her feet, and walked over to the captain, carefully stepping over those who slept.

The captain watched her approach. "Good morning, Miss Bennet. Did ye sleep well?"

"Yes, I did, thank you." She glanced briefly up into his face, smiling as she did.

He looked down at her and then said, "Ye must've 'ad some pleasant dreams."

Elizabeth gasped and felt her cheeks warm. *How could he know?*

"I cannot imagine what you mean, Captain."

He placed one hand under her chin and gently lifted her face. With the other, he touched the inner corner of her eyes with his thumb and finger.

"Ye 'ave a remnant of yer dreams in yer eyes."

Elizabeth swallowed hard and could barely think. She again thought of the difference between his soft, smooth hands, and Lockerly's coarse, rough hands. As the events of her dream became even more vivid, she wondered what it would be like if he were to actually lean in and kiss her.

"I… I have never heard that before," she said, trying to disguise her inexplicable feelings with a soft laugh.

"Me mother used to say that to me. She said that when we 'ad a good dream, it left a remnant in our eyes so that we wouldn't forget it."

"Oh," Elizabeth said shakily. She felt as though she might crumple in a heap to the ground. Their eyes locked in a gaze; his were dark, shadowed by the brim of his hat. She began to fear that she may have called out his name aloud in her dream and he had heard. She forced a smile and said playfully, "Perhaps... perhaps you should not have removed it, then, as I have absolutely no recollection of any dream."

"'Tis a shame, then." Captain Smith suddenly straightened and looked back out of the cave. "You rise early, Miss Bennet."

Elizabeth laughed, hoping to dismiss her confused feelings. "I have the unfortunate habit of rising with the sun. There is simply nothing to be done about it!" She looked up at him with a smile.

"And there's no reason to do anythin' 'bout it. 'Tis a good thing, rising early in the morn. I do it meself."

"Ah, but I would think a captain needs to be awake at all hours of the night."

The captain nodded. "'Tis true, but when I'm not sailing an' I have the privilege of sleepin' through the night, there is nothin' I like better than to waken early an' take a walk." He pointed outside the cave. "Unfortunately, 'tis quite muddy out there this morn an' a leisurely walk is out o' the question."

"For some, perhaps, but I have been known to walk in the mud on more than one occasion."

He chuckled. "Yes, I..." he stopped abruptly and took a breath.

"Yes, Captain?"

He crossed his arms across his chest. The same scowl she had noticed last night returned to his face.

When he said nothing more, she continued, "It is good to see the storm has passed. Does this mean we shall make an attempt to reach one of the ships today?"

The captain rubbed his bearded chin and looked out. "It is... 'tis not easy to say, Miss Bennet."

"I hope we shall be able to. Are you concerned we might be stranded on the island yet another day?"

"'Tis much to be concerned about in our circumstances. But I'll do me best to get ye safely off this island an' sailin' home."

"I am confident of that, Captain. I want to express my appreciation, from myself and all of the ladies, for how safe you have made us feel and how obliging you have been towards us. I know it has not been easy."

She looked up at him, but he only nodded while seemingly intent on staring ahead.

"How is your wound, Captain? May I look at it?"

She heard a deep sigh. "It is well enough."

"You must know I am truly sorry for what I did. Especially after how good you have been to us."

He turned to face her. "Pray, do not berate yourself."

She reached up and removed his hat. She could readily see how much the wound had swollen, and there were blue and purple tints of colour that spread over the top and side of his head. Dried blood was caked around the edges of the wound.

"It looks quite ghastly! I fear you shall probably have a scar and will have a dreadful memory of me and what I did every time you look at yourself in the mirror."

The captain inhaled sharply and looked down at her intently. "As long as I ken get you safely off this island an' back home, I shall not dread the memory o' our encounter in the slightest."

Elizabeth smiled, and a blush tinted her cheeks. "You are too kind, sir. Do you mind if I tie the sash back on over it?"

He looked at her, weighing what to say against what he was thinking. "Me thinks I'll leave it about me neck fer now, as the bleeding 'as ceased."

She turned to gaze out at the sky, the rocks and dirt and sand – anywhere but at his penetrating eyes. "I fear Lockerly will also end up with quite a scar, as well, but will not have such a forbearing estimation towards the person who inflicted it."

The captain chuckled. "No, I should imagine not."

"Since the others are still sleeping, Captain, would you be so kind as to allow me some privacy out there? I shall return shortly."

"Aye. I'll make certain no one steps out 'til ye return."

"Thank you." Elizabeth dipped a curtsey and left.

Elizabeth walked carefully through the mud to a shelter of rock and shrubbery. The only sounds were the rustle of the breeze through the leaves and the waves crashing onto the beaches off in the distance. She closed her eyes and allowed the peace of this place to soothe her soul.

She thought about Captain Smith and how she had on numerous occasions blushed in his presence. He evoked something within her

– a sense of familiarity, as if he was a long-time close acquaintance; a deep appreciation for the concern he obviously had for her welfare and the welfare of others; and a feeling of admiration. Sometimes when she looked up into his eyes, she felt drawn into them.

She let out a long sigh and put her hands up to her warm cheeks as she considered how silly this was. Of course she appreciated him, but he was a lowly sea captain with very little education. While it was apparent he enjoyed her company, she could never return his affection.

She crossed her arms in front of her as she walked back to the cave. It was a silly, groundless attraction that could never amount to anything.

The sound of the captain's voice stirred her from her thoughts. More people must have awakened, so she hurried back.

When she returned to the cave, Captain Smith welcomed her return with a smile and sent off two of his men, one of whom was Bellows. They were carrying the trunk.

Elizabeth nodded at them as they passed and then asked the captain where they were going.

"They're headin' down to the beach to make sure Lockerly hasn't returned, an' then they'll row out to our ship an' sail it back 'round to the merchant ship. Once there, they'll have 'em send out the dinghy to pick us up if they haven't already."

Elizabeth bit her lip, feeling admittedly a sense of disappointment. "And so we are to go back to the merchant ship. Do you think it repaired, then?"

"On the contrary, it is not."

Elizabeth looked up at him, startled. "How do you know?"

"Just as it was gettin' light, I walked down to the beach. It is still listin' quite a bit."

"And shall you then leave us there?" she asked softly. "On the merchant ship?"

"Do ye think I would?"

Elizabeth shook her head slowly. "Not, perhaps, to fend for ourselves, but perhaps you shall leave to go get help."

"'Tis dangerous to remain with me – especially on Lockerly's ship! I fear Lockerly will return to exact revenge."

"So our choice is to remain on a crippled ship and face pirates who know where it is, or risk encountering pirates intent on finding and retrieving their ship?"

"'Tis not an easy choice." He looked down at her with those piercing eyes. "If I have me say, I shall insist ye come aboard with us on the *Devil's Seamaiden* so we at least 'ave the ability to escape from the pirates should they return!"

"I am inclined to agree with you. Lockerly knows where the merchant is and that it is helpless. It is an easy target, but then he may have the greater wish to seize his own ship to get it back!"

"'Tis exactly my thought," the captain concurred in a low, coarse voice.

Elizabeth narrowed her brows and looked down. "There is one thing I fear I do not understand, Captain. Why were you impersonating Lockerly, and why do you have his ship?" She tilted her head as she looked up at him. "I do confess that I see the resemblance between the two of you, but why?"

The captain crossed his arms in front of him and leaned against the wall of the cave. "I was mistaken for Lockerly an' thrown into a cell. Spent a night in that foul place. Fortunately, someone saw me the followin' day an' realized I wasn't him."

"You truly were mistaken for him?" asked Elizabeth, astonished.

The captain nodded. He then began to tell her more of the story, omitting certain details that would reveal his identity.

"Oh, my!" she said when he finished. "So you had not intended to go to sea at all?"

The captain shook his head.

"Heavens!" Elizabeth exclaimed. "If you had not gone to sea, we may all have been killed by Lockerly and his men!"

The captain nodded slowly, tightening his hands into a fist. "Or been taken onto their ship and suffered unimaginable atrocities at their hands!"

Elizabeth shuddered. "We are so very much in your debt, Captain. I shall never forget this!"

"Neither shall I…" he returned, his voice trailing off into a soft whisper.

By now everyone had awakened, and the three ladies stepped up to the captain and asked for some privacy outside the cave. He nodded his assent, and Elizabeth stood next to him as the ladies departed. They listened to the ladies moan and groan as they trudged their way through the mud.

Elizabeth heard the captain chuckle.

"Do you find their struggle walking in the mud humorous?"

"I'm merely considerin' what these ladies will say when they discover how we propose to get them aboard the *Devil's Seamaiden*." The captain shook his head and chuckled again. "If they don't like walkin' in the mud, I ken't imagine them bein' happy wi' how they'll be boardin' our ship from the merchant ship, if it come to that!"

The captain started to walk back into the cave, and Elizabeth turned with arms upturned. "How?" she asked.

"I'd rather not tell ye now," he said with a sly grin. "That way, when the ladies ask if ye knows how we're goin' to do it, ye ken honestly say ye don't know!"

"Is it truly that bad?" Elizabeth asked.

Captain Smith continued. "I will need ye to trust me implicitly, Miss Bennet. There is but one way to do it, and I beg o' ye when the time comes, you will shew the ladies there is no peril."

"If you say there is no danger, Captain, of course, I shall trust you."

Chapter 14

Later that morning after everyone had finished eating what food remained, they gathered up their belongings and walked down to the beach to await the dinghy that would take them out to the merchant ship.

When they arrived, they spied it a short distance from shore. Excitement rose among the small group as they watched it come towards them, finally being propelled the final distance by the small waves breaking onto the shore.

Darcy stood back, watching Elizabeth as she laughed with the ladies. He leaned against a rock, folding his arms in front of him. He had taken too many liberties with her this morning and had almost blurted out his recollection of her having walked in the mud to Netherfield, early in their acquaintance.

His frustration the night before when the ladies had laughed as Elizabeth spoke of his foolish proposal had been short lived. When he had seen her sit up this morning and walk towards him, all resolve to put her out of his mind evaporated. When she had lifted her face towards his, he fought off the temptation with his every ounce of resolve to lean down and kiss her.

He shook his head to clear his thoughts and joined the other men as they rushed out to pull the dinghy up to the beach. They were told that the merchant ship had been pulled off the one rock during the storm the previous night, but had come down on another, breaking through the hull in another place. It was a smaller gash, but one that would require more repairs.

It was decided that the four ladies, Mr. Joyner, and Darcy would ride back with the two crewmen. Timmons and the remaining crew would wait for the dinghy to return for them. Darcy wanted to discuss his plans with Captain Meeker on how he proposed moving the ladies from the merchant ship to his. It was not going to be easy.

The sea was calm, and the dinghy travelled smoothly over the crystal blue water as the men rowed. Mrs. Joyner held tightly onto Mr. Joyner's hand. The other three ladies searched the faces of those watching from the ship for the first sign of their loved ones. When they came up alongside the ship, the ropes were lowered and secured to the small boat. The crewmen attached the small boat to some cables, and then they, along with Darcy, climbed up the rope and wood planked ladder that hung over the side of the ship.

Hands were again grasped tightly as the boat was slowly lifted out of the water.

"Be still, now," Captain Meeker called out. "Ye don't want to rock the boat!"

It took a little more time to raise it than it had to lower them into the water the day before, but once high and above the railing of the ship, they swung it over and brought it down onto the deck. With sighs of relief, the women climbed out.

Mr. Dillard and Mr. Keller rushed over to greet their wives. Darcy watched as Mr. Bennet and a young man with a bandaged arm rushed up to Elizabeth.

Mr. Bennet drew Elizabeth into his arms. Tears ran down the older man's face. Seeing the love and care he had for Elizabeth and his relief at being reunited with his daughter, moved Darcy. He realized then how much her father loved her.

Darcy then watched with narrowed brows as the young man grasped Elizabeth's hands in his good hand and brought them to his lips. He stepped closer to hear what he was saying.

"Cousin Elizabeth! We were so worried about you! It has been the most helpless feeling not to be able to do anything to ensure your safety!"

"Thank you, David, but what happened to your arm? Did you injure it?"

The young man looked down and nodded. "I took a tumble in

the storm last night when the ship lurched from the rock's grip. The man who calls himself the doctor on board does not think it is broken, but he wrapped it, and I will need to go to a doctor in London once we arrive."

"I am so sorry!" Elizabeth said.

Darcy turned his attention away, rubbing his bearded chin with his hand. He certainly did not like the way Elizabeth and her cousin looked at each other. He walked to the back of the ship, where the *Devil's Seamaiden* was slowly approaching. As it drew close, he watched some of the ship's sails being furled to slow her down.

One of his crew held a grappling hook and called out, "Ahoy!" With all his might he threw it across the distance of the sea separating the two ships. It came over the side of the merchant ship, landing with a thud. As it was pulled back, the hook gouged into the side railing. The *Devil's Seamaiden* was slowly pulled as close as it could get without hitting the rocky outcroppings lurking just below the sea's surface. Then they stopped and dropped anchor.

As Darcy supervised this manoeuvre, Elizabeth came over with her father and cousin.

"Captain Smith, may I introduce my father, Mr. Bennet, and my cousin, David Adams? This is Captain Smith, who is a great deal responsible for our safety." She bit her lip and then added with a wry smile, "Please do not ask him how he received the bruise above his eye. It will not speak well of my behaviour when we met."

Darcy bowed. "If I recollect, Miss Bennet, 'twas before we met, and as I 'ave said many times already, ye were doin' what ye thought ye must." He looked at the two men. "'Tis a pleasure to meet ye."

Elizabeth walked to the ship's railing and looked out at the *Devil's Seamaiden*. "Can your ship be brought any closer? I cannot imagine how we shall get over to it, especially with all the rocks below."

"An' that is where I need ye to trust me... all o' ye need to trust me." He gave a slight bow and said, "If ye will excuse me, I must speak with Captain Meeker."

~~*

Elizabeth watched as Captains Smith and Meeker seemed to be engaged in a lively discussion. They pointed up to the masts and over to the *Devil's Seamaiden*. After much back and forth conversing, pointing, and alternately nodding or shaking their heads, they finally seemed to agree on something. Elizabeth was quite certain it pertained to getting the passengers off the crippled merchant ship and onto Captain's Smith ship.

David spoke in a hushed whisper. "Do they truly expect us to travel on that? It looks to me like a sinister pirate ship!"

"Oh, that it is!" Elizabeth said with a smile. "In fact, it used to belong to one of the pirates that captured us!"

"How can you laugh about this? You could have been killed!" David said.

"True. When we were in the midst of it, we were very much afraid. But we are exceedingly grateful that Captain Smith and his men were very brave, freed us from our captors, and made us all feel very safe."

Mr. Bennet turned to Elizabeth. "So, my dear Lizzy, you had your pirate adventure after all. What shall your mother say? She will blame me for it, of that I am certain." His eyes rolled up to the heavens, and he gave his daughter a weary smile.

Elizabeth raised her brow and said in a conspiratorial tone, "Unless she chooses to divert us with stories about how *she* once knew a most dashing pirate and how forlorn she was when he left her for the sea."

Mr. Bennet let out a hearty laugh. "Oh, be assured of it, she will have *some* story to tell, if only to impress upon us how she always *longed* for a dashing pirate to carry her away!"

At length, Captain Meeker called the nine passengers over. Captain Smith stood next to him.

"We regret that this voyage 'as proven to be so calamitous for ye all. Unfortunately, storms arise with little warning, but wi' major implications. Addin' in the presence of pirates in this area an' we know not what we will encounter. We cannot guarantee yer safety if ye remain on this ship while we continue to repair it. We 'ave no other choice but to move you to the *Devil's Seamaiden*. Please go to your cabins an' pack up yer belongings. Our crew will bring 'em up 'ere fer ye as ye transfer to the other ship." He bowed and turned back to Captain Smith.

"But shall you be safe if the pirates return?" asked Mrs. Joyner.

"We're 'bout finished repairin' the ship an' most likely will be able to set sail on the morrow. We 'ave cannons that ought to hold 'em off without any problem if the pirates do show up. We all agreed that it would be best if the passengers were on a ship that could get them back to St. Mary's directly."

With that, the ladies and gentlemen rushed to their rooms. The ladies were grateful for the opportunity to freshen up and change into clean clothing. They quickly gathered their belongings and packed them up. When they stepped out of their rooms, there were some crewmen waiting to carry the luggage up for the ladies.

Elizabeth joined her father and cousin, who had already come up on deck. The three looked up at the men who were climbing the rigging of the ship and untying some ropes. A large wooden plank was brought over and propped up to one of the lower yardarms. Despite being a narrow round beam, the crew travelled across it with seemingly little concern.

As they watched, a sudden movement caught their eye. They turned to see someone fly across the bow of the ship on a rope attached to a yardarm on the *Devil's Seamaiden*. He landed with a thud on the ship's deck.

Elizabeth looked back up at the men and the plank and the ropes. "Oh, my!" she exclaimed. "Is that how we are to get across? Now I can see why Captain Smith told us to trust him!"

Captain Smith approached the passengers and addressed the four men who had not been with them on the island. "For those o' ye who 'ave not met 'im, may I introduce ye to me first mate, Bellows. If ye noticed how 'e came over, this is how we'll be gettin' all of ye over to our ship."

Mrs. Joyner let out a cry of protest.

"'Tis only two ways of getting' over to the ship, either that way or goin' across in the dinghy. To go in the dinghy, you'll 'ave to be climbin' up the rope ladder on the *Devil's Seamaiden*. If ye aren't used to climbin' up a ladder that is swayin' up an' down an' back an' forth, I suggest you allow us to help ye over this way, as fright'nin' as it may seem. But I assure ye, ye'll be safe."

Elizabeth glanced over at Mrs. Joyner, who had placed one hand over her heart and grabbed her husband's hand with the other.

"Oh, dear! I cannot do either, I fear!"

Elizabeth quickly strode over to her and placed a reassuring hand on her shoulder. "I am sure they will take good care of us."

Mrs. Joyner bit her lips and looked warily at her. "But you are so brave and can do anything. I know I will not be able to hold on to the rope!"

Elizabeth patted her shoulder. "I know the crew will help."

"Please, ladies, 'ave no fear," Bellows said. "Ye shall be perfectly safe as ye shall be tied to a gentleman for safety."

As Elizabeth walked back to her father and cousin, she saw that they were engaged in a fervent conversation with Captain Smith.

She stepped up to them, and Mr. Bennet smiled down at his daughter. "It seems as though you are to be first, Lizzy. Since I cannot be counted on to hold you, and David has an injured arm, it appears as though you shall have to go across with Captain Smith."

Elizabeth raised her brows at this. "Go over with Captain Smith?"

"I asked ye to trust me," he replied softly. "Miss Bennet, would ye be so kind as to join me as we take the plank up to the yardarm?"

Elizabeth laughed nervously. "As long as you are not ordering me to walk the plank out into the depths of the sea."

"Indeed, no." The captain turned to walk to the mast.

Elizabeth turned to her father and cousin. "So I am to go first to prove to the ladies that all will be well?"

"Elizabeth, I know how dreadful this will be for you, and I would do it if only I were able..." David paused. "It should be no more than a few seconds that you shall have to endure it."

Elizabeth reached out for David's good hand and grasped it. "Thank you, David. I appreciate it."

Elizabeth joined the captain, who now stood at the base of the wooden plank. She cast a sly glance up at him. "Pray, tell me how is it that I am not going to fall?"

Captain Smith swallowed and looked intently at her. He answered slowly and softly, "I'll be holdin' ye."

Elizabeth felt her cheeks warm, and her mouth went dry. "You will be..." Her voice trailed off. She was at a loss to explain the myriad of feelings that surged through her, the strongest of which was something she had never felt before. At least not before encountering Captain Smith.

As she looked up into his face, he slowly nodded. His dark eyes sparkled, while at the same time exuding a beguiling intensity. She unwittingly trembled.

"No need to fear, Miss Bennet. Do ye think ye ken prove to the ladies that there is nothin' to worry 'bout?"

Despite the tremor that passed through her, Elizabeth nodded and said, "Yes, Captain Smith. I believe I can!"

Captain Smith took her arm as they made their way up the steep wooden plank. The strength of his grip reassured her, and she found herself inexplicably looking forward to being held tightly in his embrace.

Two crewmen stood on the yardarm waiting for them. One held the long rope that Bellows had come across on, and the other held a smaller rope.

As they stepped onto the narrow yardarm, Elizabeth suddenly realized just how precarious their footing was. She looked down at her father and cousin, and then over to the ladies who were watching intently. Not wishing to give them any sense of alarm, she smiled and waved.

The captain helped her over to the edge of the yardarm closest to the *Devil's Seamaiden,* steadying her with his hands. She was struck again with how soft and smooth... and strong they were! Someone who regularly swings on a rope from one ship to another certainly would not have such smooth hands!

Her thoughts were interrupted when the captain looked down at her and whispered, "Miss Bennet, we are goin' to be tied together with this short rope. I'll hold ye with one arm an' onto the long rope above this knot up here wi' me other hand. When we're in the air, I'll secure my feet against the rope above the knot down below." He took in a deep breath and let it out slowly. "Ye'll be safe, Miss Bennet. I'll make sure o' it."

Elizabeth tilted her head up at him and silently mouthed, "Thank you."

The crewman with the short rope wrapped it around them snugly. As he cinched it tight and knotted it, the two stood as close as any two people could be. Elizabeth felt her heart pound as she considered she had never been so close to a man before. She felt weak and precariously close to collapsing in a heap at his feet, despite being tied together at their waists. To prevent herself from falling, she quickly reached up and wrapped her arms about his neck, holding on tightly.

The captain responded with a deep moan and quickly brought his one arm around her. She felt him draw her in even closer than she had believed possible. A sensation of euphoria swept over her, and she found herself readily resting her head against his chest. She could hear his thundering heartbeat and wondered if it was beating more vigorously than hers.

"Now hold on tight, Miss Bennet." His lips brushed the hair by her ear as he huskily whispered these words. She felt her legs begin to tremble and suspected he felt it as well, as he gripped her even more firmly.

"Are ye ready?" he whispered softly; his breath seemed to warm her to her innermost being.

"Yes," she said, as she lifted her head to look up at him. She saw his dark eyes looking down at her, a single brow raised.

"Ye are not afraid?"

"On the contrary, I believe I shall enjoy this immeasurably!"

He inhaled deeply and whispered, "As will I."

As he was about to step off, she asked with a nervous laugh, "You have done this before, have you not?"

"Never!" he said, and the next thing she knew, she was lifted off the ground, and they were swinging through the air. She held on tightly, wanting desperately to keep her head snuggled up against his chest, while at the same time wishing to look up, down, and out to see what was happening.

She finally turned her head and opened her eyes, just as they came over the *Devil's Seamaiden's* bow. She felt the rope lower, and the next thing she knew, they had come to a stop. The captain landed squarely on his feet, but he continued to hold her up in his arms. He finally relaxed his grip around her waist slightly, allowing her feet to touch the deck.

Despite standing solidly on the deck, she felt as though she were still flying through the air. Countless other feelings assaulted her, none of which made any sense to her.

The crew rushed over and began untying the rope that bound them together. Elizabeth knew not where to look, as she felt that if she looked up at the captain, he would see the storm of emotions she felt.

Once untied, she released her hands and quickly stepped away. She turned her head back towards the merchant ship to give an encouraging smile and a wave, but more to turn away from the captain.

She walked to the railing of the ship and looked out. Her hands braced the ship's railing, and she felt unsteady and confused. But more surprising than that, she inexplicably felt bereft of the captain's arms about her.

She smiled and waved again at the other passengers, a wave of melancholy overwhelming her that soon she and the captain would go their separate ways. It made no sense to her that she would find herself attracted to a man such as Captain Smith. She could not even say that he was handsome, as his beard covered the lower part of his face and the bruise she inflicted upon him distorted one side of it.

"Are you feeling all right, Miss Bennet?" The captain was standing at her side.

"Yes!" she answered abruptly. "I am quite well." Looking down at her hands, she noticed they were shaking. She clasped them tightly together. To herself she had sounded breathless, and so she took in a deep breath and let it out in a light laugh. "Rest assured, Captain Smith, I was not alarmed in the least."

The captain nodded. "I'm glad to hear that." He rocked back and forth on his heels, as if waiting for something. He finally said, "You did quite admirably. Hopefully you have assured the other ladies that they will be safe."

Elizabeth nodded and murmured to the affirmative. She could not bring herself to look at him. She had enjoyed her time on the island with him a little too much and enjoyed their rendezvous through the air a great deal too much.

After a few moments of silence, he returned to assist those coming over.

The next to come across was Mrs. Keller, followed by Mrs. Dillard, who each were held by their husbands. The captain and several other crewmen assisted in making their landings smooth and safe.

When Mrs. Joyner nervously walked up the wooden ramp to the yardarm, it was not her husband that accompanied her, but

Bellows. Elizabeth surmised that Mr. Joyner must not have felt strong enough to carry his wife with him. Mrs. Joyner let out a high-pitched scream as she flew through the air, landing with a rather white face. She was shaking from head to toe. Elizabeth stepped up to her and congratulated her for being so brave.

Elizabeth quickly returned to the rail and watched nervously as her father stepped up onto the yardarm. Her heart thundered as she wondered whether he would be able to hang on. She bit her lip and clasped her hands in front of her, offering up a silent prayer for his safety.

When her father flew over the deck of the *Devil's Seamaiden* and safely landed on his feet, Elizabeth breathed a sigh of relief. As they untied the rope from around his waist, he looked over at Elizabeth.

"That was certainly a memorable feat! What say you, Lizzy? Was it not thrilling? Would you not wish to do it again?"

She could not prevent her cheeks from overspreading in a blush, and her gaze turned unwittingly to Captain Smith, who looked upon her with a laugh in his eyes.

"Come!" her father said. "David is to come across next! Let us watch!"

David was secured with the small rope, and he grabbed the hanging rope tightly above the knot with his good hand. He nodded his head and stepped off the yardarm, his feet struggling to find the knot below to anchor him.

Elizabeth's eyes widened, and she placed her hand over her mouth as she watched him flounder as he sailed across. Just as he was about to lose his grip, he came across the bow and was caught by the crewmen.

She rushed over to him. "I was so worried about you!"

David waved his hand through the air and said breathily, "Oh, it was nothing. Quite easy, in fact."

Elizabeth noticed that David's face had lost all colour, and he rubbed his arm above the elbow.

"Come, David," Elizabeth said. "Let us sit down and wait for our belongings to be brought over."

He wholeheartedly agreed, and they walked over to a bench by the ship's railing.

Once everyone had made it to the *Devil's Seamaiden* safely, their belongings were secured to the rope and sent across. The crew from both ships did a proficient job.

When everything was on board, the anchor was brought up and sails were unfurled. The passengers waved to the crew of the merchant ship as they began to sail away. They then turned to Captain Smith to await his direction.

Chapter 15

Darcy gathered the passengers together. He welcomed them aboard the *Devil's Seamaiden*, but then added, "This 'ere is actually a pirate ship, previously belongin' to Lockerly, the pirate who took the ladies, Mr. Joyner, and Timmons captive."

Everyone's eyes were upon him and they listened intently. Darcy continued, "Because of that, 'tis not in yer best interest of safety to take ye all the way back to London, so we shall make the shorter journey back to St. Mary's."

Several people let out frustrated sighs.

"'Tis not ideal, I know, and the accommodations on this ship are likely not what yer accustomed, but we think it is best."

David turned to Elizabeth and laughed. "Imagine us sailing on a real pirate ship! I wish I could see Melanie's face when she finds out!"

Darcy glanced at him, but did not feel that same sense of excitement. He took a deep breath and continued, "Fortunately there is a cabin especially fer the ladies. 'Tis ideally suited for jest one or two ladies at the most, but me thinks you will be pleased for the night." He looked to Bellows and called him over, asking him to give an account to the group of where they were now and when they would reach their destination.

Bellows gave a quick, nervous bow. He was not used to speaking in front of such fine people. "Because o' the storm, we didn't know where we was, not bein' able to see the stars an' such.

We was blown off course, jest as ye were in the merchant ship. What we 'ave now determined is that we were blown to the north o' the Isles of Scilly an' a quick jaunt south will take us to St. Mary's. We'll travel as long as we 'ave any bit o' light tonight, an' then lay anchor 'til morn. We'll travel the rest o' the way at first light. Should pull into the port at St. Mary's a'fore ye know it."

"Oh, dear!" exclaimed Mrs. Joyner. "I just know we will get caught in another storm!"

Darcy looked about him. "'Tis clear skies now, Mrs. Joyner. Me thinks it'll be smooth sailin' the rest o' the way." Darcy clasped his hands together. "Now, if ye'll follow me. I'll shew ye to yer cabins."

They took one short flight of stairs down and walked down a hall. Darcy pointed out the dining area. "I shall have tea and some refreshments ready for you. You may come in at any time this afternoon to eat." He began walking towards the back of the ship and then stopped in front of a door.

"Gentlemen, I hope ye'll be reassured as ye see how nice the cabin for the ladies is." He opened the door and stepped aside.

The ladies rushed in and gasped.

"Oh my!"

"I cannot believe this!"

"I have never seen anything like this!"

Mr. Bennet stepped in and let out a hearty chuckle. "My, my! Who would have guessed? On a pirate ship, no less!"

"I'll 'ave some extra blankets brought to ye. 'Tis not meant to sleep four, but me thinks ye'll be comfortable 'ere and 'ave the utmost privacy."

The ladies looked about, fingering the silk counterpane, the polished wood and brass, and inspecting every nook and cranny. Elizabeth walked over to a door on a side wall and tried to open it. It was locked.

"What does this lead to?" she asked.

Darcy felt his heart begin to race, and his mouth went dry. "That door... will remain locked." He took in a deep breath and let it out slowly. "It connects to my cabin."

Elizabeth quickly pulled her hand away. "Oh!" she said as a delightful blush tinted her cheeks. "I see we have a lock on our side." She cast a sideways glance at Darcy and in a teasing voice said, "I know we can trust that you do not have a key that would open it."

"Indeed, I don't. And the ladies can lock the door that goes out to the hallway from the inside, as well."

Darcy waved for the men to step out. "Now, gentlemen, if ye'll follow me, I'll take ye to the berth below where ye'll find yer beds. We'll leave the ladies to themselves fer a bit."

~~*

When the men left, the ladies began to giggle and then laugh.

"Oh, this is exquisite!" exclaimed Mrs. Joyner. "So much lovelier than our accommodations on the merchant ship!"

"Yes, but I fear the men will have poorer accommodations down in the berth!" Mrs. Keller announced. "At least it is only for the night."

Elizabeth braced her hands on her hips. "I suppose we ought to discuss our sleeping arrangements. The bed can readily hold two ladies, and the chair in the corner looks to be quite comfortable. But if you ladies do not mind, I shall sleep on the floor on the rug. I shall leave it to you to decide who will sleep on the chair and in the bed."

"I shall sleep in the chair!" announced Mrs. Keller. "It looks perfectly inviting to me. Mrs. Joyner and Mrs. Dillard, the two of you can sleep in the bed."

Relief spread across Mrs. Joyner's face. "Oh, thank you, so much!"

Mrs. Dillard sat down on the bed. "Oh, I believe I shall sleep like a baby!"

"Unless we have another storm!" Mrs. Joyner's earlier elation about the room gave way to a look of worry lining her forehead.

Elizabeth put her arm about her. "There is no sign whatsoever of a storm, so let us not worry about something now that might not even happen." Elizabeth wondered whether this lady ever went a complete hour without fretting about something.

Much like Mama, she thought. Then she wondered whether her family at home worried that they had not yet arrived in London. They would have no way to know where they were or if they were even still alive!

A decision by one of the ladies to take a short rest before going out was settled upon by all. They felt it was a greater necessity than eating. Soon the ladies, in their respective sleeping arrangements, closed their eyes for some much needed sleep.

Elizabeth awoke first at the sound of footsteps coming from inside the captain's quarters. She could see just enough under the door to observe the bottom of Captain Smith's boots as he walked across the floor. He seemed unsettled, pacing and stopping, and then pacing again. Elizabeth chewed her lip as she surmised that it was likely due to the fact that he was responsible for the safety of the four women in the room next to his.

She slowly sat up and looked around her, admiring the cabin, although she could never admire the pirate who had so painstakingly designed it for obviously dissolute purposes. The captain began moving about again, and she crinkled her brow. How had she come to find herself so enamoured of him?

She let out a soft sigh and heard from the next room a rather deep exasperated sigh.

She brought her legs up and wrapped her arms about them. Tomorrow morning they would each go their separate ways. She imagined her father would want to remain on St. Mary's before setting off again for London, and then Hertfordshire. The captain would likely go back to his ship – if he even had one – and return to a normal life again. She bit her lip as something inside of her ached at the thought of not seeing him again.

As Elizabeth stirred, so did the other ladies in the cabin. The last to waken was Mrs. Joyner.

They freshened up and then went up on deck, where they found the men anxiously waiting for them.

"We thought you would never come out of your cabin!" David said, rushing over to Elizabeth. "You slept for hours!"

"I think we all needed the rest," Elizabeth said. "You forget that we slept in a cave last night during a storm. We were quite without the normal comforts!"

"As *the men* are now!" laughed Mr. Bennet. "Oh, Lizzy, if you could see what we must endure for the night, but I will spare you after what you had to endure! I am grateful the ladies have such pleasant accommodations for the night!"

"Are you hungry, ladies?" Mr. Keller asked. "You can probably still get some of the refreshments we had earlier."

The ladies all declined. It was such a beautiful afternoon, they preferred to enjoy it on deck and would wait for dinner to eat.

Elizabeth looked up at the sails on the ship. Despite every sail being unfurled, the ship moved slowly through the water. "There is not much wind, is there?" asked Elizabeth of no one in particular.

"Unfortunately, no." The captain came up behind her. "The sails are spread to every inch of their canvas to catch every bit o' wind. We don't seem to be havin' any luck wi' the forces of nature, but at least 'tis not a storm sendin' us off in the wrong direction again!"

"It makes me wonder," said Elizabeth, "that anyone can sail when so many forces can affect it – strong winds, no wind, stormy seas, fog... and pirates."

"We jest seem to be encounterin' 'em all, don't we?" The captain looked at her with a melancholy smile and then turned to the others. "Let me know if there's anythin' I ken do fer ye." He turned and walked away.

~~*

At six o'clock Elizabeth walked into the dining room with her father and cousin. She sat across from her father, and David sat down next to her. The other passengers joined them, leaving the chair at the head of the table and the place on the bench next to Elizabeth vacant. Bellows entered and took the place next to Elizabeth. When the captain came in, he took the seat at the head of the table.

They were served a simple meal of roasted beef and vegetable ragout, bread, and some assorted fruit. Everyone seemed to enjoy it, especially the women, who had not enjoyed a good, hot meal in over a day.

As the dinner plates were taken away, the guests were pleasantly surprised when lemon custard was brought out.

Elizabeth turned to Bellows, who had just finished what seemed to be a lively conversation with her father and cousin.

"Tell me, Mr. Bellows," Elizabeth began, "Captain Smith informed me that he was impersonating this Lockerly in order to capture him. That it was all a scheme of a River Thames Police official. This seemed quite odd to me."

"Indeed, an' the captain was not 'appy about my part in the

whole thing."

"I can imagine," Elizabeth said.

Bellows took a sip from his cup of coffee and wiped his mouth with his sleeve. "Oh, pardon me manners, Miss Bennet."

"It is quite all right, Mr. Bellows. Does the captain have a ship of his own?"

"No, in fact," he leaned in to whisper, "he ain't even a real sea captain!"

Elizabeth looked at him in surprise. "If he is not a sea captain, what is he? What does he do?" She picked up her tea and took a sip.

"That's the thing, miss. He don't do anything. He's one of those fancy estate gentlemen who spends 'is whole life bein' all social and bein' seen in all the right places wi' all the right people. No, he didn't even want to do this, not really."

"But his speech, certainly…"

"All part of 'is disguise." Bellows let out a laugh. "An' I know he's been sufferin' in all this as he told me once that disguise is an abhorrence to 'im."

Elizabeth's breath caught and her hand began to shake. She put down her cup of tea and slowly looked back up at Bellows. "What did you say?"

"He tol' me disguise o' every sort is 'is abhorrence."

Elizabeth's heart pounded, and she felt almost light-headed. She picked up her napkin and dabbed her mouth, turning her eyes first to her father, and then casting a sly glance at the end of the table. When she saw the eyes of the captain upon her, she wondered why she had not noticed before!

She quickly looked back to Bellows. "Tell me, Bellows, is Captain Smith… is that his real name?"

"Oh, no, miss. But 'e made me promise not to tell a single soul what 'is real name is."

Elizabeth slowly nodded. "Thank you, Mr. Bellows. I have enjoyed our conversation immensely."

~~*

Darcy made an attempt to attend to the conversation between the Kellers and the Dillards at his end of the table, but it became almost impossible.

He found it increasingly difficult to keep his eyes from Elizabeth and wished he was seated by her, enjoying her liveliness and wit. She seemed very intent on what Bellows was telling her. He hoped his first mate would not divulge anything about his true identity to her.

He drained his cup of coffee of its last drops. Tomorrow morning this whole charade would finally be over! His heart sank as he realized his time with Elizabeth would be, as well.

Elizabeth excused herself from the table and walked out. Darcy had to force himself to remain seated and not go after her and confess everything. When he watched David get up and follow her, it helped his resolve to remain where he was.

After the passengers finished their meal, the rest of the crew came in to eat. It was a much more raucous atmosphere, and Darcy was grateful he had his guests eat with just him and Bellows.

He and his first mate spent some time with the crew and then went up to the quarterdeck, replacing one of the men who had taken the helm. Bellows took the wheel, and Darcy looked about him with the spyglass pressed to his eye. He scanned the horizon watching for any sign of approaching ships. He then slowly lowered it to the port side of the ship, catching Elizabeth in its scope.

She was looking out on the horizon while engaged in a conversation with the ladies. The setting sun behind her painted the sky and spattering of clouds an ever-changing array of colours.

It was a peaceful evening, and as the sun dipped down in the western sky, the passengers gathered at the railing to watch. A warm light breeze made the evening air pleasant enough to remain on deck. But Darcy felt anything but peace within. He wondered whether he would fall back into his former destitute state when he returned to London. He had allowed himself to enjoy Elizabeth's presence and person too freely. He wondered what had happened to the man he believed was so regulated, who lived sensibly and rationally, and who – he believed – would only behave with the utmost decorum.

"See anythin' o' interest?" Bellows asked, a knowing smile spreading across his face.

Darcy put the spyglass down and looked at Bellows, a knot forming on his brow. "I know you suspect that Miss Bennet has become an object of my admiration." He spoke clearly and precisely.

"I don't suspect it, man; I know it!"

Darcy shook his head. "What you do not know is that I have admired her for quite some time. Since autumn of last year, in fact."

Bellows looked stunned. "Ye're acquainted wi' her? She knows who ye are?"

"No," Darcy answered. He took in a breath. "It was a brief acquaintance, and I doubt with my manner of speaking and my appearance that she has recognized me." Darcy leaned in to Bellows. "You did not reveal my true identity at dinner, did you?"

Bellows shook his head. "No, I promised I wouldn't. But why not tell 'er who ye truly are?" Bellows nodded his head towards Elizabeth. "If yer feelings are what ye say they are... It appears as though this Mr. Adams is quite fond o' her, too. I'd let her know, I would!"

Darcy narrowed his eyes at David Adams. Shaking his head, he said, "There are some complications to my doing so." He shook his head. "I cannot tell her who I am."

Bellows let out a moan. "I ken't imagine what that could be when she seems as enamoured wi' ye as ye are wi' her."

Darcy turned sharply at his first mate. "What?"

"Ye must be blind as a bat!" he exclaimed. "Here, ye take the helm. I must needs attend to somethin'."

"You are not going to go tell her, are you?" Darcy demanded. "I will not deal lightly with you if you do!"

"No worry, Captain. I jest think the crew and our guests need some lively diversion!"

Darcy kept an eye on Bellows to make sure he was not going to speak with Elizabeth. Instead, his first mate took the steps down and disappeared.

A few minutes later Bellows reappeared with Michael Jenkins, who went to the forecastle deck and began playing his flute. A few of the men began dancing a reel together to the lively music. At length, a few couples joined in as Jenkins played his repertoire of music.

Darcy watched from the helm as Elizabeth clasped the good hand of David Adams, and the two began to dance. Darcy let out a moan and brusquely rubbed his chin in frustration. Bellows returned and stood at his side.

"It appears as though they are enjoying themselves," Bellows said, casting a side-long glance at Darcy, who did not answer.

Darcy continued to watch as the couples danced. As each dance ended, the couples laughingly gave elaborate bows and curtseys and then moved on to different partners. He felt a sense of relief when Elizabeth was no longer dancing with David.

At length, some of the older couples grew weary and thanked Jenkins for the music. Darcy watched as Elizabeth stood by her father and David. The two men were conversing. Jenkins announced there would be one final dance.

"Take the helm, Bellows," Darcy suddenly said.

"What are you doing?"

Darcy took in a deep breath. "I am going to ask Miss Bennet for the next dance!"

Chapter 16

Darcy determinedly took the steps down and walked towards Elizabeth. He felt the same rush of excitement and silly boyhood anticipation he had felt when he first asked her to dance at the Netherfield Ball. This was quite different, however. That time, he had felt that Elizabeth knowing who he was had been in his favour. This time he had in his favour that she did not.

He came up to her and gave a quick bow.

"May I have... 'ave the pleasure of the next dance, Miss Bennet?"

Elizabeth turned to him with a look of surprise. He half expected a lively retort, but she was silent for a moment.

"Thank you. I... I should like that very much," she said.

Darcy bowed and claimed her hand. His fingers enclosed about hers, giving them a gentle squeeze as they took their places in the set. Jenkins began to play a slow, rhythmic tune, allowing the couples to walk and turn with each other, providing ample time for conversation. Darcy, however, could not conjure up one thing to say. It was enough to enjoy her sparkling eyes, ready smile, and radiant face.

"Do you not talk as a rule while dancing, Captain?"

Darcy started, observing her expression as she spoke these words. He searched her face, wondering whether she had any recollection of him asking her a very similar question when they danced at Netherfield. He wondered whether she knew that the man dancing with her now was the one who had danced with her then.

"'Tis the purpose of the dance, I suppose, to git a little more acquainted wi' yer partner."

"I am quite glad you feel that way, as I must admit I have found you a most perplexing character to sketch."

Darcy raised a single brow as they parted for a few movements. When they came back together, he continued, "So ye are a studier of character, are ye? An' why is mine so perplexin'?"

"For one, you are a very peculiar *pirate*! I am hard pressed to know what to make of you!" A smile touched the corners of her mouth.

"Well, ye know I'm *not* a pirate," he said softly.

Elizabeth laughed. "So you say, but you chose to impersonate one. I find that peculiar, indeed!"

"I 'ad not planned to do it; it jest 'appened. As there was an apparent similarity in our looks, I agreed to it."

"Oh, yes, I noticed the similarity," Elizabeth said as they parted again. She walked around the couple beside them, and she came back to stand across from Darcy while that couple walked around them. When they stepped closer, she said, "In your appearance, I will concur, but that was the extent of it."

"An' what do ye mean by that?"

Elizabeth looked up into his face, as if searching for something. "Your manner of speaking, while at times is in the way of the commonest man, at other times hints of refinement and education. You occasionally exhibit mannerisms of a well-bred gentleman, as well. It puzzles me exceedingly!"

He took her hand as they promenaded down the line. "Per'aps," he said softly, hoping for more time to keep his identity from her, "I've been makin' an attempt at speakin' in a more refined manner to impress a young lady."

They turned again to face one another and a lovely blush covered Elizabeth's cheeks, but she did not look away. "At times you behave like the perfect gentleman, and at other times... I do not know whether you are teasing or brazenly flirting."

"I rarely flirt," Darcy said in a grave tone. He shook his head slightly. "An' if I do, 'tis never brazen."

Elizabeth's brows pinched together, and she tilted her head. "It certainly begs the question of who truly is this Captain Smith."

The curls that framed her face bounced; one fell across her face. Darcy was tempted to reach over and gently pull it aside with his fingers.

They parted again, giving Darcy a moment to collect his thoughts – or perhaps to gather the fortitude to confess all to her. They returned to their place in the set, and he stared across at her. He would take this image of her and burrow it into his heart forever. Once she knew who he was, it would change whatever regard she held for the captain.

He had to wait a few more movements before he was close enough to speak to her again. They stepped forward and joined their hands. Darcy met Elizabeth's raised brow with one of his own.

"Who do *ye* think Cap'n Smith is?" He held his breath as he awaited her answer.

She bit her lip and looked up at him intently. "Do you truly wish to hear my thoughts? No, I shall refrain for the moment. But my curiosity impels me to insist you tell me more about him."

Darcy drew in a sharp breath, fearing she have guessed his true identity. "I fear it would be of little interest to you." Darcy winced, realizing he had not spoken with an accent.

"No," Elizabeth said softly, "perhaps the life of a ship's captain would *not* prove interesting, but tell me, have you had other adventures at sea as exciting as this one?" Elizabeth tilted her head and looked at him with questioning eyes.

"Nothing at all like this."

"No storms, no pirates, no crashing upon the rocks? What about mutinies or dealing with an unruly sailor?"

Darcy shook his head briefly.

"Hmm," Elizabeth murmured. "I would think a sea captain would deal with at least some of those on a regular basis." She sent him a challenging look. "Another peculiar piece of the puzzle."

Darcy felt his heart begin to race, as he contemplated what she might suspect. They parted again and when they came together, there was silence between them for several movements.

Finally, Darcy asked, "Is there anything else ye find peculiar?"

Elizabeth glanced down at their hands, and just as they released them to step around the dancers on either side of them, Elizabeth exclaimed, "There most definitely is."

It was several movements before they came back together, and as they did, the music came to an end. Michael Jenkins thanked everyone for indulging his playing, but said he had to report to duty. Everyone thanked him for the lively diversion.

Elizabeth curtseyed, and Darcy bowed, taking her hand. They walked to the rail of the ship.

"You were saying?"

Elizabeth looked down again at their joined hands, lifting them up. She turned his hand over in hers. With her other hand, she ran her fingers softly across his open palm. "Would you say that a ship's captain does a lot of hard work?"

"Aye," he answered, barely able to formulate a coherent thought. His mouth was dry, and he fought every impulse to pull her close. "Do *ye* flirt brazenly, Miss Bennet? For ye are treadin' in some deep an' dangerous waters here."

Elizabeth quickly released his hand. "Pray forgive my impertinence. But I fear I cannot come to understand how your hands could be so soft and smooth. It is almost as if you have never done a day's worth of hard work in your life." She sent him a challenging look.

Before he answered, Elizabeth stopped. She looked intently up into his face. "It is not important." She looked towards the stairs and said, "The men have gone to the dining room. I can go on from here." Curtseying, she said, "Thank you, again, for the dance, Mr. Darcy."

Darcy bowed. "It was my..." He gasped and he widened his eyes. He felt as if his heart had stopped. "You know?"

"Oh, I was not certain," she said with a nervous laugh, her eyes reflecting confusion, however, instead of glee. "It was just as we ate dinner that I began to suspect. It was something Mr. Bellows said after the meal that gave me pause."

"Bellows? Did he tell you who I was?"

"No," Elizabeth reassured him. "He merely recounted to me that you told him disguise is your abhorrence. I recalled you saying that very thing to me when... well..." Elizabeth trailed off, and she cast her eyes down.

Darcy lowered his brows. He knew exactly when he had uttered those words and felt anew those feelings of despair and awkwardness that had marked their last meeting at Rosings.

"I am grateful you can laugh about it now. I, unfortunately, cannot."

Elizabeth lifted her eyes in confusion. "I am not laughing, Mr. Darcy. Pray, I do not know what you mean."

"Last night... Mrs. Keller..."

Elizabeth tilted her head at him. "I fear I do not understanding your meaning." A moment later, she gasped. "Oh, my!" Elizabeth drew her fingers up over her lips.

Darcy looked intently at her. "You remember what she asked you."

"Yes, I do," she whispered fervently. "But I assure you, the proposal I told them about was not yours!"

Darcy raised his brows in curiosity and drew back. "You received another proposal more foolish than mine?"

Elizabeth sent him a sympathetic smile. "It was Mr. Collins over whom we shared a laugh last evening!"

"Mr. Collins?" Darcy could not check his reaction. His eyes widened. "Mr. Collins? He made you an offer of marriage?"

Elizabeth nodded. "The morning after the Netherfield Ball. I refused him – of course – and he moved directly out of our house to the Lucases' home, where Charlotte was more than ready to convince him to seek *her* hand in marriage."

"Mr. Collins?"

"I am so sorry! I can only imagine how much humiliation you must have felt, thinking we were speaking about you!"

"Well, I cannot doubt that I deserve as much. I was as much of a fool in my entreaty as Mr. Collins most likely was."

"Oh, pray, do not be so hard on yourself, Mr. Darcy," Elizabeth said softly.

They stood silent for a moment, and then Darcy said, "Please, Miss Bennet, I do not want word of my identity to get out to my crew. Bellows is the only one who knows who I am. I would beseech you not to inform anyone of this until we are off the ship."

"You have my word, Mr... Captain Smith."

"I thank you. But, I would tell your father and cousin. Please, would you be so kind as to bring them directly to my quarters? I wish to explain all to you."

"I shall."

"I shall escort you to the dining hall and then meet you in my quarters."

He walked her down to the stairs, bowed, and then walked away.

~~*

Elizabeth stood stunned for a moment, as she considered that what she just recently had come to suspect was true. Captain Smith was, in fact, Mr. Darcy! She knew something about why he had agreed to impersonate a pirate, and then to pass himself off as a ship's captain, but there was a greater question pressing on her. Why had he not revealed his true identity to her?

She was barely able to put one foot in front of the other as she took the few more steps to the dining hall. All she could think about was how she had enjoyed the captain's smiles, his kindness, and his brave acts of valour. As she reached up to open the door, she suddenly thought of being held tightly in his arms. She brought her hands up and covered her warm cheeks. And all along it was Mr. Darcy!

Could he still have feelings for her? She shook her head.

Not after everything she had said to him the last time they saw each other in Kent. She had lashed out at him in anger, accusing him of acting despicably, only to discover when she read his letter that she had foolishly believed Mr. Wickham's lies.

Elizabeth turned to look in the direction he had walked, her mind in turmoil. He could not still care for her! Perhaps he had been hoping to humiliate her once she knew it was him. After all, she had refused an offer of marriage from the illustrious Mr. Darcy, one which most women would have yearned to receive.

To still her shaking hands, she clasped them together as she walked into the dining hall. She found her father and David playing cards with Mr. Joyner and Mr. Dillard.

"Your dance is over with the captain, is it, Lizzy?" her father asked. "I wish he had been a true pirate. It would have made the story much more entertaining!'

Elizabeth bit her lip. David looked up at her, and his brows narrowed. "What is it, Elizabeth? Is something amiss?"

Elizabeth let out a nervous chuckle. "No, but the captain wishes to speak with the three of us."

"Now?" asked Mr. Bennet. "I have such a good hand!" He slapped a card down on the table.

"Yes, now, Papa."

Mr. Bennet resignedly put down his cards. "So what is this matter that is so pressing?"

They stepped away from the others, and Elizabeth drew her father and cousin close. "You may not readily comprehend this at first, even I am somewhat mystified by the whole affair…"

"What is it?" David asked.

She turned to David. "It turns out that Captain Smith is not a pirate, not even a ship's captain. He is actually a slight acquaintance of ours."

"Who?" both men asked at once.

She turned to her father. "You will find this difficult to believe."

"Come, Lizzy, pray tell! I am not getting any younger!"

"He is Mr. Darcy," she said softly, watching her father closely to gauge his reaction.

A smile formed on one corner of his mouth, and he was soon laughing. "Certainly you jest, Lizzy!"

"I do not, Papa, but he does not wish for anyone else to know his real identity. He wishes to speak with us in his quarters. I believe he will explain."

David stepped up alongside Elizabeth. "You are acquainted with Mr. Darcy? Of Pemberley?"

Elizabeth nodded. "His friend leased a country home near ours last year, and we found ourselves moving in the same circles."

"Mr. Darcy?" he asked again.

Elizabeth stopped and faced him. "You seem more surprised that we are acquainted with Mr. Darcy than you are that he was Captain Smith!"

"I confess that I am equally astonished! Do you realize how sought after that man is? Both by women who will do anything to secure his attention and by men who hope that association with him will elevate their own status?"

"Well, he did nothing to elevate our status, did he, Lizzy?" her father said.

Elizabeth stared down at her feet as they walked the remaining distance to the captain's quarters. Her stomach felt as if it were tied in knots. If only her father knew…

They reached the captain's quarters, and Mr. Bennet gave a few taps on the door.

Darcy opened it and extended his hand. "Thank you for coming. Please come in and have a seat."

The party stepped in, and their eyes quickly scanned the room, admiring the fine wood, bronze, plush rugs, and carpets.

"Quite impressive!" David said.

"It is very comfortable," Darcy replied. "But please remember, it is not mine."

"No, but it is fine, just the same." Mr. Bennet turned to look squarely at Darcy. "My Lizzy has made a most astounding claim that you and Mr. Darcy are one and the same! Could this possibly be true?"

Darcy nodded. "It is as you say, Mr. Bennet."

Mr. Bennet let out a laugh. "My, this adventure gets more entertaining with each passing hour!"

"I feel as though I owe you an explanation, but I beg you, once you step from this room, do not speak my real name. I would not want word of this reaching my sister before I am able to see her in person."

"We understand, Mr. Darcy... Captain Smith," Elizabeth said. She could barely bring herself to meet his eyes.

Darcy took in a deep breath and began. "There are two things I must explain. The first is why I impersonated Lockerly the pirate, and the second, why I chose not to divulge my true identity. I shall begin with the first." Darcy's hand went up, and he fingered his beard. "I had, unfortunately, neglected my appearance for some time and sequestered myself away from all that I held dear. I will not go into the reasons for this; suffice to say that I wished to be invisible as I stumbled through the streets of London, much like any other destitute reprobate. I was in a deplorable state!"

Elizabeth's brow dipped in worry, and she chewed on her lip as she contemplated his words. She wondered whether *she* may have been the cause of his anguish. Could her refusal have affected him so profoundly? She had been certain that any regard he might have still had for her after her refusal would be soon driven away. Had she been wrong?

He went on to tell them much of what he had already told her. Of course, she had not known at the time his *true* identity, which added a whole new dimension to the story.

He concluded with how, when his ship encountered the merchant ship, he had to disclose to his crew that he was not Lockerly, hoping they would continue to abide by his directives. He was grateful that the men appeared willing to follow him whether he was a pirate or just a ship's captain. Thus they were able to drive off the real Lockerly and his band of pirates and successfully rescue the captives.

Darcy clasped his hands together and looked down at them. "And now for the reason I did not wish my true identity to be known." He took in a deep breath and shot a quick glance at Elizabeth. "I did not want anyone on board to know who I was because I am not particularly proud of how I neglected my person. I did not want those dearest to me to ever find out about this. I am not proud of it, and I felt that if anyone knew... if *you* knew... there would be a greater chance of someone finding out."

"Your secret is safe with us!" David said.

"I am confident of that, and I am most grateful."

"We owe you so much, Mr. Darcy," David said. "I do not know what I would have done if Elizabeth had not been saved." He reached out and clasped Elizabeth's hand.

Elizabeth saw the twitch in Darcy's brow before he stood up and walked to the door. "You owe me nothing, Mr. Adams. Every one of the crew played a part. I only wish we had been successful in capturing Lockerly." He opened the door and stood to the side. "If you would please excuse me, I need to attend to some matters and then relieve Bellows at the helm."

They stepped out, and Darcy closed the door behind them. David and Mr. Bennet chatted enthusiastically about such a novelty as encountering Mr. Darcy impersonating both a pirate *and* a sea captain. Elizabeth, on the other hand, only felt confused.

As they passed her cabin, Elizabeth stopped, prompting David to turn and ask, "Elizabeth, are you unwell?"

She nodded and brought her hand up to her forehead. "I am tired and have a headache. If you will excuse me, I think I will bid you both a good night."

David squeezed her hand. "You have had a more taxing adventure than either one of us."

As Elizabeth opened the door, David took a lit candle from the passageway. He handed it to Elizabeth, saying, "Take this and light one of the candles in your cabin. Then you can light the others as it gets darker."

"Thank you, David."

He nodded. "Get a good night's sleep, Elizabeth. You probably need it. We shall see you in the morning."

"Thank you. Good night. Good night, Papa." She reached up and kissed her father on the cheek and walked into the cabin, quickly shutting the door behind her. While she looked with eagerness to a good, comfortable night's sleep, she was also looking forward to some time alone to contemplate all that had taken place the past two days. Finding out that Captain Smith was actually Mr. Darcy was something that had her completely unsettled!

Chapter 17

When Elizabeth closed the door, the single candle she held cast a soft glow about the cabin. She was grateful no one else was there. She hoped the ladies would remain with their husbands for a little while longer to allow her some time to reflect on this startling revelation. She lit a wall candle and then blew out the one in her hand.

She sat down on the chair that was to be Mrs. Keller's bed, leaning her head back and closing her eyes. Suddenly images of Captain Smith – Mr. Darcy – were before her. She heard his voice and saw the twinkle in his eyes. She remembered his kindness, bravery, and occasional teasing manner.

She grabbed a nearby pillow and wrapped her arms tightly about it. She felt her eyes pool with tears. Since first suspecting the captain's true identity, she had made every effort to put on a calm – even smiling – face, but it was far from what she felt on the inside.

A tear trickled slowly down her cheek, and she drew a shaky breath as she buried her face in the pillow.

Why had he not entrusted her with the truth of his identity? She shook her head and narrowed her eyes, as if that would help her understand. A few months ago he had entrusted her with a troubling family secret regarding his sister's near elopement with George Wickham. Did he feel that he could no longer trust her?

Elizabeth let out her breath in a long sigh. Just that morning he had held her close to him as they flung across one boat to the other on a rope! As she thought about being held so tightly by him, her head pounded with indignation, her mind tossed about in confusion, her cheeks flamed with mortification, and... what was it? She shivered as she contemplated this new sensation that coursed through her at the mere thought. The tumult of all these emotions assaulted her, vying for prominence.

Elizabeth dropped to the floor, pulling a blanket over her as she curled up on the rug. When she brought her head down to the pillow, an onslaught of tears trailed down her cheek. A few found their way to her lips, and she tasted their saltiness, much like the seas in which they sailed. She thought – as another tear made its way to her lips – that the sea and her tears would from this day forward be inextricably linked to Mr. Darcy.

~~*

Darcy returned to the helm, adjuring Bellows to go below and get some rest.

"Ye ken't git rid of me without first telling me what happened with Miss Bennet. Did ye tell 'er during yer dance?"

"Tell her what?" Darcy asked with a blank expression.

"Ye know exactly what ye needed to tell 'er!" Bellows said, leaning in to him. Poking Darcy's chest, he said, "Did ye tell 'er that yer Mr. Darcy?"

Darcy sighed and shook his head. "I had no need to. Miss Bennet had grown suspicious of who I was and spoke to me by name when the dance ended." Darcy raised a brow at Bellows. "No thanks to *you*!"

"Me? I didn't tell 'er who ye was!"

"No, it was not your fault. How were you to know that I once uttered those same words to her that I did to you?"

"What words?" Bellows asked.

"Disguise of every sort is my abhorrence."

Bellows eyes widened, and he slowly nodded his head. "Aye! I told 'er ye said that."

"Well, it sparked her memory and gave rise to her suspicions. I have since spoken with not only her, but Mr. Bennet and Mr. Adams, as well, telling them what happened, and admonishing them not to divulge my identity. To them I shall still be Captain

Smith."

"Well, I'm glad to hear that. I shall go below an' git some rest. It should be easy sailing. The winds are mild, but the sails are catchin' what little there is, movin' the ship steadily along. Jest keep us headin' in this direction. Furl the sails an' lay anchor when darkness falls. Call me if ye need me."

"I will. My thanks, Bellows."

Darcy was grateful for the time alone. He trusted that the men manning the sails were fairly competent. Being at the helm would allow him time to think about the past two days. He gripped the wheel as he wondered what Elizabeth thought, knowing now that it had been him who had received her tender ministrations as she nursed his wound, teased her, watched her unabashedly, brazenly flirted with her... He shook his head. Yes, for him it had been brazen, as she had no idea of his true identity or his intentions. The mere thought of holding her in his arms powerfully stirred him.

He let out a huff and gripped the wheel tightly as he recollected holding her close to him as they swung from one ship to the other. He could not have done anything more indulgent of his desires, and yet he had asked her to trust him. He had convinced himself that no one else could be trusted to do it. Only he could do it.

He jutted out his jaw and fingered his beard as he considered his recent conduct. Elizabeth would certainly have every reason *now* to accuse him of ungentleman-like behaviour.

As his mind turned over thought after thought and accusation after accusation, he noticed Mr. Bennet walking up to the helm.

"Good evening, Mr. Bennet," Darcy said with a nod of his head.

"And a good evening to you, too, Mr... Captain Smith!" Mr. Bennet raised a brow and then let out a chuckle. "Not much of a wind, is there?"

"Not enough to get us to St. Mary's before dark. But we ought to arrive first thing in the morning."

"Good, good."

"Mr. Bennet, do you mind if I ask you something?"

"No, no! Go right ahead!"

"I did not have the opportunity to inquire of Miss Bennet, but I wondered how you came to be in these seas? It is quite far from Hertfordshire."

Mr. Bennet braced his hands on his hips and looked out to the darkening skies. "My sister lives on St. Mary's, and we received word that she was in failing health. I wished to visit her and brought Lizzy along. She is the most adventurous of my daughters, and I must confess, my favourite."

Darcy nodded his head. "Yes, she is... adventurous, that is."

"I know a father ought not to have favourites among his children, but how can one not love her wit, good sense, and liveliness?"

Mr. Bennet let out a long sigh, which was echoed by Mr. Darcy.

"You know not how distressed I was that something might have befallen her with those pirates!" He turned to Darcy with eyes filled with intensity. "We owe you so much, Mr. Dar..., Captain Smith. I shall always be grateful for the risk you took to save my girl."

"You owe me nothing, Mr. Bennet."

Mr. Bennet let out a hearty laugh. "For that, I am thankful. I could never repay you what my Lizzy's safety is worth!"

"She is a priceless jewel, I am certain." Darcy took in a deep breath trying to calm himself before asking the next question. "And Mr. Adams?" He thought he heard his voice crack. "Does he reside on St. Mary's?"

"David? No, he is my cousin's son. My sister and his mother were always very close cousins *and* friends. He was there visiting with his parents from Staffordshire, and I must confess that he was quickly taken with Lizzy."

Darcy kept his eyes ahead, but his brows lowered. "And does she... return the affection?"

Mr. Bennet laughed. "Oh, I think she likes him well enough. He's returning with us to Longbourn so they can further their acquaintance, and he can meet the rest of our *esteemed* family."

Darcy pursed his lips together. His mouth went dry, and his thoughts whirled about in his head.

His reflections were interrupted by Mr. Bennet, who turned to him with his arms folded across his chest. "You asked me a question; now may I ask you one?"

Darcy raised a brow and nodded. "You may."

With a crooked smile, Mr. Bennet scrutinized him from head to toe. "I wonder how you came to find yourself in such a dire sea of neglect." With a wave of his hand downward he continued, "This all seems quite removed from the style of dress and exacting neatness you exhibited in Hertfordshire. Pray, what possibly could have wrought this change?"

Darcy's cheek twitched, and he brought his hand up to rub it, his fingers getting tangled in his coarse beard. He studied Mr. Bennet's face, wondering whether Elizabeth might have told him about his proposal and her refusal. Judging by the man's composed deportment, he doubted she had. That made him wonder how he should answer him.

He gripped the wheel and turned to look straight ahead. "I... I found myself in a rather trying state. I was faced with some hard truths... about myself, in particular..." Darcy let his voice trail off. Shaking his head, he said, "At length, I succumbed to an excessive neglect of my person and an excessive attention to brandy. Consequently, in the condition in which I found myself, I was mistaken for Lockerly, and... you know the rest."

"So it seems!" Mr. Bennet laughed. "I still find it difficult when I look at you to find the man we all knew in Hertfordshire." He shook his head and put up his hand in a slight wave as he turned. "I always enjoy a good laugh, Captain, and this shall divert me for many years to come, I am certain."

Darcy watched the man as he walked down to the main deck chuckling all the way. He let out a groan and looked down at his knuckles. They had turned white from tightly gripping the wheel. "I doubt it shall do the same for me!"

As darkness cloaked the ship, Darcy ordered the anchor to be dropped and sails to be furled. It was a moonless night so all sailing would cease. The soft flicker from candles in lanterns and the soft tossing of the ship was like a balm to Darcy's weary soul. He decided he would remain on deck as long as possible to allow Bellows more rest.

Bellows returned to the helm a few hours later. "I'm rested an' ready to do yer biddin', Cap'n. I shall remain on watch through the night an' bring us into port in the morn."

"Thank you, Bellows. "You are a good man, and I appreciate all the help you have been to me."

"Especially wi' Miss Bennet?"

"No, not wi' Miss Bennet!"

Bellows shook his head. "I saw that all the passengers but her were in the dinin' hall enjoyin' themselves. Mayhap she's makin' herself perty fer ye!"

"I think not," Darcy replied. He let out a huff as he considered she most likely retreated to her cabin so she would not have to encounter him again. "Take the helm, Bellows. If you need me – I doubt that you will – I shall be in my cabin."

Darcy was grateful to enter the sanctuary of his cabin where he could be alone with his thoughts. In truth, he needed sleep, but he doubted his cabin would provide it. The thought that Elizabeth was in the very next room caused his heart to beat wildly. Wondering what she must be thinking of him made him shudder.

He lit a single candle in a wall sconce, which barely illuminated the room. It flickered lazily as the ship rose and fell on small waves and it gave the cabin – in all its sinister opulence – a dreamlike feel. Unfortunately, it felt more like a nightmare than anything else.

Darcy was restless and could not sit, let alone try sleeping, so he began to pace the floor. Earlier he had removed his sword and baldric and now flung off his vest. He pulled the large white shirt from his breeches and unbuttoned it. He wished for nothing more but to toss these clothes overboard! He greatly looked forward to returning to some form of normalcy when he returned to London.

Darcy walked over to a small wall mirror. He leaned into it and studied his dim reflection as he fingered his beard. He wished his valet was on the ship and at the ready to shave it off! He touched the bruise above his eye tenderly. A scar was likely, and he knew that every time he would look upon it, it would be a painful reminder that although he would have a part of Elizabeth with him forever, he did not have her.

He collapsed into the large chair at the desk. He had hoped that in agreeing to this scheme, he would rid himself of all his feelings for her. Yet now, he seemed tied to her forever. He closed his eyes and shook his head as it fell back.

Moments later – at least he felt it was moments later, for he knew he had not fallen asleep – he felt the odd sensation of being lifted up, followed immediately by suddenly plunging down. The ship groaned and shuddered, and a thunderous crash sounded above him on deck. He jumped up, reached instinctively for his sword, and rushed out of his cabin.

~~*

Elizabeth had heard Mr. Darcy come to his room and pace. She had tried futilely to keep her thoughts at bay, but her mind replayed everything that had transpired the past two days. She simply could not fathom why he would have agreed to such a scheme as impersonating a pirate and why he did not choose to tell her who he was. But an even greater mystery was why she had begun to have such ardent feelings for this man. Mr. Darcy, of all people!

Perhaps she had read too many gothic novels about women kidnapped by ruthless villains who were then rescued by a handsome, gallant hero. He had certainly come to her rescue. Had she merely seen him as her gallant hero? She bit into her bottom lip as she reflected that she had always considered him handsome, just too disagreeably arrogant for her to value it.

She bunched up her pillow and turned her head. She could see beneath the door and watched with curiosity as Mr. Darcy walked back and forth in his cabin. He seemed restless. Perhaps now that she knew who he really was, he wanted nothing more than for this ordeal to be over with!

He finally stopped pacing, and Elizabeth surmised he had probably sat down. Again she tried to close her eyes and put every thought out of her mind, but she suddenly felt something odd. The ship began to rise steadily and at once came down hard. The ship moaned ominously as if it might rip apart! Something on the deck above crashed down in a deafening thud, prompting her to cover her head, thinking something – or someone – might come through the ceiling!

Elizabeth immediately jumped up, her heart pounding. Were they encountering another storm? Was the sea churning up again? Was it something worse?

She swung the door open and rushed into the partially darkened companionway, colliding with something… or someone.

"Ooh!" Elizabeth cried out, as she stumbled sideways from the collision. Hands quickly reached out to steady her and keep her from falling to the floor.

Her hands flailed about her as she was pulled upright, and they came to rest on a solid, bare chest. She was helpless to do anything about it, as the ship still jostled. In the dim light of the hallway,

Elizabeth looked up into the face of Mr. Darcy. A look of shock was emblazoned on his face. She surmised hers must have looked the same when she realized the state he was in.

Darcy kept his hands on her shoulders, but stepped back slightly as she quickly drew her hands away. "Pray, forgive me, Miss Bennet."

"I... um... the ship... we seemed to fall!"

"Yes, I was..." Darcy let go of her shoulders, and he quickly began to button his shirt, albeit in the wrong holes. As he fumbled with that task, he tried to gather his thoughts. "I was in my cabin and... I am..." Darcy took in a deep breath and shook his head. "Pray forgive my appearance. You must think me devoid of every trace of decorum!"

"No, no," she said, grateful for the dim light in the companionway. She was too disconcerted to meet his gaze, but instead found her eyes riveted to his chest, and curiously, to the hairs that peeked out through the now crooked opening at the top of his shirt. She had the oddest desire to reach up and button his shirt correctly.

"Please, excuse me, Miss Bennet. I... I must see what that was!" His eyes met hers when she shyly looked up, and he paused a moment before setting off.

"Yes, of course!" she replied, hastily stepping aside. She put her hand over her heart, as he rushed past, trying futilely to quell its insistent pounding. Whether it was from the ship's movement or the encounter with Mr. Darcy, she could not determine.

Elizabeth followed Mr. Darcy as he rushed towards the stairs, struggling to finish buttoning his shirt. He took the stairs briskly, two at a time, overtaking the passengers that had come out of the dining room to find out what had happened.

As everyone came up on deck, it was dark. Several crewmen were relighting the lanterns whose flames had been extinguished either in the ship's abrupt descent or by the water that had washed over the ship at its forceful encounter with the sea again.

"Bellows, what happened?" Darcy shouted, taking care not to slip on the watery deck. "What caused the ship to do that? And what fell? Are the crew safe?"

Bellows looked at the captain and then to the group of passengers standing behind him. "It were jest a barrel that fell." He then looked out to the sea. "An' it were a rogue wave that caused the ship to rise an' fall like it did."

"A rogue wave?" Darcy asked. He gave his head a quick shake, and then said, "Ah, so I thought! Tell the passengers, 'ere, what a rogue wave is."

Bellows' brow twitched, and a slight curl formed on his lips as he turned to the passengers.

"'Tis a large wave that has come from a far-off storm or..." Bellows paused and leaned in to his listeners. With a low voice he added, "'tis a warnin' to a ship that somethin' bad is a comin' its way."

Darcy heard the gasps and looked across at the fearful faces of the passengers and some of the crew who were standing nearby.

"Bellows knows that is jest an ol' seafarer's tale an' there's no truth in it!" He shot a warning look at his first mate. "Tell 'em, Bellows, that there's no grounds to such a tale!"

Bellows shook his head. "Well, I've only once 'eard of it happenin' to a sailor I knows, and within a few hours of it, most of the whole ship had come down wi' the plague."

"Thank you, Bellows. That is enough!" Darcy turned to address those standing there, whose number had grown. "'Tis nothin' but far-fetched believin' and superstition. It was likely jest from the storm we encountered the other night. I'll put me trust in the Sovereign Lord an' His ways much more'n a silly wave. Now, everyone ken get back to what ye were doing." Darcy turned to go and then stopped. "Jest be careful in case we encounter another one!"

Darcy marched away, angry at Bellows for upsetting both the passengers *and* the crew. He obviously had no common sense concerning what he should say and should not say.

As the crew dispersed, and the passengers returned to the dining room, conversations flew back and forth concerning what had happened and what they had just heard. Most took the words of the captain and reiterated their soundness. Mrs. Joyner, however, was certain that the wave signalled the likelihood of a gravely ominous occurrence.

As the evening wore on, there were no more rogue waves, no ominous incidents, and at length, everyone said goodnight for the evening. The ladies repaired to their cabin and settled in for a much hoped for good night's sleep. For Elizabeth, however, a new memory of Mr. Darcy was added to all the others, and with it more confusion, more mortification, and much to her distress, more awakened longing.

Chapter 18

Elizabeth opened her eyes, surprised that she had finally fallen asleep the night before. She knew not how long she had lain awake, for in addition to the turmoil of her feelings, she had heard Mr. Darcy's continued pacing in the adjacent room. She looked at the small window and could see the faintest early morning light coming through. Elizabeth quietly readied herself while the other ladies continued to sleep soundly. Rather than remain in the cabin, she decided to go out and see if she could find someone to prepare her some tea.

When she came into the dining hall, crewman Michael Jenkins was in there.

"Good mornin', Miss Bennet. Ye're awake early."

She smiled at him, remembering Mr. Darcy's – *Captain Smith's* – similar comment at the cave. "Do you know what time it is?"

"Yes, Miss. 'Tis almost six o'clock. All hands will be called to breakfast at six bells."

"Have you been up on deck yet this morning?"

"Aye. 'Tis foggy out there." In a soft voice he slowly added, "Hangin' over us like a ghostly veil."

"Ah," she replied, smiling softly at his sombre expression. She wondered if he was worried about what Bellows said last night. "Are you just coming off your watch?"

"Oh, no, I 'ave first watch this morn. Git to swab the decks." Jenkins seemed to suddenly remember his manners. "Would ye care for somethin' to eat an' drink?"

"I should like that very much. Is it possible to get some tea?"

Jenkins nodded. "I'll git it fer ye right away."

Elizabeth walked over to the window and looked out. She could see nothing outside but a blanket of grey. When Jenkins returned, she walked back to the table and sat down. He placed tea and a biscuit in front of her, and she thanked him.

She picked up the warm cup of tea and held it in her hands. "We certainly enjoyed your flute playing last night, Mr. Jenkins. It gave everyone such pleasure – the passengers *and* the crew."

A blush covered the young man's face. "Thank ye, Miss. I enjoy playin' it."

Elizabeth pinched her brows together in thought. "Tell me, Mr. Jenkins, how has sailing been under Mr... Captain Smith? What kind of a captain is he?"

"Oh, he treats us all good an' decent. All the men 'ave a great deal of respect fer 'im. Me thinks each one of us would always want 'im... or someone like 'im... to always be over us." The young man looked down and shuffled his feet. "It 'asn't even been ten days since I first met 'im, but I almost consider 'im to be like me dad, if ye knows what I mean. Even when we thought 'e was a pirate, we was amazed at 'ow good 'e was to us. Now that we know 'e is *not* a pirate, we can understand better why he weren't cruel and ruthless. Some of the men 'ave talked about other captains they have served under that were tyrants. Not Captain Smith."

Elizabeth brought her cup of tea up to her lips and smiled behind it as she listened to the young man's effusions.

The sound of bells suddenly rang out. At the sixth bell, men began to dash to and fro.

"Thank you for your time, Mr. Jenkins. It has been a pleasure to speak with you."

Jenkins nodded his head. "A greater pleasure fer me, Miss." He gave a short bow and walked away.

Elizabeth bit her lip as she pondered the young man's words. The dining hall was soon busy with men coming down from the main deck and others coming up from below. As she sipped the tea, she noticed her father come in.

"Good morning, Papa!" she said. "Did you sleep well?"

Mr. Bennet waved his hand through the air. "Our elite sleeping accommodations aboard the *Devil's Seamaiden* consisted of a hammock in a room full of a dozen other smelly and snoring men."

Elizabeth smiled. "The thought of getting back to Longbourn and sleeping in my own bed sounds better and better each passing moment."

"Ah, but you, Lizzy, have such splendid accommodations. Did you not sleep well?"

Elizabeth let out a long sigh. "No, not particularly well." A soft laugh escaped. "I slept on the floor."

Mr. Bennet placed his hand on his daughter's shoulder. "I knew you would allow the older ladies to sleep in the bed."

"It was the least I could do."

"So was Mrs. Joyner able to sleep last night after hearing about some ominous occurrence happening because of the rogue wave? I suppose she fretted about it all night."

Elizabeth shook her head. "I know it was of grave concern to her, but I think she was able to fall asleep despite it. At least I did not hear anything from her after we extinguished the candles."

"Good." Mr. Bennet turned to the door. "Look, it is David!" He waved his hand. "Here we are, young man!"

David cheerfully walked over to them, rubbing his injured arm. "Good morning!" He sat down next to Elizabeth. "When I woke up, I had to pinch myself to make sure I had not dreamt all that happened in the past two days!"

"It has been an adventure," Elizabeth said softly. "How is your arm this morning?"

"Sore. But not enough to be a nuisance."

Elizabeth smiled warmly. "I am glad. Perhaps you should have a doctor look at it when we are back in St. Mary's, now that it will be a couple more days before we get to London."

David placed his good hand over one of hers. "I shall, but it is nothing compared to what you went through. I am so grateful nothing happened to you." He gave her hand a gentle squeeze.

Mr. Darcy stepped into the dining hall and looked about. His eyes settled on the three of them, and he nodded, but instead of coming over, he poured himself some coffee and quickly exited the room.

Mr. Bennet shook his head. "I still find it inconceivable that Mr.

Darcy, who would not look upon anyone in our neighbourhood without disdain, would have agreed to do something so completely beneath him."

Elizabeth slowly nodded. "It is odd."

"So our pirate adventure has had danger, intrigue, and a masquerading hero! This will certainly divert Mrs. Bennet and the girls for quite some time, eh?" Mr. Bennet said with a laugh.

Elizabeth forced a smiled. "And yourself, I would imagine," she said, feeling somewhat disappointed that Mr. Darcy had not come over to speak with them.

"Ah, you know me, Lizzy! Always looking for something... or someone... of whom to make sport!"

At length, the remaining passengers came to the dining hall and enjoyed a filling meal. Excitement was high as everyone anticipated coming back into port at St. Mary's and then boarding another ship for London.

The only thing that would hamper their journey was the fog. As the passengers came up on deck, they saw that the ship was encased in a thick, enveloping shroud which barely allowed them to see the bow from the stern of the ship. The very top of the masts were completely hidden from those on deck.

The ship was moving slowly, not so much because of the light wind, but because about half of the sails remained furled. They did not wish to sail at a swift pace since they could not see what might be ahead of them hidden in the mist.

Darcy stood at the helm with Bellows, looking in all directions through the spyglass. The passengers walked to the rail of the ship and looked out, hoping for some sort of break in the heavy grey curtain surrounding them.

After a bit of discussion amongst the passengers debating whether they would arrive at St. Mary's that morning or afternoon, David extended his arm to Elizabeth. "Come, Elizabeth," he said. "Let us take a turn about the deck. I know the view is not much, but I could use the diversion."

Elizabeth slipped her arm through his, and they began walking down the length of the ship, stepping over and around ropes, capstans, cleats, and crewmen. They came to the bow of the ship and stopped, looking out into a vast nothingness.

David turned to Elizabeth, resting his elbow on the railing and cradling her hand in his.

"Elizabeth, you must know how grieved I am that all this has taken place. If I could, I would blink my eyes and drop us back into London this very moment!" He let out a long sigh. "In all the years my family sailed to St. Mary's, nothing like this ever happened! I would do anything to erase the past few days!"

Elizabeth smiled. "I know you would, and I appreciate it." She glanced down at their joined hands and pinched her brows together.

"I can see that you are sad, Elizabeth. This has taken a great toll on you!" His eyes searched her face. "Pray tell me, what can I do to help you forget this? I long to see your vibrant smile again."

As his one hand gripped hers firmly, the fingers of his other hand gently stroked the back of her hand. Very slowly, he brought her hand up and pressed his lips against it. David's eyes were shining as he gazed down at her, and his smile widened. "I hope you know you have become very dear to me."

Elizabeth opened her mouth to reply, but a movement caught her eye. She turned to see Mr. Darcy walking around from the quarterdeck. He came to a halt and seemed almost ready to turn around when David called him over.

"Captain Smith! Do you know how much longer before we arrive at St. Mary's?"

Darcy pulled off his tri-corn hat and ran his fingers through his hair. His eyes remained focused on David as he shook his head. "Unfortunately, no. We cannot sail at the speed we would like because the fog prevents us from seeing too far ahead. We hope it shall burn off as the day warms."

"I understand perfectly." David said. "I want to thank you again for everything you did. I know you risked your life to save Elizabeth and the other ladies."

"I was glad to do it and am grateful for the outcome." He stole a glance at Elizabeth and then made a quick bow. "If you will excuse me."

David extended his arm to Elizabeth, and they began to walk back towards the stern. Elizabeth shivered in the cool of the morning.

"Are you cold? Perhaps we ought to go inside."

Elizabeth shook her head. Her eyes narrowed as she gazed out into the foggy mist. She paused, looking out past David.

"What is it?" David asked.

"I am not certain. I thought I saw something."

David looked out, searching the fog for any sign of what Elizabeth may have seen.

"I only see fog. Fog and more fog!" He chuckled. "I doubt anything is out there."

"I suppose," she said. She was not as certain as David was, however, and her heart pounded. She was certain she had seen something, if only a fleeting glance that disappeared as quickly as it had appeared.

They stopped just opposite the helm, where they saw that Mr. Darcy had returned. They looked out towards the sea, which merged with the sky in a muted vapour of grey.

"There it is again!" Elizabeth said excitedly, pointing off to the distance. "I think it is another ship!" She grasped David's hand. "It appears to be coming directly towards us!"

As passengers and crew came to the port side of the ship where David and Elizabeth stood, Darcy grabbed the spyglass and looked out.

"I think I saw it!" said Mrs. Joyner. "Oh, I hope they are not going to hit us! Do you think they saw us?"

A brown image slowly appeared from the haze, but only enough for them to see that it was a ship, and it appeared to be turning. Once again, it vanished.

Mrs. Joyner clasped her hands together. "Oh, good! They have seen us! They are turning the boat away from us!"

To the passengers and crew on the ship, it seemed a novelty, and they watched with curiosity for it to appear again. Fingers pointed when they thought they saw it again, and others searched intently into the fog, but could see nothing.

"Nonsense!" said Mr. Bennet. "I do not see a ship or anything like it!"

Elizabeth glanced up at the helm and saw Mr. Darcy and Bellows in a tense conversation. They seemed much more concerned than anyone else. Darcy raised the spyglass, as if determined to see what was out there as soon as it showed itself again.

The curtain of fog lifted slightly, and at once everyone could see a good part of the ship. It now was sailing almost parallel to the *Devil's Seamaiden*.

"Well, look at that, Lizzy," Mr. Bennet said. "We *do* have fellow travellers. I wonder if they have had the adventure that we have had!"

Bellows called out to the crew to unfurl the main sail and gallant sail. In an instant those sails unfurled in a snap and billowed out as they caught the wind. Elizabeth watched as Darcy turned the wheel, causing the ship to slowly veer away from the other ship. With more sails unfurled, the ship picked up speed.

"Why do you suppose they did that?" David asked. "I thought they did not want to sail at a brisk pace because of not being able to see ahead of them."

Elizabeth looked back towards the ship, which was now disappearing into the fog again. "I am not certain, but I think it has to do with that ship," she said softly.

Mr. Keller nodded his head. "Captain Smith probably wants to put some distance between us and them to prevent any unforeseen collision." He pointed off into the nothingness. "Did you see how that ship appeared and disappeared in the fog? If that ship has not seen us, there might still be the possibility of it coming upon us without any time to swerve out of the way." He let out a laugh. "A ship cannot turn as quickly as a horse-drawn carriage, you know."

"No, it cannot." Darcy approached to the passengers. "I do not wish to alarm any of you, but I would ask that you all get below deck. If you would be so kind as to follow me, please."

"What is it?" Mr. Dillard asked. "Why do you want us to do that?"

An explosive boom came from within the depths of the fog, and a fiery light was all the answer that was needed.

Darcy peered through the mist. "There!" he hollered, pointing out to sea towards the bow of the ship. A cannonball fell from the sky just short of the ship, sending water over the railing.

"Come quickly!" Darcy ordered. "You must get below deck now!" His eyes met Elizabeth's, and she could readily see the alarm on his face. She knew not what was going on, but her heart pounded with the fierceness of that same apprehension.

Elizabeth heard Mrs. Joyner mumble something, and she immediately went to her side, taking her arm. "Come, Mrs. Joyner.

We must go below!"

"Oh! Where is my husband?" Mrs. Joyner said, her face drained of all colour.

Elizabeth pointed. "He is just over here. Mr. Joyner, your wife needs you!"

The group quickly began to move to the stairs. Elizabeth found herself next to Mr. Darcy, being propelled along by his hand at her back.

"What is it?" she turned to him and whispered. "Are we under attack?"

Darcy nodded. "Possibly." As he led the group down below, he gave explicit orders.

"I am taking you down to the hold where you will remain until I come for you. Everyone is to stay there with the door locked." As they reached the companionway, he stopped. "Continue down these steps. I need to get something from my quarters and will join you there!"

Darcy rushed down the hall towards his cabin as the group hurried down the next set of stairs. The passengers mumbled and fretted amongst themselves about what might be happening. Elizabeth stood at the rear, behind Mrs. Joyner, nudging her along while Mr. Joyner was practically holding her up with his arm.

Mr. Darcy soon returned and came up alongside Elizabeth, holding a rifle and a pistol.

"Oh!" she exclaimed. "Is it that bad?"

"It never hurts to be prepared."

Elizabeth nodded. "But who is it?" she whispered. "Why did they shoot at us?"

Darcy took a deep breath. "The ship is the same one we saw Lockerly and his men sail away on. I fear it is Lockerly, and I know he must be intent upon reclaiming his ship!"

Alarm swept over Elizabeth's face. "Will you be able to keep him at bay?"

Darcy nodded. "We should have more men," he said, as they took the stairs down. "We should be able to hold him off."

"Does this ship have cannons?" she asked.

"Stop right there!" Darcy called out to the group ahead. Turning back to Elizabeth, he whispered, "It does have two, but unfortunately, there is no one who has the expertise to shoot them."

Darcy moved to the front of the group of passengers and opened the door to the hold. He then issued some orders. "I want each one of you to remain inside. I have a key and am going to lock the door, but you will have a key, as well." He handed the extra key to Mr. Bennet. "I beg you to please keep the door locked until I – or one of my crew – returns and tells you it is safe to come out."

"Can we not stay up on deck and help – the men, that is?" It was David asking.

Darcy looked down at his arm. "With your injury, I think it would be best if you remained down here." He looked up at the others. "I do not suppose that any of you men are proficient at fencing."

The group sheepishly shook their heads.

"Then I would ask you to remain here. You can at least give some protection to the ladies. For that, I will be grateful."

As the passengers stepped into the hold, he handed the guns to two of the men. "Use these if you have to." Darcy glanced down at Elizabeth as she came through the door.

"Be safe," she said softly, pleading with her eyes.

He nodded and offered her a reassuring smile. He turned to the others and said, "Again, no matter what you hear or how long you have to wait, do not unlock the door unless I or one of my crew comes and tells you it is safe."

"And if no one comes for us?" Mr. Dillard asked.

Darcy narrowed his brows. "Say a prayer and use your key."

The door slammed, and the click of the lock was heard. Mrs. Joyner cried out and collapsed onto the floor with a thud.

Chapter 19

Darcy rushed back up onto the deck. His heart pounded so thunderously he thought it would burst out of his chest. He looked out into the heavy mist searching for any further sign of the ship. Not seeing anything, he took the stairs up to the helm and joined Bellows.

"Have you spied it again?" he asked.

Bellows shook his head, a dire expression on his face. "No, but I'm sure it were the same ship we saw yesterday."

"I am, as well," Darcy said, rubbing his jaw. "Perhaps we have lost them."

"Perhaps." Bellows gripped the wheel tightly. "Ye must think Lockerly ain't goin' away, puttin' the passengers down below like ye did. Ye don't think 'e sent off a warnin' shot 'oping to scare us, an' they 'ave set sail in the opposite direction?"

Darcy narrowed his brows and his jaw tightened. "I would hope so, but until we know for a certainty what he is up to, I want the passengers safely below."

"Ye don't think 'e 'as left, do ye? Ye thinks 'e is still out there."

Nodding his head, Darcy said, "I am of the opinion he is staying just out of sight." He let out a huff of air. "We have his ship. We took his prisoners. I believe he is going to try to take them from us."

Darcy picked up the spyglass and gazed around him into the mist. All hands were on deck silently at the ready, anxiously awaiting orders – or for something to happen. Several tense, quiet moments passed, the only noise being the soft rustle of the sails as the wind alternately caught and then released them and the lapping of the waves against the ship.

Suddenly another explosion came from the starboard side, a cannonball falling just short of its target. As it plummeted into the sea, the seawater crashed over the stern.

"There she is! She is on our starboard side!" Darcy yelled.

"Come about!" Bellows yelled as he turned the wheel sharply. "We'll give them a narrow target!" His eyes darkened under furrowed brows. "We ken't outrun 'em, they is smaller and ken sail faster." He then began to slowly nod his head. "But we ken certainly try to disappear into the fog before they ken turn to follow."

Darcy kept the spyglass fixed on the stern of the ship. "They are turning!"

"We should be safe for a short while. Their cannons won't be aimed at us. I doubt that ship has a bow-chaser."

"Bow-chaser?" Darcy asked tersely.

"A smaller, single cannon at the bow of the ship used to shoot an enemy in front of 'em." Bellows' eyes remained fixed ahead. "From the size of that ship, they likely only 'ave a single cannon on each side."

Darcy watched the ship intently as the distance between them widened. It was soon swallowed up in the fog. "Good!" Darcy exclaimed. "We are out of sight of them." He called out an order, "Thirty degrees more to port!"

The crew scrambled to adjust the sails. Bellows looked at Darcy and nodded as he turned the wheel. "Ye are thinkin' like a true cap'n. We'll change our direction while we are outta their sight, an' hopefully they'll keep sailin' towards where they last seen us."

Darcy nodded. "As long as we remain veiled by the fog, there is hope we can escape." Darcy continued to look about him, ready to give warning at the first sign of them. "I wonder if he purposely missed hitting us with his cannons. I believe he will want to take his ship back in one piece."

"I 'ope yer right, Cap'n."

The ship moved briskly along. Darcy kept watch aft of the ship and both sides, while Bellows peered into the mist ahead of them.

The last thing they needed was to encounter another unsuspecting ship; they would have little time to respond.

As they made their way steadily along, they veered occasionally more to port, hoping to completely lose their enemy. Turning slowed them down, so at length, Bellows issued the command, "Lay forward!" and the *Devil's Seamaiden* set off speedily in the direction of St. Mary's port.

Darcy and the crew remained alert and kept a watchful eye out for any signs of the ship. It had been several minutes since they had made their last turn, and everyone looked around, wondering whether they had successfully evaded Lockerly's ship.

An uneasiness pervaded the crew. They were sailing into an unnerving nothingness, and knew not if or when Lockerly's boat might reappear. As much as they had earlier hoped the fog would soon dissipate, now they all hoped it would cloak them until they were safely out of harm's way.

Everyone looked about for signs of the ship, but their fearful expressions displayed a hope that they wouldn't encounter it again. There was an eerie silence, broken only by an occasional wave that crashed against the ship or the sails that rustled in the light breeze.

Darcy swung the spyglass around just as another explosion shattered the silence. The fire from the blast painted the grey mist with fiery shades of red, orange, and yellow.

Webber, who was up in the top crow's nest suddenly called out in his loud, booming voice, "Incoming!" He pointed to the bow of the ship.

Everyone instinctively ducked as a cannon came over the ship, entangling the sails and masts. Two of the crew jumped out and away just as the rigging they were on came crashing down.

The tangled mass of wooden beams and shredded canvas fell across the ship.

"Is any man hurt?" Darcy called out.

Several men called out that they were not, and the ones who had leapt from the rigging stood up and brushed themselves off.

"Chain shot!" Bellows hollered.

Darcy looked at him with a raised questioning brow.

"'Tis cannons with chains attached to do as much damage as possible to the rigging." Bellows struggled to turn the wheel as he hollered out to the men on the main sail to come about.

"So they do not care that they damage the ship. I was wrong," Darcy said.

"No, you was right. Their intent is to cripple us. Masts an' spars an' yards an' sails are easy enough to replace."

"Can we manoeuvre away from them?"

Bellows' countenance was grim. "No. We must now arm our men an' prepare 'em fer battle."

"Any chance we can use our cannons to ward them off?" Darcy asked.

Bellows tossed his head in the direction of the ship. "No. They're now coming at us headlong. They know exactly how to approach us so even if we knew how to fire those things, they wouldn't be in our line of fire."

Darcy let out a huff. "Foster did not think through this scheme as thoroughly as he should have. He has put us all in danger!" He turned to Bellows. "Let's arm the men, then!"

~~*

The passengers heard the first explosion. From the hold, the muffled sound seemed far enough away that they were not too concerned, especially when it did not seem to hit the ship.

Mrs. Joyner was sitting on the floor leaning against a wall despairing. Mrs. Keller tried to reassure her they would be all right. "Captain Smith will know what to do. After all, remember it was he who came to our rescue on the island!"

Elizabeth, her father, and her cousin exchanged worried glances. Knowing Captain Smith was not a real sea captain was something they did not want anyone to know. It would only add to their concern. She walked over to Mrs. Joyner and sat down on the floor next to her.

"We are all worried, Mrs. Joyner, but have faith. All shall work out for the best." Elizabeth was not sure even she had the faith now to believe that. She nervously ran her fingers along the smooth wooden planks of the floor as everyone conversed and conjectured what might be happening on deck. As she did, she felt one of the planks move.

"What is this?" she said, leaning forward and giving it a pull. The plank cleanly came out after a few tugs. She pulled out two more on either side, revealing a deep cavity. She leaned over and peered in.

"I think there is something down there!"

Mrs. Joyner let out a joyful cry, suddenly diverted by such a discovery. Everyone stood around them watching as Elizabeth reached in and felt around. Her fingers brushed against some sort of fabric, and as she stretched in as far as she could, she was able to grasp it and slowly began to pull it up.

A few more planks had to be removed to lift it completely out, but at length she placed it on the floor. They all simply stared at the white fabric bag, probably made from sail canvas, which was tied together at the top with rope.

"It is a treasure, I am certain of it!" Mrs. Joyner said. "Hurry! Open it!"

Elizabeth smiled at the sudden change in Mrs. Joyner's demeanour. Her hands shook as she tugged at the knot, trying to pull apart the strands of rope. When it finally gave way, there was not a sound in the cabin as she slowly opened the bag.

The onlookers gasped as they beheld the treasure before them. There were glittering diamonds and a vast array of jewels in a variety of colours and sizes.

"Heavens above!" cried out Mr. Dillard. "It is likely worth a fortune!"

"Do you suppose anyone knows about this?"

"Since we found it, does it belong to us?"

"I cannot imagine what this might be worth?"

"Do you think they are real?"

Questions abounded amongst the passengers. Elizabeth stood up and quietly went to her father and cousin, who were enjoying the merriment.

Her brows pinched together in concern.

"Well, Lizzy, our pirating adventure now has the final element!" Mr. Bennet said jubilantly. "A hidden treasure!"

In a hushed voice, she said, "Yes, but do you not realize that this belongs to Lockerly, and he will most likely do whatever he can to get it back?"

The smiles evaporated from both men's faces. "You are right," David said. "But do not say anything to anyone. Their elation at finding a treasure will be short lived and replaced by even graver concern if they hear that."

"No, I shall not. But I think somehow we must warn Mr. Darcy that Lockerly has more than just his ship that he will attempt to reclaim for himself!"

At that moment, a second explosion was heard. This time, however, they felt the ship shudder at the impact.

Everyone's merriment quickly dissolved back into fright.

~~*

Lockerly's ship swept down upon the *Devil's Seamaiden*, and the men watched with wide eyes as it veered starboard at the last minute to avoid crashing into them headlong. Within minutes they had come alongside, and the two vessels collided into each other's sides with a jolt. Lockerly's crew threw a grappling hook over, and as the hooks dug into wood, the two ships were anchored together firmly.

Confusion reigned as men scrambled from Lockerly's ship to the *Devil's Seamaiden*, either by jumping as the two ships jostled together or by swinging over on a rope. Shots were fired, but went wild, due either to a lack of expertise or the inability to take aim because of the tossing of the ship. Pistols were soon discarded and knives, cutlasses, and swords were drawn as the adversaries came together.

Darcy and Bellows pulled out their swords. Bellows was the only crew member Darcy felt was proficient to fight these men. However, as he assessed Lockerly's crew, he felt the pirate was in the same quandary as himself. His crew, although now greater in number than had been on the island, appeared to be just as inept.

From his vantage point at the helm, Darcy searched the motley group of men for Lockerly, who most likely was also looking for him. From what little he knew of the pirate, he was probably already on the ship, plotting its takeover. But as unrelenting as his thoughts were about what Lockerly might do and where he was, just as pressing was the thought of Elizabeth and how to ensure her safety.

Darcy looked at Bellows and nodded. There was nothing left to be done at the helm; the ship was sitting helpless in the water. They both took to the deck and entered the fray.

As Darcy made his way through the fighting men, he kept a lookout for any of his crew that seemed most in need of assistance.

It was overwhelming, at first, not knowing where to turn. He was grateful for the lack of proficiency exhibited by all men. The last thing he wanted was a massacre, especially when these men – both his and Lockerly's – were young, and likely did not have the same evil propensity that drove the merciless pirate.

He fought off a couple men as he made his way around the ship. He saw a movement out of the corner of his eye and realized someone was headed towards the ship's stern. He quickly followed, and when he cautiously came around the corner, he found himself face to face with Edward Webber. The young man's eyes were wide, his face ashen, and his hand gripped his shoulder.

"Are you hurt, Webber?" Darcy asked.

"Jest a small slice, Cap'n. I feel a bit dizzy. Need a moment."

Darcy lifted the man's hand and saw the blood ooze from his wound. "Get yourself below. Go to the hold and announce to the passengers it is you. Someone there should be able to tend to you."

"But the fight…"

"Do not worry about the fight!" Darcy took his pistol out of his belt and handed it to the young man. "Take this and use it if you have to! I need you to stay down there and guard the passengers. Do not let anyone get past you!"

"Aye, aye, Cap'n."

The two walked back towards the bow of the ship, with Webber slipping down the stairway as they passed.

~~*

The activity in the hold came to an abrupt halt when footsteps were heard, followed by a knock at the door.

Mr. Dillard pressed his fingers to his lips to silence everyone. They were not sure whether they should say anything, in case it was Lockerly or one of his pirates.

"It is Webber," came the voice at the door. "Ken ye open the door? I'm hurt."

The door was unlocked and opened just enough for Mr. Dillard to cautiously peer out. When he saw it was indeed Webber, he slowly opened the door. The young man walked in. Blood trailed down his shirt, as well as his fingers and hand. They quickly locked the door once he was inside.

"'Tis not much, but…"

"What happened?" Mr. Dillard asked, helping him in.

"Lockerly's pirates come aboard and we be fighting 'em, but I..." He face turned white, and his eyes rolled back. "I..." Mr. Dillard caught him as the young man collapsed onto the floor.

Mr. Dillard tore open the young man's shirt and saw a gash across the top of Webber's shoulder. He pulled out a handkerchief and pressed it to the wound. Turning to his fellow passengers, he said, "It is only a slight wound. It has been bleeding, but I doubt that he lost enough blood to cause him to pass out."

"Then what did he pass out from, dear?" his wife asked.

Mr. Dillard glanced up and said, "My guess would be fear. I think the poor lad is plain frightened!"

Webber began to stir, and his eyes slowly opened. Then he bolted up. "What 'appened?" he asked, looking around him. The colour began returning to his face.

"You were injured," Mr. Dillard said. "Rest a little and tell us more about the fighting up on deck."

Webber nodded. "Pirates... I've never 'ad to fight like that before."

"Are there many?"

"Seems like a lot." Webber winced. "Me thinks they 'ave as many as we 'ave."

Mr. Dillard nodded. "You just rest a little, lad."

Webber began to sit up. "Cap'n Smith gave me the pistol to protect ye down here, but me thinks I should go back up an' 'elp."

"But you yourself said you have never fought before."

Webber sadly shook his head. "I know Cap'n Smith is dependin' on me. I ken't let 'im down."

Elizabeth stepped forward. "Mr. Webber, I believe I saw you climbing the ropes and masts like you had done it all your life. Am I correct?"

Webber nodded. "Aye. Me brothers used to call me Monkey 'cause I loved to climb."

"I think I have an idea of how you can be a big help to Captain Smith," Elizabeth said. "Do you think you can slip out carrying a bag and climb up one of the masts quickly without anyone seeing you?"

Webber nodded. "I know I ken do it quickly. I ken certainly try to do it without them seein' me."

"What do you have in mind, Lizzy?" Mr. Bennet asked.

"Hand me the bag," she said to Mr. Keller, who had a tight grip on it. As she looked back at Webber, she said, "And I also recall that you have a fairly loud voice, which could easily be heard from up on the mast?"

"Yes, me ma always had me call me brothers when she needed 'em."

As the bag was passed to her, she explained to Webber what they had found. The young man's eyes grew wide as Mr. Keller opened the bag and he saw all the jewels.

"I think Lockerly has come back for this, and it probably is worth a great deal more than this ship!" Elizabeth pointed to some of the jewels. "It appears there are diamonds, sapphires, rubies, emeralds, and other gems that I could only guess at."

"You think he can use them to distract Lockerly?" Mr. Dillard asked.

Elizabeth nodded. "I also wonder if his crew, who apparently he only recently engaged, even know about it. We could use this to turn his crew against him." Elizabeth leaned in to Webber. "I have no idea if this will work, but I have a plan!"

Chapter 20

Darcy shook his head in frustration. Webber had been scared to death and should not have been forced into a situation like this! He was as unprepared as anyone but was younger than them all! He was grateful he had received only a minor wound, and he hoped that sending him down to the hold would spare him from being injured even more!

Darcy searched for any sign of Lockerly, as well as any crewman who might need help. It was difficult, in the confusion and action, to even differentiate between his and Lockerly's men. The blades of their weapons crashed between the crewmen, but he could see no skill exhibited in their manoeuvres. In their faces he could see no real thirst to do their opponent harm. He felt he was watching a sparring match, where injuries would be unlikely. For now he was satisfied with that.

He saw smudges of blood everywhere, but fortunately, no one was down. He saw that young Jenkins had taken a fall and a pirate stood menacingly over him brandishing his sword high enough above him not to pose a real threat. Darcy rushed over, however, and sliced through the air with his sword, knocking the pirate off balance. Darcy and Jenkins quickly subdued and bound him.

As Darcy scanned the ship, he noticed someone moving stealthily towards the stairs. His heart pounded thunderously as he feared that whoever it was might reach the passengers in the hold. He ran up behind the man with his sword drawn and hollered,

"Halt!"

The figure spun around. In a blur, he came at him with his sword swinging, knocking Darcy backwards. The man came at him again, swinging his sword high and low. Darcy's jaw tightened in anger as he stared back into the face of Lockerly!

Lockerly lunged back at Darcy. "How dare ye hornswaggle me out of what be rightfully mine!" Lockerly yelled.

The two danced around each other as their swords clashed between them. "You own nothing, Lockerly!" Darcy countered. "You ought to be dead like your former shipmates. A dead man owns nothing!"

Lockerly's face twisted with rage, and the two men continued their fight at a much greater intensity than before. The stature of the two men, and their proficiency at fencing were equal. Darcy was determined to keep the ruthless pirate at bay and not allow him any sort of advantage. The thought of protecting Elizabeth from this vile monster gave him added strength and endurance. He would not allow Lockerly anywhere near the hold and especially nowhere near Elizabeth. In that moment when he thought of her, he vowed that he would even give his life to save hers.

The two men battled ferociously, steel meeting steel with a resounding clank. Their swords met high and low as each man attempted to successfully thrust, parry, and outwit the other.

Lockerly suddenly lunged at Darcy with his sword pointed at him. As Darcy quickly swung his sword to ward off the blow, he jumped back and stumbled over the grappling hook that had been thrown earlier from Lockerly's ship. He struggled to keep himself upright, but could not, and fell to the ground. Lockerly slowly approached him, a sinister sneer etched on his face.

Darcy inwardly chastised himself for not paying attention to his surroundings, a vital element in fencing. He surmised that Lockerly expertly planned and executed the manoeuvre that unknowingly directed his own movements towards the hook, which consequently brought him down.

He looked around for Bellows and finally saw him cornered at the bow of the ship by two of Lockerly's men. He would be of no help to him now, but he seemed perfectly capable of holding off the two men.

Lockerly let out a vile laugh as he hovered over him. "So, me inferior impersonator, me thinks you'll be visitin' Davy Jones' Locker by day's end!"

"I would not count on that, Lockerly!"

Darcy was grateful for his years of fencing lessons. Despite his one misstep, he was confident he could hold off Lockerly, even though the pirate now had the advantage over him.

Darcy kept his eyes fixed on his adversary. He fought him off as he watched and anticipated every move Lockerly made so he could quickly respond with the best defensive tactic. He was getting weary, the sword held up in his arm feeling heavier with each passing moment. He only needed to wait with patience for the precise moment when he could knock Lockerly off balance and leap back up to his feet.

As Darcy continued to fight from a prone position on the deck, watching for the right opportunity to present itself, a sudden cry from up in the main mast caught everyone by surprise.

"Lockerly!" the booming voice called out.

Darcy glanced up at the mast and narrowed his eyes, realizing it was Webber.

"Is this what you 'ave come aboard fer?" Webber called out as he walked out across the yardarm to the edge. He held out a white bag, dangling it precariously out over the water.

"Where'd ye git that?" Lockerly demanded.

"I bet ye would like to know!"

"What ye got in there?" one of Lockerly's pirates asked.

Webber smiled triumphantly. "So Lockerly did not tell ye, eh? 'Tis jewels. Lots of 'em. They was 'idden in the ship's hold! There be diamonds, rubies…"

"Don't ye dare drop that!" Lockerly yelled, glancing from Darcy to Webber, and then to his men. "An' I *was* gonna tell 'em!"

"When?" demanded another. "When ye took most of 'em fer yerself?"

Webber smiled. "Ye give yerself up, Lockerly, an' I won't drop these." He peered over the edge of the ship. "Looks to be perty deep down there." He raised and lowered the bag a few times. "An' it seems perty heavy. Me thinks it'll sink straight to the bottom!"

Lockerly's face grew red with anger. "You bring me that bag right now or I run this imposter through wi' me sword!" He moved closer to Darcy with a threatening glare.

Webber slowly shook his head. "No, Lockerly. Ye put yer sword down an' give yerself up, an' I'll *think* about comin' down wi' 'em!'

Lockerly let out a string of curses and pointed his sword up to the sailor. "Ye and yer cap'n will both meet your maker t'night if ye don't drop it! Now!"

Darcy quickly jumped up when Lockerly was distracted by Webber. Lockerly noticed and swung his sword back around. Darcy held him off with a swing in the opposite direction.

Webber's eyes widened. "Ye really want me to drop it?"

"Right now! Throw it to me! I've only been playin' games wi' yer cap'n. He'll not live to see another day if ye don't do as I say!"

Webber looked from Lockerly to the bag, and then back to Lockerly.

"As ye say!" With that, he heaved the bag over the heads of the pirates, the crew, and Lockerly. As it sailed over his head, Lockerly yelled and dropped his sword. Sprinting to the rail of the ship, he jumped up to try to catch it as it went over, but it was too high for him to reach. As it hit the water with an impressive splash, Lockerly quickly hopped over the railing of the ship and crashed into the water, just as the bag began to sink.

Darcy rushed to the rail and looked out. Lockerly held onto the bag with one hand, and was struggling to keep himself afloat. His arms flailed about, in an unsuccessful attempt at staying above water.

Lockerly's men looked about sheepishly, unsure what to do. They began grumbling amongst themselves how their captain had not been honest with them about this valuable treasure, and now they did not know whether he would even be pulled from the waters alive. They reasoned their best course of action was to surrender, and they all despondently dropped their weapons and raised their hands.

Darcy issued the order to tie the men up. He watched as Lockerly struggled for a while, and then he finally threw a rope over.

As much as he was curious about what was in the bag, Darcy hollered out, "Let go of the bag if you want me to pull you up."

"No!" 'Tis mine! All of it belongs to me!"

Bellows rushed over to the railing. "Then ye ken go down to the bottom of the sea wi' it!" He let out a laugh. "If ye think *we* won't take it from ye, *yer men* certainly will! They ain't too happy wi' ye right now!"

Darcy almost laughed as he watched Lockerly weigh his options, as if he really was considering whether or not to go down to the bottom of the sea just to be in possession of his precious jewels. He went underwater a couple more times, spitting out water each time he came up.

Darcy was grateful that the ship Lockerly had been on was on the other side of the *Devil's Seamaiden*. Seeing how Lockerly could barely keep himself above water, even if he considered trying to swim around to his boat, he would not make it.

Finally, in a moment of desperation, he released the bag and watched it sink. He let out a howl before grabbing onto the rope with both hands. Darcy and Bellows pulled him up.

Lockerly coughed and heaved as he came over the railing. Darcy kept a firm grip on him as Bellows quickly bound his hands behind his back with rope. They took him over to the rest of his crew and tied him to one of the masts.

Bellows swiped his hands against each other in a gesture of success. "Ye shall pay this time, Lockerly! An' ye won't escape!"

It seemed that Providence knew that evil had been vanquished, for the fog slowly began to burn away. A few rays of sunlight began to shine down upon the ship. Darcy felt a great deal of satisfaction, but he also knew that they were not going anywhere in the condition their boat was in. He was not sure whether Lockerly's ship was large enough to carry the crew of both ships and his passengers, but that might be their only option.

He glanced up at Webber, who was coming down from the mast, a triumphant smile on his face.

Darcy slapped him on the back as he came up to him. "You did a good job, Webber! You had a capital idea!"

"Where did you find those jewels?" Bellows asked, and then let out a laugh. "And how could you bring yourself to throw them all overboard?"

"The passengers… they found 'em hidden in the hold… oh, we must tell 'em their plan worked!"

"*Their* plan?"

Webber nodded. "Actually, Miss Bennet came up wi' the idea. She's very clever."

"Too bad those jewels are now at the bottom of the sea, though," Bellows said.

"Oh, no!" Webber laughed. "That's the best part! They took out the jewels an' replaced it wi' junk they gathered from down in the hold! The jewels are safe!"

"You are to be commended for your bravery, Webber," Darcy said with a broad grin. "Now, if you will please excuse me, I must go to them!"

Darcy hurried down the two flights of stairs and rushed through the companionway to the hold. He tapped at the door and announced himself as he unlocked the door. As it was opened, he heard a loud sigh of relief.

"All is safe, you may come out. Webber performed admirably, and the pirates are all bound!"

A cheer went up, and they hurriedly gathered at the door.

"Be advised, however, that Lockerly and his pirates are still on deck. They are tied up, but I suggest the ladies either repair to your cabin or the dining hall. I beg you not to come up on deck and be subjected to them."

Mr. Dillard handed Darcy a bonnet filled with jewels as he walked past. "I hand this over to you, Captain. Every last jewel is there." He then laughed. "The bonnet belongs to Miss Bennet. She willingly gave it up, and I believe she will gladly receive it back when you find something else in which to store the treasure."

As Elizabeth walked past him, he touched her arm to stay her. "I thank you, Miss Bennet. I understand you were responsible for coming up with Webber's scheme."

Elizabeth shook her head, causing the curls around her face to bounce. "I fear it is likely from reading too many novels."

Darcy softly laughed. "And a level head, I would suspect, as well." Darcy took in a quick breath and let it out. "It was a superb plan."

When the group came up the stairs to the galley, they were met by Bellows. "Come, Captain Smith, you must see this!"

Darcy and Bellows took the stairs up to the deck, followed by the passengers who wanted to see what was happening.

At the top of the stairs, the most beautiful sight awaited them.

The fog had dissipated, the sun was shining down on them, and a ship was slowly approaching.

"Please tell me it is someone who has come to rescue us and not fight us," Darcy said to Bellows.

Bellows nodded. "From the signal flags, it appears to be a small ship belongin' to the British Navy." He smiled triumphantly. "I believe, Cap'n, that our adventure is finally over an' has met wi' success!"

Darcy lifted Elizabeth's bonnet filled with the jewels. "And I shall be most grateful to hand this precious cargo over to someone else!" He stole a glance at Lockerly, who obviously did not realize his jewels now resided in a green bonnet.

The first mate's eyes widened. "Ye best not git anywhere near Lockerly wi' that!" He leaned over and peeked in. "I 'ave never seen anythin' like that before!"

Darcy shook his head. "I can honestly say, neither have I!"

~~*

The passengers watched the naval ship as it drew close to the *Devil's Seamaiden.* Their excitement rose as she came alongside the port side of the ship, opposite from the ship Lockerly now had. They threw over a grappling hook, and the ships were pulled close together.

Men began to make the easy swing from the naval ship to the *Devil's Seamaiden.* As men continued to board, they watched as a small boat was extended out over the bows of both ships and lowered. It was carrying an officer and two other sailors.

"My!" exclaimed Mrs. Keller, "that shall be so much easier than carrying us across on a rope!"

Elizabeth smiled. *Yes, but not as much fun*, she said to herself.

The officer walked over to Darcy and Bellows. They soon were engaged in a rather intense conversation. Both men were pointing to Lockerly, but the officer shook his head.

Darcy glanced over at the passengers who were drawing near. He let out a huff and shook his tousle of hair. "I most certainly will not!"

"I wonder what they are talking about," Elizabeth said. "I wonder what he does not wish to do!"

"I am curious about that, too!" David replied. "I am going to go over and see what I can hear."

Darcy, Bellows, and the officer walked over to Lockerly, followed by David, who drew close to listen. After a few minutes, David came back chuckling.

"What is it?" everyone asked.

"It seems that they have orders to verify that they actually have the right Lockerly as their prisoner. Apparently he has a scar that runs from his shoulder to the centre of his chest. Both men are being asked to open their shirts, but it seems our captain does not see the need to do so, as everyone on the ship knows it is Lockerly who is tied up."

Elizabeth checked her smile. The poor man most likely considered this to be humiliating, baring his chest before everyone on the ship.

"If you would, Captain," the naval officer said.

Darcy turned to see the passengers watching. All eyes were on him as he slowly unbuttoned his shirt. When he pulled it opened, the officer nodded his head.

"My!" whispered Mrs. Keller, who stood behind Elizabeth. "He certainly is a nice specimen of a man!"

Elizabeth's eyes widened, and she brought her hand up to cover her mouth, but not in time to hide the mischievous smile that appeared. Mr. Darcy glanced over at her and scowled, quickly buttoning his shirt again.

The passengers were told to pack up their belongings and then return to the dining hall. They were to wait to be summoned, for the prisoners were to be taken over first and securely locked up.

At length, the passengers returned to the deck. Some of the crew helped carry their belongings up. As Elizabeth stepped out into the warm sunshine, which now glistened across the waters, she looked about for Mr. Darcy, but did not see him.

They were more than ready to climb into the small boat that was swung across for them. Mrs. Joyner actually laughed as they were swung over to the naval ship. Elizabeth could only suppose that she had been through so much already, this was nothing to fret about at all!

Once on board the naval vessel, the passengers were hurried off to some cabins that had been prepared for them. They were assured they would enjoy every comfort and to let the crew know if there was anything they needed. From what the captain said, they were just an hour from docking at St. Mary's port.

Elizabeth took time to freshen up, and then went up on deck with her father and cousin. She desperately wanted one more opportunity to see Mr. Darcy. As they walked about and greeted the crew, enjoying the warmth of the sun on their backs, Elizabeth grew concerned that she did not see him.

She did not see Bellows, either, and finally asked Webber about them. "Oh, they've been taken in to be questioned by the naval captain. They prob'ly won't be long."

Elizabeth hoped they wouldn't be long. She did not wish to disembark the ship without first expressing her appreciation to Mr. Darcy. In truth, she wished to express more, but knew she could not.

Chapter 21

Darcy and Bellows were whisked away to the officers' quarters by Captain Newton. He asked the two men question after question and took detailed notes about what had transpired with Lockerly that would be used as evidence against him. Lockerly had been a daunting nemesis to the navy and the ships sailing in British waters, and Newton was pleased to finally have him in custody.

As the men were questioned, Darcy grew more impatient for the interrogation to end. When the ship finally came into the harbour at St. Mary's, the captain assured them that they would not be much longer. The questions, however, continued unabated, and Darcy grew more anxious to depart, knowing the passengers and his crew were likely going ashore.

There was a knock at the door, and at the captain's acknowledgement, Foster burst in. He nodded at the men in the cabin and sat down. Looking at the captain, he said, "I hear we have Lockerly in custody."

Newton nodded and smiled. "The seas will be safer now. He shall hang, as he should have before."

Foster turned to Bellows. "I have arranged for you and your crew to sail to London on the naval ship in the next berth. It is set to sail at four o'clock. You and your crew may go gather your things and report to the captain on board that ship." Foster then turned to Darcy. "Unfortunately, I need you to remain with me a little longer."

Darcy looked at Bellows, who stood and was about to take his leave. "Tell the crew to gather on deck once they have their belongings and wait for me before leaving. I shall not be much longer." He said the latter as much to Foster as to Bellows, his voice and expression indicating he would brook no opposition. "I would like to express my thanks to them before they return to London."

"Aye, Cap'n." Bellows nodded at the men and walked out.

Foster turned to Darcy, looking at him pointedly. "I know you are angry at me for what I did, and I confess I had no idea all that would transpire as a result. I do apologize for deceiving you and getting you out to sea through such trickery. It was wrong of me."

Darcy raised a brow. "But you do not seem at all repentant. In fact, I believe you are quite pleased!"

"How could I not be? Lockerly was captured!" He leaned back in the chair and folded his arms across his chest. He looked at Newton. "I trust that you will transport the pirates to London and ensure they do not escape this time."

"I will."

He turned back to Darcy. "I thought you should know that there is substantial prize money for capturing Lockerly. It will be divided up amongst you and your crew as you see fit."

Darcy's eyes widened in surprise, and he felt his anger lessen... just a little. "I had no idea. I am pleased to hear that, but I will decline any for myself. I would like to have a say, however, in how it is distributed amongst the crew."

"There is also this!" Captain Newton interjected, placing a leather pouch on the table in front of Foster. "It was found on the ship and is filled with jewels. I assume there will be a reward for this?"

Foster's eyes widened as he looked at the immense treasure before him. "I would imagine there will be a fairly good sized reward for this, as well!" He looked at Darcy. "Where did you find this?"

"In the hold."

"We will add the reward to the prize money."

"Foster, it was the passengers who actually found this. If I can have a say in this matter, as well, I should like the reward to be divided up amongst the passengers, with a greater portion awarded to Mr. Bennet and Miss Elizabeth Bennet. It was she who actually found the jewels and devised the plan that stopped Lockerly."

Foster nodded, cradling his chin. "We can do that. I am not certain what the reward might be, but let us talk theoretically and decide how you want the reward and the prize money divided up."

Darcy spoke with Foster on how to distribute the rather substantial sums of money. He hoped to help out not only his crew, but the Bennet family, particularly Elizabeth, as well.

When they finished, Darcy requested a reprieve so he could express his thanks to the passengers and his crew for their bravery in the midst of several dire situations. He hoped to see them again before they went their separate ways.

Foster reluctantly agreed, but added, "You may do so, but there is one more thing we need to discuss. You may go now to say what you will."

Darcy glared at Foster before rushing up on deck. He looked about him and saw his crew standing just off the ship on the dock with their belongings. When they noticed him, they rushed towards him.

Darcy met them half way. "I am glad you are still here. Where are the passengers?" he asked, looking around him. "They have not left the ship yet, have they?"

One of the men nodded. "Aye! Some are gittin' right back on another ship to take 'em back to London, an' others are spendin' the night an' will leave at a later date."

Darcy's brows lowered as he looked out at all the people walking about the harbour. "And what of Mr. Bennet and his daughter and the young man? Do you know what has become of them?"

One of his men nodded. "That's them in that carriage, there. They is settin' off to spend a couple days wi' family before they return to London."

Darcy watched as the carriage disappeared around a bend. He let out a huff.

"Cap'n?" Another of his crew looked at him with a worried expression. "What's to become of us when we git back to London?"

At this, Darcy was able to smile. "You are all to receive prize money for capturing Lockerly. It will be divided up amongst all of you, with each receiving a fair share."

"That's mighty good to hear, Cap'n. Are ye goin' to sail back to London wi' us?"

Darcy shook his head. "I regret that I am not. But I want you all to know how grateful I am that you trusted me and were willing to do all we asked. You are, all of you, good men!" He turned to Bellows. "Take care of them, Bellows!"

"I will, Cap'n."

Bellows held out his hand, and Darcy took it in a firm grip. "And you take care, my good friend. I owe you a lot!"

Bellows shook his head. "No, ye were the hero – to me, the crew, an' to the passengers."

"Well, we shall just have to agree that we disagree on that point. God speed, Bellows!"

"Thank ye! An' God bless ye!"

As Darcy turned to leave, another man called out to him.

"Cap'n? Do ye mind if I asks ye a question?'"

"No, go right ahead."

"Why is it that ye suddenly started talkin' all good an' proper like?'

Darcy took in a deep breath and gave them a half-hearted smile. "'Tis a rather long, complicated story, me mate. I'll let me good friend Bellows tell ye what 'e knows. Me thinks ye'll be together for some time."

The men parted, and Darcy returned to the officers' quarters, disappointed that he had not been able to see Elizabeth before she left, but grateful to have shared with the men what would be theirs as a result of their service. He sat down and met Foster's stare.

"In addition to the prize money, I also want me men… my men to receive a high commendation. I am resolute on this matter."

Foster nodded. "I can do that."

"They deserve it. They deserve an exceptionally *high* commendation."

Foster was silent for a moment, chewing his bottom lip.

It gave Darcy the opportunity to ask Captain Newton a question. "Would it be possible for me to reclaim the bonnet that held the jewels when we turned them over to you? I should like to return it to the young lady who owns it."

"Certainly!" The captain retrieved the bonnet and handed the neatly folded bundle to Darcy.

"Thank you." Darcy looked down at the pale green bonnet. He could not help but run his fingers over it and down the length of the ribbons. He smiled as he considered how Elizabeth's bonnet, when holding the jewels, had contained a vast treasure. His smile was bittersweet, however, as he considered how the bonnet belonged to an even greater treasure, in the person of Miss Elizabeth Bennet.

Foster nervously rubbed his hands together as he watched Darcy finger the bonnet. Finally, he said, "Mr. Darcy, you may be wondering why you are not sailing back with the men."

Darcy looked up and waited for Foster to continue, although he was not particularly sure he wanted to hear what he had to say.

"We have Lockerly, but we do not know who helped him escape the last time, and we think they may try again."

Darcy looked from Foster to the captain and back to Foster with a questioning look. "He should be secure in the hands of the British Navy. Captain Newton said so himself."

Foster clasped his hands tightly together, bringing them down onto the table. "Oh, he will be, but I should like to arrest those who were involved in the escape last time." He took in a deep breath and said, "There is just one more thing I would like you to do."

~~*

Elizabeth's heart sank as the carriage conveyed them away from the dock. She had searched futilely for Mr. Darcy and could only conjecture he did not wish to be found by her. She looked out the window, scanning the harbour one last time to see if she could spot him. Her heart was heavy; she knew it was futile to think that he might have feelings for her still. Yet she could not dismiss the way in which he had treated her all the while she thought he was Captain Smith.

Both her father and cousin had been anxious to return to the comfort and refuge of the Clowers' home and did not wish to remain a moment longer than was necessary. They were disappointed they could not personally thank Mr. Darcy, but he was nowhere to be seen. As the arrangements were being made to secure a carriage to take them to their relatives' home, they had sent a message ahead informing them they were returning and would explain all once they arrived.

They had also sent letters home, one to the Gardiners and one to Longbourn. They chose merely to tell them that a storm had thwarted their plans to sail back to London and they would attempt to make the journey again in a day or two – by way of Portsmouth. From there, they would take a carriage to Brighton, pick up Lydia, and then travel by road the remainder of the way to London. It would take longer, but Mr. Bennet had had his fill of sailing. A shorter journey at sea was much preferable. A final letter was written to Lydia, in care of the Forsters, informing her to be ready to travel home with them in about three or four days.

Once the harbour was out of her sight, Elizabeth looked over at David, whose eyes were bright as he talked with Mr. Bennet about how much Melanie would enjoy the stories of their adventure. He laughed as he said, "I believe, at first, she probably will not believe any of it, but then she will become so envious of our adventure, that she will likely wish she could have been a part of it!"

Elizabeth tried to smile, but felt a heavy weight upon her. Much like an anchor that holds the ship in place against the battering waves in a storm, she felt as though it would be difficult for her to move forward as her emotions continued to pound against her.

When they arrived back at the Clowers' home and told them briefly what had happened, the conversation rose steadily to an uproar as questions were asked, every detail and sentiment related, and each different perspective shared.

David was correct about Melanie's response. She listened with rapt attention and responded in disbelief. This was followed by heartfelt sighs, saying how much she envied them for their adventure and wished she had been with them. She teasingly expressed resentment that despite having lived all her life in a place known for pirates, she had yet to see one.

Elizabeth retired early that night, looking forward to her first good night's sleep in two days. She longed to be home, but it would still be nearly a week before she would be able to enjoy the solitude and sanctuary of her own room at Longbourn. It could not come soon enough.

~~*

At first light the next morning, Darcy, still dressed as a pirate, set out with Foster on a small ship to Portsmouth. Foster made sure word was spread that Lockerly was being transported from the port, then on through Brighton, and finally to London. The plan was to travel the exact route Lockerly had travelled when he was boldly snatched out of their hands the last time. That time they had not been ready. This time they would be, and it was Darcy who was going to be in the carriage, not Lockerly.

They made the crossing from St. Mary's to England's mainland without any difficulty, and Darcy was hurried away to a waiting carriage. He was handcuffed, to ensure the appearance of him actually being the captured pirate.

As the two men began their journey towards Brighton, Foster removed the cuffs that bound Darcy's wrists. He stretched out his arms in front of him and opened and closed his fists. He enjoyed this bit of freedom, as they would be replaced at the first sign of something unusual. Seven men followed at a short distance on horseback and in an additional carriage. If anything happened, they easily would be able to capture those involved in the escape attempt.

Darcy leaned back in the seat and looked out the window, his arms tightly crossed. Foster had done it again, and he was just as angry with him now as he had been a few days back. Darcy's jaw tightened as he recollected Foster informing him that there was just one more thing he wanted him to do. He had agreed, however, when Foster told him his crew would receive the highest commendation and even greater prize money for their efforts on behalf of the Crown if they were successful in apprehending the culprits.

Darcy propped his elbow up at the window and rubbed his forehead between his brows. He mumbled, "I hope you know what you are doing."

Foster glanced over at him. "There is nothing for you to worry about, Darcy. The driver and I are both armed, but we plan to readily release you into the hands of anyone attempting to set you free, to lessen the chance of bloodshed." Foster looked at Darcy pointedly. "You, of course, have no reason to fear, as they believe you are Lockerly. Rest easy."

"I assure you, Foster, I will *not* rest easy until I am safely back in London."

Darcy rubbed his chin and let out a groan when his fingers tangled in his beard. He was tired of the disguise and wanted nothing more than to return to London. He looked forward to a good shave and bath before he did anything else. He had already written his valet requesting him to return to his house in London. He had also sent a quick letter off to Georgiana, asking that she come to London at her earliest convenience. He was anxious to see her.

They were about an hour outside of Brighton when the driver of the carriage called out. "I think this is it! On the left! Get ready!"

Darcy and Foster looked out the window, seeing a young lady waving a handkerchief. She was lying on the ground holding her ankle, as if she were injured.

"Ahh," said Foster. "Very cunning. A young lady in distress." Turning to Darcy, he said, "This may be nothing, but we shall put the handcuffs on you just in case."

Darcy reluctantly agreed, placing his wrists together in front of him so Foster could snap them on.

"You shall likely be on your own for a short time in the carriage. Could be others hiding up ahead. We shall follow close enough so we will not lose you, but far enough back that we won't be seen."

The carriage came to a stop, and Foster and the driver hopped down.

They walked over to the young lady. Darcy watched as they bent over to talk to her.

From out of the bushes came the sound of gunshots, and Foster and the driver put their hands up quickly in mock surrender. A man rushed out, grabbing the girl by the hand and pulling her up. They both rushed to the carriage.

Darcy's heart pounded as he watched the scene unfold outside the window. He tightened his fists, hoping they would not realize he was *not* Lockerly. But he hoped to a greater degree that the men on horseback would arrive in time to make an arrest before these two evaded them!

He turned his head to the door as it opened.

"Get in, quickly!" a voice ordered. The man shot the gun wildly into the air. Foster and the driver stood unmoving with their hands in the air.

Once the girl was in, the man looked up and smiled. Darcy's eyes widened as he looked into the face of George Wickham!

"You're safe now, Lockerly!" Wickham's eyes were wide and his voice shook. "Your friends are waiting for you just up the road!"

Darcy was grateful Wickham had not recognized him, but he was sickened at the thought that his onetime childhood friend had stooped to such depravity. Yet he was fairly certain the man was not acting brazenly. He was terrified. Wickham jumped up to the driver's seat, taking the reins and setting off.

Darcy turned back to the young lady who now sat across from him. She was looking down at her hands, and the brim of her bonnet covered her face. He stared at her, wondering what sort of young lady would agree to do such a thing!

"This was so much fun, but I hated having to get down in the dirt!" she said laughingly as she wiped her hands. She let out a huff as she fluffed her dress about, looking for smudges.

When the young lady looked up, Darcy had a second shock in as many minutes. He had to restrain himself from calling out her name. It was Elizabeth's sister, Lydia! His jaw tightened as he considered what this meant. She met his glance with a raised brow.

"Pray, excuse my dirty dress," she said as she began to wipe away some dirt. "George told me I had to make it appear as if I were really in distress. I do believe I did a splendid job!" She bounced on the seat and gave a nod of her head.

Darcy had to loosen his jaw to speak. "Do you know who I am?"

Lydia lowered her brows and tilted her head. "No, but I should like to find out!" She let out a flirtatious laugh and looked down demurely at her hands, which she quickly folded.

"So… George… did not tell you anything about me?"

Lydia shook her head. "I don't think he knew anything about you. He only told me he was doing a favour for some friends… well, I don't think they were real friends… I think he owed them money. He just said he desperately needed my help to get someone out of the hands of some ruthless people."

Darcy raised his brows. "Ruthless people? So that is what he told you?"

Lydia nodded. "I think George was so brave to do this! There are a lot of wicked people in this world. Why would someone hold you like they did?" She leaned towards him, her eyes wide, and she whispered, "Were you kidnapped? Did they want a ransom?"

Darcy shook his head at this naïve and foolish young girl. "Do you see my hands?" Darcy asked, lifting up his arms to show her his cuffed wrists.

"La!" she exclaimed. "These men certainly did not mean for you to get away! I don't think George has a key to open them, but maybe your friends do."

Darcy knew that Lydia could face a severe punishment for her participation in this crime. Perhaps even death. He hoped he could find out more about this scheme before the authorities stopped Wickham. He let out an incensed huff. He would leave Wickham to fend for himself.

"Do you know who these men are that Wick... that George owes money to?"

She shook her head. "No, but I think they were kind to forgive his debts, don't you? And I think they are going to give him a reward, as well."

Darcy debated what to tell Lydia. He did not want her to know who he was, but he desperately wished to teach the foolish girl a lesson. "Did you ever consider," he said leaning towards her with a piercing gaze, "that I might be wearing these handcuffs because *I* am the ruthless one, and I was being transported to gaol by the police?"

Lydia's face drained of all colour. She tried to smile, but it appeared she could not. "George would not do something like that!"

The sound of horses' hooves pummelling towards them prompted Darcy to nod at the window. "The authorities will not look kindly on what you and your friend have done. I suggest you tell them everything you know and perhaps they will go easy on you."

The carriage came to a halt, and several men on horseback surrounded it. Foster ordered Wickham to drop his pistol, put his hands up in the air, and step down. "If you try anything stupid, we'll shoot you without a second thought!"

Another carriage pulled up and stopped alongside theirs. Darcy and Lydia watched as Wickham was handcuffed. She turned back to Darcy, her eyes filled with fear. "This cannot be happening!"

The door to Darcy's carriage was thrown open, and Lydia drew back with a cry, recoiling from the two men reaching in for her.

"Come, ye little pest!" One of the men grabbed her by the wrists to pull her out, as she tried to wrestle from his grip. She was not strong enough, however, and the two men were easily able to extricate her. Darcy watched as they took her to the waiting carriage. At least she was helped into it a little more politely than Wickham had been.

Darcy's insides writhed as he considered Lydia's plight and what this would mean for the Bennet family. He slowly climbed out of the carriage and called Foster over.

"We got them!" Foster said. "Thanks, Darcy. I owe you a great deal."

Darcy shook his head. "You did not catch the ones truly responsible. These two were merely doing the bidding of the real culprits. They were going to take me to them. You need to find out where those men are."

Foster narrowed his eyes. "Are you certain?"

Darcy nodded. "I am. And Foster, I have a favour to ask of you since you *do* owe me a great deal."

"Certainly. What is it?"

Darcy blew out a frustrated puff of air. "I shall tell you, but first, would you kindly remove these handcuffs?"

Chapter 22

There were innumerable emotions two days later as Elizabeth, her father, and cousin set off for the docks at St. Mary's to make the return voyage to the mainland of England. It had not been easy to say goodbye to their loved ones a second time. Staying with the Clowers had been a well-needed respite, and yet while being asked again and again about their adventure, their only thought now was to return home. David had visited the local doctor, who felt that his arm had not been broken, but still needed to be kept wrapped up for another day or two, to insure its complete healing.

While there was much anticipation to finally reach London, the dread of another sea voyage loomed over them, particularly Mr. Bennet. They were all grateful for the shorter journey.

They were thankful for the beautiful sunny day as they boarded the sailing vessel. If the winds remained favourable, they would reach their destination at the port of Plymouth by day's end.

As they sailed across the shimmering blue waters, Elizabeth remained on deck, enjoying the warmth of the sun. Her thoughts were somewhere else, however, as a myriad of emotions were a constant reminder to her of how she had begun to feel about Mr. Darcy, from the small tingles that rippled through her to the deepest warmth that made her feel as though she might melt.

She kept watch for that first sign of land, and by late afternoon she was rewarded with the sight. She, her father, and David breathed a sigh of relief as the ship finally pulled into the dock just before twilight. As they made arrangements to spend the night at a nearby inn, a beautiful sunset welcomed them home.

~~*

Another day and a half of travel brought them to Brighton. Travelling by carriage was certainly not as quick, nor as pleasant for the body, as one was confined in a small space for hours on end. It was more reliable, however, and while there was always the possibility of being waylaid by accident, a break down, or even highwaymen, they were pleased that their journey to Brighton was tediously uneventful.

As they made their way through the town to the Forsters' address, they began to see more and more redcoats walking about. Elizabeth kept her eyes to the window, wondering if she would recognize any of the soldiers who had been in Meryton. She let out a sigh as she concluded Lydia would have certainly had her share of dances, balls, and parties these past few weeks.

The carriage pulled up and stopped in front of a modest home. As they waited for the door to be opened, Mr. Bennet looked at Elizabeth and David, a single brow raised. "What say you that we do not tell Lydia, her sisters, and especially Mrs. Bennet about Lizzy being held captive by pirates? I suppose there is no way we can avoid telling them about the pirates attacking the ship, but let us not allow Mrs. Bennet the delight of imagining that we were in the gravest danger." He sat up as the driver came to the door. "She need only know that we were safely locked up in the bowels of the ship as our crew victoriously fought off the pirate's crew." They all agreed, and the door was opened so they could step out.

"I hope Lydia will be ready to leave with us and not squabble about it," Elizabeth said. "You know how stubborn she can be!"

"Is Lydia stubborn?" Mr. Bennet asked with a laugh. "I cannot imagine why you would say that, Lizzy!"

David looked at Elizabeth quizzically. "I have not heard much about this sister. Is there anything I need to know?"

Elizabeth's curls bounced about her face as she gave a quick shake of her head. "I beg you, David, please do not take her behaviour to be an example of that of the rest of our family."

"Come, come now, Lizzy. Is she that bad?" Mr. Bennet turned to David. "She is young and a bit immature, but she shall outgrow it."

David nodded his head at Mr. Bennet, but gave Elizabeth a sympathetic smile.

They came up to the door and knocked. It was opened, and they were brought into a small parlour, where Colonel Forster greeted them. "Welcome! Come in, we have been expecting you."

Mrs. Forster was there as well. After she greeted her guests, she walked to the back of the room wringing her hands, a worried expression on her pale face.

Mr. Bennet introduced David to the Forsters. When Mr. Forster did not seem inclined to say anything, he said, "I hope my daughter was not too much trouble during her stay!"

The look between Mr. and Mrs. Forster did not go unnoticed. "Please, sit down."

They sat down, and when the Forsters said nothing more, Elizabeth asked, "Is something amiss? Where is Lydia?"

Mr. Forster, who was still standing, came up to them, his hands tightly clasped together. "Something of a most unexpected and rather… dreadful nature has occurred."

Mr. Bennet shot out of his chair, his face as white as his shirt. "What has happened?" he demanded. "Where is my daughter?"

Mr. Forster raised his hands. "She is all right. She is upstairs." He looked to his wife. "Would you please bring her down?"

Mr. Bennet was visibly shaken as he slowly sat down. "Please tell me what has happened!"

"Your daughter was involved in a rather unfortunate incident with one of my officers which resulted in criminal activity and arrest."

Mr. Bennet bolted out of his chair again. "What? I cannot believe this of Lydia!"

Elizabeth widened her eyes and brought her hand up to cover her mouth. She could not bring herself to look at David, who, she was certain, was just as shocked and appalled as she and her father were.

"Apparently she was asked to participate in a scheme to rescue someone they believed to be in the wrong hands. As it turned out, it was a prisoner being transported to London to face criminal charges."

"No!" Elizabeth cried out, burying her face in her hands. "How could she do such a thing?"

Mr. Bennet was unable to move or formulate one thought. Finally, he asked, "Was my daughter caught and arrested?"

Mr. Forster nodded. "Yes, she was."

"Yet, she is free?" Mr. Bennet asked.

"Yes. It was determined she was acting out of ignorance and a foolish desire to please Mr. Wickham."

"Mr. Wickham!" Elizabeth exclaimed. "Oh, poor, stupid Lydia!"

"She was released yesterday. No charges will be brought against her. I am convinced she has had her share of punishment, as she had to spend several days in gaol while it was sorted out."

Elizabeth could sit still no longer. She stood up and walked to the window and looked out. She could not trust herself to say anything, as angry as she was. Yet it was anger directed at herself, as she had chosen not to divulge Wickham's true character to her family several months ago when she had come to know of it.

The sounds of footsteps drew everyone's attention. Lydia walked in, rather sheepishly, at first, but when she saw her father, she ran to him and threw her arms about him.

"Oh, Papa, it has been most upsetting! I can't wait to get home and away from here. Such a misunderstanding!"

"We shall talk about this later, Lydia. Are your things packed?"

Lydia nodded. "Yes, I'm ready. Oh, I can't tell you how happy I am to see you... to see you all!" She suddenly looked at David. "La! Who is this?"

"Lydia, this is my cousin's son, David Adams." Mr. Bennet turned to David with a look of resignation. "David, may I introduce you to my youngest daughter, Lydia!"

Elizabeth raised an eyebrow and smiled at David as he cordially and most civilly greeted Lydia. "I am pleased to make your acquaintance. I have enjoyed getting to know your father and sister."

Lydia's belongings were brought down, and Mr. Bennet turned to the couple. "We shall trespass on your hospitality no longer. I regret that my daughter caused you such consternation, and I hope that Wickham will receive the punishment he deserves!"

"I am certain he will," Mr. Forster said. "If not from the court system, then from me!" He shook his head in disgust. "I will not tolerate such lawless conduct!" Mr. Forster's chest heaved. "Please know how grieved we are that this happened while your daughter was our guest."

Mr. Bennet only nodded. His brows were tightly knit together and a frown etched his face. "Come, we must take our leave."

They walked out quickly and silently, each feeling the mortification of Lydia's actions. Elizabeth could not imagine a more dire circumstance than what they had just discovered. She could only imagine what David now thought of her family.

They boarded the carriage, and Lydia's belongings were secured with the others. As they drove away, there was a deafening silence in the carriage. Lydia played with a strand of her hair, repeatedly twisting it around her finger. Mr. Bennet stared out the window, his fingers rubbing the bridge of his nose. David read a book, but he did not seem to be making any progress, as Elizabeth had not seen him turning a single page.

Elizabeth leaned back against the seat and stared out the window, glancing only occasionally at the others. She was pained that her father seemed unwilling to confront Lydia, although it might have been because of David's presence. She was humiliated that David had to witness this and was fairly certain he would think long and hard about what his relationship to the Bennets would be in the future. If news of this circulated, it would bring disgrace to their whole family.

When Lydia began humming a merry tune, Elizabeth could keep her frustration to herself no longer.

"Lydia, have you no shame? Do you not realize that what you did was terribly wrong?"

Lydia looked up in surprise. "Did Colonel Forster not tell you?" She pounded her hands into her lap. "We thought we were helping someone! How was I to know that the person was in trouble with the law?" She shook her head. "It's the fault of those men that put George up to it!"

"George!" Elizabeth said in disgust. "Are you on such intimate terms with him that you call him by his first name?"

Lydia shrugged her shoulders. "And why not? I don't see anything wrong with it."

Elizabeth let out a huff and turned her face away.

"You have greatly disappointed me, Lydia," Mr. Bennet said.

"You should have known better. You could have been killed! It was very foolish and very dangerous!"

Lydia cocked her head back and forth. "Well, it wasn't really all that dangerous." She let out a chuckle. "It turns out the man in the carriage was not the man we were supposed to free. It's a good thing, too, because we later found out the man we were after was a pirate! Can you imagine that?"

"A pirate!" Elizabeth said, her face turning white. "Whatever do you mean?"

Lydia's eyes grew wide. "Calm down, Lizzy! I told you we didn't know he was a pirate. But we found out that it wasn't really him…in the carriage… I think his name was Lockerby… but it was someone else dressed up to look like him!"

Elizabeth felt the world about her begin to swim. Her cheeks grew hot, and her heart pounded wildly. A very real pain grew in her stomach as she comprehended what Lydia was saying.

"Mr. Darcy!" her father and David exclaimed at the same time.

Lydia responded with a look of astonishment. She shook her head, "No, I said Lockerby. He was…"

"It's Lockerly," Mr. Bennet said tersely. "And you can count yourself lucky, indeed, that it was not him you encountered."

Lydia twisted her head. "How do you know who he is, and what does this have to do with Mr. Darcy?"

Elizabeth slowly shook her head and felt her eyes well with tears. She knew what this meant. Now Mr. Darcy was acquainted with her sister's injudicious actions. She felt as though she might get physically sick.

Mr. Bennet's jaw tightened, and he pointed his finger at Lydia. "Young lady! You have no idea what we suffered at the hands of Lockerly, and to think that you would have helped him escape has me…" Mr. Bennet's whole being shook. "I am so upset I can barely think straight!"

Lydia drew back into her seat. It was not often that Mr. Bennet got angry, but when he did, one could readily see it in the redness of his face, the way his body shook, and the raised tone of his voice. This was one of those times.

She waited a few moments before asking her question again. "What does this have to do with Mr. Darcy?"

Elizabeth listened as David very calmly and patiently told her that it was likely Mr. Darcy in the carriage; that they had encountered him at sea when he had been impersonating Lockerly.

Lydia's eyes widened. "Mr. Darcy was in the carriage?" She looked at David with incredulity. She then turned to her father. "The Mr. Darcy who was Mr. Bingley's friend? *That* Mr. Darcy?"

"Yes, Lydia!" Elizabeth replied harshly. "*That* Mr. Darcy!"

Neither Elizabeth nor her father seemed capable of explaining to Lydia about their encounter with Lockerly and how Mr. Darcy played a part in the whole affair, so David was the one who calmly told her of their adventure.

Lydia listened to all the particulars of the adventure, which – from the entranced look on her face – she most likely wished could have been hers. As they had agreed before, he omitted the part about Elizabeth being held captive by pirates on the small island.

Elizabeth knew that neither she nor her father would have been able to say more than a few words without their anger towards Lydia spilling out, so she was grateful that David was there to tell the story.

She could think of nothing save what Mr. Darcy must now think of her family. She could hardly breathe as she grasped that this would certainly preclude him from ever wishing to see her again.

~~*

The journey to London, with an overnight stay at an inn, progressed at a pace too slow for everyone's comfort. Elizabeth could barely bring herself to speak to Lydia. Her father buried himself in the pages of a book, thereby separating himself from all his aggravations. David remained in polite, but stilted conversation with the young girl.

Lydia's impertinent and inappropriate outbursts gradually tempered. Elizabeth glanced up at her occasionally and actually saw evidence of worry. She would bite her fingernails, which was odd because she was always so concerned about her appearance. At other times she would furrow her brows as if a thought distressed her. Elizabeth was not certain her sister was worried about herself and the gravity of her actions, but feared her sister's concern was about Wickham. His fate would rest in the hands of the courts, and his sentence would likely be harsh.

She wondered whether Mr. Darcy was concerned at all for his

childhood friend. Would he have been willing to step in and help his friend? Elizabeth's eyes shot wide open. Could it be? She turned slowly to Lydia. Her youngest sister should have faced a judge and been sentenced for her part in breaking the law. But she had not.

Elizabeth felt her face flush as she considered that perhaps Mr. Darcy may have had some influence over the charges against Lydia being dropped. She looked at her father, David, and then back to her sister. She let out a shaky breath.

She suddenly felt an onslaught of tears threaten to spill out. The man that she had so callously refused to marry was certainly not the man she had thought he was. She turned her head away from the others, closed her eyes, and let the tears trail down her cheeks.

~~*

It was almost dusk when the carriage pulled up to the Gardiners' home. Everyone was weary from the days of travel and looked forward to a decent meal and comfortable bed in which to sleep.

The Gardiners welcomed them all, and then heard about the storm and an abbreviated account of their pirating adventure. When everyone repaired to their rooms to ready themselves for dinner, Elizabeth remained behind and told them about Lydia, so it would not have to be done in front of everyone. The Gardiners were astonished that she would do such a thing, but were also quite perplexed about Mr. Darcy's involvement in all of it. Elizabeth then explained how they encountered him at sea.

"It is odd, is it not, Lizzy? Everyone thought him so proud and above everyone else!" Mrs. Gardiner said. "Perhaps he is not as bad as you once thought him to be."

Elizabeth shook her head, her brows knitted together. "No, Aunt. We were all wrong about him. I was especially wrong about him and have much to regret."

Mrs. Gardiner patted her niece's hand. "You need not be so hard on yourself, Lizzy. The man most likely never had the slightest idea how strong your dislike was."

~~*

As they gathered for dinner that evening, Elizabeth felt a great deal of strength just being with her aunt. She was a lady for whom she had a great deal of respect, and she always appreciated and benefited from her reassuring words and sage advice.

As they ate, a letter was brought in and handed to Mr. Bennet.

As he took the letter, he said, "Ah, Mrs. Bennet must have known we arrived!" He laughed as he looked down at the missive. "But it is not anyone's handwriting that I am familiar with! Such neatness and exactness! Who could it be from?"

They all watched him eagerly as he opened it. "Hmmm," he said in a drawn out tone. "This is rather interesting!"

"What is it, Papa?" Elizabeth asked.

"It seems as though you, David, and I have been invited to Mr. Darcy's town home tomorrow afternoon. Shall we accept?

Chapter 23

Darcy paced nervously in his study, watching the mantel clock that seemed to move at an unreasonably slow pace. He lifted his fingers to rub his chin and was surprised – as he had often been of late – to find it clean shaven. On the journey back to his town home, he had spent the night at an inn, where he had enjoyed a much-needed bath and employed the innkeeper to cut off his unruly long hair and give him a shave. He also had bought himself some new clothes so when he stepped into his house in London, the servants would not be shocked at his appearance. If he had arrived in his previous state, he doubted they would have even recognized him!

He had not felt as though he would be quite back to himself, however, until his valet tended to him. Stewart had been waiting when Darcy arrived and immediately had set forth to improve upon what the innkeeper had done to his hair and beard.

It was almost two o'clock, and he knew that at any minute his guests would arrive. He was anxious to tell them about the reward, but his excitement was tempered by what had happened with Lydia. He would not divulge knowledge of the situation unless he found they had become aware of it.

There was a light tap at the open door. He smiled, knowing that tap well.

"Come in, Georgiana."

The young girl walked in and glanced at the clock. "They ought to be here soon."

"Yes."

A gentle smile tugged at her lips. "What are their names again?"

Darcy leaned casually against the wall, not wishing to give rise to any suspicions on Georgiana's part. "Mr. Bennet, Mr. David Adams, and Miss Elizabeth Bennet."

Georgiana pursed her lips and nodded her head. She walked over to her brother's desk and picked up a pen, twirling it about in her fingers. "And they somehow were involved in this pirating adventure of yours."

He nodded. "Very involved. One of the reasons I invited them today was because they are to receive a portion of the reward for finding some jewels Lockerly had hidden in the ship."

"I am certain they will be very pleased."

"I believe they shall be."

Georgiana suddenly furrowed her brows and looked askance at her brother. She reached into the pocket of her dress and pulled out some paper. She looked down at it, and Darcy realized it was a letter.

"Would you mind if I asked you a question?" She smiled sweetly at him, and Darcy almost detected a slight quiver in her voice.

"Does it have to do with that letter?"

She nodded and took in a deep breath. "You wrote this letter to me last autumn while you were visiting Mr. Bingley at Netherfield."

Darcy slowly nodded his head, not realizing his sister kept his correspondence. His heart began to race a little faster than it already was.

"In it, and in several other letters, you mention – quite often – a Miss Elizabeth Bennet." She looked up with beseeching eyes. "Is this the same Elizabeth Bennet who is coming today?"

Darcy again nodded, wondering what all he had written about her.

"I do not have all your letters here, as some are at Pemberley. I believe there were others that were written this spring when you were in Kent, and she was there." She unfolded the fine linen paper and looked down. "You say, 'Miss Bennet is one of those fine ladies that one seldom meets, who is lively and intelligent and does not seem to care for all the trappings of the fine circles in society. She is a rare and delightful find.'"

Darcy actually felt his cheeks warm as she read this. He wondered what he should tell his sister. As he contemplated this, she continued.

"While I do not have the letters written while you were in Kent, I do recollect you mentioning that you were about to ask for her hand. And yet, I heard no further mention of her. When you returned and seemed so distraught, I was so concerned for you that I forgot all about your letters. I do not think I would have ever suspected that she – or any lady, for that matter – would refuse you." Uncertainty wrinkled her brow. "Tell me, Brother. Is that what happened?"

Darcy's hands began to shake, and he clasped them tightly together. "Yes, but please, there is so much to tell; I do not have the time now. Please welcome her as a guest and say no more about it."

"Oh, Brother, I am so sorry," she walked to him and wrapped her arms about him, leaning her head against his chest. "Now I know why you were so downcast when you returned from Kent. Is there any hope for...?"

"Nothing can ever come of it," he interjected. "She and her cousin, Mr. Adams, are likely to marry." He leaned down and kissed the top of her head.

Georgiana looked up at her brother, a twinkle in her eyes. "Shall I like her, do you think?"

Darcy tousled the young girl's hair. "I think you shall like her very much."

When he pulled away, he placed his hands on her shoulders. "I need to meet with our guests privately, and then I shall come for you and make the introductions."

Georgiana smiled and stood on her toes to reach up and give him a kiss on the cheek. "I shall be eagerly waiting."

Darcy watched his sister walk away. His heart pounded thunderously, and he felt a real sense of grief that his sister would never know Elizabeth as the kind sister he knew she would have been to her.

He heard the sound of the bell and gave a tug on his coat. He took in a deep breath and walked out of his study to the parlour, where he would meet his guests.

On the way, he stopped in front of a hallway mirror and looked at his reflection. He was not interested in the fact that he had often been told that he was handsome, but he only hoped he would look presentable to Elizabeth. He reached up and touched the scab above his eye. The swelling and redness were gone, but he would likely have a scar. He hoped she would not be distressed by what she had done. If only he could tell her how it allowed him to think of her each time he looked upon it.

He took in another deep breath and tugged again at his coat. Shaking his head, he thought, *It was so much easier for me when she did not know who I was!*

He walked into the parlour, sat down, and then bolted to his feet when he heard voices approach.

His butler, Godfrey, appeared at the door and announced the guests. Darcy walked to the door and gave a quick bow, inviting them in. His breath caught when he saw Elizabeth. He wondered whether it was finally being able to see her again after so many days or that he had feared she might not come.

"Welcome. Please, come in and have a seat."

Mr. Bennet took Darcy's extended hand. "Now there is the Darcy we all knew back in Hertfordshire!" He turned to David. "He is a completely different man, is he not?"

"Very different! The only thing I recognize is the bruise above his eye! Otherwise, I would have never known he was the same man! It is no wonder you did not recognize him." He let out a laugh as he shook hands with their host.

Elizabeth winced at the reference to his bruise. She dipped a small curtsey as Darcy gave her a short bow and a reassuring smile.

"I am glad you have come."

"How could we not?" Mr. Bennet interjected. "We owe our lives to you, well, my Lizzy's, at least, and now we come to find out you were somehow involved in my other *esteemed* daughter's venture into lawlessness. We understand Lydia had a rather unexpected encounter with you."

Darcy grimaced at the mention of Lydia, and he saw Elizabeth cast her eyes down and bite her lip. It pained him to see the shame that tinged her cheeks a rosy pink. He wondered how much they knew of the extent of his involvement. He had to change the subject and improve the mood, and he knew exactly how to do it.

"Mr. Bennet, all that is forgotten. I did not invite you over this afternoon to discuss Miss Lydia, but rather because I have some news to share with you that I believe you all shall be delighted to hear."

"You have my attention, Mr. Darcy, and I, for one, am eager to change the subject."

"Good!" Darcy clasped his hands together. "I do not know if you are aware, but there was prize money for my crew for the capture of Lockerly."

David spoke up. "I understand that crewmen are often rewarded in that way. But what does that have to do with us?"

Darcy stood up and walked over to a small desk. He opened the door and pulled out some paper.

"These are banker's cheques that are being bestowed to you and the other passengers for the return of the jewels." Despite being completely the truth, he did not wish for them to find out he had had a say as to how it would be distributed amongst them. He handed the cheques to Mr. Bennet and Mr. Adams. "He looked at Mr. Bennet, holding up one last cheque. "I have one more, sir, that with your permission, is reserved for your daughter, as Miss Bennet found the jewels and was instrumental in coming up with the scheme that brought Lockerly down while keeping the jewels intact." He looked with questioning eyes at Elizabeth's father.

"Well, Lizzy, if you promise not to tell your mother or any of your sisters about this, you certainly deserve it." He gave a nod of his head in affirmation to Mr. Darcy's request.

Elizabeth took the cheque, and her eyes widened as she looked at it. "Thank you, Mr. Darcy," she said nervously. "I am not quite certain what I will do with it…"

"I trust that you are wise enough to handle it judiciously."

She looked up to see him smile briefly and give a few nods of his head.

"Oh, be assured she will," Mr. Bennet said. "And I thank you, too. I barely consider myself worthy of it, but I know what I shall do with it. Since, due to my own neglect, my daughters do not have decent dowries, I intend to make it up to them." He then let out a huff. "I am not certain, however, that Lydia deserves any part of this unless she improves in character."

David then added his thanks.

Mr. Darcy nodded. "You are indeed welcome, although I was merely the bearer of the good tidings." He clasped his hands together. "Now, if you do not mind, I should like to introduce you to my sister. Would you please excuse me while I go get her?"

Elizabeth looked up and smiled. "Your sister is here? I would love to meet her."

Her soft smile warmed him, and her eagerness to meet his sister delighted him. "She is eager to meet you, as well."

He began to walk out, but Elizabeth stopped him. "Does she know about your pirating adventure?" She gave him an encouraging smile. "I would not wish to enlighten her on a subject you wished to keep from her."

Darcy nodded. "I have informed her of it, yes, Miss Bennet." He gave another single nod of his head and walked to the door, but then stopped and looked back at Elizabeth. "I tell my sister everything."

~~*

As she watched Mr. Darcy confidently stride out of the room – much unlike his stride as Lockerly or Captain Smith – her heart pounded relentlessly. Could he have told his sister about her refusing his offer of marriage? If she was as proud as Mr. Wickham had led her to believe, would she treat her with contempt for slighting her brother?

She had been a fool. She stood in a handsome room, decorated with beautifully carved wood mouldings and furniture with intricately embroidered tapestry coverings. She had been struck by the simplicity of the outside of the house when their carriage pulled up, but upon entering, she readily saw its fine qualities.

A marble entryway welcomed them, but there was warmth in the reds and golds of the area rugs and window coverings. A small flower print wall covering added a cheery feeling against the heavy wood of the furnishings. It was all very pleasing to Elizabeth's senses.

She walked over to the window, which looked out at the park on the north side. It was more extensive than any she would have imagined in town. A beautiful garden was in full bloom, with a rock path that wound through it to the back. She could just see a small pond with a few benches placed near it. The prospect from this vantage point was very pleasing. She imagined that walking within the garden would be a pure delight.

She shook her head slowly as she realized how all of this could have been hers. She could only imagine what Pemberley must be like. And yet, it was not these things that caused her to regret her earlier decision. It was that the man she had thought was full of pride and arrogance was truly a man of integrity, generosity, and compassion.

The sound of a young girl's cheery laugh drew her attention from the window. Mr. Darcy walked in with a tall girl, whose features were very different than his. She had blond, straight hair that was pulled up into a tight knot on the back of her head. Not a stray curl was in sight. She had deep blue eyes that hinted of shyness but were welcoming. She stood in the shadow of her brother, whose dark features and muscular build seemed to radiate strength to her.

"May I introduce my sister to you? Mr. Bennet, Mr. Adams, and Miss Elizabeth Bennet, this is Miss Georgiana Darcy."

She curtseyed and nodded shyly, but her smile was pronounced. "It is a pleasure to make your acquaintance," she said, walking over to a small couch. Turning to Elizabeth, she said, "Come, please, have a seat by me. I have asked that tea and cakes be brought in."

Elizabeth studied her as she walked over. The young girl was obviously shy and had not an ounce of pride in her. She absently shook her head as she chided herself for even considering that Wickham's estimation of her would have had the slightest bit of truth in it. Their eyes met and Elizabeth smiled.

As Elizabeth sat down, Miss Darcy leaned over and whispered, "I so much enjoy the conversation of a lady and do not often have the opportunity."

"I will gladly oblige you." Elizabeth felt as though Miss Darcy was terribly shy, rather than proud, so she was determined to set her at ease.

"I understand that you play the pianoforte," Miss Darcy said.

Elizabeth shook her head. "I do not pride myself on my abilities. I play only tolerably. But I understand that you are most proficient. I have heard much praise for your talent."

The young girl looked down and blushed. "I do so enjoy it, but my favourite times to play are when I am alone or for my brother." She glanced at him with eyes filled with admiration and then turned back to Elizabeth. "I am often asked to perform before others, and I hope someday I will overcome my fears."

Elizabeth smiled warmly. "I am confident you shall!"

Miss Darcy seemed uncertain what to speak about next.

Elizabeth leaned in towards her. "I understand that your brother told you all about our seafaring adventure."

Miss Darcy's eyes lit up. "Oh, yes! It must have been so terrifying while at the same time exciting!"

Elizabeth shook her head. "I cannot say I felt those things at the same time, but I definitely felt both."

"I can hardly keep my countenance when I think of my brother as a pirate." She chuckled softly. "It seems so unlike him."

Elizabeth laughed and looked over at him. "I agree! It was so unlike him, that even though my father and I were acquainted with him, we did not realize for some time that it was him."

Darcy seemed to notice the laughter and glanced over. His eyes met Elizabeth's, and she quickly turned back to Miss Darcy, feeling a rush of emotion brought on by the intensity of his gaze. She hoped the young girl would not notice.

The two talked on a variety of subjects, and at length the tea and cakes were brought in. Georgiana excused herself and went to inspect the savouries.

Elizabeth found her gaze settling on Mr. Darcy as he spoke to her father and David. He was sitting back in a chair, leaning casually on one arm, one leg crossed over the other. His voice resonated with eloquence. She smiled as she thought of how he had disguised not only his looks, but also his voice, affecting an accent and even a different tone. He had a very calm and reassuring voice, and he spoke with great insight and intelligence. His hair had been neatly trimmed, and his face shaven smooth. He was handsome. She had always thought so, but her dislike had not allowed her to appreciate it. Now, when it was in all probability too late, she did.

She began to wonder just how smooth a man's face could be. His looked so smooth. She suddenly wished she could walk over and stroke his face with her fingers.

Her eyes widened at the direction of her thoughts. She looked about her, trying to rein in the emotions that prompted such a desire. She doubted that they would evaporate any time soon. Fortunately Miss Darcy walked back over with a servant carrying a silver tray.

"Miss Bennet, would you care for a piece of lemon cake, apple tart, or some plum pudding?"

"An apple tart, please. It is my favourite."

Miss Darcy's eyes widened. "Oh? It is my brother's favourite, as well." She smiled as she directed the servant to serve her.

The two ladies found themselves drawn into the men's conversation. Elizabeth had to refrain from shaking her head in astonishment as she saw such a different side of Mr. Darcy. He exhibited gracious hospitality, far different from his behaviour in Hertfordshire. She recollected him saying to her in Kent that he found it difficult to speak to those with whom he was not acquainted. He certainly seemed comfortable and at ease speaking with her father and cousin.

When they had finished tea, Mr. Bennet stood up. "Well, Mr. Darcy, we would not wish to overstay our welcome. We really ought to take our leave."

Mr. Darcy pulled out his watch and looked at it with a frown. "I had hoped another acquaintance of yours would have been here by now. He wished to see you and said he would try to be here by three o'clock."

"Who is that?" Elizabeth asked.

Mr. Darcy turned to her, his dark eyes reflecting something she could not decipher. "Mr. Bingley," he said softly. He studied her as if to gauge her reaction.

"Oh," she said. "I am sorry we will miss him." She wondered whether he was now attempting to right the wrong he had committed when he separated Mr. Bingley and her sister.

"Whom did you miss?" Mr. Bingley stepped into the room, a smile lighting up his face. "I am sorry I am late, Darcy."

He walked in and shook hands with Mr. Bennet, was introduced to David, and came up to Elizabeth.

"It is good to see you again. It has been too long," Bingley said with a smile, as he seemed to search her face.

She returned his smile. "It *has* been too long." She stole a glance at Darcy, who was watching the exchange. "We had hoped that you would return to Netherfield."

"You had?"

Elizabeth nodded and stole another glance at Darcy. "Yes, we *all* did."

There was a bit more conversation, but at length Mr. Bennet announced that they really must leave. They expressed their thanks to Mr. Darcy for the reward, to Mr. and Miss Darcy for their hospitality, and expressed their fervent desire to see Mr. Bingley back at Netherfield.

They all walked towards the front door, and then Mr. Darcy stopped. "Oh, I forgot something. Miss Bennet, I have something for you back in the parlour." He looked up at the others, saying, "I shall return her to you in a moment."

Walking alongside Mr. Darcy again gave rise to emotions that ranged from a quickening pulse and tingling sensation to a real fire burning within.

When they walked into the parlour, Darcy picked something up from a chair on the far side of the room. When she saw the light green colour, she knew it was her bonnet.

He brought it to her and placed it in her hands, their fingers touching, causing an even greater rise in her feelings. She kept her eyes down, eyeing his fingers which lingered. She knew he likely could see her rosy cheeks and did not know what to do about it. She felt her hands begin to shake as he pulled away. She wished to thank him, but knew that her voice would tremble with emotion if she did.

"I wanted to make sure this was returned to you."

Elizabeth tightened her grip on her bonnet as she attempted to mask her turmoil. She felt as though her heart would burst if she did not express how drastically her feelings towards him had changed. She looked up, and her eyes locked with his.

"Mr. Darcy," she said softly, "I want you to know…"

The clanking of dishes startled her, and she turned to see two servants removing their tea and cakes. "So sorry," one said as she dipped a curtsey. "We thought everyone had left."

Elizabeth took in a deep breath. "Yes, yes. I was just leaving." She looked up at Mr. Darcy and tried to smile. "Thank you, again, for all you have done."

Elizabeth turned and walked out of the room and the short distance to the door, where she joined the others. She knew not whether they could see the effects of the warmth in her cheeks, the trembling of her hands, or the clamorous pulsing of her heart. She could only hope she would not be required to speak, for she could not trust herself to have one coherent thought or express it without her voice unduly quaking.

Chapter 24

Mr. Bennet suffered an attack of a stomach ailment that left him quite unwell the morning the party had planned to leave for Longbourn, and they were compelled to delay their journey. He was indisposed to any sort of interaction, eating, and especially travelling. It was all Elizabeth could do to get him to eat and drink just a little to keep his strength from waning.

When not caring for her father, Elizabeth enjoyed spending time with her aunt. She had several opportunities to stroll through the parks and streets of London with her and David. Lydia accompanied them on only one occasion. Since walking without a particular destination was not a favourite pastime – and she would only be satisfied by a destination that included at least four shops – she usually remained at the Gardiners. Because of her behaviour in Brighton, they felt it incumbent to ensure she was under her uncle's close scrutiny at all times.

After four days, Mr. Bennet finally felt well enough to leave his room, join the family at meals, and visit. He still felt weak but was certain he would be ready to leave on the morrow.

An early morning start allowed them to make the journey at a leisurely pace, in deference to Mr. Bennet, who still felt the effects of his illness. By afternoon, everyone was eagerly anticipating arriving home.

As they passed through the small town of Meryton, just a few miles from Longbourn, Elizabeth let out a sigh and addressed

David. "This is Meryton, an easy walking distance from our home." Elizabeth pointed out stores and other places of business in the small town as they passed.

"It is a charming town, Elizabeth. I know I will enjoy my stay here."

Lydia gave her head a shake as she looked out the window. "But it shall be so dreary! The militia is gone, and there shall be nothing to do!"

"Lydia!" Elizabeth scolded. "You should be looking forward to seeing Mother and your sisters again!" She clenched her jaw and took in a breath between her teeth. "I believe that even if the whole army were in Meryton, you would not be allowed out after what you have done!" She looked to her father for corroboration

Mr. Bennet wearily waved a hand through the air. "She is correct, young lady. Until you learn to apply yourself in a useful employment for at least one hour a day, you shall attend no balls, no parties, and no soldier shall come within five miles of Longbourn!" His leaned his head back and closed his normally animated eyes, which were now dull and slightly sunken. He pressed his fingertips to the bridge of his nose and rubbed them in a circular motion.

Elizabeth believed that his illness had been exacerbated by his deep anxiety over what Lydia had done. She wondered whether he would ever fully recover from the disgrace that came very close to overshadowing their family.

"You won't tell Mama, will you? She does not need to know. It was not that bad, and it will only upset her, thinking I could have been killed."

Elizabeth leaned forward in the seat and looked pointedly at her sister. "Lydia, getting killed was not the only thing that could have happened! You could have been sentenced to serve time in prison."

Lydia huffed, folding her arms across her chest. "I think you are making too much of this!"

Elizabeth stole a glance at David, who was staring out the window, and then to her father, who was either sleeping or pretending to be asleep. "I do think Mother must be told, as well as our sisters."

"Well, Kitty will think it awfully brave of me. She will be jealous that I had some excitement while she had to stay at home with nothing to do!"

Elizabeth pursed her lips together to refrain from blurting out what she truly wished to say. Fortunately, David intervened.

"Miss Lydia, we all make mistakes in life, but when we do, it is best to learn from them and not idly dismiss them. Granted, the gravity of this could have been must worse, but unless you comprehend that, you have learned naught."

He ended with a smile, and Elizabeth thought she saw a glimmer of understanding in Lydia's eyes. It was good he was here to gently admonish his young cousin without being overly consumed with the exasperation she and her father felt.

As the carriage pulled up in front of Longbourn, Jane and Kitty rushed out, followed by Mary. The weary travellers stepped down from the carriage and Mr. Bennet began introducing David to his three other daughters. Once introductions were done, Elizabeth turned to Jane, embracing her.

"Oh, Jane! It is so good to be home!" She pulled away and looked at her, noticing something different in her countenance. "You seem especially radiant! What is it?"

Jane bit her lip and her eyes welled with tears. "It is... it is Mr. Bingley. He has returned!"

Elizabeth's joy matched her sister's. "I am so pleased to hear that! Did he tell you we saw him?"

Jane nodded blissfully, her eyes revealing the depth of her joy.

After giving Kitty and Mary a kiss on the top of their heads, Mr. Bennet walked up to Jane. He smiled warmly and whispered, "It is good to see you, my dear." He then leaned down and kissed her, as well.

Lydia said something to Kitty, and the two squealed and ran to the house. Elizabeth let out a long sigh. "I am so glad to be finally home. How I have missed my favourite sister!" She squeezed her sister's hand and noticed David walking over. "We have so much to talk about, but we shall talk later.

David came up and took Jane's hand. "Miss Jane Bennet, I feel as though I already know you. I have heard so much about you from your sister."

Jane smiled. "It is always a pleasure to meet family."

As Jane and David talked, Elizabeth walked over to Mary and greeted her. "How have you been, Mary?" she asked.

Mary bit her lip. "It has been quiet, which satisfied me quite well, but poor Kitty has felt the loss of Lydia and the militia."

"And Mama?"

Mary chuckled. "At first, she fretted every day about you and Papa, but she soon found other things to occupy herself and her thoughts."

Elizabeth raised her brows as she considered that most likely when they were in the most dire situation, her mother had no concerns about them at all!

As the family gathered for tea and cakes in the dining room, everyone wanted to know about the trip, how Mr. Bennet's sister was faring, and what St. Mary's was like. Since they had agreed to divulge to the family only the barest details about their journey home, they each had to think carefully before answering. Mr. Bennet had even decided he was not going to mention the reward. He would, at some point, surprise everyone with the news that each of his daughters now had a suitable dowry.

Lydia shared with tempered enthusiasm about her time with the Forsters in Brighton. There was no need to communicate the news of her scandalous behaviour in front of the whole family when they were so excited everyone was home. Mr. Bennet decided he would speak to Mrs. Bennet alone in the morning. He was certain Lydia herself would spread the news to the others.

When everyone finally retired for the evening, Elizabeth found herself sitting on Jane's bed, eager to share some of the unspoken details of their time away.

"Mr. Darcy was very gallant in coming to my rescue when the pirates had taken us captive. Of course, I had no idea that it was him until later."

Jane shook her head in amazement. "So you were again thrown into his presence. I imagine you were quite troubled when you found out it was him."

Elizabeth softly chuckled. "Troubled in ways you cannot imagine." She grasped her sister's hands. "But tell me about Mr. Bingley!"

Jane was more than willing to share her good news.

"We received news that Mr. Bingley had ordered Netherfield to be opened and ready for his arrival. I had been fairly certain my feelings for him had long faded and that I would not allow his return to raise my hopes, but…"

Elizabeth took her hand. "But you found that your feelings were just as strong as they had been when he was here before."

Jane slowly nodded her head and smiled. "Mrs. Long was very neighbourly and informed us the day he arrived. I almost felt sick from wondering whether he would ever pay a call." She looked down at their joined hands. "And Mother complained all day that if only Father were here, he could visit him."

"Little did she know that we had seen him."

"Yes, when he came, he told us he saw you and Father." Jane's cheeks coloured in a faint blush. "And he has come to call each day since."

Elizabeth leaned in and hugged her sister. "I had no doubt he would!"

Jane shook her head and she pinched her brows together. "He told us something about Mr. Darcy and a pirate and a disguise, but I could not quite understand it. Finally, from what you told us tonight, I was able to piece things together. I still cannot fathom it all."

"Neither can I."

"But Lizzy, I must tell you. Not all is right with Mr. Bingley."

Lizzy's heart began to pound. "What do you mean, Jane?"

Jane began to smooth the coverlet on the bed. "He said that he and Mr. Darcy had a terrible argument, and he does not know if he can ever forgive him!"

Elizabeth's brows pinched together in a frown. "Did he say what the argument was about?"

Jane took in a deep sigh. "He said that last year, his wish was not to be gone from Netherfield for long. He wanted to come back and further our acquaintance, but both Mr. Darcy and his sister convinced him that I did not return his affection."

"I always believed he truly cared for you," Elizabeth said.

"Mr. Darcy confessed to him that he had been in error in his presumption, asked for Bingley's pardon, and for that, Mr. Bingley forgave him."

Elizabeth tilted her head. "But there was something else?"

Jane nodded. "Mr. Darcy apparently knew I had been in town in the spring, and was even aware that I paid a call to Mr. Bingley's sisters and they returned the visit. But they all kept it from him. It was that deception that Mr. Bingley finds difficult to forgive."

Elizabeth could barely manage a smile, knowing that until the two men made peace with one another, it was unlikely she would see Mr. Darcy. "What about his sisters?"

Jane shook her head. "He is very angry with them, as well. They have not joined him at Netherfield. He is here alone."

"Ahh, so that gives you that much more time to spend with him."

"Yes, but he always comes here, as there would not be a chaperone for us at Netherfield."

"No, I imagine not." Elizabeth's smile turned into a chuckle. "You have a good man, Jane. He is not readily provoked by certain members of our family."

"He is good," Jane said with a sigh. "But now that *you* are here…"

"So *that* is the real reason you are so happy to see me!" She leaned in and said with a laugh, "I am no longer your closest confidante, but your chaperone!"

"Oh, Lizzy, you know that is not true. I have missed you terribly!"

"I know. And how I missed you, dearest Jane."

Jane looked down at their joined hands. Pulling a hand loose, she began gently stroking Elizabeth's hand. "And David?" She lifted her eyes to her sister. "I would imagine he shall make the tedious chore of being our chaperone a trifle more bearable?"

"David?"

Jane laughed. "This is perfect! You can be our chaperone while we are chaperoning you and David." She leaned in, and her eyes widened. "Tell me, Lizzy, what do you think of him? He seems very amiable."

Elizabeth pursed her lips together and looked away. "He is all that is good and amiable and kind."

Jane tilted her head at Elizabeth, the way she always did when she felt her sister was not telling her all. "But?"

Elizabeth pressed her fingertips together and brought them up to her chin, as if in prayer. "I believe…" she began slowly, "that if I had met him a year ago, I would have found myself hopelessly in love." She took in a deep breath and swallowed. "But I have… I have fallen in love with another." The melancholy in Elizabeth's eyes did not equal the smile on her face.

"Lizzy!" Jane said, placing her hands against her cheeks. "You have not fallen in love with Mr. Darcy, have you?"

Elizabeth nodded and slowly shook her head. "He is a good man... a most surprising, unpredictable, generous, and gallant one." She took Jane's hands again. "I have been such a fool!"

"But certainly there is the chance that he still loves you, after all you went through recently."

She let out a slow breath. "Yes, there were times, looking back, when I thought he might still care. But..." Elizabeth shook her head and wiped a tear that trailed down her face. "He cannot want anything more to do with our family after what Lydia did."

Jane remained silent for a moment. "What did Lydia do?"

"Oh, Jane!" Elizabeth said, as her tears flowed freely. "Our sister has done the most unthinkable thing, and Mr. Darcy was witness to it all!"

~~*

The following day, when Mr. Bingley called upon Longbourn, he was treated with the news that Mr. Bennet, Elizabeth, and David had returned. He was delighted to be able to walk up to Oakham Mount with Jane, having Elizabeth and David as their chaperones, rather than Mary or Kitty. He also invited them to return with him to Netherfield for the afternoon.

When Elizabeth stepped through the door at Netherfield, memories of her stay there last autumn swept over her. She almost expected to turn her head and see Mr. Darcy gazing out one of the windows or standing by a fireplace with his elbow propped up on the mantel.

She turned to David, who was engaged in a lively discussion with Mr. Bingley, and smiled. He was a good man. Perhaps she could convince herself to love him, knowing that Mr. Darcy would likely never have anything to do with her again. She was certain Mr. Darcy was the type of man who had the principles that would compel him to disassociate himself with the Bennet family and their taint of disgrace.

David and Mr. Bingley both turned at that moment to look at the two sisters, who were sitting next to each other on the sofa. They were both grinning, but David's smile did not seem as fervent.

Elizabeth shook her head imperceptibly. How could she not have realized that David no longer had the feelings for her that he had exhibited at St. Mary's? Or even on the ship? Ever since discovering what Lydia had done, he had been distantly polite, kind, and even understanding. But did he now have doubts that uniting with her family was wise?

She smiled back and wondered when he might suddenly announce he had to depart. She sighed as she almost wished it would happen sooner than later. Then, at least, she would know.

As they stood there, the butler walked in carrying a salver and presented it to Mr. Bingley, who picked up a small card. He thanked his butler and looked down to read it. He began smiling, said something to David, and the two walked over to the ladies.

Mr. Bingley sat down, taking Jane's hand. "It seems there is going to be a Masquerade Ball at the Meryton Assembly in two weeks. I cannot think of anything more delightful!"

Jane returned his smile, her eyes dancing. "Sir William Lucas hosts this every year. He prefers a summer masquerade ball over an autumn or Twelfth Night Ball, so it can spill outside into the courtyard in the mild evenings." She turned to her sister. "We must begin thinking of our costumes! How shall we dress up?"

David sat down on the other side of Elizabeth and folded his hands, resting them on his legs. "I fear I will not be able to join you. It does sound like fun, but I shall likely be on my way to Staffordshire by then."

Elizabeth tried to sound surprised and disappointed. "Truly? I am sorry to hear that."

David nodded. "I shall remain a few days longer, but I really ought to leave no later than the end of the week. I am sorry."

Elizabeth now had her answer but was truly able to smile, however, for she saw the love and admiration that her sister and Mr. Bingley both had for each other. It might be some time before she felt anything close.

Elizabeth bit her lip. No, she *had* felt something very close to what her sister felt, possibly even more, but it was something she would only be able to treasure as a memory.

Chapter 25

Two days later, David and Elizabeth were once again acting as chaperones for Jane and Mr. Bingley at Netherfield. Elizabeth suspected that the two gentlemen had been conspiring together on some seriously clandestine plot. Later, as they took a walk about the grounds, David nudged Elizabeth ahead at a quicker pace while Mr. Bingley seemed to linger with Jane.

After they had been walking alone for quite some time, Elizabeth looked back and then smiled up at David. "Do you think we ought to wait here for Jane and Mr. Bingley? We are not being the most attentive chaperones."

David shook his head. "We can wait if you wish, but I doubt they will catch up with us any time soon."

Elizabeth tilted her head and looked up at David. "What do you mean, Mr. Adams?"

A guilty smile appeared. He leaned in and whispered, "I think he might be asking her something of great import."

Elizabeth clasped her hands together, and she squealed with glee. "You cannot imagine how happy this makes me!"

David looked down at her and smiled. "I believe the two of them shall be very happy together. I have enjoyed getting to know them."

Elizabeth turned to look towards the path they had just walked down. "I think they are perfectly suited for each other."

Taking Elizabeth's hand, David gazed at her warmly. "You know I shall be leaving on the morrow."

"Yes, and I have so enjoyed our time together and deepening our acquaintance."

He gave her hand a squeeze. "You believe that I am leaving because of your sister's indiscretion."

Elizabeth pinched her brows. "I must admit that has crossed my mind."

David walked around and stood in front of Elizabeth. "No. But I do have other reasons."

Elizabeth turned her gaze up to him. "What other reasons?" She braced herself, expecting to hear him say he no longer cared for her.

His expression was solemn. He looked down at the ground, bit his lower lip, and finally said, "I believe that you are in love with someone else." He took in a deep breath. "And I believe that gentleman is very much in love with you."

Elizabeth felt her face grow pale, and she slowly shook her head. "I am so sorry, David, although I doubt..." She let out a shaky laugh. "I doubt that *anyone* would continue to have a strong sentiment for me after what Lydia did."

David gave his head a toss. "Well, Mr. Darcy probably has his scruples – I cannot say what he might feel about what your sister did – but I doubt that I would ever find a way to replace that man who seems to reside so deeply within your heart."

Elizabeth turned her eyes up to look at him. "I am so sorry, David. I never meant..."

"Lizzy!" Jane called out as she and Mr. Bingley hurried around a bend in the path towards Elizabeth and David.

"I want you to know, Elizabeth," David said as they watched the happy couple approach, "that I truly enjoyed getting to know you, and I wish you all the happiness in the world. I am in earnest."

"Thank you, David. I feel much the same for you."

Jane came up and hugged her sister. "Oh, Lizzy! I am so happy! You cannot know how happy I am!"

The two men shook hands as David congratulated his new friend. "I assume she said yes?" he asked.

"Of course! There was no hesitancy at all!"

Jane and Elizabeth walked back to Netherfield, arm in arm, with the men just behind them. Jane told her that Mr. Bingley had visited their father earlier that morning to obtain his permission, which he readily gave.

"When we had dropped far behind you," Jane gleefully told her, "he stopped and asked me a very odd question."

"What did he ask?" Elizabeth wanted to know.

"He asked me how we should dress for the Masquerade Ball." Jane shook her head. "I had not even had time to think about it and could not give him a reply."

She told Elizabeth that Mr. Bingley had taken her hand and then asked, "What would you think about us going as a bride and groom?"

Jane beamed at Elizabeth with wide eyes. "I did not know what to think!"

"Tell me more, dearest Jane! What did he say next?"

Jane giggled. "It is not what he said, but what he did! He got down on one knee and said, 'I would be honoured if you would accept my hand in marriage.' Oh, Elizabeth, I thought I would faint! Fortunately, I did not!"

"And you said yes?"

Jane giggled. "I gave him an unequivocal yes! I was determined there would be no misunderstanding."

With great joy, Elizabeth listened to her sister as she continued to proclaim the extent of her happiness. She was amazed at the level of Jane's excitement, something she had rarely seen Jane exhibit.

Jane let out a long sigh and smiled.

Elizabeth quickly leaned over and gave her a kiss on the cheek. "I am so happy for you, Jane. So happy!"

~~*

When they returned to Longbourn, Jane, Charles, and David repaired to the sitting room, while Elizabeth went in search of her parents. She approached her father's library, knowing he would likely be there, and heard both her parents' voices coming from inside.

"We are likely to have a guest for dinner tonight, Mrs. Bennet, who will soon be a member of the family, but it is not Mr. Adams."

"Not Mr. Adams? But he leaves on the morrow! I thought

before he departed, he would have asked for Lizzy's hand!" Mrs. Bennet let out a moan. "Is that not why you brought him here?"

Mr. Bennet shook his head. "We never have a guarantee of those things, and we must not dwell on what might have been. But are you not inclined to hear who the person is?"

"Oh, yes, Mr. Bennet! I was so distressed over David, that I forgot there is someone else!"

Mr. Bennet smiled. "It is our neighbour, Mr. Bingley, who is this very day asking for our Jane's hand."

"Mr. Bennet! I am delighted with such news! But what can we do about David? I am so disappointed he is about to leave us."

"We are going to do nothing about David. Let us be happy for our Jane and share in her joy this evening."

Elizabeth waited, listening at the door, until she was certain her mother was thinking about Jane and Charles, and not David and her. She finally walked in and announced that the newly engaged couple had returned and were waiting for them in the sitting room.

~~*

Later, as they gathered in the dining room for dinner, the mood continued to be joyful, and everyone talked about the engagement and wedding. David did not wish to take away from the elation everyone was feeling, so he spoke little about his departure.

They had just finished their meal, when there was a knock at the front door. A few moments later their butler walked in carrying two letters.

"A missive for Mr. Bennet, and one for Mr. Adams." He handed each of the men their letter, bowed, and stepped out of the room.

"Oh!" cried Mrs. Bennet, who began fanning herself. "It can only be about your sister, Mr. Bennet. I just know she has died! It is always bad news when one receives an unexpected letter!"

They both opened their letters, and David abruptly stood up. "Heavens! This is grave, indeed!"

Mr. Bennet read his letter, slowly shaking his head. "How very sad!"

"When did she die, my dear? I am so sorry!"

Mr. Bennet looked up. "She did not die; she is still very much alive, for if you look closely, the letter is from her. But there *was* a recent death."

"Who?" everyone in the room asked.

David softly answered, "Robert Mintner, the young man in the navy whom Melanie loved."

Elizabeth brought her hand up over her mouth. "Oh, this must be so hard on her. Does it say how she is faring?"

He nodded. "My mother says she is taking it hard and is very despondent."

Mr. Bennet looked down at the letter in his hands. "Viola says she does not know what to do to help her through this. She only wishes she had the strength to do everything she would wish for her daughter."

Elizabeth looked at David and could readily see the concern he had for Melanie. He began to pace, reading the letter again and again. She stood up and walked over to him.

"I am so sorry to hear this. It sounds as though she would benefit from the support of a very close friend." She bit her lip and watched him, but he said nothing. Finally, she added softly, "Do you really have to go on to Staffordshire? Perhaps... perhaps you ought to return to St. Mary's?"

David pinched his brows. "I do not know if I should. I would not want to interfere. I would not want her to think..."

"No, I know you would not. But you are a good friend and care deeply for her." Elizabeth took in a deep breath. "If you go and allow her to grieve... just be there for her... she might come to return those same feelings you have for her." She lifted her brows and gave him a nod of encouragement.

"Has it been that apparent?"

Elizabeth silently nodded and smiled. "I know how much you care for her."

"I do not know..."

She placed a hand on his arm. "Of course, you cannot expect her to suddenly switch her affections from this young man to you, but if you let her know you are there only to give her comfort and support, be a listening ear, and give her a shoulder to cry on, she will treasure that."

David slowly nodded. "I should really like to do that, but do you suppose she will come to love me?"

"I believe she already does. She needs to realize that what she feels for you is something that two people do not often have." She gave him a smile and tilted her head. "You will not know until you try."

His brows furrowed as he considered her words. Finally, his brows lifted. "I believe I shall! Thank you so much, Elizabeth." He turned his head towards her. "I wish…"

Elizabeth gave a quick nod of her head. "Yes, I know."

David spread his lips in a smile. "I hope all things work out for you, as well, whether it is Mr. Darcy or someone else."

Elizabeth let out a long sigh. "Yes," she replied wistfully. "Perhaps someone else!"

~~*

The following day, David departed for London, planning to return to St. Mary's. Mrs. Bennet, of course, did not understand how he could settle upon making another trip across the sea after all that had happened to them on their previous journey. She was still disappointed that Elizabeth had not secured the young man's affections, or if not his affections, at least an offer of marriage, for certainly love could come later. She blamed Elizabeth for not having made a greater effort in securing his hand.

Elizabeth could only silently laugh at her mother's absurd grievances.

~~*

Nearly everyone in the Bennet household was in an uproar the days before the Masquerade Ball as they excitedly planned their costumes. Since this was a yearly event, the same costumes were usually worn year after year, if not by the same person, then passed down to another. They were always altered in some way, with embellishments added, changed, or removed.

Mr. Bennet had decided to allow Lydia to attend, as he always looked forward to a pleasant evening alone on the night of the Masquerade Ball. His idea of enjoying the evening was to remain at home with a good book in front of his face instead of a mask. The last thing he wanted was Lydia there to disturb his solitude. While Elizabeth did not agree with his decision to allow Lydia to attend, she was not surprised by it.

Previous years' costumes were brought out, haggled over, and snatched up. Kitty and Lydia immediately began pulling out ribbons, lace, beads, and feathers and adding new ones. They did not care what they were dressed up as; they only cared that they and their costumes would be noticed.

Mary's costume always consisted of the same muslin dress and a mask which was adorned with a simple flower. She did not care to dress up as something she was not, but she conceded to enter into the masquerade festivities by covering her eyes.

Jane chose to dress up as an angel, because that had become the endearing name Mr. Bingley continued to call her. She wore all white, and Elizabeth made a halo decorated with white ribbons and small white flowers. The wings were somewhat problematic, but a solution soon presented itself. They attached sheer white fabric to the sleeves, so when Jane lifted her arms, the wings spread. She was eager to see Charles dressed as a soldier, borrowing the uniform from one of the families in Meryton, whose father had been in the army in the late 1700s.

Mrs. Bennet was dressed as a lady from the early 18th century, with a dress that had been handed down for several generations. It came complete with wide domed hoops, which took up most of the room in the carriage every year when they rode to the affair. Elizabeth always thought that was the main reason her father never wished to attend, as there was always very little room, and her mother fretted whether the hoops would get crushed. Every year the dress had to be tailored, however, to allow for her ever expanding body, but she was still able to wear it.

On the day of the Masquerade Ball, Mr. Bennet could not enjoy one moment of silence as the ladies spent all day making sure their costumes would be ready on time. Mrs. Bennet wailed and fretted the most, as she continually asked for someone to advise her concerning some aspect of her costume. At length she entered Mr. Bennet's library to seek his opinion.

After a rather lengthy discussion about the embellishments that might be added to her dress, he stood to his feet and pointed to the open door. "I have had enough! Oh, that you all could have been like Mary and just worn a mask!"

"But that would not be so much fun!" exclaimed Lydia, who ran past his library with Kitty after picking some flowers. "I am so glad the Masquerade Ball is in the summer and not winter, as so many others are. Flowers add so much to the costume!"

Kitty giggled, and the two girls ran upstairs.

Elizabeth had been standing nearby, and felt a pang of regret for her father that he did not have a son. He had seemed to enjoy David's level-headed conversation and steady demeanour. The Bennet household was certainly influenced by all the feminine sensibilities, which sometimes drove their father to his wit's end. The day of a ball was always the most trying for him.

She stepped into her father's library after her mother stomped out.

"Now what?" Mr. Bennet asked as he glared up from his book. "Oh, Lizzy! Now you certainly look splendid." He gave her a brief smile and tilted his head. "What are you supposed to be, again?" He narrowed his eyes. "I believe you were a *Parisienne belle*, last year, but this is certainly different."

She shrugged her shoulders. "I think I am a Spanish gypsy."

She had taken a multi-coloured dress, sewed ruffles onto the bottom, and tied a large shawl about her waist that hung down her dress at an angle. She tied a smaller, narrower shawl around her head and decorated it with flowers and ribbons. She also wove flowers and ribbons through her hair, which was pulled together to one side and over her shoulder to the front.

She fingered the rather large necklace, which came from her mother's jewellery box. She would never wear something like it except to an affair such as this, as she preferred a small chain and dainty cross or pendant. She laughingly held up her mask to her face, which was decorated with more flowers and a few feathers.

"I cannot say I know what a Spanish gypsy looks like, but I daresay you make a beautiful one. Come, give your father a kiss and then be on your way."

~~*

The Bennet ladies made the short ride into Meryton in as much discomfort as they always did. Mrs. Bennet sat in the middle of the seat to allow her hoops to extend out on either side. Mary and Kitty had to sit on the very edge of that seat next to her so as not to ruin the dress. Jane, Elizabeth, and Lydia sat across from them.

When they arrived at the Assembly Hall, they stepped out of the carriage with care so as not to ruin any part of their costumes. There were no announcements at the ball, as part of the fun was to try to guess the identities of the attendees. Since their neighbourhood was small, however, it was not difficult to recognize nearly everyone there.

They stepped in and were amazed, as they were each year, at the array of glamorous and creative costumes. Even though the summer days were longer and it was not yet dusk, candles were lit about the room. Flowers decorated the hall in elaborate arrangements and hung in garlands. A small orchestra was playing, but the first dance would be announced shortly.

When Mr. Bingley came up and bowed, the ladies giggled. The uniform was a little large for him around the waist and was different from the uniforms worn now, but he certainly looked handsome. His eyes sparkled through his mask as he gazed at his *angel*. He spoke a few moments with the Bennet ladies, and then took Jane's arm and ushered her directly to the centre of the room to await the first dance.

Mary walked to the side room where the refreshments were being served and chairs were set up to visit. Mary preferred not to dance, but merely to observe and enter into conversation with anyone willing to join her.

Kitty and Lydia quickly set off in search of any new acquaintance that might be made. They usually were good at guessing who everyone was and were excited about the possibility of there being someone in attendance from outside their neighbourhood.

Elizabeth watched as the dancers lined up and the music began, but she also found herself looking about her. It was such a festive atmosphere, however, she felt anything but. She could offer up a smile and friendly conversation, but her heart felt heavy. Perhaps she should just join Mary, for even the thought of dancing did not appeal to her at the moment.

As she turned to go to Mary, she came to an abrupt stop, her heart beating wildly. She saw a man across the room. He was facing the other way, but she could see his black oilskin coat and tri-corn hat. She watched as he talked to those around him. Then he slowly turned around. She held her breath.

Her heart sank. It was not Mr. Darcy, but Mr. Goulding. Her shoulders rose and lowered as she let out her breath in an audible sigh. She shook her head in disgust as she recollected that he came to the ball every year as a pirate.

She suddenly felt someone behind her, and a tremor passed through her.

"If ye are not otherwise engaged, may I 'ave the pleasure of the next dance?"

Elizabeth stood frozen and was unable to move. Her eyes had only a moment ago deceived her; had her ears just done the same?

Chapter 26

Elizabeth clasped her hands tightly together to calm the trembling that beset her. She took in a deep breath but could not keep from whirling about. She found herself looking up into the face of Mr. Darcy. He stood before her, dressed as the pirate she had come to love, albeit with a few changes. He wore his tri-corn hat, but his trimmed hair did not peek out at the sides, and curls did not trail down his neck. His face was clean shaven, and he wore a patch over his eye instead of the red sash. She could see the scar peeking out at the top. The red sash had resumed its function around his waist. His shirt, complete with white billowy sleeves, had the addition of exceptionally large ruffles. His baldric hung across his chest, but without the scabbard to hold sword, dagger, or pistol. His oilskin coat hung loosely at his sides.

She could not trust herself to utter one word, but it was very easy for her to smile.

"You must know I find this all infuriatingly arduous, standing in the midst of people that I do not know." He smiled weakly. "It would be a great help to me if you accepted my invitation to dance."

Elizabeth felt a sense of euphoria at being asked to help him feel at ease, while at the same time, the desire to enter into a bantering dialogue with him tugged at her. "And why should you feel that way, Mr. Darcy, when you *are* acquainted with several in this Assembly Hall."

Mr. Darcy looked at her sheepishly. "Because I cannot tell the difference between those I have been introduced to and those I have not! I cannot recognize *anyone* behind these wretched masks!"

Elizabeth tilted her head. "How, then, did you know it was me standing here? I have a mask on, and I was facing away from you!"

He allowed a smile. "When I entered the ballroom, ye were the only lady pirate I saw! I knew me first dance would 'ave to be wi' a lady pirate."

"Lady pirate! I beg your pardon, Mr. Darcy, but I am a Spanish gypsy!"

Darcy took a step back and lifted a brow as he took in her attire. "'Tis me error, m'lady." He bowed his head briefly. "Pray, excuse me. But ye 'ave yet to answer me question. May I 'ave the next dance if ye are not otherwise engaged?"

Elizabeth could not keep back her giggle. She felt as though at this moment, she could giggle all evening. "I am not otherwise engaged, and yes, you may have the next dance, Lockerly, or Captain Smith, or Mr. Darcy. May I inquire what your name might be tonight?"

"Who would you prefer I be?"

Elizabeth felt her cheeks warm just from the intensity of his gaze – even though one eye was covered! She laughed nervously. "You know I think you are a very odd pirate and a most excellent captain, but I should prefer to call you Mr. Darcy."

"Then Mr. Darcy, it is."

She tilted her head and fingered a single strand of hair that had fallen across her face. "I did not know you were in Hertfordshire."

"I only just arrived." He spoke in his normal voice, very mellow and smooth.

"Did your sister come with you?" Elizabeth bit her lip. "I should very much like to see her again."

"And she returns the sentiment. I hope the two of you are able to renew your acquaintance."

Elizabeth found it difficult to breathe. Was he merely being polite, or was there deeper meaning to his words?

Darcy continued. "She will be arriving on the morrow. I rode on horseback, and she is taking the carriage."

"On horseback? With your pirate costume in hand?" Elizabeth felt she needed to keep things lively between them, or she might declare her ardent love for him right there!

He gave his head a shake. "What makes ye think I didn't wear it as I rode?"

Elizabeth laughed gaily. "Certainly you did not!"

"And why should I not?" He smiled and shrugged his shoulders. "I brought it along in a satchel. A rather large satchel."

Elizabeth wondered if he knew he was alternating speaking like Captain Smith and then like himself. "Has your pirate attire now become a standard part of your wardrobe? Do you carry it along with you in case you are required to impersonate one at a moment's notice?"

Darcy laughed. "Bingley informed me of the Masquerade Ball."

"So Mr. Bingley has forgiven you? I understood he was quite angry."

Darcy nodded. "I believe your sister had a good deal of influence over his decision to accept my apology."

"I am glad."

"I am, as well. I deeply regretted the possibility that I might lose his friendship over my actions. I know that it..." He took in a breath and looked away, then returned his gaze to Elizabeth. "I know that it cost me the loss of something of even greater value earlier this year."

Elizabeth felt her face flush, and tears began to sting her eyes. "I..."

At that moment the music came to an end, and the next dance was announced. "Come, Miss Bennet, let us take our place."

As they walked over to join the other dancers, Elizabeth had time to think how to respond. Before they took their place in the line of dancers, Elizabeth said, "I have long ago forgiven you, Mr. Darcy. Your letter helped me understand where I had been seriously mistaken."

"But I was in error, as well." They separated to stand opposite each other in the line.

The couple stared at each other in silence as they waited for the music to begin. After a short introduction, the couples on the dance floor stepped towards each other, grasping hands. As they began to promenade around another couple, Mr. Darcy looked about the room. "I do not see Mr. Adams here. His disguise must be quite good."

Elizabeth smiled. "Well, unless he is dressed as an invisible man, he is not here. You see, he returned to St. Mary's."

Mr. Darcy's started. "He... returned?"

The dance required them to separate and join hands with their neighbouring partners.

As they passed each other, Elizabeth nodded and said, "There was an unfortunate death..."

Darcy turned sharply, but he was too far from her to say anything.

When she returned to his side, his face was grave. "Your father's sister, of course. Pray, accept my condolences."

"No, no!" Elizabeth shook her head. The flowers in her long locks were tossed about. "It was a young man our other cousin, Melanie, had a strong attachment to. He was in the navy, and she had hoped to become engaged when he returned. Unfortunately, he was killed while at sea."

"I am sorry. Was Mr. Adams acquainted with him?"

"No, but he and Melanie were very close."

Darcy looked at her with questions in his eyes but was prevented from asking those questions when they turned in opposite directions.

When they came back together, he took her hand in a tender, but firm grip. "What do you mean they were very close?"

She looked down at their joined hands and then stole a peek up at him. "They have known each other all their lives, and he has always been very much in love with her."

Darcy almost stopped in the middle of the dance, and his jaw dropped. "He is... I thought..."

Elizabeth prodded him along with a gentle tug. "To the right now, Mr. Darcy."

They had to separate again, and Elizabeth felt the release of Mr. Darcy's grasp at the very last moment. Her hand felt cold at the loss of his touch, but she felt a great deal of warmth inside. When they came back around, Mr. Darcy looked at her earnestly.

"But I was under the impression that he had a... a strong affection for *you*." His voice cracked and hinted at a sense of urgency.

She smiled warmly as they parted again. Her heart pounded with the hope that Mr. Darcy still cared deeply for her.

They came back together for one final promenade down the line of dancers. Their hands reached out for each other, and they began walking. "I believe," Elizabeth said softly, "that David and I both esteemed one another, but it was not love."

When Darcy took her hand this time, he did not simply hold it. He cradled it in his hand in a warm grasp. His fingers softly caressed it, and his thumb stroked the inside of her palm. Although no one would be able to notice it but her, she felt as though everyone in the room must have been able to see the clamour of emotions that were pulsing through her at his touch.

Any thought as to what she might say evaporated. She glanced up at him and smiled, hoping that would be enough to convey everything she was feeling.

When the dance ended, they walked over to a refreshment table, Darcy still holding her hand.

"Have you, Miss Elizabeth, ever successfully completed your sketch of my character?"

Elizabeth laughed while at the same time shaking her head. "I fear that is an impossible task, sir. There are too many layers of contrasts and hidden hues, and ever-changing properties that appear and disappear depending on the light. I fear it has proven quite impossible to sketch a true likeness."

"Mmm," Darcy grimaced. "It makes me sound perfectly monstrous!"

Elizabeth smiled and glanced down at their hands. "On the contrary, it makes you an excellent study."

Darcy raised a brow and leaned in, tilting his head as he said, "Perhaps one that might take a lifetime to complete?"

Elizabeth felt her heart jump into her throat at his words. Her mouth was suddenly dry, and she moistened her lips with her tongue. She cast her eyes down, as if that would prevent him from seeing her flushed cheeks. When she looked up at him again, she saw him take in a deep breath.

"Pray, forgive me, Miss Bennet. Would you care for something to drink?"

"Thank you, no. But I fear that word is currently being circulated that Mr. Bingley's friend, Mr. Darcy, is the pirate who danced one dance with me and has continued to hold my hand since that dance." She looked down at their hands.

Darcy winced. "I am sorry. Again. I clearly need to work on my manners. Pray, forgive me for my unpardonable conduct." He released her hand.

"Have no fear, Mr. Darcy. I did not back then on the island nor do I now find it unpardonable."

She glanced out and noticed more and more people watching them. "Now, Mr. Darcy, I would make a gentle request that perhaps you dance a few more dances with some of the other ladies who are here."

"But who?" he asked, a crease appearing in his brow.

"Well, you certainly can ask Jane to dance, and any of my sisters. Perhaps even Mary would consent. And then, of course, there is my mother."

"Your mother?"

"Oh, yes. You will find her quite the dancer."

"Truly?"

Elizabeth curtseyed. "Thank you very much for the dance, Mr. Darcy. Perhaps I shall see you later?"

Darcy leaned in and whispered, "Will you promise to have one more dance with me?"

Elizabeth curtseyed slightly as she nodded. "If you insist!"

~~*

Darcy walked away from Elizabeth determined to make an effort to dance. He first asked Jane to dance with him, and when he did, Bingley took the opportunity to dance with Elizabeth.

"You must tell me, Miss Elizabeth," Bingley asked as they took their place in line, "how my good friend behaved as a pirate. I am completely flummoxed by his behaviour of late, and I cannot reconcile the man I know and this..." he pointed over to Darcy, "*this* man!"

"Well, I only believed him to be a pirate for a very short while, but even when I believed him to be Captain Smith, he was very polite and honourable." Elizabeth laughed gaily and met Darcy's eye, as he stole glances at her occasionally from where he and Jane stood. "He did speak quite oddly, however. I think that is why I did not readily recognize him."

The music began, and Bingley stepped forward and bowed. Elizabeth returned it with a curtsey, and then he took her hands.

239

Bingley let out a huff. "He is so different. He has said nothing to me, but my angel... my Jane... has informed me that he once asked for your hand in marriage."

Elizabeth let out a long breath. "Yes, but I would not mention it to him. Let him be the one to tell you what happened. I assume she told you I refused him?"

Bingley's eyes grew wide. "Yes! Confound it all! These things completely baffle me, but I shall not pry into your private affairs." He smiled and looked down at her. "I am now very glad my friend and I have sorted out our differences. He is a good man, you know. Very good. No one like him."

Elizabeth pursed her lips together to suppress a smile. "Yes, Mr. Bingley, I am quite certain he is."

Elizabeth changed the subject and directed Mr. Bingley to talk about the wedding, or Jane, which he did, with great enthusiasm. Every once in a while, however, praise for Mr. Darcy poured forth from him, and Elizabeth believed he felt it incumbent on him to convince her of his great worth.

After a dance with Kitty, Mrs. Bennet, and Maria Lucas, Mr. Darcy finally returned to Elizabeth's side. She grimaced at the look of exhaustion on his face.

"Mr. Darcy, I fear you have quite overdone it tonight."

He waved his hand through the air and shook his head. "I am not so much physically tired as I am emotionally spent. There is a difference. Trying to keep up with the conversations during my last three dances has completely fatigued me! I spent a great deal of effort trying to comprehend what one lady was saying, what to say to another who would not utter one word and seemed terrified of me the whole dance, and I finally gave up saying anything to the third because she talked non-stop!"

Elizabeth looked at him with pity. "I think I can guess who each guilty party was."

She glanced over at Jane and Bingley, who were sitting out. "Look, there are Mr. Bingley and Jane sitting out. Let us go join them so you can rest."

"I confess I would enjoy the brief respite, but I think I would prefer to remain here. Besides, you promised me another dance."

"Yes, I did. And so that you will not become more fatigued, I also promise that I will not speak during the whole of the dance and will not oblige you to talk at all... as I was determined to do during our very first dance at the Netherfield Ball last year."

Darcy's brows shot up. "Truly? That was your object, then? I can assume you thought it would be torture for me, but I assure you it was not." He leaned in towards her. "You must realize something, Miss Elizabeth. There are some people with whom I find it difficult to converse, who wear me down to the point of exhaustion and try my patience, while others – a *few* others – invigorate me and make me feel very much alive. I can speak with them with the greatest ease... and pleasure, and enjoy the silence between us, as well." He paused and breathed in deeply. "I think you know how I have long felt about *our* conversations."

Elizabeth listened in rapt amazement at Mr. Darcy's insight as he offered revelations about himself and a hint at how he felt about her. The look of admiration on his face almost said more than his words did, and it took all her power to not reach up and stroke the face that looked down at her.

Before she could find the words to reply, he asked, "Miss Elizabeth, is there some place where we can go to talk?"

"Oh," Elizabeth said softly. She could not think of one place they could go where they would not have a crowd of people staring and eavesdropping. She finally gave her head a shake. "Not around here. I cannot think of any..."

As the throng of people increased around them, discouraging any further conversation, Darcy let out a low humph.

Elizabeth took in a deep breath and swallowed, wanting somehow to further this discussion. Suddenly, with a carefree voice, she said, "I certainly hope the weather remains warm and sunny. I do so enjoy a long, solitary walk in the mornings up to Oakham Mount. It is always such a pleasant way to begin my day. I believe I shall take a walk first thing tomorrow."

"Oh, I see," Darcy said in almost a whisper. "So now we are on the safe topic of the weather." He folded his arms across him and looked out across the room.

Elizabeth gave her head a slight shake, and then looked at him with a pointed gaze. "You see, Mr. Darcy, I enjoy taking a morning walk, and rarely – if ever – do I encounter anyone! It is really something that *you* ought to try. I think you would enjoy it, as well."

The light of dawning appeared in Darcy's eyes – or rather, his one eye – as he looked down at her. "Yes! Yes! You are most correct! I know I should like it very much! Very much indeed!" He nodded at a couple as they walked past.

"I thought you would."

"When would you suggest is the best time to go? I mean, since I am not from around here, I am certain you would know these things better than I."

"Oh, I think the best time would be at about seven o'clock. I would conjecture that since the ball will most likely continue on into the early hours of the morning, seven would be a very good time."

"Yes, I do appreciate your assistance in this matter, Miss Elizabeth."

Elizabeth nodded her head slowly, despite the rapid pounding of her heart. "It was my pleasure, Mr. Darcy."

Chapter 27

The next morning Elizabeth opened the large wooden door at Longbourn as quietly as she could and slipped outside. She breathed in the fresh morning air, glorying in the songs of the birds, and squinted her eyes as the rising sun greeted her. She walked down the dirt path, kicking a small rock and sending it into the shrubbery that bordered it. Once she was out of the gate, she turned and looked to the east, towards Oakham Mount. Her heart thundered as she considered who she was going to meet.

Elizabeth's incessant thoughts and the strength of her feelings after last evening had not waned. She had hardly slept at all as she recounted every word Mr. Darcy had spoken to her at the ball, weighing them against the words her heart longed for him to say.

A smile brightened her face and her eyes danced with joy as she recollected him complimenting their conversations. She winced as she realized she had had no idea that when she purposely provoked and challenged him, he was greatly enjoying their lively banter. She let out a chuckle as she considered that the times they had walked in silence, it was because she had no desire to speak to him. He, on the other hand, had cherished those times because he felt she had understood that he needed quiet as well as conversation. She shook her head. He was a complex man!

As she drew closer to the base of Oakham Mount, her pace increased in time with the pounding of her heart. She looked about her, hoping to catch a glimpse of Mr. Darcy, but did not see him.

As she began to take the dirt path up the small hill, she thought she heard footsteps behind her. She stopped and turned her head, narrowing her eyes against the sun's glare, but she did not see anyone. Suddenly a deer sprang forth from the shadows of the dense woods, startling her, but prompting her to laugh. She turned and continued to walk.

She would soon come to the turn which would give her the view towards Netherfield. From this vantage point, she would be able to look out and see the direction from which Mr. Darcy would come. Her steps hurriedly carried her along, and at length, she reached the lookout and could see the path that came up from that direction.

A rough-hewn wooden fence had long ago been erected along the path here, as there was a steep cliff on the one side. She walked over to the fence and gripped the top beam, looking out. When she did not see him, she suddenly felt apprehensive that he might not come. Perhaps he realized he had said too much to her and decided he could not go through with it and finish telling her all he had planned to say. Her fingers tightened around the beam, and she felt herself begin to sway as she leaned over to look farther out towards the path Mr. Darcy would have taken.

There was the sound of footsteps again, and before Elizabeth could turn, she felt a hand grasp hers.

"Ye aren't thinkin' of jumpin', are ye, m'lady?"

Darcy pulled her gently towards him, and elation flooded her. She stopped within a few of inches of him and looked up into his smiling face.

"You know I was not." She could not conceal the nervous laugh that accompanied her words. "I was... I wondered... I did not know whether I should wait here, go back, or continue on."

Darcy rubbed his jaw. "Do you often find yourself faced with such dilemmas and decisions to make when you walk up to Oakham Mount?" His eyes held a tender glint. "I understand you walk up here quite often."

"I do, and no, I am not often faced with such dilemmas." She peeked up at him. "Only when I am anticipating a clandestine encounter."

"Is that what this is?"

She bit her lip. "Some may consider this rather shocking, coming out here to meet... without a chaperone."

"I most certainly would!"

Elizabeth winced. "Do you think me imprudent to have agreed to it, then?"

Darcy laughed and shook his head, giving her a pointed look. "You did not agree to it, Miss Bennet. You suggested it!"

Her eyes widened. She looked up and saw that his piercing dark eyes were smiling. "You are incorrigible, Mr. Darcy. But, yes, I did! You must believe me to be quite a disreputable lady!"

"I think no such thing. Come." Darcy nodded his head in the direction of the path, and he tucked her hand within his arm, while still holding onto it with his other hand. They fell into step, walking slowly up the hill.

They walked in a contented silence, and then Darcy asked, "Did you fear I might not come?"

Elizabeth looked straight ahead and then turned her head away. She finally looked back and admitted, "It crossed my mind."

"Hmm…" He gave her hand a gentle squeeze. "I have been out here walking for some time. I set out at first light, actually."

Elizabeth looked down at the path in front of them but knew his gaze was upon her. "I see."

"I cannot say that I got much sleep last night. I was rather…"

Elizabeth waited for him to finish. He looked away and let out a sigh. She could only conjecture what he had been about to say. If his night had been anything like hers, it had been one of joyously recounting every moment of the previous evening and eagerly anticipating the coming morning.

"Neither did I sleep well," Elizabeth volunteered.

They walked on a short distance with neither saying a word. Elizabeth decided she would wait until Mr. Darcy broke the silence, despite wanting – no, needing – answers to so many questions. They came to a fork in the path, and Darcy gently guided her to the left, which she knew would take them to a small clearing.

Elizabeth finally stopped. "Mr. Darcy, we have not spoken at all of Lydia's shameful actions since it happened."

Darcy's head lowered, his brows pinched together, and he looked off to the side. "There is nothing about which to speak."

"Oh, but there is." It grieved her to see the pained expression on his face, but she had to know. "You see, my family may not have considered this, but I certainly have. I cannot help but think that my sister was spared any arrest, trial, and possible conviction by your hand." She shook her head. "I do not know how you may have done this, but I find it incomprehensible that she was merely released. I cannot believe that she did not have to suffer any of the consequences for doing such a horrid thing."

Darcy looked down at their hands. "You are correct," he said solemnly. "But for the most part, I did nothing but make it perfectly clear to the authorities that she was an..." he paused and looked up. "Pray, forgive me for my words, here, but I fear I told them she was an ignorant and silly girl who was merely following the directions of Mr. Wickham, out of love, or lust, or whatever you want to call it." He took in a deep breath. "I told them that she knew nothing about what it was she was being asked to do."

"You had no reason at all to do that, Mr. Darcy. My family thanks you, even though I do not believe they fully comprehend this."

He paused and took in a slow breath. "You know I did it all for you." His tender words washed over her and filled her with a flood of warmth.

Elizabeth opened her mouth, but nothing came out.

"Miss Bennet, if your feelings are what they were in the spring, just say so. I would hope those impressions I came away with last evening were everything I believed them to be, but I will not speak words of my love and devotion for you if they are still unwelcome."

Elizabeth's eyes welled with tears. She shook her head slowly. "No, Mr. Darcy, they are not unwelcome. Not in the slightest. In fact, I can think of nothing I would rather hear you say."

They began walking again, and he did not seem inclined to say anything further, which left Elizabeth somewhat perplexed. But again, rather than breaking the silence, she would wait until he did.

At length, came upon the clearing. It was a natural small meadow of grass, bordered by low shrubs. Wild flowers grew in patches throughout, adding a myriad of colours to the serene setting, and a bench was situated on one side. A coverlet was laid out in the middle of the clearing, and a basket had been set on the coverlet. Her heart leapt in her chest at the sight.

"Mr. Darcy, this is lovely!"

He patted her hand. "I am glad you think so."

He led her over to it. "Would you care to sit down?"

"Yes, that would be very nice."

He directed her to the coverlet and helped her down, finally releasing her hands as she sat. He stood for a moment merely gazing at her. Then very slowly, he lowered his tall frame down to her side. Instead of sitting, however, he came down on one knee.

Elizabeth had to tell herself to breathe and hoped that her heart would bear the excitement she now felt, after the exertion this morning of the climb, the momentary fear she had experienced, and the pounding that accompanied all the feelings that this man evoked.

"Miss Bennet... Elizabeth, I do not know what I have ever done to warrant a second chance with you, but I am grateful for it, all the same. I have never ceased to love you, and that love has continued to grow with each passing day. I will not bore you with details about how I have changed... how I hope I have changed. I can only hope you have seen it for yourself and can be assured that I desire nothing more but to make you happy. I ask you, Elizabeth, will you make my joy complete and consent to be my wife?"

Elizabeth's shoulders began to shake as her tears began to fall. She nodded her head and mumbled, "Yes, I will!"

Darcy drew to her side and pulled out a handkerchief. He gently wiped her eyes with it. "Come, Elizabeth, I had hoped this would make you happy, not sad!"

Elizabeth laughed between sobs. "I am happy. I am very happy! You cannot know how deeply I have come to love you!"

Darcy sat down next to her, a wide smile gracing his face. He opened the basket and pulled out a bottle of wine and two goblets. Then he set out a plate with cheeses and breads. "Would you care for something, Elizabeth?"

She smiled and looked up at him with brows raised. "Yes, that would be very nice... Fitzwilliam."

Darcy had just tilted the bottle of wine to pour it, but stopped. He looked up at Elizabeth, his dark eyes shining. "I like the sound of that, Elizabeth. I have often wondered what it would be like to hear you say my name."

They sipped some wine and ate the bread and cheese in silence. Elizabeth actually began to enjoy the silence between them, as if they shared something special.

When they had finished, he took her hand and cradled it between both of his. "You have no idea how happy this has made me." He patted her hand, causing her to look down.

Elizabeth placed her other hand over his and studied them. "You know, Fitzwilliam, it is the way you held my hand that made me realize how much I adore you."

"It all began when I reached out and grabbed it, then?"

Elizabeth chuckled. "I may not have fallen in love with you then, but you know that I noticed your hand. I could not ignore how soft and smooth it was; I told you that. I came to realize how warm and protective and strong it was. I believe from that very moment you clasped it, there was nothing that would get in the way of my falling in love with you."

Darcy smiled. "Truly? And what of David? I saw him holding your hand on several occasions." He raised a brow as he asked.

Elizabeth licked her lips. "Hmm. Yes, he did hold my hand. But..." She gave him a sideways glance. "I realized that when he held my hand, I did not feel all those things I felt when you held it." She bit her lip and widened her eyes. "It felt like any other gentleman who had ever held my hand." She looked up and saw his brow lift. She quickly added, "I will have you know that has occurred solely during a dance; so pray, do not fret about a dozen men who have taken my hand in theirs."

"Oh, I will not fret, but I do wish to know more about how you felt." He looked down at their hands, then stole a sly upward glance.

She blushed, wondering how she would ever explain those feelings that were so personal, so intimate. She also knew it was something she should not discuss with him – at least now. She raised a single brow. "I shall only say that when I held your hand in mine at the end of our dance on the ship and you warned me that I was in dangerous waters..." She paused and waited for him to acknowledge it.

"Yes?"

"I have often felt very much the same way when you hold my hand in yours." She glanced up and met his penetrating gaze. "Or look at me in that intense way." It was true. The way he looked at her made her feel as though she would melt away.

Darcy began to move towards her, lowering his gaze to her lips. When he was but a few inches away, Elizabeth pushed herself up and walked over to the edge of the clearing.

"Is something wrong?" Darcy asked, standing up and walking over to her. "You do not wish for me to kiss you?"

Elizabeth laughed. "On the contrary. I have desired your kisses since…"

Darcy leaned in towards her. "Since when?"

"Since you held me on the merchant ship as we prepared to swing across to your ship." She tossed her head casually. "As improper as that would have been."

Darcy's eyes widened. "You wished to be kissed then?"

Elizabeth nodded and watched him take a step closer.

"Does this mean you desired Captain Smith to kiss you?" His eyes held incredulity. "How do I know you have not fallen in love with him, instead of me?"

Elizabeth's mouth opened, and she covered it with her hand. "Oh, my! This is wretched, indeed! I had not thought of that!"

Darcy folded one arm across his chest and rested the elbow of his other arm on top of it. He brought his fisted hand up to his chin and tapped it a few times. "This is grave. What am I to think?"

Elizabeth looked up with mock despair and just a little bit of teasing. "Perhaps you can help me forget my little infatuation with the captain."

He took another step closer. "And how am I to do that?"

"Well," she said as she stepped towards him, closing the distance, "you may begin by putting your arms about me, much like he did." She helped him along.

Darcy smiled. "Now what?"

"Well, I believe I had to put my arms about your neck, much like this." She stood on her toes and brought her arms about him. They stood staring into each other's faces. Elizabeth could feel his breath upon her and again felt that she might collapse if he loosened his grip.

"Now?"

"Heavens, no. We were then tied together."

Darcy shook his head. "We have no rope."

"That is true. We shall have to pretend, then."

Darcy tightened his grip and pulled her even closer. He leaned down and asked huskily, "Is this pretend enough?" His breath brushed her hair by her ear, sending shivers through her.

"Yes, I believe so," she whispered trembling, looking up at him with wide, expectant eyes.

Their gaze remained locked for some time, and Darcy lowered his head. Just before his lips touched hers, he suddenly stopped. "You are not afraid?"

"On the contrary, I believe I shall enjoy this immensely."

Darcy tilted his head. "I believe the word was immeasurably."

"Oh, yes. I believe I shall enjoy this immeasurably."

He took in a deep breath and let it out slowly. "I believe I shall, as well."

He drew back and looked at her. He drew a strand of hair away from her face. "I have a question I must ask you, Elizabeth. Have you ever done this before?"

Elizabeth felt a sense of light-headedness at his question. "Never!" she said, and his lips came down to meet hers.

If Elizabeth had believed she had felt everything a woman could feel in the arms of a man she loved, she was wrong. She felt as if she were swinging across the sea again, flying, soaring to new heights and new depths. Her heart pounded from her head to her toes as his lips moved from her mouth to her cheeks, up to her ears, and down her neck. With each kiss, a new sensation revealed itself and rendered Elizabeth breathless.

She clung to him as if her life depended on it as he sought her lips again, this time with more fervency. She felt as if she would collapse into a puddle if either let go. When he finally lifted his head, he asked hoarsely, "Did that work?"

Elizabeth was somewhat confused. "Did what work?" she asked meekly.

"Did that erase any feelings you might still harbour for Captain Smith?"

Elizabeth smiled and leaned her head against his chest. She could both feel and hear the pounding of his heart. She nodded her head but then looked up. Her brows furrowed. "I think I can readily recall – with a great deal of fondness – the curls that peeked out of his tri-corn hat and trailed down his neck." Her fingers lightly played around his neck.

Darcy gave her a cautioning look before coming down and

claiming her lips again. Then without warning, he suddenly picked her up.

"What are you doing, Mr. Darcy?" Elizabeth asked, feeling both anticipation and just a little uncertainty.

"I am going to make certain you forget about Captain Smith." He sat down on the bench and cradled Elizabeth on his lap. Wrapping his arms about her he said, "I daresay you never sat on the captain's lap, did you?"

Elizabeth bit her lip and shook her head, speechless. She could not prevent a smile from appearing.

"Good." He looked at her with deep longing in his eyes as he drew close to her, kissing her with a passion that stirred them both.

She leaned her head against him as he stroked her back. She felt his kisses on the top of her head.

He finally pulled away. "Now, Elizabeth, I must know. Have I removed every ounce of feeling for Captain Smith?"

Elizabeth swallowed, her mouth suddenly very dry. She allowed a smile and said, "There is one more thing, I am certain, that will take away all memory of him."

"What is that?" he asked with feigned distress.

She reached up and stroked his clean-shaven face with her fingertips. She felt breathless as she met his intense gaze. "I doubt that his face was as smooth as yours."

Darcy shook his head and captured her hand in his, pressing it against his cheek. "I can assure you, it was not!" He closed his fingers around hers and then brought them to his lips, kissing the tips of each.

After a moment, he continued, "Can I now be assured that Captain Smith is completely out of your heart and mind?"

Elizabeth slowly nodded. Her face felt flushed and a wave of emotions swelled through her. "Utterly and completely," she replied weakly.

~~*

They lost all track of time as they remained in their secluded hideaway, laughing, holding each other, and kissing. At length, Darcy slid her off his lap and onto the bench. He stood up and sent her a meaningful look.

"Come, Elizabeth. If you are to remain virtuous until our

wedding night, I suggest we leave now. We have moved from the dangerous waters into the fire, and I, for one, do not think I can control my behaviour if we do not cease now. In addition, the longer we remain here, the greater chance there is that someone might come upon us."

Elizabeth tilted her head at him. "But we still have so much to discuss!"

"Ha!" he exclaimed. "We have been here for quite some time, and very little discussion has taken place!"

"You are correct," she said with resignation. She began to stand and was grateful for Darcy's hand. Every nerve within her trembled.

He leaned over and gave her a very chaste kiss when she was on her feet. "There is something I need to ask you, Elizabeth."

Elizabeth looked up at him. "Yes?"

"I should like to marry as soon as possible. Do you think your sister would mind if we made it a double wedding?"

Elizabeth rewarded him with a wide smile. "I think Jane would be delighted to share her wedding day with me."

Chapter 28

While Elizabeth folded the coverlet, Darcy placed the glasses and remaining items into the basket. They then set them behind a nearby bush, making sure they were well hidden, so he could retrieve the items on his return to Netherfield.

As they made the short descent down Oakham Mount, Elizabeth tucked her hand through the crook of Darcy's arm. She was content to walk quietly, but she needed some answers, so she decided she would begin with one easy question to see if he seemed inclined to talk.

"Tell me, Fitzwilliam, what will Georgiana think of me as a sister?"

He turned and tapped Elizabeth on the nose. "I believe she will like it very much. She told me she was very fond of you, and I told you last evening that she looks forward to furthering your acquaintance."

Elizabeth smiled. "I am glad. I found her delightful." She stole a glance at Darcy, who had turned to look ahead. He did not seem inclined to add anything, so she allowed him a little silence.

After a short while, Elizabeth took in a quick breath and held it briefly. She knew asking the next question – the one she really needed an answer to – might prove problematic. She looked up at Darcy and smiled, receiving one in return.

"And what of your aunt?" she asked with a light tone. "What will she think?"

Darcy's brow lowered, but he continued to look straight ahead.

"My aunt?"

"Yes, Lady Catherine." Elizabeth looked down and then back up. She stopped walking and turned to him. "I understand... I heard that there were certain expectations about you marrying Anne."

Darcy rubbed his jaw and then clasped his hand over Elizabeth's, where it still rested on his arm. "What you heard is correct, but..."

Suddenly he released her hand and began feeling around in his coat for something. He reached into a pocket and pulled out a letter. He gave her a pointed look as he opened it. "This is from my aunt. I received it just before I left London. I will not bore you with everything she writes, but I shall read one part. I will summarize what she said, however, by telling you that somehow she heard about my little pirate adventure, about my appearance, my speech, and a few more things that somehow had been added or grossly exaggerated."

He moved his finger down the letter. "Here, this part might be of interest to you."

You can be at no loss, my nephew, to understand my reason for writing. Your own heart, your own conscience, must tell you why. But I shall account for it anyway. This alarming report about your pirating activities, your manner of dress and talk that I understand was utterly despicable, makes me wonder if you have forgotten what you owe yourself and all your family. I believe your mother would be deeply grieved, as am I, as this cannot turn out good for my Anne. Even though your mother and I wished for your engagement and marriage from the start, I must now declare that this marriage would be impossible to take place! Honour, decorum, and prudence forbid it! Pray, Nephew! Tell me this has all been a scandalous mistake, that the rumours circulating are untrue! Otherwise, I shall have no other alternative but to remove my consent.

Darcy lifted his eyes to her over the top of the letter. "There is much more, but I do believe that she has released me from her expectations. I daresay, my mother released me even before she died."

"I imagine she still will not be pleased."

Darcy let out a huff. "I can assure you she will not. There is very little that pleases her. I would not be concerned."

"How do you suppose she found out?"

Darcy deliberated for a moment. "Any number of ways. Perhaps Georgiana told someone in our family, and they told her."

Elizabeth bit her lip. "Or I suppose my mother could have told Mrs. Lucas, who then told her daughter…"

"Who told her husband, who then told my aunt."

Elizabeth laughed and took Darcy's arm again, giving it a squeeze. "I would imagine if that were the case, each one likely added their own little element to the story, making it quite a tale by the time it reached your aunt."

Darcy nodded with a smile. After a moment of silence, he asked, "Who told you about the expected engagement between Anne and myself?"

Elizabeth felt her cheeks warm and a sense of discomposure flooded her. She said, almost in a whisper, "It was Mr. Wickham."

Darcy frowned. "I thought as much."

Elizabeth realized this was the perfect time to ask her next question, although she knew it would upset him. Speaking as carefree as she could, she said, "Speaking of Mr. Wickham," she paused as Darcy's head jerked towards her, "what is to become of him for his part in the attempted escape?" She patted his arm. "I only wish to know so we can determine whether Lydia is in any danger of encountering him again."

Darcy raked his fingers through his hair and the crease on his forehead deepened. "You will likely not see him for five to ten years."

Elizabeth's eyes widened. "Oh!"

"He has yet to stand trial, but Foster told me he would likely receive a sentence of that approximate duration. He is fortunate in that he will not hang. Lockerly and the others certainly will."

Elizabeth mutely nodded, and they continued in silence.

Darcy stopped and turned to her. "I suppose you have an unrelenting curiosity about why I was in such a destitute state when I was mistaken for Lockerly."

Elizabeth looked at him with a sheepish grin. "I suppose I did wonder that."

"Can you conjecture why?"

Elizabeth shook her head. "I would not wish to."

Darcy licked his lips. "Well, you are most likely correct." He paused and looked away. After a few moments he returned his gaze to Elizabeth. "It was because of you."

Elizabeth felt a surge of regret and knew her face reflected how she felt. "I am so sorry. I had no idea…"

"That I would take it so hard?" After Elizabeth silently nodded, tears pooling in her eyes, Darcy continued. "I came to you expecting a favourable reply because I had a very elevated opinion of myself, erroneously so. What you said and did – as painful as it was – helped me see the person I truly was – as others saw me – rather than who I thought I was when I looked at myself."

"I truly believed you would readily forget me and, of course, would want nothing to do with me ever again."

He touched a finger to her face, catching a tear that fell. "I was angry, of course, at first, and I had hoped to put you out of my head and my heart. When our paths crossed again on the island, I knew I could not, but did not know if you would ever return my affections." He glanced down at her. "Especially when I saw you with Mr. Adams."

"Oh, yes…" Elizabeth said, "Mr. Adams. I believe it has turned out quite providentially in his favour for him to return to St. Mary's. I do hope he is able to secure Melanie's love."

Darcy laughed. "I do, as well! I would not want him returning to claim your love!"

Elizabeth smiled and looked down, taking his hand in hers. "He knew I loved you."

Darcy tilted his head as he looked down. "Did he?"

She nodded, adding, "And he claimed that you loved me, as well."

"Bright, young man! Always liked the fellow!"

Elizabeth shook her head. "But I did not believe him. How could I expect you to still feel the same way after what I said to you that evening in Kent?"

Darcy lifted his head up to the heavens. "I think the bigger question is why did our paths cross again in such an extraordinary way? What would have happened if life had just gone on as usual for us? Would we have had this second chance?"

Elizabeth shuddered. "I would hope so, but I have no idea how it would have occurred."

Darcy shook his head. "Neither do I." He clasped his hand over Elizabeth's, again, and they walked, all conversation for the moment ceased.

After walking quietly for some time, Elizabeth determined that Darcy must have had enough of her questions. They were almost to the base of the hill, where they would make the turn to set out for Longbourn, when she felt him squeeze her hand. He looked down at her, a look of concern in his eyes.

"What is it?" Elizabeth asked.

Darcy's brows drew together. "I have a confession to make."

"You make it sound serious."

Darcy slowly nodded his head. "There was another reason I did not tell you who I was."

Elizabeth bit her lip and tilted her head. "What was that?"

Darcy drew in a breath. "I rather enjoyed how you treated me as Captain Smith. I felt if you knew who I was, that would change."

Elizabeth raised her brows. "I do not know how I would have acted or felt if you had told me." She squeezed his arm. "But I assure you, I had already begun to rethink my opinion of you."

Darcy smiled. "What shall you think of being Mistress of Pemberley?"

Elizabeth leaned her head against him as they continued to walk. "Since I have never seen it, can you tell me what it is like?" She looked up with a teasing smile. "Is it much like Rosings, would you say?"

Darcy laughed heartily. "It is nothing at all like Rosings!" He grew serious. "It is a wonderful home. It is larger than Rosings, but not as ornate. I think you will be pleased. There is a lake on one side, gardens on the other, a ridge behind the house, and acres of woods surrounding it. You shall never lack for a new path to explore."

"It sounds lovely." Elizabeth let out a long, soft sigh. "I think I shall love it as much as I can see you do."

"I believe, my dearest Elizabeth, that you shall."

She stood up on her toes to kiss him on the cheek, but at the last moment he turned, so her lips met his. She was somewhat startled, but relaxed in his arms as he drew her into an embrace.

~~*

When they reached Longbourn, Elizabeth directed Darcy to her father's library, and she scurried up the stairs to Jane's room. She tapped on the door, and Jane welcomed her in.

Jane was sitting in a plush chair, still dressed in her night clothes and robe. Her slippered feet were propped up on an ottoman, and she was gazing out the window.

"Good morning, Jane." Elizabeth walked over to a mirror that hung on the wall. She placed her fingers on her cheeks, noticing their flush, but knew there was nothing she could do about it now. She fiddled with her hair, attempting to tidy it. "How are you this morning?"

"I am well, but a little confused."

"Why?"

Jane motioned for Elizabeth to sit down on the bed. "I just saw you walk to the house with Mr. Darcy."

Elizabeth looked down at her fingers, which she was nervously knitting together. She bit her lip and nodded her head. "Yes. That is why I have come to you. He is presently with Father."

"Why is he with Father?"

Elizabeth laughed and threw back her head. "Why would a gentleman go to see a young lady's father?"

Jane shook her head. "Well, I can only think of one reason, and I doubt that…" Jane suddenly gasped and clasped her hands over her mouth. Her eyes widened. When she lowered her hands, she said, "Did he?" She rushed over to the bed and grabbed her sister's hand. "Lizzy! Did he ask for your hand in marriage again?"

When Elizabeth nodded, Jane let out a squeal and wrapped her arms about Elizabeth. "Oh! I am so happy! I do not know what to say, but I had hoped this would happen! I had hoped so much!"

Elizabeth returned her sister's hug, and Jane joined her on the bed, making it bounce as she plopped down. "Tell me all about it, dearest Lizzy!"

After Elizabeth had finished telling her about their morning – leaving out certain details – Elizabeth grew solemn. "Jane, there is something I must ask."

Jane's eyes grew wide. "What?"

"Would you mind terribly… what would you think… if we had

a double wedding ceremony? If Mr. Darcy... Fitzwilliam... and I, were to get married at the same time as you and Mr. Bingley?"

"Oh, Lizzy!" Jane cried as she wrapped her in an embrace again. "I would like it very much, very much indeed!"

~~*

Mr. Darcy chose to slip out quietly after speaking with Mr. Bennet and getting his consent. Mr. Bennet called Elizabeth down once he had left, informing her that he was pleased beyond measure with the man who would marry his favourite daughter.

He gave her a hug, kissed her on the top of her head, and then told her, "Now, go tell your mother. I shall take a stroll outside and return in about fifteen minutes. That shall be enough time for her to get her flutterings all over with, do you not think?"

"Is she awake?" Elizabeth asked. "Should I go to her now?"

Mr. Bennet gave a solemn nod. "Might as well get it over with. There are not many things that will put her in good spirits as news such as this."

Elizabeth watched her father leave and pursed her lips. As much as this would please her mother, Elizabeth expected she would react with vehement gushing.

Before going up, she went to the kitchen and armed herself with a cup of steaming tea and some sweet biscuits. She knew her mother would have her smelling salts at her side. She then straightened, drew her shoulders back, and marched up the stairs.

When she came to her mother's room, she placed the cup and saucer on a nearby table and tapped lightly on the door.

"Oh, my head!" came the agitated voice from inside. "Hill, did you bring my tea?"

"It is Lizzy, Mother. May I come in? I have tea and biscuits."

Without waiting for a response, she opened the door, picked up the cup and saucer, and entered the dark room. She placed them on the table at her mother's side and promptly went to open the curtains.

"Lizzy! It is too bright! If you have to open them, just a little."

"Yes, Mother, but I have something to tell you, and I wish to see your face when I do."

"Oh, dear! Another terrible missive has come, has it not? Where are my smelling salts?"

"They are right at your side, where you always keep them."

Her mother's face drained of all colour. "Something terrible *has* happened?"

Elizabeth gave her head a toss, a smile forming on her lips. "No, Mother. Something wonderful has happened. Mr. Darcy has made me an offer of marriage, and I have accepted!'

Mrs. Bennet went rigid, the only movement being the slow widening of her eyes as she comprehended her daughter's words.

Elizabeth reached for the smelling salts. "Do you need these, Mother?"

She took a deep breath and lifted her hands towards them, but stopped. "Of course not! Why should I need smelling salts after hearing news as wonderful as this?"

"I am glad you are pleased!"

"Pleased? I am ecstatic! I am... I am..." She waved her hands through the air.

"Speechless?" Elizabeth asked with a smile.

"Heavens, no!" Mrs. Bennet quickly sat up. "Oh, there is so much to do! Two weddings! Is this not the finest way to start your day?"

Elizabeth had to agree it was.

"Give me my robe, Lizzy." Mrs. Bennet clasped her hands together. "Imagine Mr. Darcy marrying my Lizzy! I always thought he was the most distinguished gentleman, so gracious and attentive." She pointed her finger at her daughter. "I can only say it is the most splendid thing that Mr. Adams departed. I was growing quite tired of him. What if he had asked for your hand? I never believed him to love you! Oh, I am so glad he is gone!"

Elizabeth sighed and shook her head. Her wedding day could not come soon enough.

~~*

Later that day, Georgiana arrived at Netherfield with her companion, Mrs. Annesley. Darcy brought her to Longbourn without delay so she and Elizabeth could begin to further their acquaintance before the wedding.

Since Jane had already begun planning her wedding, Elizabeth's main objective was to have her dress made. Darcy arranged for the banns to be published, announcing their upcoming nuptials, not only in the Longbourn parish, but also in his Pemberley parish.

Darcy remained at Netherfield a few more days before he had to depart. He made sure his sister was well situated before he left. Mr. Bingley's sisters had arrived, and although he knew his sister was not particularly at ease around them, he knew they would likely leave her alone now that there was no longer a reason to impose themselves on her. Miss Bingley had always hoped for her brother and Georgiana to marry, thinking that if that had occurred, she may have been able to secure his hand in marriage. As both gentlemen were now getting married, there was no need to ingratiate herself with the young girl. He was also confident that Georgiana would be spending a good amount of time with his betrothed and, therefore, would not be subjected to those two ladies.

The Gardiners arrived the week of the wedding, just as Darcy returned. Elizabeth was pleased to introduce them to Fitzwilliam and his sister. They shared many stories about Pemberley and nearby Lambton, where Mrs. Gardiner grew up.

As the wedding day drew closer, Darcy's family descended upon Netherfield. Elizabeth enjoyed meeting them all, but took great delight in seeing Colonel Fitzwilliam, again. He had become a very special friend when she had met him at Rosings in the spring.

The only person noticeably missing was his aunt, Lady Catherine de Bourgh, and her daughter, Anne. When Elizabeth inquired about her, Darcy winced, informing her that he had received another letter from his aunt after she had heard about his upcoming wedding.

"What did it say?" Elizabeth asked.

Darcy pressed his lips together and shook his head. "She is not happy, of course. She claims I have shown no consideration for her, her daughter, and for the reputation of my family, and she adamantly refuses to attend such a disgraceful affair." He gave his head a slight toss as if to show he cared little for her accusations. Looking up at Elizabeth and smiling, Darcy added, "Anne sent her regards in another letter. She is delighted with my choice of bride and wishes us great joy."

He leaned in and kissed the tip of Elizabeth's nose. "I cannot believe, my dearest, loveliest, Elizabeth, that my most heartfelt dream is going to come true."

Chapter 29

On the day of the wedding, everyone and everything in the Bennet household was in an uproar, mostly due to Mrs. Bennet's nerves. Elizabeth was grateful for her aunt's calming presence. Mrs. Gardiner had the unique ability to assist with the tasks Mrs. Bennet fretted over, all the while making her believe that she was taking care of them herself. Elizabeth did not think she and Jane would have survived the days before the wedding without her dear aunt's encouragement to them when they needed it most.

Elizabeth had been pleased that she and Jane had similar tastes and were of one accord in their wedding plans. The two men left all the decision making to their brides-to-be. Elizabeth knew that Fitzwilliam's only care was that they be married when they left the church.

Despite Mrs. Bennet's qualms that some great catastrophe would occur, the two couples were married in what everyone said was a lovely ceremony.

After the wedding, everyone set out for Netherfield for the wedding breakfast. The beautiful August day allowed the two couples to ride in open white phaetons decorated with ribbons and flowers and drawn by stately white horses. The procuring of the phaetons was the one arrangement Darcy insisted upon making himself. He brought them in from a neighbouring town, wanting his bride to ride in elegance and be shown off to everyone who saw them pass by. As Darcy drove, he and Elizabeth enjoyed their time alone together – conversing, laughing, and stealing kisses when no one was near to see them.

~~*

When they arrived at Netherfield, the throng of well-wishers greeted them. Since the guests included Darcy's family and close friends, as well as those of the Bennets and Bingleys, there were many introductions to make.

Elizabeth held tightly onto his arm and gently encouraged him when he showed signs of fatigue and stepped back into a reserved deportment. She knew how to invite him into the conversation, especially when they were speaking with someone she knew well.

The wedding breakfast passed in a flurry of activity, and by early afternoon, many of the guests began to take their leave. Darcy suggested to Elizabeth that they do the same. Her mouth went dry as she contemplated what this would mean, but she was just as eager to be alone with him as he was to be alone with her.

They bid family and friends farewell, spending more time with the other wedding couple. Jane and Elizabeth hugged tightly, as they knew it would be a while before they would see each other again.

"Take care, dearest sister," Elizabeth said. "I know you shall be delightfully happy."

"But how I wish we lived closer! I shall miss seeing you."

Elizabeth smiled and took her hand. "Perhaps someday we shall." They kissed and parted.

The Darcys boarded the Pemberley carriage and waved once more to everyone as the coachman drove away to the inn Darcy had selected. He pulled Elizabeth close and kissed her. As he drew back, he said, "I did not think we would ever get away."

"You were eager to leave, then?"

Darcy eyed her longingly. "Very much so. You know how wearisome I find these things."

"You performed admirably. Elizabeth lifted a brow and tilted her head; a teasing look touched her features. "But is that the only reason you wished to leave?"

His response was to pull her close and kiss her again.

When they drew apart, he looked down at the necklace she wore. "Are you pleased with my gift? I think it suits you perfectly."

Elizabeth fingered the diamond necklace Fitzwilliam had given her. "It is the most beautiful thing I have ever seen, aside from the ring." She held her hand up so the large marquis diamond, flanked on either side by two sapphires, shone with brilliancy.

"I thought you would like my grandmother's ring best."

"You have excellent taste, my dear Fitzwilliam."

"Yes, I do." Darcy let out a contented sigh and looked into her eyes.

"And speaking of gifts, I have one for you!"

"For me? Elizabeth, you should not have done that!"

"And why not?" She reached down at her feet, pulling out a wrapped parcel. She held it out to him. "It just arrived last evening. I thought it would not get here in time."

"What is it?"

"I believe you must open it to find that out!" Elizabeth laughed gaily.

Elizabeth held the bundle while Darcy slowly pulled at the ribbons. Finally growing impatient with the slow pace in which he was proceeding, she opened it the remainder of the way.

Elizabeth peeked sideways at her husband as she watched him pull out a beautifully carved wooden ship. It was a faithful replica, laden with unfurled sails and even tightly wound cordage. He reached over and carefully ran his fingers against the polished wood. "Elizabeth, it is beautiful!"

Elizabeth bit her lip. "I thought it might look nice on one of the mantels and be a reminder of our adventure."

"It will look splendid in the library! You could not have chosen a more perfect gift! But this must have cost you a fortune!"

Elizabeth shook her head, her eyes flashing with mischief. "Are you not aware that you married a lady of great fortune? The reward for the jewels was more than enough needed to make the purchase."

Darcy shook his head. "You should not have spent your money on me!"

"And why not?" she asked. "You specifically told us we could spend the money however we wished. Did you not?"

Darcy chuckled, fingering a loose strand of her hair and bringing it back to the side. "You are correct. I did say that."

He slipped his hand behind her neck and pulled her close.

"Thank you very much, my angel!" He then met her lips with his.

Elizabeth's eyes widened, and when he drew away, she exclaimed, "Angel?"

"Most definitely! You looked just like a heavenly angel, robed in silver, as you walked towards me this morning." He let out a sigh of contentment and looked at her with a wide smile.

"That will not do, my dear Fitzwilliam," Elizabeth laughed.

His smile wilted. "What will not do?"

"Charles has already claimed *angel* as his endearment for Jane. You must choose another."

"Oh, dear," he replied. He eyed her from the top of her head down to her feet. "Well, if you are not an angel, you are then the very substance of my dreams."

Elizabeth cocked her head. "Would that be a *remnant of your dreams*, then?" When he turned to look at her, she pressed her finger into the corner of each of his eyes. "I fear I see no remnant, now."

Darcy smiled and took her hand, giving it a gentle squeeze. "That is because my dreams have come true. Oh, Elizabeth, if you only knew how often you were in my dreams. If this is a dream, I hope never to waken."

~~*

They rode for several hours, arriving late in the afternoon at the inn Darcy had selected for their first night. The carriage door opened, and Elizabeth and Darcy stepped out. As he walked her to the inn, Elizabeth looked about her, admiring the secluded area surrounded by dense trees.

She smiled. "This is lovely, Fitzwilliam!"

"I hoped you would be pleased. There is also a lake on the other side of the inn we can walk down to."

"It sounds heavenly."

They entered the inn, preceded by Darcy's valet, who was securing the key to their room. The servant then got the key to the room for him and the footman.

Darcy decided that Elizabeth would use a lady's maid from the inn. He wanted her to take her time in choosing her own once they arrived at Pemberley.

The valet and footman led the way to Darcy and Elizabeth's

room, where the footman opened the door and stepped aside to allow them entrance. He carried in their overnight luggage and set it down in the bedroom.

"The meal is served in the dining room at six o'clock," said the valet. "We are down the hall at the end on the right. Feel free to summon us if you need us. We shall be ready to leave by nine o'clock tomorrow morning, as you requested."

"Thank you," Darcy said and closed the door.

Elizabeth looked about her. She suddenly felt awkward and wondered what she was supposed to do.

She walked over to the window and gazed out. "Oh! You can see the lake from here! It is lovely!"

Darcy came up behind her and put his hands on her shoulders. "It is an easy walk down to it. We have plenty of time to do that before dinner." He leaned down and kissed her on the back of her neck, then wrapped his arms about her, clasping them at her waist.

"Yes, that would be nice," Elizabeth said, clasping her hands over his.

"Shall we change into something less formal and set out? Shall I send for the lady's maid to assist you?"

Elizabeth moistened her lips with her tongue and shook her head. "No, I shall not need her now." She directed Darcy to a large overstuffed chair. "You can wait here for me while I get ready." She looked nervously about her. "I shall return directly."

Elizabeth began to walk into the bedroom but stopped. She looked behind her at her husband. "Would you mind terribly unbuttoning the back of my dress? In that, I believe I do need some help."

She watched him slowly rise and come towards her. She turned back to look straight ahead as his fingers seemed to fumble with the tiny buttons. Neither said a word; the only sound Elizabeth heard was her heart pounding and Fitzwilliam's deep breaths. As he quickly became quite adept at unbuttoning it, she also felt his breath along her back.

When he finished, she felt his lips press against her back between her shoulders.

"Do you need any more assistance?" he whispered in her ear.

Elizabeth's breath caught. "I… I… perhaps later."

She quickly walked into the bedroom and shut the door behind her. She was nervous and filled with anticipation at the same time.

~~*

It was some time before Elizabeth stepped out of the bedroom. She walked into the sitting area, where she found Darcy holding a newspaper that his valet had left for him to read. He did not seem to be reading, however, as he was staring at the wall.

He heard her come in and asked, "Are you ready?" When he turned and saw her, he bolted to his feet. "Elizabeth!" He sucked in a breath and held it, finally letting it out in a soft whisper. "Elizabeth." He quickly walked towards her.

She reached out her hand, and he took it. She had no desire to walk around the lake now, and she was fairly certain he had other things on his mind. She had gone to their room and pulled out the sheer nightdress that her aunt had given her that morning. She and Jane had each received one, along with a gentle talk about what to expect that night; a talk that had been so much more beneficial than the one their mother had given them. Elizabeth had loosened her hair from its upward styling, allowing it to flow down her shoulders and back.

She felt very exposed, but the reaction of her husband was well worth it. She began to pull him closer to her, but he resisted.

"No, allow me the pleasure of just feasting my eyes on you for a moment."

Elizabeth felt her cheeks blush at his perusal, but when he gave her hand a gentle squeeze, she smiled. He drew her to him and wrapped his arms about her, stroking her back and shoulders.

He then pulled back and placed his hands on either side of her face. He searched her eyes and then leaned down and met her lips in a kiss. His fingers wound their way up through her hair and out to the ends. He pulled back and asked breathlessly, "Are you certain, Elizabeth? It is only four thirty."

Elizabeth looked up at him with beguiling eyes. "I was not aware of there being any rule as to the time one…"

Darcy pressed his lips to hers again as he nudged her towards the bedroom. When he reached the door, he picked her up in his arms, and then with his foot closed the door behind them with a decisive thrust.

~~*

At the first sign of light the next morning, Darcy awakened and turned to his bride. He still could not believe she was his. The most magnificent and satisfying thing about it was that she appeared to love and desire him just as much as he did her! He could not now imagine what would have happened had she accepted his first offer of marriage out of an obligation to her family or because she merely wished to marry a man of fortune.

He let out a sigh as he watched her sleep. Her hair was splayed across both pillows, and a smile tugged at her lips. He thought back to the joys of yesterday and her willing playfulness when their coming together could have been something she had looked upon with trepidation. He was completely sated and contented.

He leaned down and kissed her on the cheek. Her eyelids fluttered, and the small smile that had played around her lips widened. She wrapped her arms around him and pulled him close.

"What time is it, Fitzwilliam? Must we get up and hurry to ready ourselves?"

"It is a little after seven, but it is up to you to decide whether we need to hurry. The earlier we get to Pemberley, the more you shall be able to see of it before dusk."

Elizabeth let out a long sigh and stretched her arms out as she did. "Yes, I suppose we should try to leave as soon as possible." When she brought her hands down, she fingered the scar above Darcy's brow and leaned in to kiss it. Then she took his hand and brought it up to her lips. She turned it over and began to kiss his palm, stroking his fingers with hers.

"Elizabeth…" Darcy said, thinking to warn his wife that she had best know what she was doing. She looked up at him with a teasing glint in her eyes. He softly chuckled, knowing his wife knew full well what her actions would lead to.

~~*

They left the inn at ten o'clock. The trip would take them almost the full day, and they each had brought books to help them pass the time. Elizabeth, however, was fascinated with the scenery they passed and found great delight in imagining herself amongst the woods and trails. She enjoyed studying her husband, as well, in the quiet moments of solitude they shared.

He often looked up and smiled as he noticed her looking at him and finally asked what she found so intriguing.

Elizabeth tilted her head. "When an artist does a portrait, I imagine he has to look at his whole subject in various lighting so he can fully do it justice. I am merely getting ideas to put into my sketch of your character."

"So you are sketching my character again?"

Elizabeth tossed her head back with a laugh. "You said it might take a lifetime; I had best begin right away, do you not think?"

"And what is your success?" he asked.

She laughed with a quick shake of her head. "Oh, I agree with you. It *shall* take a lifetime."

Darcy leaned in to her with a raised brow. "I might request, Elizabeth, that you not sketch my character at the present moment."

Elizabeth's eyes widened and met his teasing gaze. "Why?"

"I would ask that you wait until you see me at Pemberley. It is there that I feel I can be my true self and am more comfortable in those surroundings."

"Then I look forward with great anticipation to observing you there!"

At length the carriage came to a stop. Elizabeth had fallen asleep in her husband's arms, and she awoke with a start. "Have we arrived?"

"Not quite yet, but I wish to show you something."

The door was opened, and they stepped out. He took her arm and guided her across the road. They were surrounded by a deep, dense wooded area, but walked a short ways to a clearing.

Elizabeth looked out and gasped. Her jaw dropped as she looked down at a magnificent structure. "Is that... Pemberley?"

Darcy murmured the affirmative. "This is one of my favourite views, although not many see it as it cannot be seen from the road."

Elizabeth cast her eyes across the expanse. Her grip around her husband's arm tightened. "Oh, my dearest, it is just as you described, and yet..."

"Yes?"

"It is far grander than my imagination allowed it to be."

"Are you pleased with Pemberley, then?"

Elizabeth turned back and mutely nodded. "I know I shall treasure it as much as you do."

"Good!" He wrapped his arms about her. "Welcome, Elizabeth, to your new home. We have just entered Pemberley Woods, my dearest. Of all this, you are now Mistress!"

Epilogue

One Month Later

Elizabeth sat on a bench seat and rested her arms on the railing of the sailing ship. She looked out at the glassy waters and felt the fresh spray on her face. An occasional gust of wind prompted her to hold down her bonnet with one hand. She looked back at her husband, who was enjoying manning the ship as it sailed across the waters of Windermere Lake.

The scenery was ever changing as they sailed across the largest of the lakes in the Lake District. The green meadows contrasted with the blue sky above and crystal waters below. In some parts, the lake mirrored the large bluffs across from them. They passed alder-fringed meadows, wooded islets, cottages, and an occasional farmstead off shore.

"Is this not the loveliest sight?"

Elizabeth looked up and saw her Aunt Gardiner coming towards her. "It is wonderful! I am delighted that my husband invited you and Uncle Gardiner to accompany us."

Mrs. Gardiner bit her lip and she looked at the helm of the ship towards her niece's husband. "That was so kind of him. I had no idea he would invite us to join you when I told him he could thank us that the two of you met in the Isles of Scilly. It was all due to the necessity of us having to cancel *our* trip to the Lake District."

"It was a delightful surprise to see you here!"

Looking back at her niece, she asked, "Speaking of the Isles, what have you heard from St. Mary's?" Mrs. Gardiner asked.

Elizabeth clasped her hands and smiled. "Melanie writes that her mother is doing tolerably well. She is still weak, but they are grateful that she seems somewhat stable."

"Does she speak of David?"

Elizabeth silently nodded and smiled. "She is grateful that David returned to help her through this. She does not know what she would have done without him."

"Can this be taken as an indication that she might grow to love him?"

"I think she already does. She needs only to realize it. When I replied to her, I gave her some strong encouragement in that area."

Mrs. Gardiner looked again towards the helm. "Both of our husbands seem to be enjoying taking turns manning the ship with Captain Bellows."

"It was so good to see him again. I think they came to respect each other a great deal, having to depend on the other to get them through quite a bit."

"Captain Bellows is certainly fortunate that he and five of the crew were able to purchase this ship with the prize money they received."

"Yes, I believe they shall have a good business here. In addition to providing tourists with a wonderful outing on the lake, they will be transporting people and merchandise from one port to another.

"Would ye care fer some tea?"

Elizabeth looked up and saw Edward Webber standing before them with some refreshments. "Why thank you, Mr. Webber. Are you enjoying your new employment under Captain Bellows?"

"Very much. We was very grateful to Bellows fer allowin' us to go into business wi' him. Me thinks he was tired of sailin' the high seas and is enjoyin' this so much more."

At the sound of a flute, they all looked up to see Michael Jenkins playing while sitting casually up on the main mast. They smiled as they listened to the lively tune. Despite the fact that this ship was quite a bit smaller than the *Devil's Seamaiden*, the six men were doing a fairly good business.

At length, Darcy came over and put his arm around his wife. "Are you enjoying your visit, my dream?"

Elizabeth's eyes brightened. "I most certainly am, but I must say, Fitzwilliam, I do not think I have ever seen you enjoy yourself more, even at Pemberley."

"Truly?"

Elizabeth gave a firm nod of her head. "I believe that I will need to add to my sketch of your character this whole new side of you; one that I shall have to call *Captain* Fitzwilliam Darcy."

"But you already have a lengthy description of me as Captain Smith!"

Elizabeth laughed. "Oh, no, my love. You were suffering from a great deal too much concern, trying to protect a bunch of silly passengers and a novice crew from the treacherous Lockerly. Besides, you were in a most abhorrent state of disguise." She shook her head firmly. "No, despite performing admirably in such dire conditions, this is quite different."

He leaned in and kissed her cheek, rewarding her with a warm smile. "Me dearest Lizzy, as long as ye promise to always remain by me side as me most precious first mate, I shall always be the 'appiest of men."

THE END

ABOUT THE AUTHOR

Kara Louise lives outside Wichita, Kansas with her husband and a variety of animals, including a dog, several cats, goats, and horses. They have a married son who lives in St. Louis.

Other books by Kara Louise:

Darcy's Voyage

Only Mr. Darcy Will Do

Assumed Engagement

Assumed Obligation

Master Under Good Regulation

Drive and Determination

and

Pemberley Celebrations: The First Year

~~*

www.karalouise.net

23451187R00149

Made in the USA
Lexington, KY
11 June 2013